The Collapsing House

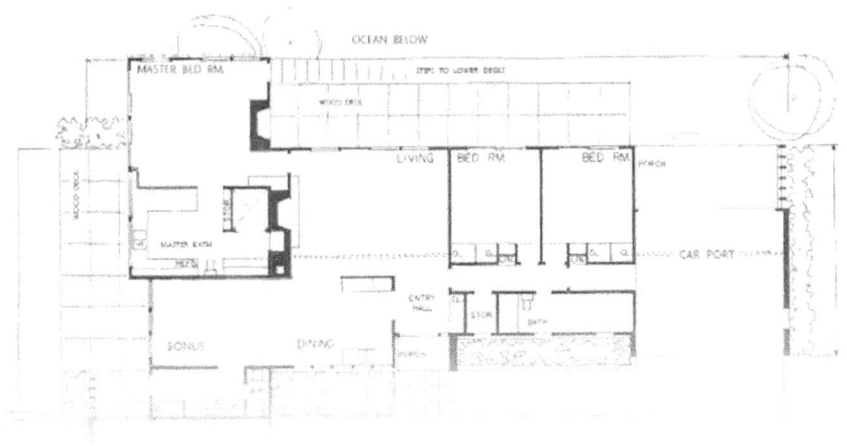

Farley Dunn

🍳🍳🍳 THREE SKILLET

THE COLLAPSING HOUSE, Dunn, Farley L

First Edition

 THREE SKILLET

www.ThreeSkilletPublishing.com

Cover design by Farley L Dunn
Back cover photograph by Farley L Dunn

ISBN: 978-1-943189-19-9

The Collapsing House

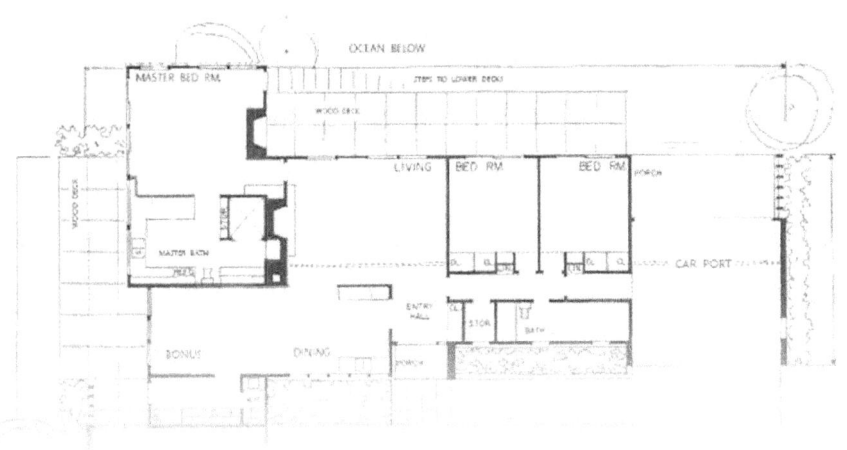

Farley Dunn

Chapter 1

THE MID-CENTURY MODERN house hovered, perched on the barest sliver of steep hillside, its foundation of tall, angled pilings of wood and steel reaching for the sloping ground far below, unleashing stunning views of the Pacific a hundred feet farther down. Decks leaped down the hillside, revealing the concrete footings anchoring the bottom of each piling. The music of the pounding surf drifted through an open sliding glass door.

Inside, Geraldine Gossamer Ridgway sat at the dining room table, her eyes half closed and oblivious to the sounds of the surf, with her thoughts far away. The floors were bare, and furniture was almost nonexistent. The massive windows spanning the back of the house were all the embellishment the old place needed.

An outsized Golden Retriever charged past, his four paws pounding the floor in a lumbering run, a pair of blue-checkered boxers in his mouth. The room vibrated as he tore past, belying the robust appearance of the building that clung stalwartly to the side of the steep incline. Half a century boasted stability. The shaking said otherwise.

The table began to skip to the rhythm of the big dog's feet, and the chattering of the table's legs was the staccato beat of a Cuban rumba. In that moment of musical musings, Geraldine found herself on a beach far, far away.

"Ah, Pablo. Another one of these." She held up her empty glass, its paper umbrella askew, the clear, scalloped lip catching in the late afternoon sun. She and Daggett always had their afternoons by the pool, and later they would wander to the sea. To wade in the warmth of the Caribbean surf was heavenly, unlike the cold California waters of home. "With rum, if you please, Pablo."

"Si, Senorita." He backed away, his head bowed.

She twirled her fingers in the air. Of course, she knew he understood no English, and he would bring her whatever he wished. However, rum seemed so, so . . . so very Ernest Hemmingway. It was all so very *exotic*.

Then, as Cuban rumbas will do to unattached crockery, her plate began to vibrate violently.

"Flotsam," she cried, catching sight of the dog disappearing into a hallway. Her sand and waiter were gone, stolen from her, and she was dismayed. She'd enjoyed her time on her tropical beach. Just before her dish vibrated off the table, she grabbed it, lifting it into the air.

"Daggett?" she called.

She refused to think about the floor, and what might happen in the next earthquake. The bedrock that made up the side of the hill had dropped again in the last one, and now the table was several inches lower on the left than on the right. Soon she'd need to put bigger blocks under the two legs on the far side.

Even worse, the master bedroom was yet another foot closer

to the ocean.

Holding the plate, and not hearing Daggett's reply, she shrugged. The house was standing, if precariously, and the view from the windows was as stunning as the day she'd moved in. For now, she was satisfied simply to save her breakfast.

She peered into the plate and picked up three peas, the most she could grab with her fingers at once. With a quick movement, she popped them into her mouth. When the floors began to vibrate again, she let out a short laugh. It seemed that Flotsam had snagged her boyfriend's last pair of boxers. She expected Daggett to appear within seconds.

With a grin, she heard him. Today, it seemed that Daggett Damon Priestly had no patience for the big animal's shenanigans.

"Flotsam! I can't even take a nap without you snatching my underwear! Where are you, you big, ugly, shorts-stealing mutt?" With curses flying, he came running through the living room, bare-skinned as the day he was born.

"Daggett?" Geraldine smiled and waved as he stood highlighted against the brilliant sky.

"Morning, Baby," he called with a wave of his hand, and then he was gone, leaving only the sparkling of the waves in the distance for her admiration.

Setting the plate down and closing her eyes, she let herself return to her beach, with the sun shimmering in the island heat. Warmth twisted through the trees, and the only pockets of cool were in the shade of the palms. She reached for her replenished drink, and it was refreshing against her fingers. Oddly structured island music hovered in the background. She looked forward to a night on the town in brightly colored clothing, with a flower in her hair.

"Pablo, have you seen Mr. Daggett this morning?"

"Si, Senorita." He smiled, and he laid a fresh towel at the

foot of her chaise lounge. Dipping with a half bow, a white cloth formally draped over his arm, he backed away.

She smiled to herself, letting the expression spread languidly over her lips. Mr. Daggett? Of course, Pablo knew where Mr. Daggett was. He knew the answer to any question she might ask, as long as the answer was *si*.

The sun drifted behind a solitary cloud, and with a chill down her arms, the beach was gone. Opening her eyes, the familiar old house that she had called home for the past two years surrounded her once again, its vanilla and wild rose smells pungent and wonderful. One of the sliders at the back of the house was open, and sea air gusted in, washing her with the memories of days spent on the water surfing with Daggett.

The table began to vibrate again. She turned to see Daggett barrel back into the room. He braked to a stop in front of the bank of windows stretching across the back wall of the living room. The glare of the sun silhouetted his trim waist against the vastness of the ocean in the distance. Golden hair perched in a tousled mess atop his head, with longer strands curling along his neck. It would need to be cut before long, but for now, she found it raggedly charming. Freckles sprinkled his golden shoulders, the result of days on end during which she had watched him attempt to tame the wild California surf. Sinewy, muscled legs spoke of hours on any number of favored surfboards.

Surfing was his life, and this house allowed him to be on the water every day. The awkwardly askew floors whispered of the foundation's compromised integrity, but the view was twenty-eight feet of the most beautiful Pacific Ocean on God's green earth. Once the house came down, he'd never be allowed to build on this site again, but as long as the hillside held firm, it was home. To take time to repair it? Anything that took him away from the ocean was a waste of his time.

Geraldine was content with that. After all, she loved the

ocean almost as much as Daggett.

She popped another pea into her mouth and smiled. She also suspected it was part of the reason why she was still here after two years. He'd not felt the need to "fix" her, either. Thank God for that!

"Daggett?"

He turned to face her, a puzzled look on his face.

"Um, have you forgotten something?" She pointed. "Your underwear?"

He looked down, then turned back to her as if just noticing for the first time. "That dog! What does he want with my clothing, anyway?" With a growl, he was off again.

This time, nearly two hundred pounds of human flesh shook the dining room floor instead of a mere eighty of animal, catching her by surprise. She reacted when she saw her plate jump, but not fast enough. It bounced once, then skittered in a series of clattering leaps to the edge of the table. Finally, it teetered for a moment, almost as if teasing her. She grasped for it, hoping the plate, the last of the heirloom dinner service from Daggett's grandmother, could be saved, only to realize her peas were still dashing toward the Pacific side of the dish. At the last possible moment, the plate leaped from her touch, flinging its bounty of green peas across the room. She cringed as she heard the china dish shatter on the floor. Across the room, a chorus line of rolling peas danced across the wood, searching out the lowest points in their dash over the canted boards.

She sighed, closing her eyes and letting it go; and she smiled at the new scene that leaped into her vision. A sailboat plied the waters in the distance, and her rum and umbrella were at her side once again. A quickening breeze blew a strand of hair across one cheek, and the equatorial sun was sharp against her skin. She caught her napkin before it fluttered from the table, but she couldn't catch her drink decorations. The small, colorful

11

umbrella skittered away like a butterfly in the breeze.

With a slender finger, she pushed the hair back into place, mildly disappointed to feel the breeze drop away. Walking across the sand was her young man from earlier. His slicked hair gleamed in the sun. He grabbed at the lost items, but a freshening wind whipped them away.

"I am so sorry, Pablo," she called to him with a languid wave of her hand; and letting it drop, she sighed. It was just as well. The Cuban sun had grown warm in the fullness of the approaching afternoon, and Daggett was probably at the beach already. He'd said he planned to surf if the wind picked up.

She glanced up to see Pablo back with the tiny paper umbrella. She smiled when he closed it with a flourish, pushing it firmly into the sand-filled ashtray at her side. He backed up a step and waited, as if he required a word from her before he could head elsewhere.

"Thank you, Pablo. You are very kind. You take such good care of me." She smiled and fluttered her fingers, watching her ring flash in the sun.

"Si, Senorita."

"Pablo, I'm headed to the beach. I'm sure Daggett will be there ahead of me already. May I sign for the tab?" The gold pen sparkled in the sun, and her name pirouetted across the paper, a ballroom dance of exquisite proportions. She stepped to the edge of the decking and looked out over the sea. It was the most beautiful view she had ever seen. She pressed her eyelids closed and turned into the sun.

When she opened them, the beach and Pablo were gone once more. The peas were not, though. Three of them disappeared into a crack in the wide wooden planking that had appeared when an aftershock had shaken the house several months before. That very crack had saved the house, she was sure. Wood floors flexed when they shook, giving under the stresses of an earthquake, and then returning to their original location. However, in the aftershock, a fifteen-foot long gap, about half an inch wide at the center, had opened in the living room just past the dining room door.

That gap had just eaten three of the peas.

"You stupid dog! I'll pull every hair from your tail if I get my hands on you!" A door slammed. Flotsam bounded back into view, the checkered boxers still flapping from his muzzle.

The man was yet to be seen.

The big dog looked at her, his great, long tail wagging in excitement. She could have sworn he grinned at her. Then he dropped the shorts, a length of tongue leaped out, and seven more of the peas were gone. The rest continued on their march toward the far wall.

"Flotsam!" Daggett panted at the door, sweat from the chase gleaming on his skin. His nostrils flared. Seeing Geraldine sitting at the table watching his antics, he snorted a quick laugh of recognition before his eyes jumped to the boxers lying on the floor. They were finally out of the dog's mouth, and he locked on them with an intentness that rivaled that of a hunting cat. His muscles, honed by a lifetime's dedication to his surfboard, tensed, and he flung his body smoothly across the room. With one arm outstretched, he did his Superman thing in order to reclaim what was rightfully his.

Flotsam was a smart animal, either that or too stupid for anyone to tell the difference, and with the seven peas gone, his quick teeth snatched up the boxers once again. His feet scrabbled on the wooden surface, and he was gone, this time turning a corner toward the front door.

Daggett crashed to the floor, his shorts already in flight before he could reach them. He yelled, "No, Flotsam! Not outside!" Leaping up, he threw his long body after the dog, disappearing from Geraldine's sight. Then, a sun-bronzed hand grasped the doorframe, and a grinning face reappeared.

Geraldine caught Daggett's eyes, and she saw them twinkle. A wink told her more than words could say. The screen door slammed, and she knew his drawers had exited to the front yard.

"Go," she called, waving him way. "Your dog wants to play."

He winked a second time at her and whispered theatrically, "Elvis has left the building." Then he yelled, "Flotsam!" With a scrabble of his feet, he was out the front door after him.

She laughed and glanced back into the living room. Four of the peas had been taken out by Daggett, and she was pretty certain that had been during his Superman landing. The final three peas had made it to the far wall and now rested against the glass just under the view painted across the back side of the room. She stood, stepping around the broken bits of china. That would have to be cleaned up, but she was still hungry. Reaching the windows, she knelt and picked up the peas.

Holding them in the palm of her hand, she looked out the window. Off in the distance, layers of wispy clouds wove patterns of lace through the sky, and whitecaps rippled along the surface of the ocean. To the left and right, breakers tore at the rocks strewn along the bottom of the escarpment. It was a great day for surfing, and she knew that if the weather held, Daggett wouldn't be able to resist.

A rough trail heading toward the shore marred the lushness of the coastal vegetation. There was a small beach below the house, but it was just out of sight. Somewhere in between was their washing machine that had fallen through the floor in the last aftershock and tumbled down the side of the hill.

She chuckled at a flash of blue. It was Flotsam running down the path. Not far behind was the man she had grown to love, one hand cupped between his legs, and the other raised in a fist over his head. He'd never catch the dog, she knew. To

Flotsam, it was all about the chase.

With a certain sense of satisfaction, she turned from the window. She grabbed one of the peas between two fingers and popped it into her mouth. After all, they were undamaged. She might as well eat them while they were still warm. No one else would.

Walking back to the table, she wound carefully around the broken bits of crockery on the floor, seating herself at the table. She chewed the final two peas slowly, looking out across the living room, enjoying the view, and waiting.

Then, when she was about to give up, the front screen opened and slammed to, and she heard the scramble of toenails on wood. Flotsam tumbled into view. He immediately stopped to lick at the remains of the peas smeared across the floor.

Almost without a break, a tall, tanned body wearing blue-checkered boxers flung itself into the room. With flailing arms, unable to stop, he crashed into Flotsam, tripping over him, and sprawling across the floor. When he came to rest, he was on his back, and a grin was on his face. He looked at Geraldine and winked.

"Surf's up, Geri. Gotta change. I can't go around in my underwear all day. Are my board shorts clean?"

She moved to stand over him, her willowy limbs telling their own story of sun and the beach. She smiled and stuck out her tongue before answering. "As clean as they were when you took them off yesterday. Do you remember losing the washer in the last big quake? I only visit the Laundromat every other Friday."

He held out a hand. "Yeah, that's right. How could I forget? Help me up, won't you?"

"Say uncle." She put a bare foot on his chest and grinned. When he just laid his head back and laughed, she insisted. "Uncle, Daggett. Say it if you want up."

He grabbed her leg and yanked, throwing her off balance, catching her as she came down on top of him. He wrapped his arms around her and rolled her over so he was on top of her. With a kiss on her lips, he leaned his mouth to her ear before whispering, "Uncle."

She laughed, and it was breathless. "Want to play for a while with your uncle?"

"I just got my shorts on." He nibbled on her ear, and his answer wasn't no at all.

Flotsam had different ideas. Having finished the pea paste on the floor, he saw the two adults he lived with wrestling together, and he wanted to be part of the action. With a leap, he was in the pile, and his long tongue let them know how much he enjoyed their attention.

Daggett let go of her and wrapped his arms around the big dog. "So, you want to be part of the action, too? Then come and get it." He laughed as he rolled with the animal, until they crashed against the windows. He reached for Geraldine, only to find air.

"Geri," he called, seeing her heading into the kitchen. "I thought you and me, um, were playing uncle."

"With the dog? I don't think so." She shook her head.

"He just wants to be part of the fun."

"And that breaks the mood for me. You have fun with your dog, and your board shorts are in the bathroom. If you get in the tub, bounce a few times before you turn on the water. I think the floor's getting weak, and it'd be a long way to fall. Before long, we may be down to the shower in the master." She leaned her head back into the room for a moment. "I'll be watching for you out on the water. Oh, and remember, I have to go in at five today. Sweets!" She put her finger to her lips and flicked a kiss toward him. Flotsam leaped up as if he knew just when to intercept it.

16

"Flotsam! Give that back!" Tanned arms grabbed the dog, pretending to snatch the kiss from the air. When Daggett looked toward the kitchen with a grin, Geraldine was gone. He turned to the dog, "You love me, don't you, boy? You've always loved me, no matter who else was around. Well, I love you, too."

Geraldine had paused just around the corner. She bit her upper lip and quickly blinked several times to clear the sting away. She wanted that wonderful man out there to say those words to her, but he never had. He was a wonderful, crazy fool, and when he acted like he loved that dog more than her, she wanted to run away before he abandoned her.

She brushed a tear from her eye, knowing it was her own fault. She'd meant to be strong and keep her distance, to not get hurt again, but here she was. She loved a man who cared for his dog more than he cared for her. How could she have been so stupid?

She dealt with it the best way she knew. She opened the broom closet and grabbed the sweeper and dustpan. The last of Daggett's heirloom china was on the floor, and after all, it did have to be cleaned up, didn't it? And it would get done, if she had to smile and pretend her eyes weren't the teeniest bit raw.

Chapter 2

"HEY, BOY! Want to go for a swim?"

Daggett was in the bathroom to change, and the dog was with him. The room was large, one of two in the big old house. The decor dated from decades before and hadn't been redone in the years in between. He pulled a piece of old gum from his mouth. When the big dog barked and jumped forward, Daggett admonished playfully, "Down, boy!" The animal jumped on him, a tongue finding one of his eyes. He laughed, rolling the dog off and pushing him away.

Flotsam barked rapidly several times, leaping on Daggett once again. In the roughhousing, the gum was lost, and he turned to see it resting at the back of the toilet.

"Flotsam! Bad dog!" He laughed, pushing on the animal's chest and reaching for the messy wad. "I could have gotten one more day from this." He held it in front of the dog. "You want it, boy? Would you like to have a go at some gum?"

"No, Daggett. I can hear you in there, you know. Do not

give that dog your gum. It sticks in his stomach, and it'll make him sick." A rapid series of brisk taps vibrated the door, and Geraldine's steps were rapid staccato drumbeats as she walked down the wood-floored hallway.

"Quiet, boy," Daggett whispered. "Now, if you want this, you have to keep it a secret from Geri. She'll be all over us both if you chew it to where she can see. Here. Take it if you want it."

The dog seemed to wink, lifting one side of his upper lip, then his tongue lapped out, and the gum was gone. His front paws pulled at the sides of his face as he dropped to the floor and smacked at the treat.

"Like it, boy, do you?" Daggett ruffled the dog's fur down one side, then he rolled his lean body and stood in a smooth and easy motion. He flipped the water on and splashed his face with water. With a wet hand, he ran his fingers through his hair before turning to the swim suit on the side of the tub.

"Trunks time." Holding them to his face, he wrinkled his nose. "Maybe they'll smell better after an afternoon in the ocean."

Flotsam wagged his tail, nudging Daggett as he changed from his boxers to the trunks. He barked twice, then attempted to wrestle the undershorts out of Daggett's hand.

"Want to play, boy?" Daggett held them high overhead, shaking them.

The dog growled and barked again. Daggett opened the door and threw them down the hall, laughing to see the animal tear out of the bathroom and down the hall after them.

"That's why the animal takes your shorts, you know."

Daggett turned to see Geraldine standing at the back bedroom door, one shoulder against the doorframe, her arms crossed. The wall of windows behind her flooded the room with light, reaching out to wrap its fingers around her, surrounding her with an ethereal glow. In that moment, she was as beautiful as the night he'd first set eyes on her, down at San Jose, just over two years ago.

What a weekend that had been!

Chapter 3

DAGGETT'S most recent girlfriend had bailed on him several weeks earlier, and he'd been alone. With the emptiness of the house, he'd felt the need to get away. There was a big blowout on the beach down near San Jose, and he hitched a ride with his cousin's girlfriend, Ronnie Bertram, in her Volkswagen Beetle. His cousin was already there, and she'd welcomed the company for the ride down.

The Beetle was circa 1964 and had been flooded out in a storm once, sitting half buried in the surf for two days. Her brother had torn the engine apart and crudely rebuilt it. The body was hopeless, though. It was little more than rust held together by occasional pieces of metal. There was a hole in the passenger side floorboard covered by an old piece of plywood. Safety first, Ronnie always laughed.

The little Bug ran, though not well, spitting black smoke and occasionally coming to a coughing stop on the side of the highway. Still, it was more of a car than Daggett had. She'd even let him strap his surfboard on top for the Moonlight Surf Tour. They arrived after dark, as pockets of fog began to reach fingers along the beach, and there were cars everywhere. Daggett had unstrapped his board, and they'd made their way through the maze of vehicles, aiming for the light of the bonfire in the distance. It was red and brilliant, blurring in the haze, and flickering against the darkness of the star-studded sky. Somewhere along the way, they picked up another couple, not that he and Ronnie were a couple, but they were together, and that made them one. The other couple had sticks of weed in their hands, and they offered Daggett and Ronnie a toke. Ronnie laughed and said she was game, but Daggett intended to be on his board all weekend.

Then Daggett's cousin appeared from inside a van, with a girl on his arm, one who looked about fifteen, and Ronnie went berserk, smashing the joint into the girl's face, and kneeing Daggett's cousin in the groin. She left a few scratch marks on his face in the process, and Daggett was glad he'd done nothing to upset her on the drive down. With the blood, Ronnie started to cry, and she wanted to make up, apologizing for kneeing him so hard.

Daggett couldn't take the drama, so he wandered off toward the party. The other couple hadn't waited as long as he had, already high on their weed, so he was alone with his board. Before he'd gotten past the next car, the girl from the van stepped from a patch of fog and latched onto his arm. She had on swimsuit bottoms, with only a thin shirt on top, with one button fastened just below her breasts. She leaned into him, pressing against his arm, and when she looked up at him, he could smell the liquor on her breath.

Poor girl, he thought, a surf groupie who should be in her bedroom doing her homework.

Once he got to the beach, he sloughed her off, letting her

find her own way through the night. She was just a kid, and she'd find a friend somewhere to keep track of her. If not, he couldn't watch over all the stupid people in the world.

"Daggett! You young whipper-snapper, you!"

He snorted, surprised to be recognized in the dark. The owner of the voice was no stranger. A burly redhead with bare shoulders and wearing giant flower-print shorts came stumbling out of the fog, a can in his hand. The big man owned a board shop up in San Fran, and when Daggett was about sixteen, they'd made a surfing run down to Baja, spending six weeks on the beach, doing nothing except chasing the perfect wave.

He should have known he'd find Corky Maiterson here. Beach, water, beer, and a roaring fire equaled one Corky. Always. And those four things were present that night in full measure.

Of course, Corky had been half the man he was now, but Daggett was glad to see him. Corky was the parent he'd never known, even when his mother had still pretended she loved him, occasionally showing up at his grandparents' to pick him up for a Sunday afternoon ice cream cone.

"Corky!" Daggett dropped his surfboard, throwing a long arm around his old friend's neck, and slapping him on the back. Stepping away, he laughed. "I could have caught a ride with you, you old surfer, you. I probably would've had a pleasanter trip." He pictured the VW that had spent as much time on the side of the road as traveling down the highway.

"I'm sure. I would've loved a young pup along to navigate. Like when you and me went down to Mexico. Remember then?"

They were back to Corky's resting spot, and the big man pulled a sausage off a small grill. Slapping it into a toasted bun, he handed it to Daggett.

"Yeah, I remember." It had been the first time in his life that he'd felt like someone loved him for who he was instead of who they wanted him to be. "Good sausage. Ones you made?"

"Stuffed them myself."

That was Corky, independent and with a hand in everything, including grinding and stuffing his own meat. Daggett also knew he made his own boards to sell in his shop. Nothing was too gritty for the big man to delve into.

Laughter closer to the bonfire caught Daggett's attention, and he turned to see a group of bare-shouldered surfer boys crowded around a fog-shrouded girl he couldn't quite make out. One of the surfers looked like Zac Dirkson from Big Sur— American born, Aussie honed, and deadly on the water.

"What's going on there?" He turned back to Corky, biting into the meaty sausage, ducking his head and dodging the dripping juices as he watched them dribble at his feet.

"Going on?" Corky reached to the fire to pull the rest of the sausages free.

Daggett nudged him and nodded at the boys by the fire. The girl was still in the center of the crowd, but in the flickering flames and the dancing shadows, she seemed more a ghostly vision, a goddess of the night, destined to be hidden from mortal man. One of the boys on the edge of the group laughed. His voice had a rough sound, one that spoke of hours of falling into the cold water just off shore. Laughter rang from the girl. She must be beautiful, Daggett was certain, to have garnered such a crowd of spectators.

"There?" Corky nodded toward the goddess, at the same time digging in an ice chest for a moment, and handing Daggett a cold can. "She won't have time for you, you know. She's been here all day, and everyone on the beach wants her attention. Come on. I've brought a new board. I was hoping you would work your way down for the surfing contest. This board is one I built just for you."

"And if I hadn't shown up?" The sausage was about gone,

24

and he stuffed the end of it in his mouth. His next words mumbled out, "Would it still be just for me?" He grinned.

A shower of sand was his only answer. It was going to be a fun night, and it was only beginning.

Chapter 4

DAGGETT struggled out of the sleeping bag he'd borrowed from Corky. It smelled like the beach, and that wasn't necessarily a good thing. He bunched the front of his shirt and pressed it to his face, taking a deep breath and coughing at the intense aroma of fire and sausage. There were also overtones of an unwashed, sleeping man.

"That bad, huh?"

His eyes found his inquisitor, and for a moment, the ceaseless surf just down the sand quieted its incessant pounding, his shirt no longer antagonized his nostrils, and he forgot all about his rumbling stomach. The goddess from the crowd stood in front of him. Her limbs were long and lithe, and flowing hair with the texture of silk cascaded in a sweeping waterfall from her head. Then he caught her eyes. They were deep pools of ocean blue with just a hint of a summer shower. A shimmering wrap enclosed her torso, and what a torso it was!

He was in love.

"Okay, what does that look mean? I don't see any head-lights, but if it were nighttime, I'd guess we were in Colorado, and I'd just caught a deer in mine." She laughed lightly, brushing one hand through her hair, the silken strands gliding through her fingertips like hot butter across an ear of corn. As she lifted her arm, she was silhouetted against the foggy sea, and she was exquisite in every way.

He coughed roughly, laughing at himself. He glanced at his sandy feet, and sudden pressure on his bladder made him aware that this wasn't heaven, even if he had an angel standing in front of him.

"You know, you stuck that shirt to your face for some reason, and then you screwed up your nose like you'd never smelled anything that bad. No man should be forced to wear anything that distressing. Here. Let me help you."

And sucker his soul if she didn't walk right up to him, grab that shirt just where it lay against his waist, and pull it hard up, forcing it over his arms and his head.

She stepped back, holding the shirt at arm's length, and she surveyed him critically. He rubbed his arms, suddenly cool in the California morning. It was early yet, and there was no sun. He felt goose bumps rise on his skin.

"Not bad. Your board, I'm guessing." It lay beside his sleeping bag. "With that body, I'm guessing you've been on the water since your first flight of puberty. What, twelve, thirteen?" She laughed brightly, tossing the shirt off to the side, as far as it would go.

"Hey," he cried, taking a step forward, then stopping himself for some reason he couldn't quite define. "That's my shirt."

"You'd wear it again? Don't bother. If you can't stand the smell, it's not worth washing. Buy you another if you need it."

She untied her wrap and adjusted the strap. As she did so, he could see the shadowed outline of her form darker within the thin cloth. Then she pulled the belt tight again, and she disappeared back into the wrap, the tease just that—a tease.

She continued, "You've known Corky long?" The man lay to the side wrapped in a dirty quilt, snoring softly. She chuckled. "He's quite a character."

"Pretty long. Corky and I go way back." A lifetime, he thought.

"Way back, huh? You're twenty-six, maybe, twenty-eight at a stretch. How far back can you two go?" She reached for his hand and pulled him away from the sleeping bag. "I want to know all about my way-back boy."

She smiled, and he couldn't resist.

They didn't talk for a time, though. The sand scrunched under their feet, causing them to crab along in a sideways walk until they reached the wet sand closer to the shore. Foam had built up in little piles, forming ridges like miniature breakers on the sand. Every now and then they were forced to step over piles of drying seaweed, the remains of the tide that had risen during the wee hours of the morning.

At one point, he picked up a sand dollar and made to toss it out to sea like a skipping stone. Before he could release it, she grabbed his arm, and she brought it to her, turning his wrist and slowly opening his hand. She held it for several minutes, the sand dollar lying in his palm, as she brushed her fingers along his wrist.

"Nice," she said, and then after a moment more, she picked the shell up and slipped it into a hidden pocket in her wrap. "For luck," she said.

It was unclear whether her first word had meant the shell was nice, or that touching his skin felt so, but to him the luck was obvious.

"So, how do you know Corky?" She had his hand in hers again, holding it as they walked along. With her free hand, she kept pushing her hair from her face. Occasionally she would brush it over her shoulder, only to bend down and have it slip past again. Once he knelt beside her and lifted it over her shoulder for her, and he noticed a blush leap into her skin just at the base of her neck.

"Corky's my father." He said the words softly.

She laughed. "Now *that* is not the truth."

He let go of her hand and crossed his arms over his chest. He tried to contain his grin, but it escaped from him regardless.

"Is so."

He turned and started off down the beach, faster this time. Just once he turned to see if she followed.

She did.

"Explain how." Her hand pulled at his arm, and she worked her fingers back into his. "But before you do, you must understand that I know Corky. You can't pull anything over on me." She leaned against him, her fingers entwined with his.

"Okay, he's not my real father, but he's my only father. Does that suit you?"

"Only father? That tells me a lot. Does that mean you're adopted?"

"Yeah, adopted." In spirit. In love. In his heart. "In the best way possible."

"Yet, you don't call him much, do you?"

He stopped walking and looked at the girl with him. How could she know that? Was she a girlfriend? Worse, a wife?

"Nah. You can't be." He chuckled as he began to walk again. Corky was twice this girl's age. People did that, he knew, but he couldn't imagine his friend in a May-December marriage. Besides, she wouldn't be walking with him here, holding his arm so tightly, if she were involved with Corky.

"I can't be what?" There was humor in her words, as if she knew more than she let on.

29

He took a chance. "Corky's girl." He looked her way, grinning. The pressure on his bladder was long forgotten. This girl was the cause.

"You could say that." She looked down and straightened the fabric of her wrap before she looked him in his eyes. "Yes, you could say exactly that, except Corky doesn't know." Her eyes were redder than they'd been moments before, although the difference wasn't obvious, not to anyone who hadn't just looked into those blue eyes and wanted to fall inside them forever.

"A secret love? Or just an admirer?" He couldn't help himself. He'd never dreamed Corky to have a secret admirer. Corky was just Corky, a good friend, an even better surfer, and the man he considered his father. He wouldn't trade him for a hundred other people, but to be the sole focus of a girl's admiration, one half his age? It boggled the mind.

"Both." Her word was whispered. Off in the distance, a sea lion could be seen on a distant rock. It brayed its defiance to the sea, or perhaps it was a love song, and no one except a sea lion could tell. Pulling a slender strand of hair from her lips, she murmured, "All of the above, actually."

"You've never told him?" He'd heard her words and chuckled. "Does he know he has a secret admirer?"

"Oh, he knows." She brightened her voice. "He knows every bit of who I am, well, almost every bit. There are a few secrets I keep hidden deep inside. The thing is, you don't know who I am." She held out her hand as if to shake.

"You hold my arm all the way out here, and now you want to shake my hand?" He couldn't help himself, and he laughed.

"Introductions, you know. They must be done formally. Don't be afraid. If I haven't bitten you by now, I think you can safely assume you will emerge from this handshake unscathed." Her hand was still in the air between them, and she nodded at it.

Grasping it, he bowed in his bare-shouldered, surfer-best

form, intoning, "Daggett Damon Priestly, like Jason the actor, except much better looking."

"Oh, I can certainly agree with that." Laughter imbued her words. "Geraldine Gossamer Ridgway, named for a children's book character. My middle name, anyway. Geraldine is for my grandmother. Most people know me as Geri."

"I'm glad to formally meet you, Geri Gossamer Ridgway." He bowed again, making as if to tip an imaginary hat.

"And the same to you," she giggled, "Daggett Better-Looking-Than-Jason Priestly." She glanced at his askew hair and the freckles scattered across his skin, and then she giggled again.

He wrapped her arm in his as if on a formal Victorian stroll. "Now, my beautiful Geri, what else do you wish to know about your exceedingly handsome companion?"

"Thank you, good man. Now, how's Corky your father? I'm unaware of any children he claims as his own, and as far as I am aware, he has none that are adopted."

"Ah, what does adopted mean? That's the question, my good woman." His eyes turned sideways to her, and he pumped his eyebrows in teasing.

"Like a son. An adopted son. Are you really Corky's?"

"Really Corky's?" He made as if to ponder the question, his lips pursed, his eyes raised to the skies. After a moment, he put his finger to his chin and frowned. "Am I really Corky's?"

"Come now. It's a very easy question. You're making this difficult on purpose."

"I'd like to turn your question around. Is Corky mine? I have no compunction at all in saying that I've adopted Corky as my own, and he is indeed my father." He smirked as if that settled it. He knew he thought of Corky as a father, and he hoped Corky felt the same about him. He was pretty sure most of the time, but still, he'd never pushed the matter with the older man. He didn't dare risk something so fragile.

"Bully. I still don't know my answer." She pretended to pout, but her expression was washed away before too many steps were gone.

Over the next rise, they were surprised to see a small waterfall, a storm drain still shifting runoff from the interior of the city to the wide ocean. It tumbled over several stone steps, and it was quite pretty. It burbled like a country creek.

She turned to him, a frustrated smirk on her face. "Daggett, seriously. What's your relationship with Corky? I have to know."

She didn't get her answer. With the sound of the burbling water, his bladder did a somersault, and it reminded him that he hadn't relieved it, yet. With a yelp of impending disaster, he tore for the nearest sand dune, diving over the top, leaving only the sound of his actions to reveal the reason for his sudden exit.

LISTENING to a double waterfall, one natural, and the second very man-made, Geraldine giggled. She quite liked this guy, and she barely knew him. She would be green with envy if he really were Corky's. It would be so unfair for Corky to claim this man as his son, especially if he had no biological connection to him. However, anyone involved with Corky couldn't be too bad. And if so, then that was a chance she would simply have to take.

Chapter 5

"YOU REALLY care about Flotsam, don't you, Daggett?" Geraldine stood against the doorjamb, with her arms crossed. Her question flayed his moment of fun, laying bare his flouting of her earlier demand.

"Care about my best friend?" He stood contritely, although mimicking her stance. "How can you even ask that?"

"I see what he has in his mouth. Gum." She left her final word hanging in the air.

A dozen years before she'd owned a miniature pincher. Just a kid, she had doted on the animal, taking it everywhere with her, letting it sleep under her covers, and feeding it from her own plate. She had even shared her gum with the animal, and it had been funny to watch it chew the sticky substance until it managed to swallow it down.

When the dog was two, it began to have stomach problems, throwing up and enduring bouts of constipation. One night after constant retching, the vet in the animal hospital's emergency room told her the gum had clogged its digestive track, and there was nothing she could do.

Until Flotsam, that was the last dog she had owned. Of course, Flotsam was Daggett's, not hers, but still, here they were. For all practical purposes, the animal was hers just as much as his.

"Come on, Geri. It's just a bit of gum. Flotsam loves it." With loose joints and a grin on his unshaven jaw, he wrapped long arms around her, planting a quick kiss on her cheek. "Wind's up. I'm out on the water in a bit. See you, Baby. I'll wave to you. I want you to be looking."

He took off down the hallway, his bare feet slapping the floorboards. One hand grabbed the frame of the door into the living room, and just before he disappeared, he turned, winking at her.

Off behind him, she could see a sliver of ocean through the living room windows. The sun glittered on the waves, darkening his face to near invisibility. His wild hair glowed, a halo of golden light around his head. He blew her a shadowed kiss, one hand flinging it her way.

Immediately calling to Flotsam, he bounded out, the house shivering as he ran. Barking came from somewhere unseen, and a few moments later, the screen door slammed a second time.

The house was quiet once again, and Geraldine leaned her head against the wall, closing her eyes.

"Puis-je vous aider?"

The exotic words washed over her. With a smile, she let out a breath she didn't know she was holding and opened her eyes. She realized she could see her breath in front of her face. Rubbing her arms, she wasn't surprised to feel a down jacket covering her arms.

Laughing, she whispered, "What else would one wear on a ski vacation in the French Alps?"

After all, there was snow all around, a steaming cup of dark cocoa on the small bistro table at her side, and the air was crisp and cold.

"Puis-je vous aider?" The smooth sounds wrapped her once again, cajoling her, drawing her attention.

She turned to see a liveried waiter at her side holding a tray of steaming beverages. His black hair was slicked against his head, and a handlebar moustache dripped from around his mouth. He didn't seem cold, although there was a thick layer of snow covering the ground just past the portico.

"Yes. Could I possibly get you to check on my skis? I gave them to the maître d'hôtel for a quick wax. I would like to go out on the slopes this afternoon, and I didn't bring my backup pair." She could just see his name on his jacket. Paul. She had known it would be.

"Oui, mademoiselle." He reached out and deftly slipped her cup from the table, sliding it among the filled ones on his tray, and placing a fresh offering at her side. Atop its dark surface, a billowy dollop of whipped cream floated languidly. "Avec ceci?"

Avec ceci? She had no idea what that meant, and she giggled. She didn't know what *puis-je vous aider* meant, either. It was just as well. At least Paul always gave her one answer she understood. Oui. Yes. As long as she asked him questions he could answer with *oui*, then she could have anything she wanted.

"Rum, Paul? I do believe I would like some rum in my chocolate. Just a bit, please, as I intend to visit the slopes as soon as my skis arrive. Oh, and I haven't seen Daggett since arriving. Could you please locate him for me?" She smiled brightly, and in that moment realized she was wearing a woolen scarf. She tightened it around her neck, sheltering against the chill of a stiffening breeze.

"Oui, mademoiselle." Paul flipped a cloth off his arm and pressed it against the tabletop, neatening up some perceived affront to the perfection of the small restaurant. With equal aplomb, he adjusted the second chair at the table as if for an anticipated arrival, setting a second cup of cocoa next to hers.

"Thank you, Paul." She touched him gently on his white sleeve, her gratitude made stronger in that one small motion. The second cup meant Daggett was on his way.

Paul turned, and in a fraction of a second, he was gone, as were her down jacket, the blanketing snow, and the steaming cocoa. The doorjamb pressed into her shoulder, and her calves ached from standing too long. The sound of a dog in the distance caught her attention, and she moved down the hall. This bedroom opened to ocean vistas matching those seen through the living room windows. Far below, Daggett ran down the trail, his board held in both hands high over his head, followed by a mass of barking dog. It was Flotsam that had drawn her from her French vacation. What amused her were Daggett's knees as they jerked high in the air with each step, dodging roots and branches on the overgrown trail. Flotsam nipped at his heels, bouncing along like he was part of a pinball machine. The animal had energy, enough to keep pace with his master like few others could.

She placed her hand flat against the glass, and she smiled as she turned away. Soon Daggett would be far out in the waves, and she could watch him, using the binoculars in the kitchen if she wished. Except for needing to be at work later in the day, she might consider joining him, but there would be other times.

It was then that she felt the floor shift under her feet, and she knew another earthquake was underway.

Chapter 6

"DAGGETT!" Geraldine let the word loose as fear grabbed her stomach and forced it into a knot. Moving away from the glass—always sensible—she prepared herself as best as she could with no warning.

Then, as her world twisted out from under her, she felt her arms go wild, and her vision begin to spin. Outside she could see the tips of the trees begin to sway, and strange popping sounds echoed throughout the house. This time she was certain the old building would dance off its foundation supports and leap skyward, flung at the distant ocean like a Frisbee in flight.

Something somewhere crashed to the floor, and in that blistering moment of fear, the world became still once again. After a tense moment of silence, she released the tightly held breath she didn't even know she clung to. Looking outside, the sea continued its rhythmic journey toward the shore, and the occasional cloud overhead hung serenely still. A speck on the water could easily be Daggett, paddling out as if he hadn't a care in the world.

In reality, he probably didn't. The house could come crashing down, and he'd crawl under the surviving floorboards, using whatever remained of the structure as shelter, surfing his days away.

As her heart pounded in her chest, she realized she was perspiring, and she ran a finger just under one eye, the motion one she remembered from long ago. Her mother's funeral. What made her think of that?

The phone began to ring.

She laughed, and it sounded hysterical, even to her. The phone! It was ringing, just as always, as if nothing had happened. She laughed again before covering her mouth with her hand and regaining control. How she loved the phone telling her that the world was still in one piece, and she wasn't all alone!

Moving to the bed, she picked it up and breathed into it, murmuring, "Geri, here." With her words, she let the moment of the impending disaster slip away.

"Excusez-moi, mademoiselle. Jusqu'à présent nous avons un problem. Un avalanche." The genteel voice over the phone exuded polite help, and she looked up to see snow piled high outside her window. Glancing back, the bed, clearly one in a high-priced luxury hotel suite, was rumpled in a fashion showing two people had recently nestled between its linen sheets. Her eyes jumped to a bathroom visible through a double door. She wondered whether Daggett was inside. Peering through the opening, she found a sunken marble tub with two Doric columns flanking each side and extensive mirrored walls, but there was no Daggett to be seen.

"Daggett?" She called to him, waiting a moment on his answer. He might be able to talk to the person on the phone. Surely he knew French, as he'd been the one who had planned this trip.

"Mademoiselle?" The receiver called to her.

"Certainly!" She spoke brightly into the hand piece, as if she'd understood every word spoken to her. "That will be fine. Si! Or rather, Oui!"

It bothered her that Daggett hadn't come when she called.

Feeling rather foolish, she placed the receiver gently on the cradle and stepped to the window. Three of the words she thought she knew. Excuse . . . problem . . . avalanche, although she didn't see what that had to do with her. Did the resort have regular drills, like on cruise ships? Perhaps that's what the man was telling her.

Looking down to the parking lot, she noticed someone walking across the drifts, and he carried a snowboard with him. Daggett! She rapped on the window firmly, hoping to get his attention, finally resting her palm against its cold surface. He'd snuck out without her, leaving her alone in the room. He could have at least kissed her and reminded her to have a good day.

She felt the glass begin to quiver, and looking up, she realized what the phone call had been about. Coming down the mountain was a wall of snow a hundred feet high, and Daggett was directly in its path. He had to see it and run. He glanced back at the building and waved to the window where she stood. He wasn't watching ahead, simply walking forward, a smile on his face, not a care in the world.

"Daggett," she pleaded, the sound useless, even to her.

Then, an ear-splitting crack echoed throughout the room, and she closed her eyes, not wanting to see the disaster that she knew must have torn the outside world apart.

"Geri? Honey, are you there?"

The phone prodded with its gentle words, and she opened her eyes, not sure what she would see. There before her was sunshine, a plate glass window stretching from floor to ceiling, and on the other side, ocean as far as her eyes could see.

Placing her palm on the window, she let it rest for a moment, then slid it across the smooth surface. Frowning, she retraced her hand's path, realizing she'd felt something unexpected. Finding it again, she ran her fingernail across the spot. It was what she thought, a hairline crack.

"Did you survive the quake?" The voice on the other end of the phone tittered nervously. "Geri? Honey?"

"I'm here, Mrs. Nettleworth. We've got a cracked window, I think. I haven't inspected anything else."

She hated the window damage. Structural plate this thick was hard to come by, and besides, if the quake had cracked the glass, what else in the house had taken damage? The glass had never cracked before, not in any of the windows. Why this one just now?

"At least you don't have a cracked head. My son tells me that all the time, with me living near the San Andreas Fault. I tell him that's in Southern California, near those crazy movie stars!" Mrs. Nettleworth giggled until she coughed. "Is Daggett doing okay? I knew him when he was just a boy, you remember. He spent more time with his grandparents than he ever did with that unusual mother of his."

"Hm." Geraldine let the comments go. She didn't intend to discuss Daggett's past life with anyone. Mrs. Nettleworth might feel free to express her opinions, but Geraldine didn't have to get involved in them.

Something sparkled on the windowsill. Small slivers of glass. The crack seemed to be on the inside only, though. The lamination sandwiched between the panes had held. She felt relieved.

"Not injured, is he? You can tell me if he is." Mrs. Nettleworth seemed lonely, as if the quake was her chance to strike up a conversation.

"He's fine. He went down to the beach, and I'm sure he

40

doesn't know we've had another one. I appreciate you asking about him, Mrs. Nettleworth. He'll be pleased to know how much you care."

"Well, I'm bringing him down a strawberry pie. I had some in the freezer, and I decided I needed to use them up. It's for you, too, dear. Don't go hungry just because you and Daggett aren't, well, married. It'll happen when the time's right. I know about that. I didn't marry Mr. Nettleworth until I was twenty-five. It'll come to you. Trust me, dear."

Then the voice over the phone was gone, and she replaced the receiver. Apprehensive in spite of her reassurances to Mrs. Nettleworth, she scanned the water in the distance, looking for Daggett. Something was out there, catching the light, brighter than the sparkling whitecaps.

Hurrying to the kitchen with a speed she didn't think was exactly safe—and didn't care particularly if it was—she opened the top cabinet and pulled out the binoculars. Adjusting the eyepieces, she made her way to the expanse of windows that made the house so beautiful, and she held them up, searching the sea. Then she saw him, and she smiled. He was poised on his board atop a wave, and the sun glistened on his skin. The board jerked and bobbed under his feet, a rooster tail shooting from the back, and he looked as if he were strolling down a country lane. Then his legs tensed, and he jerked. In a series of rapid switchbacks, he danced on the wave with a grace that would have shamed many a ballroom instructor. That was her Daggett, secure in his world, even if his world was the sea and the surf and a house that was falling into the ocean.

She felt a moment of intense longing, although she didn't know for what. Then she let it go. Her life was what it was. Her world had become Daggett and his collapsing house, and jinx her soul if she didn't love him for it anyway.

Chapter 7

FAMILIAR music softly swirled throughout the house, draping the walls in old memories. Geraldine dropped a well-worn knife into the sink and lifted a plate of small sandwiches—cheese, tuna, and anchovy—ready to feed the masses. Somewhere Daggett laughed, his voice carrying through an open door, probably perched outside on the deck.

Hidden in the late evening's darkness, somewhere she couldn't quite see, the ocean collided with exuberance against the rocky shoreline, and its cries of exultation rippled up the hillside. Over a hundred people had joined Daggett and her for a Juneteenth celebration, and the house vibrated with life.

As many holiday lights as they'd been able to scrounge up from the neighbors were strung along the ceilings and out onto the deck fifteen steps down the hill from the sliding glass doors. Doorways had multicolored strands dangling, and people glowed like Christmas trees as they laughingly pushed their way through. The bare plate glass stretching across the back of the house was a black mirror reflecting the miniature lights back into the interior. What little furniture the house wore was pushed to the back walls, and cheap plastic beanbag chairs had been thrown everywhere. It was a magical world, glittering with color and otherworldly effervescence.

Geraldine floated through the chattering people, her feet bare, and one hand holding her plate of hors d'oeuvres high over her head. She had on cutoff jeans, and a billowing chiffon pullover with a ruffled collar fluttered as she walked. She was in her element among crowds of people. This was what she was born for.

"Geri," a voice called to her, waving. "Fuel for the hungry?"

"Jasmine! Of course, I knew you would be here." She swung the plate low, letting one or two of the finger sandwiches disappear, lightening her load. She mouthed to her friend, "Come outside and join us. The best of the party is there."

"Geri!" Another voice called, another hand waving. She knew everyone, her innate skill at matching names one that would shine tonight. "Geri! . . . Geri! . . ." and the calls went on, the plate growing lighter and lighter. All the while, she called her responses, "Artie, and Bette, and Jolene . . . Chase . . . Ritchie . . . and Sam." Even Ronnie was there. She was still with Daggett's cousin, although Geraldine had yet to figure out why. She was happy for them, though. Anyone who could weather a relationship was to be congratulated.

Swirling outside, artfully maneuvering through the curtain of lights, she located Daggett. His golden skin glowed against the candles scattered over the deck below. He was sitting on the railing, hunched over, his forearms on his knees. His eyes were focused on something someone was telling him, and a smile kept building and fading on his lips. Once he laughed, then he turned quickly serious again, making a comment she couldn't hear. Finally he threw his head back and laughed again, exposing his long neck, and she could see tendrils of blond hair curling from inside his open-neck shirt. He lifted one arm and ran his fingers roughly through his hair, shifting his position on the railing, and turned to slap another equally golden man on the shoulder. He made a comment then rubbed his hands together. Catching sight of her, he waved and motioned her down.

He was surrounded with surfer types, the kind of people he ran with. It was his trust fund that enabled him to surf every day, but the money wasn't quite enough to allow real upkeep on the house or for him to travel to warmer climes when the winter rains kept the waters too chilly for anything except the thickest of wetsuits. Still, he shared what he had. That was Daggett, generous with what he owned, his house and his beach, and modest enough not to realize he had anything at all.

Her bare feet skipping down the fifteen steps, careful of the one that suffered from a botched repair job, she joined the crowd on the deck wedged below the house. From the crack in the living room floor, a sliver of refracted colors danced along the deck. The railing also glittered with strands of lights wrapped around the boards, and one strip blinked on and off, occasionally matching the beat of the laid-back songs melting into the night.

"Finally, Daggett." Her voice tinkled with laughter as she fell at his side. "I brought you something to eat, but I think most of it got snagged along the way."

"Nothing to drink?" He reached for the plate, and the bleached hair on his arm caught in the lights. The day had been warm, but the breeze lifting from the ocean below had goose bumps crawling over his skin. "Cocoa, maybe?"

"Cocoa, is that your secret?" One of the surfer types, skinny as a rail and red-haired as a blood moon, zeroed in on Daggett's request. Freckles shattered his complexion, looking in the darkness like shards of bittersweet chocolate.

"Geri, this is Skylar. I told him he was welcome to come

44

aboard for the summer, if he wants. He's from Carolina, Mass, or somewhere back East. Says he surfed Indonesia two summers ago, then Tierra del Fuego last winter."

"South America? Daggett will envy you." Geraldine winked at the flame-haired boy.

"He used up all his money, and he can't get home," Daggett continued. "Surf here, I told him. We can put him up." He grabbed Skylar's hand, doing a handshake that took several steps to complete, then they slapped each other roughly on the shoulder.

Skylar turned and stuck out his hand Geraldine's way. "Skylar Johnson, ma'am. It's Carolinas. South, to be exact. Presently from California. Your spare room as of tonight, if you must know, and I thank you for your welcome. I'll do you proud." He grinned, and it was the playful look of a boy who had enjoyed too much of a good time in one evening.

"I only know normal shakes, Skylar." She held out her hand. "Normal, remember?"

"Yes, ma'am." He hiccupped and took her hand, all manners and politeness. Then he leaned in, filled with seriousness. "Does he always drink cocoa? If that's the magic, then I want some, too." He nodded expectantly, as if she could bring him a mysterious brew that would turn him into the skilled surfer Daggett was known to be.

She laughed, reaching to give Daggett a kiss on the cheek. "You bamboozler," she whispered. "You've hoodwinked him."

"He's my slave," he whispered back. "I need the trail to the beach cleared, and I figure it's worth a few bucks in groceries."

She laughed, turning to Skylar. "Cocoa it is. Two cups of magic brew coming up."

As she walked away, she overheard Skylar's Low Country voice as he turned to Daggett. "Now about that big wave you caught in the spring. You say you saw a shark swimming right under you? Were you scared? Boogers, but I would be . . ."

Like she'd told herself a million times, she wouldn't trade her man for any other Joe in the world. She loved him, and that was that.

She just hoped he loved her.

Chapter 8

GERALDINE pushed at a half-burned log, and two that had been standing on end fell into her bed of coals, sending a flurry of sparks rising into the moist air. Flames leaped upward, and the sizzle of steaks wrapped in thick foil made her hunger burn.

Sitting on a portable rack next to the steaks, a pan contained red beans spiced with bacon strips; and French bread in more foil warmed off to the side. She sat on a rock half buried in the sand, and off to the side, her girly surfboard was upended against a damp, dripping cedar. Her wetsuit lay across the top in an attempt to keep it out of the sand. Behind her rose a wall of tumbled stone and rough vegetation, its steepness blocking any view up the hillside. It also blocked any view down the hillside, giving the small beach perfect and complete privacy.

Off to one side, a series of railroad tie steps sliced into the greenery, disappearing as they cut a circuitous path into the hillside, eventually winding to the house on the top of the hill.

In the direction of the sea, the wind had the breakers

showing whitecaps, and spray whipped into the air. The surf exploded against the rocks along the shore, sending up flumes of liquid iced with glittering froth. The beach trembled with each impact.

Flotsam chased the dying waves as they crashed onto land, attacking them as if he could bark loudly enough to scare them back into the sea. Occasionally Geraldine caught sight of Daggett's blue trunks, amazed that he could surf in the cold Pacific and not wear anything more to keep warm.

Less often, Skylar's orange popped into view. The man said he'd surfed Indonesia and Tierra del Fuego, but she suspected he'd paddled more than he'd surfed. He spent more time in the water than on his board. His most rousing surfing exploit since moving in with them had been hustling up the impossible hillside of the house next door, chasing a surfboard that had blown away in the wind. She kept plying him with cocoa, but not even that had brought much improvement. The path to the house was better, though. He worked it some every morning, cutting back the staggering growth, and now she could get through without needing a package of bandages to staunch the bleeding from the wild roses.

An especially large wave exploded against the rocks, catching her by surprise. Startled, she closed her eyes for a moment, only looking up when a second explosion directly overhead caught her attention. Her heart stopped. A pyrotechnic display of unprecedented proportions spread across the sky.

She immediately recognized where she was, Normandy, and the battle had clearly been engaged for some hours. The incoming breakers pounded the sand, and soldiers ran past, dodging the fire of enemy guns. She knew her only protection from the Germans farther inland came from the high wall at her back. She dared not move from her present position. Even so, in spite of the danger, she'd risk anything to offer her vital nursing

48

skills to the brave men who were fighting for the world's freedoms, especially the young and quite debonair Daggett Priestly. She'd met him at an Army social on the last night before his deployment. The word among the nurses was that his company was scheduled to make landfall today.

A man wet with the surf tumbled to the sand at her side, his uniform blackened on one side.

"Please, Miss. I can't feel my left arm. Can you do something for me?" His face twisted with pain, and in his eyes, she could see that without help, he couldn't last much longer.

"I'll do what I can, soldier. What's your name?" She glanced at the information on his shirt, hoping to tell if this was Daggett's company. The information was damaged beyond recognition, and she pulled his shirt back, only to see yellow fluid seeping from beneath burned skin. She knew she had to distract him from what she must do. She repeated, "Your name, soldier?"

"Frank," he mumbled, letting out a groan when she dabbed the oozing burn with a clean cloth.

"Do you have a last name, Frank?" She'd found a vial in her bag, one her superiors had assured her would heal all wounds. She opened it as she talked.

"Hawkins. Frank Hawkins, ma'am. Are you going to make the pain stop?" His arm had become a limp rag at her side, and his head lolled over, his words fading.

"Sure, Frank Hawkins. You're going to live to fight another day." Squeezing some of the vial's contents onto a bandage, she pressed it to the burned skin, securing it firmly. "Feel better, Frank?"

An expression of incredulity spread over his face, and with a deep breath, he pulled himself up. As if he couldn't believe it, he moved his left arm, gingerly at first, and then rapidly, swinging it in an outsized circle.

"You're a miracle worker. Bless you, ma'am. I think I can join the fight again." He leaped to his feet, his gun in hand, and just before he tore away, he dropped to one knee to look carefully into her face. "I know you. You're Daggett's girl. He carries a picture of you wherever he goes. He's on his way, the next transport. He hasn't forgotten you. He knows you're here, and he said for you to be patient a little longer." Then, with a jerk of well-trained muscles, the soldier leaped away, scrambled up the hill, and was gone.

The battle continued to rage around her as if in a dream world, but it was the smell of toasting flesh that brought her back to the present, that and Daggett's voice.

"Hey, Baby. How well done do we want that meat?" He shook his head violently, and cold seawater showered everything. Flotsam was at his side, and when the animal began to shake also, it was a cloudburst of staggering proportions.

"Daggett! Tell that dog to shake somewhere else." She sputtered her words, jumping from her rock to get out of the way. She reached for a towel, throwing it at him. "Dry off while I pull the meat from the fire. I have some bowls for the beans, and if you want, a couple of cold cans in the cooler. Help yourself. Is Skylar coming in, too?"

The water irritated her. It was freezing.

"Sure, Baby. I might check the cooler at that. Don't know about Skylar. He was determined to catch one more wave. This smells good. Surfing all day works up an appetite." He dipped a bare finger into the bean pot, missing anything solid on the first try, and then snagging a piece of bacon on the second. He lifted it to his mouth and sucked it inside, licking his fingers when he was done. Some of the juice ran down his chin, and he attempted to lick it away.

"You'll get a burn that way, you know." She glanced up at him as she raked the wrapped meat from the flames.

"Get a full stomach, too, if I do it right." He grinned.

Just then, Flotsam jumped on him, chasing the smell of the bacon, and Daggett stumbled backward. His foot hit a piece of driftwood, and he went down onto the sand.

The big retriever began to lick his face.

"Get him, dog," Geraldine cheered, her good mood restored. "Lick it off!"

"Get off, you mutt!" Daggett laughed. Pushing the animal away, he rolled to his side, leaving sand coating his wet skin. He brushed at some of it, and when it only made matters worse, he chuckled. Looking at Geraldine, he grinned. "I'd take a kiss right now."

"I bet you would." She snorted her brushing off of that suggestion. They'd made use of the beach's privacy quite a few times in the past, but with Skylar around, she wasn't going there. The skinny redhead had been friendly and helpful, but he was here, and that was the point. No privacy equaled no kisses. "Are you going back out, or is this it for the day?"

"I'll see what Skylar wants." Daggett rolled to his back, kicking at the sand with his feet to dig himself a footrest. He propped himself up on his elbows.

"You do that," she laughed, unwrapping one of the steaks. "I'm having food. If you're staying in, don't expect to change. Your jeans are on that rock over there, but the dog found your shorts, and they're off up the trail somewhere." She pointed vaguely the direction of the railroad timbers before turning to pat a second steak to see if it had cooled enough to unwrap. Flotsam pressed up to her side, clearly interested in the smell of the steaks, and she pushed him aside with a casual movement of her shoulder.

"Down, boy. That's my dinner," Daggett called. "Come on, Flotsam. Show me my shorts." He leaped to his feet, showering sand into the edge of the fire.

"Daggett! You're as bad as Flotsam. You nearly ruined all today's hard work!" She grabbed a handful of sand and tossed it his direction. "Take that. Get out of here, and don't come back until you're ready to eat."

"Yes, ma'am," he called as he laughed, imitating Skylar's oft-used Southern courtesy. He started toward the steps, and with a loud series of barks, Flotsam tore ahead of him. Daggett chased after him, calling him a series of names intended to egg him on.

"And go find Skylar when you return!" she called at his retreating back, but she wasn't surprised to get no response. With a chuckle, she turned to her steaks. In that instant of shifting attention, and with no one around, the war raged about her once more.

"Your name?" It was the tenth or twelfth soldier she'd treated, and each seemed to carry worse injuries than the one before. This one had a leg that was no more than ragged meat. She unwrapped it carefully, peeling the ragged cloth back like tattered tin foil, cringing at the sizzling flesh underneath.

"Careful, please," his voice whispered. "I can't stand the pain."

"I don't know your name, yet, soldier. Can I get you to tell me?" She slowed as she peeled the fabric away. It was the best she could do. She had a reputation as a caring nurse, and she didn't intend to lose it with this man. If he lived, and she wanted him to, he would tell his children stories of the kind woman who had helped him survive the worst battle of the war.

"Stephen. Stephen Starr. Can you save my leg?"

"Stephen, if you want this leg saved, then I'm going to do my best to make sure you live to fight again." She had the wound exposed, and she reached for her vial of medicine. She turned to the soldier and smiled at him, placing a hand on his arm. "This may sting for a minute, but then you'll feel better.

Are you a lieutenant or a corporal?"

"Corporal. My friends call me Steve. Corporal Steve."

That name sounded familiar to her. "Do you know a man named Daggett?"

"Daggett Priestly? Yeah. He came through on the transport ahead of me. You know him?" His eyes were closed with the pain, and sweat beaded his forehead. He let a moan escape his lips before cutting it off with a grunt.

Know him? She was waiting on him. It was the only reason she'd volunteered for this most dangerous of missions. How had she missed him? Soldiers had been running by her all day. Daggett had to have been one of them. She turned to look back up the hill toward the German entrenchments dotting the tree-covered hillside. She couldn't see any of them, but then, of course, that meant they couldn't see her.

Tearing a section of her skirt for a bandage, she answered the soldier's question. "I met Daggett once. He seemed a nice guy." She spoke her words softly as she poured out of her vial onto the piece of fabric from her skirt. She had long since run out of bandages.

"He's the best, would give a man the shirt off his back and never ask him to return it. We've been together since boot camp." The soldier winced when she pressed the cloth to his leg.

"You'll feel all right as soon as this soaks in." She tightened the bandage so it wouldn't fall off. She didn't know what was in the vial, but it worked every time. It hadn't run out, either, unlike the bandages she had carried with her. She wondered if she could simply pour the medicine directly on the wounds, if it would have the same effect. She couldn't keep using her clothes to doctor injuries. Soon she'd have nothing on at all.

"Where's Daggett, ma'am?" The words rolled over her like honeyed butter, thick and drawn out.

The question startled her, and she glanced up from the

soldier at her feet, only to find a familiar man in orange trunks. He carried a surfboard under one arm, and water glistened over his bare skin. He shivered. The rays of the sun behind him sparkled in the haze, the air clouded by the spray peeling from the breakers. The sound of the surf roared around them, muffled only by the fingers of green enclosing the beach on two sides. Just in front of her were the fire, burning down now, and the food she'd been working on for the past hour, steaks, beans, and French bread.

"Up the hill," she replied. "Flotsam stole his shorts. Again."

"It's cold out, huh?" Skylar grinned as he rubbed his hands up and down his skinny arms. Looking up the hill, squinting at the sun just high enough to catch in his eyes, he yelled, "Daggett, you up there?"

"Whoo-ee, got them!" Barking punctuated the words, and bright green fluttered high into the air. It was clearly the stolen boxers, tossed skyward by the barest glimpse of a golden arm. "Back, Flotsam, you big baby. Beat you to the beach!" The golden arm caught the bright green, and excited yelping filtered beachward.

"Eat, Skylar." Geraldine pushed a plastic plate his direction, a bowl of beans and one of the steaks perched in the center. "There's a fork and knife in the cooler if you want them. Check in the bag by the drinks. Oh, and bread. Tear off a piece, if you like."

She had her own plate prepared, and she didn't need utensils.

"You have cocoa?" He had the meat in his hand, and he bit off a chunk. "Good steak, Geri. If you weren't Daggett's girl, I'd marry you in a minute." He talked through his mouthful, and his Southern words were tangled more than usual. "I'd marry any girl that can cook a steak like this."

She reached by her side and tossed him a small thermos.

"Drink up, Skylar, and thanks, I guess."

Daggett tore onto the beach, his boxers held high in the air, with the golden retriever jumping in the air hoping to get them back again. Laughing, Daggett jumped even higher to keep them away.

"Steak's ready, Daggett. Want yours now?"

"Why's this dog do this, Geri?" He danced around, his shorts held high in the air, just out of Flotsam's reach. "Normal dogs don't steal underwear."

He waved them directly under the dog's nose, then yanked them away when the animal snapped at them. He hooted then threw the shorts into the tree just over Geraldine's surfboard, laughing when they caught on a sagging branch.

"Flotsam," Skylar yelled, clapping his hands. When the animal charged his direction, all three took off towards the water.

Geraldine turned with a fresh plate in her hand, only to find herself alone. With a blink of her eyes, the skies were once again filled with black smoke. A rattle of gunfire punctuated the leaden sky, and she involuntarily jerked, nearly dropping the plate.

"For me?" A soldier stood in front of her, and his face was streaked with black. Dirt ringed his eyes, and he licked his lips nervously. It was clear the food was an unexpected offering. From his looks, whether he could keep it down on his twitchy stomach would be another thing. Death hovered everywhere, and more than once, his stomach had come into his throat, evidenced by the stains down the front of his uniform.

"Daggett?" She frowned, peering at the soldier, doubting her eyes. The war-torn man seemed familiar, but she couldn't be certain. "You're not . . . Daggett, are you?" She'd only seen him that one night, and it had been months ago.

"No, ma'am. I don't know no Daggett. Which way to the

front? I hear there's a war going on." The man was obviously little more than a boy and frightened out of his wits. He couldn't be over seventeen. He didn't even know where he was. The war was going on all around, in the skies, along the beach, and right there at their elbows. A sane man couldn't miss it.

All that and more was written in his eyes.

She pulled the plate back, reaching with slender fingers to the browned meat. Tears came into her eyes as she tore a sliver off the steak, holding it out to him. All the poor soldiers who had passed her by, and she hadn't been able to help more than a few, her vial of mysterious medicine healing injuries that no normal man would have been able to survive. She had done that, at least, done what she could. It had been something.

"Thank you, Geri." The plate disappeared from her hand, and there Daggett stood in front of her with Skylar at his side. It was the real Daggett this time. The skies had returned to a beautiful blue, and the surf resounded in the background, filling the air with a thundering sort of peace, the kind found on a peaceful California beach on a sunny summer afternoon. He pulled an old piece of gum from his mouth and stuck it under the edge of his plate. "I think Skylar and I might head up in a bit, after we eat, of course."

A creaking sound reverberated from up the hill, and she frowned at Daggett. Then a low-pitched rumbling kicked in, vibrating the ground beneath their feet, and the sand began to shiver. The air grew ominously still.

"Daggett? Geri?" Skylar stood with his plate in his hand, a sliver of steak between two fingers. He glanced at Flotsam, who held his tail between his legs. Moisture puddled underneath the dog as he quivered in fear. Geraldine's board against the tree fell sideways, kicking up sand as it hit the ground.

"Daggett . . . another quake." She glanced up the hill at the house she couldn't see, the scent from the wild roses wafting over her. "Your house . . ." She remembered the cracked window from the last one, and she cringed, hoping it didn't come down the hill and land on top of them. She also remembered the washing machine. She hoped the fridge didn't follow it through the floor. They could live without a washer, but a fridge? Every house had to have one of those.

Something popped sharply and loudly up on the hill, and then a series of crashing noises followed. They could hear whatever it was tumbling through the undergrowth. It finally came to rest, but the silence was more eerie than it was a relief. Geraldine felt an arm around her shoulder, and she glanced down to see bronzed skin with sun-bleached hair. Daggett. Of course, it was Daggett.

"Is the house coming down?" She wasn't sure he could hear her words. She wasn't sure she'd even said it aloud. She'd thought it, more likely. She shivered, feeling the tingling start deep inside, the shaking sensation beginning at the base of her spine and working its way up through her neck.

Daggett must have felt it, because he squeezed her tight and whispered into her ear, "Don't worry, Geri. We're safe down here."

She pressed her eyes shut, and then the bombs began to fall, with all hades breaking loose. Men were dying around her, and her vial of medicine had finally run dry. The water from the pounding surf surged around her feet, and it was red with blood. Her heart caught in her throat. Were they all going to die?

A rapid series of barks caused her to turn, and there was Flotsam barking wildly at their fire. The carefully assembled logs had shifted in the quake, and flames were flaring into the sky. Skylar was on his knees, tossing sand at it as well as onto their uneaten food. The food didn't matter to her anymore. Who could eat with their home tumbling down on their heads?

"Heavens, Skylar!" She released Daggett's arm, calling to

their houseguest. "The quake's caused a bonfire, and you're the only one with any sense. We don't want to burn the entire hillside." She dropped to her knees, pushing a mound of sand directly into the fire pit. Then she sat back as Daggett took over, and she brushed a hand against her face, forcing her hair out of the way.

Looking to the sea, she watched the ocean waves for a moment, seeing but not really seeing the mounding sand as the fire slowly died to nothing. The waves continued in their restless motion, tearing at one another as if angry at the gravity that never let them have their freedom. Several birds chased each other, and she wondered why they didn't dive into the water for food and get on home. Home. Home! Did they even have a home? She laughed, even as unexpected tears coursed down her cheeks. The quake had stopped, and she hadn't even noticed.

"What's funny?" Daggett's arms were covered to the elbows with a coating of sand, and the odd thing was, it didn't really show. His hair was dry except for tendrils around his face. The sweat of his sudden burst of energy in putting out the fire had moistened them into careless curls that gave him the appearance of a charming little boy out for a day on the beach.

"You." She laughed again, leaning her head back and reveling in being alive. There for a moment she had wondered. The quake had shaken the beach, and her imagination had taken her into a darker time, one she'd never endured, but that had always intrigued her. It had felt real this time, the quake combined with the war in her head.

"Me? I'm funny?" He sat back on his haunches, and now his knees were covered with the sand that so closely matched his golden skin.

Before she could answer, Skylar leaped from his position on the other side of the defunct fire directly toward her, and he threw his arms around her. Twisting their paired bodies, he landed directly between her and the steep hillside that rose so sharply behind them. Jerking once, and then letting out a sharp and very intense gust of air, he turned loose of her and fell onto his side on the sand.

"Skylar?" Almost too quickly to be seen, Daggett stood tall against the sky, a frown between his eyes. He'd moved before she could even comprehend that she wasn't where she'd been a moment before.

"Yeah, Daggett?" His words were limp, and he groaned. Pain was apparent in the way he sucked air in and exhaled it back out.

"Skylar, are you all right?" She twisted around to look at him. His face was pale, and his eyes were tightly closed.

When he first rushed her, she'd been puzzled. A sudden attack of passion brought about by the extreme, earthquake-riven moment? Her thought had been an impulsive one, but trust first impressions, she had always been told. People did stranger things during moments of stress, and South Carolina wasn't earthquake territory, as far as she knew. This was probably Skylar's first. Now, however, his voice said something other than passion.

His face spoke even more clearly. He moved his shoulder, then he jerked it back as if in pain. "Ah! Maybe not."

Daggett dropped at his side, his hand grabbing Skylar's shoulder. When he pulled him forward was when they saw the cause of his sudden leap across the beach. Even more so, they understood the short answers and the pained expression. Blood seeped from claw marks across the man's back. The blackened culprit lay half covered with sand.

"What's that?" Her stomach turned at the blood, but she had no magic vial for this. The blackened lump looked vaguely like a piece of a machine, but she couldn't make out just what. "Daggett?"

"I'm stupid!" He hit his forehead with the heel of his hand. "It's been up there all this time just waiting to fall on us, and I never once gave it a thought."

"Gave what a thought?" Skylar's words jerked roughly from his lips. His chest rose sharply, holding the indrawn breath for a time, then slowly relaxed. "God, this hurts. I just saw the undergrowth moving, and I knew something was coming down the hill in a hurry. Geri was in the way." He grimaced as a new wave of pain lanced through his body.

"Never mind. Can you stand? We have to get you up the hill." Daggett knelt, lifting one of Skylar's arms around his neck. "Come on, buddy. Help me out."

Looking at Skylar's attacker, the unfamiliar shape coalesced in Geraldine's mind. It was a washing machine motor. Her heart sank. It had fallen from the house months ago, but it had been attached to a washing machine and working at the time. Neither she nor Daggett had searched it out, letting it disappear from their minds just as it had disappeared from the laundry room. A piece of plywood now covered the hole, and it had been forgotten, an outsized potted plant filling the space. Now, here it was returned to haunt them, a reminder that Daggett's house was slowly collapsing down the hillside with all his worldly goods inside, or outside, in the case of this motor.

"What can I do to help?" She reached for a hand towel, still folded, and she held it out.

"Thank you, Geri." Daggett took it with his free hand. "I've got Skylar covered, if you can get this down here." He blew her a kiss, the world already back under his control. This was the California coast, after all. Earthquakes happened.

"Sure. Don't worry about any of this stuff. Skylar?" She reached and pressed a quick hand against his face, and in a singular motion, brushed damp hair from his temple. "You're in good hands. I'll be up in a minute to bandage that back."

Standing, she shooed them away. Skylar limped along. She was relieved to see that the bleeding looked less fearsome than it had when he was on the ground. She watched until they were up the trail and out of sight.

She turned to the water. When she heard a bird singing, a smile crept over her face. Birds knew. If she'd listened, she would have, too. Birds never sang before an earthquake. Birds and frogs. They knew, somehow, as if they spoke Earth. The secret whispers that rumbled in the ground just before a quake were the language that told all the animals to hush, because Earth had a statement to make. Then the ground shook, its words clear and strong, and once it was through, the birds and other creatures were free to speak again.

She turned and looked up the hill, the underbrush the same as always. How had Skylar known? He said he saw the movement in the undergrowth, but what had he *seen*? She wouldn't have noticed, she was certain. Perhaps Skylar spoke a bit of Earth. Maybe that was something people in South Carolina learned. She smiled at that. Perhaps the slaver ships all those years ago had brought more than hard-working field hands to provide free labor for the Southern plantation owners. Perhaps they had brought a piece of African Mother Earth with them, and as they had tilled the dirt, something besides the sweat of their skin had remained. Perhaps when growing children walked the soil of South Carolina, the language of Earth rose out of the ground and entrenched itself somewhere deep down in their souls.

Skylar, Earth-child.

He had saved her life, of that she was certain.

The sun washed her face, and she shivered in spite of the warmth. She felt her knees tingle, her energy suddenly drained. It was the fading adrenalin, the moment of danger gone. Still, it made her aware of someone else. Daggett. She pictured him leaping to Skylar's aid, his words of concern, and the quick arm offered in help.

She whispered, "Daggett, you are a better man than you know, and I love you for it."

The wind off the water was cool, and shivering again, the sun no longer enough to entice her to stay on the beach, she turned to gather her things. Then she noticed one of the steaks still wrapped in foil. It was half buried in the sand. She picked it up and shook it, knocking the sand away. Peeling back the foil, she saw wisps of steam curl into the air, and it smelled good. Did surviving a disaster stir the salivary glands? It did hers. Sitting back on her rock, she peeled a fragment of the meat away and sucked it into her mouth.

She was halfway through the steak when she felt unexpected arms wrap around her shoulders. From the touch, she knew they were Daggett's. He might have feet of lead inside the house, but those same feet whispered on the sand. She hadn't heard a thing.

"Yes, rescuing beach angel?" She glanced up into his face, his golden, unshaven face. She rubbed her cheek against the hair on his arm, its touch reassuring. He was comforting, just being here, coming back for her when he didn't have to.

"Beach angel?" He twisted around to sit at her side. "How's that?" His fingers tore a piece of her steak free and pushed it into his mouth, licking his fingers noisily. "It's still good. No one cooks beach steak better than you."

"Never mind. Here, Sweets. It's yours." She released the meat into his fingers. "I've had enough. How's Skylar?"

"Skin deep. He was more winded than wounded. Saved your life, Baby. He'll be your hero from now on." He grinned. "Glad I invited him to stay?"

She leaned into him, resting her head on his shoulder. She could feel his muscles flex, his tendons shifting as he tore slivers of steak free, chewing them one at a time. She could smell his skin, the salty freshness of it, his body giving off a pleasing undercurrent of masculinity. She whispered, "You're my hero, and I'm glad you invited me to stay."

"What did you say, Baby?" He paused, his mouth still filled with meat. When she didn't answer, he dug his long toes into the sand, working them around, and pulling at the meat again.

She smiled. She hadn't intended him to hear, and she didn't need to repeat her words. She was content to sit at his side, as long as he would let her stay.

Chapter 9

A FULL MOON was out. The windows across the back wall of the bedroom were as wide as the ones in the living room, stretching floor to ceiling, and laminated plate, as were all the windows on the ocean side of the house. They offered an incredible, panoramic view as far as the eye could see—in the daytime, anyway. Wind just outside worked desperate fingers, afraid of the dark, trying to get in.

Geraldine lay in bed, a single sheet pushed down around her waist, exposing the white tank top she slept in. Daggett lay next to her, his arms wrapped around his pillow, and his face turned to the side. He'd twisted the sheet until only his feet were covered. Moonlight washed his skin, pooling around him on the bed, creating shadows in the darkened room, places of true night in the empty spaces where his curled body didn't quite meet the bed. His boxers were baby blue, and in the moonlight, they glowed white, the milky substance of the moon on a midsummer's night.

Gently rolling to her side, Geraldine propped her head on one hand to watch him as he slept. At night, with all the day's distractions pushed aside, was the one time he was really hers, all hers. Other times he was charming or fun, or more likely, smoke on the water, and she could reach for him but never grab hold. Not quite. She could come close, but then her fingers would slip, and he was gone again, Flotsam leading him away, or his precious ocean pulling him from her once more. Even when she was on the water with him, he wasn't with her. He was with the sea, and the surf, and he was wrapped in the magic of something she could enjoy but never truly understand in the way that he understood it.

His eyelids twitched, and she knew he was dreaming. It was of the waves, riding the incoming surf, of the latest move he'd invented out on the water. She might be in that dream, but if so, she would be in the margins, an accessory only, perhaps making the dream more pleasant, but not the center at all. With a careful finger, she reached to push a lock of his hair from his forehead, letting the moonlight flood more brightly across his face. She wanted to see this dream as it played itself out. The stubble along his jaw created small shadows of its own, and his bleached eyelashes were clear silk. Just under one eye was the shadowed line where he had long ago taken a fall on a bank of coral, and he'd refused stitches. It had healed badly, and she loved him for his scar, anyway. His eyelids twitched again, the small movement working down the side of his face to the corners of his mouth. She was tempted to brush her hand across his skin, but the wind shifted a loose board somewhere, and with the popping, she was afraid he might wake. The dream would be gone, and she wanted him to have it. All of it. And if she was in that dream, she wanted to play out her part as fully as she could.

He shifted, and drawing a deep breath, he raised his head for a moment, his eyes still closed, and turned to face away from her. With a soft sound, he relaxed onto the mattress, and his breathing evened into the restful rhythm of deep sleep.

Now all she had was his back, and she studied it for a moment. His diet kept him trim, and his surfing kept him strong. With each breath, his muscles rippled under his skin, but it was his face she loved.

She sighed and rolled away, sitting on the edge of the bed and placing her feet on the floor. She was full of wakefulness tonight, and she blinked her eyes rapidly, letting the remains of what sleep she had managed slip away.

She rubbed her hands over the surface of the bed. It was the one thing she had brought into the house when she'd moved in. Daggett had been content with a pallet and a sleeping bag for a blanket. After one night on the floor, she'd taken a portion of the money left to her by her mother and visited a furniture store. The bed and two sets of linens had been delivered that afternoon. She thought it money well spent. Some mornings she wondered if Daggett even noticed.

She did, and perhaps that was enough.

She pushed the sheet aside and stood, glancing toward the windows. The ocean was black tonight. The sound of the surf worked its way through the glass, but it was muted. In places, the moon glinted off the waves, and the glints were jagged. That meant it was dangerous to be out tonight, for ships as well as humans.

"Be safe, people," she whispered softly.

Moving through the darkened house, the moonlight more than adequate for her night-adapted eyes, she stopped to feel the leaves of the potted plant standing where Daggett's washer had once cleaned their towels and underwear. It seemed a bit dry. She would water it before returning to bed, if she remembered. A soft whine told her Flotsam had chosen the laundry room for his bedroom tonight. She knelt in the darkness and found his muzzle. "Good dog. Be quiet, now." His cool tongue licked her hand, and she chuckled. Reaching her fingers under his chin, she felt cloth and realized it was a pair of Daggett's shorts. Rumpling the fur along his head, she accepted that this dog was as much a part of Daggett as this house and the sea. For that, she loved the animal, just as she loved Daggett.

Just past the laundry room was the canted floor connecting the two sections of the settling house. She no longer noticed the uphill climb. She stepped over the crack in the living room, for the tenth time wondering if it was worth the effort to buy an area rug to cover it. Then she remembered she would also need a vacuum cleaner, and she let the idea go, as she had the past nine times it had come to her.

At the kitchen tap, she filled a glass of water and drank about a third. On the return to the bedroom, she poured part of the remaining water into the base of the plant, and at Flotsam's whine, held the glass low for him to drink what he wanted. Lapping sounds told of his thirst. When they ceased, she set it in the corner and rumpled his fur once again.

"Stay out of my bed tonight, you baby. You hear me? Stay." She smiled, even though the animal couldn't see it, and she made her way back to Daggett.

Easing herself onto the bed, she pulled the sheet over her. The moon had slipped behind a cloud, and the room had darkened. She barely noticed. She knew the space. She could move about by feel alone.

Just as she settled down, with her eyes fixed on a ceiling she couldn't really see, she felt Daggett move. He slid closer, and his hand brushed her arm.

"Missed you," he said sleepily. Then he was still once again. She smiled. She had missed him, too.

Chapter 10

IN THE DISTANCE, Flotsam ran along the shore, looking tiny, his barking carrying over the water in faint bursts that didn't quite match up with his movements. The swells under Daggett's surfboard were long and languid, the water a deep gem green that not even the best of painters ever managed to capture. Warm where the sun baked his skin and cold where his legs dangled in the water, he drew in repeated deep draughts of air. Paddling out had been hard. Nearer to shore, the surf had been rough, and he'd had to fight it for close to half a mile.

He waited on Skylar.

"Daggett!"

He turned the direction he thought the sound was from, the swells distorting his bearings, and he saw a skinny arm in the air. The water moved, and the arm fell away, swallowed by the shifting surface of the ocean. It would be back . . . if Skylar didn't lag behind too long.

Today was a test.

"This way, Skylar," he yelled, waving his arm in turn. On shore, he could see Flotsam suddenly running berserk. A short break, and barking again filtered out over the water. By the time the sounds reached him, the animal had calmed down. Grinning, he raised his hand again, waving. "Flotsam!"

The animal went wild again.

The golden retriever was the best thing he'd ever let into his life—after Geri, of course. Always after Geri. He thought back those two years and some months ago. If he'd not hitched a ride with Ronnie, not gone to the Moonlight Surf Tour, not seen Corky that night, he'd have missed out on the best thing in his life. He didn't know what she saw in a bum like him, sometimes wondering how long she'd stay.

"Daggett!" The word was gasped out, breaking the silence of the undulating ocean.

He turned and caught a spray of water in his face. Skylar's hand flipped a second spray his direction before the man laid his head on his board, letting both arms drag in the water. His skinny body barely filled out his wetsuit. He was a black stick on a floating board, his red hair and freckles brilliant in the late afternoon sun. At the party so long ago, his freckles had been burnt chocolate. Today, in the sun, they were flashing prickles of crimson fire.

"Up, boy." Daggett put his big, athletic hands in the water and pushed his board near Skylar's. He splashed water over him, the crystal green sea turning magically clear when it was thrown from the ocean. "No time for rest. The day's winding down, and I want to make the most of it."

"You're a machine, you know that?" Skylar pushed himself up, leaning forward on his arms. "And you in those trunks. Don't you ever get cold? I'm freezing, and I'm wearing a full suit." From the ankles to the wrists, he was fully insulated, with only his hands and feet exposed.

"I don't have time to get cold." He grinned, impish and playful. "Except when I'm waiting on you. Geri'll be here at dark. That gives us—" He glanced up at the sun, his brow furrowed, calculating. He pursed his lips, his eyes cutting for a quick moment to Skylar, and then back to the sky. "—about just long enough to catch a few more waves."

"Can we rest a minute, though? Boogers, but paddling out was hard." Skylar's rhythmic Low Country words seemed lethargic next to Daggett's crisp California speech.

"There's time for rest when we die. See those breakers just over there?" He pointed with a long arm, causing the sun to glint on dancing ribbons of moisture as they leaped from his hand. "Paddle over there, and those'll take us around the point and all the way in."

Skylar sighed. He shook his head, sending remnants of water sprinkling the surface of the sea around his board. His face twitched, his eyes blinking rapidly in a parody of exhaustion.

Daggett knew better. "Did you drink the magic brew Geri sent?"

"The cocoa?" Skylar frowned. "Of course, on the beach before we paddled out, but yes, I did. All of it. It was good. Why?"

"That's what gets me out here. Started drinking it at twelve, and look at me now. Strapping big, and not even you can keep up." He had drifted just close enough to jab Skylar in the chest with one wet finger, and immediately he spun and began paddling furiously toward the breakers in the distance. "See you on shore!" he yelled back. His feet were pointed high in the air, his legs bent at the knees, his chest flat on his board. Ripples spread outward from his board, painting an arrow the direction Skylar would have to follow. It was a generous gesture, although he didn't wait to see if the other man was in pursuit or not.

"Daggett! Sometimes I hate you!" Skylar shook a fist in the

air at him. "We could have paddled out a third the distance if we'd started from here. We'd have caught the same breakers and ridden them in to the same beach."

In the distance, Flotsam had seen Skylar's raised fist, and he went into a frenzy. It took seconds for his barking to reach the man on his board, and by then, Skylar had dropped to his chest, and he was paddling furiously once again.

THE WATER swirled around Daggett's feet and across the beach. One arm rested on his board, the end buried in the sand. He wanted to send a clear message to Skylar. He was here and already waiting.

At least Skylar was upright. He'd just caught a wave, and his arms were extended, the nose of his board hanging in the air, and the tail buried in the water. His knees flexed once, and the board shifted, following the direction the water took him. The wave built until the spray began to form a barrel, and ducking, his hand trailing in the water at his side, Skylar disappeared inside.

Daggett smiled. He didn't know if Geri could brew enough cocoa to make Skylar perfect. Even if she couldn't, he intended to push him until he reached whatever potential he had.

In a flash of white and black, Skylar's surfboard shot from the collapsing wave, and he knew the man's ride was over. It was time to hike back to where they'd left Flotsam, and anyway, the sun had begun to dip. Geri would expect them back at the rendezvous site by nightfall.

"Skylar!" Daggett waved, encouraging the younger man. "That was sick! I was impressed with the way you took that barrel, right until it took you!" There was a touch of a gibe in his words.

"Yeah," Skylar called, as he laughed, exhilarated. "Big wave! I caught a right good macker, didn't I? Took me right

71

inside that keg." He had his board under one arm, his knees jumping high as he danced his way to shore. He was pumped, and it showed on his face. He ran along the beach, slamming the end of his board into the sand, leaning on it and gasping for breath. Laughter broke from him, his chest shaking, and he sank to the sand, letting his board fall beside him.

Barking caught their attention, growing louder, and out of the growth at the edge of the sand burst a golden blast of fur, tearing their direction.

"Flotsam! You found us!" Daggett raised his hand in greeting. The dog dropped to a crouch at their feet, playfully nipping at exposed ankles, dancing around the two surfers.

"Hey, boy," Skylar called, holding out his hand.

"No, like this," and Daggett fell on the big animal, wrapping his arms around his neck. Rolling with him in the sand, he jumped up and took off running. Dropping back into a crouch, the dog growled, and then took off after him, the damp sand peeling from under his paws and showering Skylar's legs.

"Aren't you tired, yet?" Skylar stood and stamped sand off his feet. "We still have to hike back to the beach where we were dropped off this morning. Come on, Daggett."

"No, you come on." He was to the line of greenery. "Bring my board. I see someone I know."

Sure enough, coming down Flotsam's path was a familiar face.

"Hey, guys!" Geraldine waved. In the fading light, her hair was liquid gold, and her skin was burnished the color of amber. She held up a small bag with a delicatessen shop logo on the side. "Hot cocoa's on me."

"Oh, Geri! I love you!" Skylar beamed. He had his suit down to his waist. His skinny arms and freckles were pink with the cold, and he shivered.

"Here, Skylar. How's the magic working for you?" She

pushed her hair behind one ear; and winking at Daggett, she pulled a second cup of cocoa from the sack. Daggett already had the first.

Skylar wrapped his hands around the cup, snapping the lid open on one side, and putting it to his nose to inhale sharply. He didn't answer, but a smile was on his face.

"Skylar!" Daggett slapped him on the shoulder. "Tell Geri what you did."

"What?" The cup was to his lips, and it was half gone as he pulled it away, wiping his mouth on the back of his hand.

"The keg, you fool." Daggett was grinning, and he stood beside Geraldine, his arm wrapped around her waist. He rubbed the side of her head with his cheek. "Remember?"

"Oh, yeah! You should have seen it, Geri." His face lit up. "There I was on the lip, the face of the wave just under my feet, and it was gnarly! It opened to a giant hollow, and I zipped right in, turning on the rail, riding that keg like I'd been doing it all my life! I wish I'd had Daggett around before I wasted my time in Tierra del Fuego."

"Wasted?" She glanced at Daggett, smiling. Usually it was the opposite, the man building his exploits into impossible feats.

"You know, Geri, I've never been to del Fuego. It sure seems to me that whether in California or South America, good surfing time's never wasted." Daggett had one hand on Flotsam's head, working his ears. He chuckled when he said it, looking back to Geraldine.

Skylar grinned, shaking his red hair to knock out the rest of the water. "You're right, there. Not wasted." With a quick gulp, he emptied the cup and crushed it in his hand. When Geraldine held out the sack, he dropped it in. "I spent my college fund traveling to all the places I wanted to go, thinking I was all that, you know. I was the best in the world, would enter all the contests, and everyone would know my name. I ran out of money before I won anything, but I blamed that on the lack of cash. I still thought I was the best. I just needed the chance to prove it. Just then, out there, I did something I've never done before. Oh, man, it felt good. But now I know how much I still have to learn. I wasn't good at all before."

"You've taken the first step."

"The first step?" He chortled. "Like a baby? I don't think so." He glanced at his arm, bending it at the elbow to force a muscle to show.

"You've learned that no one knows it all. Everyone has something new they can learn, if only they'll keep their mind open." Daggett turned his head and kissed Geraldine on the cheek. "Right, Baby?"

"That's not right, not for you, Daggett." Skylar shook his head, drawing his words out in Southern disbelief. "You are the god. No one knows more than you."

This time Daggett laughed loud and riotously. That set Flotsam off, and he began going in circles, barking repeatedly. There must have been something hiding in the undergrowth, because there was a sudden scramble of something running away from their beachside noisemaking. It never showed itself, making it all the funnier.

"See, Geri, I'm a god." He picked her up and swung her around. His hair was dry by then, knotted and sticking out in ratty tails, and his suit had loosened on his hips. His feet kicked up sand, leaving ragged trails behind him. After he set her down, he swung one leg over Flotsam, sitting on him like a pony, his feet on the ground, walking along as the dog tried to get away.

Geraldine snorted, calling, "Here, Flotsam." She laughed when he ran to her, jerking out from under Daggett, leaving him sprawled in the sand. "Good boy," she cooed. "Good dog."

Daggett stood, and he shook the waistband of his suit up and down. Sand poured from inside the legs. Flotsam ran to him, thinking he wanted to play, and he jumped on him. Daggett grabbed his front legs and did a funny little dance.

"Anyone for a burger?" Skylar changed the topic as he headed off down the trail. "We're going to be hungry by the time we get back to where you're parked."

"Real hungry." Geraldine nodded. "You get the boards, Skylar. Then you catch up. We've got a long way to walk back. And if you want burgers, you're paying."

"Sure. I've got a twenty I've been saving." He stopped and pulled one out of a zippered pocket at his side, waving it in the air. Then he caught her words about the boards. "Carry them both?"

"You heard her. Just do it." Daggett pointed.

Without another question, Skylar was off.

"See, Geri," he whispered, putting his arm around her waist and moving with her into the trail. "Being a god has its perks."

"I bet." She chuckled.

"Are you parked just over the dune?" He nodded the direction they were walking.

"Of course. I found your dog where I'd dropped you and Skylar off, and when there was no sign of you, I knew exactly where you'd be. There was no sense in walking all that distance."

"Good girl."

"You didn't bother telling Skylar I always do that, did you?" She reached up and tapped him on the nose. "You are a bully of a god."

He laughed softly, keeping his steps in rhythm with hers. They'd topped the dune. The smell of the wild roses was everywhere. It was nearly dark, and on the highway, cars buzzed by, their shining eyes white lights in one direction, and rows of brilliantly lit little strawberries in the other. Directly in front of them was the car they'd be riding home in. It was Ronnie's old

75

VW. She'd long since gotten another one, but the dealer had refused the ancient car in trade. Ronnie had offered it to Daggett and Geraldine if they'd just come take it home.

He pulled her hair from her neck, and he kissed her just below her ear. He smiled when Flotsam ran by barking.

"Hm. That felt good." She reached up to place a hand on his neck, pulling him close.

"I'm not really a god," he whispered, kissing her neck once again.

"I won't tell a soul." She smiled.

"Not even Skylar? Once upon a time I wanted to be a god, although maybe not Skylar's. But he's the only one who thinks I am, and it would be a shame for him to learn the truth." He chuckled and kissed her a third time.

She didn't get a chance to reply. About that time, Skylar came walking up, dragging the surfboards along the sandy path.

"I went towards the other beach. I was halfway there when I realized you weren't ahead of me. I only found you because Flotsam barked. You should have told me you were right here." He sounded petulant.

"Ah, the life of a god. Go appease your unhappy subject." Geraldine patted the side of Daggett's face, laughing softly. She turned and pushed him away, laughing and running toward the car. "Thanks for bringing the boards, Skylar. You're a good man, and I'm glad Daggett invited you to stay."

His face brightened in the fading light. "You're welcome, Geri, I mean thanks, I think." He grinned. "I'm glad I can help out."

"Give me the boards, Skylar. You've done enough." Daggett placed a tanned hand on his and reached for the other.

"I've got them." Skylar put his hand on Daggett's board. "I carried them this far, and the car's right there."

"You sure?" He'd pushed him today, and the boy had kept

up all the way. He knew he must be exhausted.

"Trust me."

He let go of his board, shooting the other man a thumbs-up hand sign. "I guess I should know I can trust you not to bail out."

The grin on Skylar's face told Daggett he'd said just the right thing. When Daggett got to the car, he untied the passenger door and dropped inside, his feet rattling the loose plywood that still covered the hole in the floor. He groaned when Flotsam jumped in, scrambling over him into the back seat. When the dog was settled, he picked up Geraldine's hand, putting it to his mouth and kissing it.

"If anyone had ever told me being a god was so easy, I'd have tried it a long time ago." In the gathering shadows, he slouched in the seat, one knee pressing against the dash, and the other leg hanging out the door. He worked his fingers into hers, kissing her hand once again before resting it in his lap. "How do you like holding hands with a god?"

In the deepening evening, her face was shadowed, but he felt her squeeze his hand.

It was answer enough for any god.

GERALDINE had watched Daggett and Skylar from the car. Against the deepening sky, the two men had been little more than darkened silhouettes, towering Daggett, bronzed with golden hair, and skinny Skylar, ablaze with the final light of the setting sun. They had been ancient heroes from a distant age when men had worshipped the sea, and great foundries had raised statues to the gods therein.

Riding his surfboard was Daggett's first love. He was in his element on the waves, a true god. She was glad for the shadows, because she knew her eyes would tell the truth if he could see into them. Holding hands with a god was easy enough. It was holding onto his heart that she worried about.

As Skylar ran up to the car, banging the boards on top as he scrambled to tie them on, Daggett climbed out to offer him a hand. As she felt him slip from her touch, his voice ragging on his friend, she murmured, "But you are a god. To me, anyway. You just don't know it."

In the darkness, she didn't even have to wipe the tear that rolled down her cheek.

Chapter 11

"HEY, GER!"

The effusive greeting was from Marla Scott, just back from vacation. She was late, as usual, and Geraldine had taken on two extra customers to cover for her. However, there were times Marla had returned the favor, and so it was no big deal. They had become friends in the course of working together, and that was what counted.

"Hey, Marla." Geraldine was working shampoo into a matron's hair. This was Thursday, and on Thursdays she worked the late shift, five to nine, for those customers who couldn't get off during regular hours. She was straightening the woman's hair, and this was the second shampoo. After she treated it one more time, she would shampoo it a third time before finishing it off.

This was Marla's customer.

"Key West was fun." Marla stepped in front of one of the big mirrors at the back of the shop and looked at herself critically. Then she fluffed her hair with both hands, her nails glittering with bright, new polish. "I think I lost some of my perm. It's the salt water, I think. You remember my brother, Bobby? He insisted we swim in the ocean every day. I don't know why. We had a pool right there at the hotel." Reaching into her pocket, she pulled out a piece of foil-wrapped gum and began to fold the covering back.

"Fresh towel, Marla." Geraldine turned the water off and held out a hand. She had towels, but she needed something to get her friend back on track. She wanted to hear all about Key West, but only after Mrs. Bidwell was straightened and out the door.

"Sure, honey." Marla opened a cabinet that was filled with towels, and she pulled out an oversize black one. She handed it to Geraldine, then walked around the counter, crossing her arms on it, and resting her chin on her arms. She slipped the gum into her mouth and watched Geraldine, chuckling. "You're so good at that. You didn't even drip anything on the floor. Isn't she good, Mrs. Bidwell?"

"Might have her color my roots next time, too." Mrs. Bidwell tried to nod, although with Geraldine toweling her dry, it looked more like a bobble. The old woman smiled, her eyes crinkling into a mass of wrinkles.

"No, no, Mrs. Bidwell. I'm your regular, and you don't forget that. Geri's just doing me a flavor. Isn't that right, Ger?" Marla grinned. It was an inside joke about the popsicles they always traded. She unwrapped the silver foil from a second stick of gum, popping it deftly into her mouth alongside the first.

Geraldine looked hard at her as she tossed the towel into a basket. The look said she'd better take Geraldine's next customer. He was a dancer, very particular, and she'd just as soon not work him tonight.

"I know that look. Sure, if you want." She rolled her eyes.

"You haven't met my new houseguest. His name is Skylar, and he thinks Daggett is a god."

"A god? Oh, my goodness, I could have told him that." She left the counter, following Geraldine to one of the chairs, sitting down beside Mrs. Bidwell. Her face brightened. "Is your houseguest a surfer, too?"

"Oh, I just love surfers." That was Mrs. Bidwell. Her eyes were closed, and Geraldine was working more magic into her hair. Mrs. Bidwell caught a whiff of the chemicals, and she coughed.

"See, Mrs. Bidwell? Just sit quietly and breathe through your nose. We'll all be better for it." Geraldine patted her on the shoulder, but she smiled at Marla.

Marla slumped into her chair, flinging her arms wide, and she leaned her head against the headrest. "Never mind. He thinks Daggett is a god. That means he's gay. Am I right?" She looked at Geraldine, an excessively pained expression on her face. The bell on the door jingled, and she looked up. "Your regular is here, already? I just got my things put down"

Geraldine whispered over Mrs. Bidwell's hair, "Mr. Chickawaddy, the dancer. Remember, he's yours, tonight."

"Mine? Nothing ever pleases him." Marla mouthed the words, shaking her head no.

"Mr. Chickawaddy," Geraldine called out. "It's me, Geri. I'm afraid Marla will be working with you tonight." Mrs. Bidwell coughed, and Geraldine spoke to her, "You breathe through your nose like I told you."

"Yes, dear." The words were very nasal, and it was obvious she was trying her best to do as she was told.

The response from the front of the shop was less enthusiastic.

"You mean that girl with the permed hair? Oh, my! Does she even know what brand of color I use?" His words were also nasal, but that's just the way he sounded all the time.

Marla made a face, pointing to the front of the shop, shaking her head no again.

Geraldine grinned at her, nodding. "Yes, Mr. Chickawaddy. I've briefed her, and she'll do a perfect job."

"If you insist, dear. I'm sure the color will turn out all right." It was obvious by his tone that it would not be all right at all.

Marla walked right up to Geraldine, and she hissed in her ear, "I expect a date with your new houseguest. You owe me that for doing this." She made a horrid face, turning away and speaking her next words just loudly enough for Mrs. Bidwell to hear. "That is if he isn't gay."

Mrs. Bidwell's eyes flew open. "Mr. Chickawaddy's gay? Oh, my, and I never knew."

"Shush, Mrs. Bidwell. None of us knew."

Geraldine smiled. Old ladies were always the last to find out.

Chapter 12

DAGGETT tossed the rubber ball at the floor. It bounced onto the wall, arced through the air, and back into his raised hand. He tossed it again and once more caught the ball.

Two boxes of pizza had just been delivered, one pepperoni and the other cheese, but they remained unopened. Geraldine wasn't home yet.

"Let me try." Skylar held up both his hands, as if it would take both of them just to catch the small ball.

"Try what? This?" Daggett tossed the ball harder, aiming at a slightly different spot on the floor, and the ball careened into the wall, just kissed the ceiling, and with a loud smack, slammed back into his outstretched palm. He held it up, poised on the tips of his long fingers. "That?"

Skylar sat back against the wall, wide-eyed and mouth agape. The plastic of his beanbag chair—yellow for the evening—squeaked against the wood floor, echoing against the hard expanse of glass that took one entire wall away from the room.

It was dark outside. A storm had been threatening all evening, and now it seemed it might come through. One weak bulb in an overhead fixture lit the room. The party lights from June had mostly fallen down, although a few in the corners still hung by their thumbtacks. All the extension cords had been returned to the neighbors long ago. There was one faded paper lamp hanging in the darkest part of the room, just over a Mission-style armchair with a wooden frame and worn leather upholstery. There was a matching ottoman, but for now it was in another part of the house, serving duty as an end table next to a bed.

The Christmas lights in the corner began to vibrate, and in the kitchen, something could be heard shifting in one of the cabinets. The hanging lamp flickered, a short in the cord, coming on fully, then blinking out again. It stayed out. Dust shifted from behind the doorframe leading into the dining room, a puff at first, then a steady stream. A sharp, high-pitched pop came from the direction of the bedroom Skylar used, the sound of glass giving way under pressure.

A clickety sound started off small, the rapidly repeating taps growing louder, until Flotsam bounded into the room, his tail between his legs. He slammed into Daggett in a sudden crouch, his nose finding its way under the man's arm. He whined.

It's an earthquake, he seemed to say.

"It's okay, boy." Daggett ran one hand along the dog's back, working the fur gently. He raised his head to the ceiling, letting his eyes run along the corners where the walls intersected. He wasn't stupid about what might eventually happen to the house. He'd noticed the slope in the floor leading to his and Geraldine's bedroom. It was worse than it had been. The floor in the laundry room, also. He'd had to notice that, what with the trips Geraldine now made to the Laundromat. The money, too. It took money to visit the Laundromat. This house was collapsing a little more with each quake. If there was a big one? Who knew?

84

Growing up, the house had always seemed permanent to him, constant, with its views of forever, the grand vistas of the Pacific unencumbered as far as the eye could see. He'd dreamed at those windows as a boy, of pirate ships and submarine wars and giant asteroids crashing into the sea and what would happen in the aftermath. His father would come to rescue him, and they would run away, living in the hills together, a tent for their home, perfect always. Reality had stepped in, the giant eraser of life wiping his dreams clean, leaving him with only the ocean. Just that, the ocean, clean and pure and forever.

When his father had disappeared—before Daggett was born—his mother had left him here with his grandparents, only occasionally trying to parent him. Her maternal instincts hadn't been her strong suit, and each time her attempts had faltered more disastrously than the last. Finally, she'd given up, only showing up on the odd Sunday for a trip to the ice cream shop for a visit both could barely endure. Eventually she had abandoned even that, sinking into her life on the street. He'd never seen the drugs, but he'd known the marks on her arms, and her eyes were deeper, the skin darker, each time she came to call. Now, only now, he was sure there had been men, night after night, providing the money that supplied her habit. She was worn out before she was thirty. Early one day when he was fourteen, his grandfather had come into his room, the one Skylar used now, and sat on his bed. He'd placed a gnarled hand on his back, rubbing the skin for a moment. After a bit, he'd rolled over to see his normally staid grandfather looking out the window with tears running down his face.

"What, Gramps?" His heart caught. Had his grandmother . . . he couldn't think it. Had she died? She'd been full of fire the night before, chewing on him for his grades on his report card, sending him to bed early. But dead? He didn't want her dead.

"You mother won't be back to see you, son."

"So, what's new about that?" He rolled back over. He'd cared, once.

"No, it's different this time." The old man's hand was still on his back. "We're all you've got, now." He patted Daggett's back twice before standing and walking heavily out of the room.

After his grandfather left, Daggett had stared out the window. They'd never had curtains, not any time since he could remember. The sea was all the curtains his grandparents said they needed. He counted three ships, and he could tell one was a cargo vessel, piled high and looking top-heavy. He'd do that, crew on a ship like that, anything to be gone from his life, with no connections to anyone. He knew what his grandfather was trying to tell him. He buried his face in his pillow, but his tears were for what should have been. His mother had died to him a long time ago.

They never even had a funeral.

Flotsam squirmed, pushing his nose free, and he barked. The house was still again. Daggett looked at him, grinning. "Hey, boy. Better?" He rubbed his fingers under his chin.

"Has it stopped?"

"What?" He still held the ball, and he bounced it in his hand. The house was still here, clearly not having fallen into the sea, and for him, its sense of permanence was as it had always been. The house was simply here, perched on the side of the hill, overlooking the sea. It always had been, and it always would be.

"The quake?" Fear tinged the question.

"Ha!" Daggett threw the ball again, hard once more, and watched it fly into the wall. As it careened away, heading upwards to skew off the ceiling, he called, "That wasn't a quake. An aftershock, maybe. Hardly noticed it."

The returning ball missed his hand, and Flotsam leaped from his side, scrambling across the floor with his toenails clicking a merry tune, excited, and he pinned the ball in his mouth. He looked up, his tail wagging.

"Bring it to me, boy." Daggett motioned with his hand, then slapped his leg. Flotsam leaped forward, sliding across the wood and dropping the ball at his side.

He tossed the ball again, hard, and it went wild once more. Flotsam took his actions as an unusual opportunity to play, and he took off after the ball once again.

"Losing your touch?" Skylar laughed. "That was twice in a row."

"Nah. Just hungry." He wouldn't admit to worried. "Wishing for Geri to get home."

"Geri wouldn't mind if we took just one slice. You want me to get a plate?" Skylar glanced at the boxes hopefully.

Daggett grabbed the ball from between Flotsam's legs and tossed it directly at Skylar. It was well aimed and quick, catching him by surprise, and it landed on his upper arm. It hit with a smack, falling away and rolling to the side.

Flotsam jerked into motion, scrambling for it, the game on once more, and he careened into Skylar in the process. He grabbed the ball, loping with it into the kitchen, and chewing on it as he went.

"Ouch! What'd you have to do that for?" Skylar grabbed his arm, raising his sleeve to check the damage. A red spot had already formed. "What did I say?"

From the dining room came a crashing sound.

"Skylar?" Daggett glanced at his houseguest, his word sharp and pregnant.

"Daggett?" Even the freckles on Skylar's face turned pale.

Daggett leaped to his feet. In that one sound, the cracking earlier from the bedroom, the dust from the doorframe, and the wall that no longer bounced straight and true became the aftershocks that had loosened the house from its foundations. In his mind, it was already sliding down the hill. Both men looked to the windows, somehow expecting to see ocean water lapping their black surfaces, the distant white-foamed breakers come to greet them.

Barking brought them back to the moment.

"Flotsam?" Skylar's freckled eyelids opened wide.

"The pizza!" Daggett flung himself to his feet, hurling his long body through the dining room door. There, as he suspected, was one box upside down on the floor. The blocks under the table legs had shifted in the quake, and Flotsam was enjoying the treat so generously flung to the floor. Sensing the men's unwelcome attention, he swallowed his first bite whole.

"Oh, man!" Skylar looked at the pizza in dismay, and his stomach growled. "Flotsam! I was so hungry, and now you're eating it all. This is a disaster!"

"Half a disaster, anyway." Daggett could see there was half left. Probably more, if they were quick. A disaster didn't have to remain a disaster. Half a pizza left, half a family to raise a kid, half a life when everyone was gone. They were all the same.

His grandparents had been in the movie industry. That's where the money for the house had come from. However, in the fifties, like so many others in Hollywood, they'd been black-listed in the McCarthy hearings. They'd lost half of everything they'd owned, their place in the Hills, their country club memberships, and most of their friends. They'd kept half, though, and lived well enough after that.

His mom hadn't done so well trying to be half a family, but he'd been lucky his grandparents had been there to pick up the slack.

Now, as long as Geri stuck around, Daggett had more than half a life. He had everything he needed.

He reached to push Flotsam aside, slapping Skylar's ankle to get him to help. It turned out they lost only three slices. The bad thing was that they were cheese, Geraldine's favorite.

Flotsam licked the floor as they worked, and by the time the good pizza was reassembled in the box, the wooden surface was clean.

"See? Good as new." Daggett frowned at Flotsam. "You, boy, are in the doghouse." He reached and flicked his ears as the animal stole a greasy lick on his leg.

Skylar peeked into the pizza box. Pinching a lump of cheese from the box, he sucked it in his mouth. "Good cheese." He grinned, turning to Daggett.

The sound of the front door opening gave a fresh sense of urgency to the moment.

"Geri!" both men cried as one. She'd left the money for the pizza, and now half her favorite flavor was wasted.

"Quick, Skylar!" Daggett flung the lids back on both boxes. With the props gone from under the table legs, one started to slide off. He grabbed it. "Hold this."

Skylar watched as he rearranged the pizza slices, mixing the pepperoni and cheese. He left them widely spaced, filling the boxes evenly. As quickly, he closed the boxes, and then lifted the table.

"Legs, Skylar. Put the blocks underneath." When it was completed, he set the table down. "She'll never know."

"Never know what?" She stood in the doorway, and she leaned her head against the frame. Her long hair was behind her shoulders, and she'd kicked her shoes off as soon as she'd entered the house. Her dark shirt was unbuttoned, and she had on a white tank underneath. She wore a skirt, her Thursday evenings usually being her better clients. If she dressed a bit sharper, she sometimes got more tips.

"Pizza, Geri." Daggett opened one of the boxes, showing the evenly spaced slices. "I got you a soda. It's in the fridge."

"Never mind. I'm too exhausted to eat. I'm headed to brush

my teeth and go to bed." She turned, but before she walked off, she glanced disinterestedly at the pizza boxes. "I hope you didn't wait on me. I'm really not hungry. Sorry, guys. Feel free to eat it all."

"You sure, Geri?" Daggett stepped to her, putting his arms around her, and he kissed her on the forehead. "Half of that is yours. We got cheese just for you."

She kissed him back, lightly and on the lips. "No, but thanks. I just need bed. Night, Skylar." She leaned around Daggett to look at the red-haired man, then untwined Daggett's arms, and waved and walked away. Before reaching the door, she stopped. "Oh, the shop shook tonight. It felt like a quake. I guess you guys got it here, too. You'd let me know if there was a problem, right?" Flotsam whined, catching her attention, and she looked down to see him at her side with his tail wagging. She knelt and rubbed his nose. "Night, dog."

Skylar had the pizza open and was already chewing.

Geraldine paused to look out the blackened windows. The sound of the surf was faint, but it drummed through the house, a basso vibration that was always underfoot, even when the house was silent. She walked to one of the windows, placing her palm flat against the glass. "I love this place," she murmured. "I can feel the ocean, even here."

Then she stepped into the hallway and disappeared.

GERALDINE huddled under the sheet, her eyes wide awake and scratchy with need for sleep at the same time. Through the door dribbled the sounds from the living room, Daggett and Skylar arguing over who got the last of the pizza. Occasionally Flotsam joined in. It all seemed so normal.

She'd pleaded with God for the house to still be on the hillside when she got home, and the worrying had taken everything from her. Daggett had been inside, and if the house went, her life went with it. After a time, the sandman of sleep slipped into the room, brushing the unwelcome wakefulness from her eyes. The room grew blacker, and the sounds of the men in her life faded away. The sandman nestled into bed to lie at her side, holding her hand all the while.

THE ROOM was dark. The windows shined black as coal, with not even starlight to illuminate Daggett's way. Heavy clouds covered the heavens, the remains of the storms that had threatened the coast. He stepped into the enveloping blackness, its solidity swirling about him, the ebony of the bedroom complete.

His feet knew every step of the way to the bed. As a small boy, when his grandparents had slept in this room, he'd found his way between them more times than he could count, the steps measured, the distances memorized over and over.

As he reached the bed, the skies relented, although their generosity was a stingy one. Only the barest hint of a shadowy moon resting on the horizon suggested the distant and ever-present gods of the night hadn't completely abandoned the skies.

When the carpets and furniture had been sold, with only the one chair in the living room left—no one had made so much as an offer for it at the auction—he'd had to relearn his steps on the bare wood. He had, spending months with no electricity. Geri paid the electric every month, now, and he had both refrigeration and light, although he knew it would be gone when Geri gave up on him. It was like the old house, here for as long as he had it, and then gone when it was gone. Only the sea was forever.

He was at the bed by then, Geri's breathing soft in the darkness, the undercurrent of the rumbling surf at the base of the hillside a pleasing, deep-toned note.

His brightly printed tee came easily over his head, the branding logo of a surfboard company turned inside out. His well-worn jeans, the result of weather that had cooled in the night, fell to his feet.

The clouds broke, and there he stood, his shorts filled with dark stripes this night. The moon was a sliver, making him ghostly dark, baked flesh against deeply burnt sky. On the bed, Geri's face was turned to him, waiting, her hand lying just where he would soon be.

"Oh, you are beautiful," he whispered, his heart rich with the serendipity that had brought her to him. He had nothing, knew nothing that completed him as she did.

He sat on the edge of the bed, reaching for that hand, and he held it for a moment, its warmth, its softness real to him. Sliding beside her, wrapping her sleeping arm into his, their fingers entwined, he laid his head on the pillow and turned to look out the window. Just around the moon the clouds jostled for space, as if in a fairy tale dream world, caressing that glowing sliver of light, afraid to let too much of it escape to Earth, lest it awake those bathed underneath its cool glow. Without warning, the fragile puffs of effervescent dreams trailing across the sky gobbled up the moon, and the world became black and empty.

Only Geri's hand remained.

Not too many days before, he remembered sitting in Ronnie's old VW and asking Geri how it was to hold the hand of a god. For some odd reason, that made him think of Corky. At fourteen, just after his mother died, they'd found each other on the beach, surfboard riders one, catching the same waves over and over. Once, just once, Daggett had dropped in on Corky, taking the wave that should have been his. Had the older man groused? Nah. Instead, he'd hailed Daggett, taking time to explain the rules to him, and gotten him up to steam on the lingo. It was two years before they'd taken that trip down Baja, but

Daggett had been ready by then. Polished, Corky had said. Even remembering it made Daggett glow inside. Polished. He'd liked the sound of that word then, and he liked it now.

He turned his head to Geri, and he whispered, "Polished. Corky said I was polished. How do you like that?"

The clouds released the moon for a time, and its faint light dribbled through the room, sprinkling the bed with just enough glitter for his eyes to see. Geri's finely tuned features coalesced in sharp contrast to the darkened room beyond. Her eyelids were still, showing no dreams in her deepest of sleeps. Gently rounded lips quivered with each breath. Her white tank fitted her snugly, the swell of her womanly shape perfectly outlined against the bedding.

"I may be a god," he whispered, "but you are my angel."

He sank back into his pillow, the moon gone once again. He smiled. Had he said those words? Maybe he'd thought them, only. Yes, he was sure of it. Whether he ever told her or not, he was certain of one thing. Those words told of the most truthful thing he knew.

Chapter 13

"KICK THE tires, Skylar."

Geraldine held her thumb out, hoping someone would stop. She had on shorts and her ubiquitous tank. No socks. Her hair was pulled back loosely and tied in a casual knot. A piece of beach grass that was looped around one wrist reminded her of walking with Daggett along the shore, the time private, with not even Skylar along.

"I have. And the bumper and the fender—"

"Not the fender!" She dropped her hand, pressing her palm to her temple, sighing.

"Ha! That's funny," he said. "Not the fender! Have you ever looked at your car? I don't mean to make fun, but still. Don't kick the fender?"

She closed her eyes and took a deep breath. She was quite aware the car was a disaster. The fender had fallen off once already, and she'd managed to borrow a power drill, forcing new holes into the metal, then threading several mismatched bolts into the holes to hold it on. The rust was so bad, she'd barely found any good spots to drill. After she'd finished, the car hadn't looked any better, but it had been her handiwork, and for that reason, she was proud of it.

A good kick could easily cause the fender to fail all over again.

A car whisked by without slowing, its horn honking, and a blaze of excess fuel and burning exhaust slapped her in the face. She sighed. Just for one minute, she could use a break from her day. She leaned against her car, and with the brush of the sun on her forehead, she was elsewhere.

"May I have your keys, Miss?"

She opened her eyes, and she smiled. She recognized that voice. The man asking the question was in a black, double-breasted blazer, and his swept-back hair gleamed in the midday sun. Behind him rose a huge building all done up in pink marble. Arches and miniature Ionic columns surrounded each window, and small metal balconies dotted the front of the structure.

"They're in the ignition, Paul." Glancing at his nametag, she smiled. She'd known, just known, that his name would have to be Paul. It always was.

"Thank you, Miss. Enjoy your time at the tables."

He waited patiently for her to step away, and then ducked into the low-slung automobile. The powerful machine whooshed subtly as the engine started, falling quickly into a distinctive rumble.

At the door she was greeted by a young man, this time in a white blazer with navy pants. His shoes reflected like a mirror, and on his lapel was a discreet nametag. She glanced at it. Paul. Naturally.

"Thank you, Paul." She blew him a kiss. She felt generous today. She pulled out a fifty, and she tucked it in his hand.

"Thank *you*, Miss. I know Lady Luck will treat you well.

Enjoy your stay." He bowed and let the door close gently behind her. A horn honked, and she opened her eyes to find she was back in California once again.

"Why, it is you! Geri!" A tinted window on the passenger side of a very long, luxurious car soundlessly slipped the final few inches into the door. The words carried a familiar nasal whine.

"Mr. Chickawaddy?" She stepped closer, surprised to see her customer from the shop, and then not surprised at all to find the passenger seat scattered with musical scores. "You drive . . . this?"

"A rental. I usually like something less imposing. However, my normal transportation is under the weather. Are you having trouble, dear?" He waggled his fingers at her, and they were filled with gem-encrusted rings.

"My car." She laughed, glancing at her little VW on the side of the road. "It turns over then stalls. My friend and I have been stuck here for the past hour."

Without another word, he motioned for her to step back, and he pulled his big car to the side of the road just in front of the small VW. Climbing out, he marched spritely to the rear of the broken vehicle in crisply pressed slacks and open-toed sandals.

"Trouble, I hear." He touched Skylar lightly on the arm, smiling when the boy glanced at him.

"Yes, sir."

"Ah, my boy, let me have a look inside." Mr. Chickawaddy squatted at his side, placing one jeweled hand on the boy's shoulder. "This is something I'm good at." Almost immediately, Mr. Chickawaddy stood, and he wiped his hands briskly together. "Done! Start it up, my dear." He smiled brightly, immensely pleased.

"I'm sorry, Mr. Chickawaddy. I know you mean well, but we've tried a dozen times."

"Dear, I've fixed it. It'll run, now. You and your little boy here can get along to your destination with no more time wasted." He nodded his assurance, and the jewels on his fingers twinkled right along with him. "Now, dear. Try it."

He was so sure of himself that she didn't have the heart to put him off again. She slipped into the old car, and she pumped the gas before hitting the key. She heard the engine crank. Rather than dying as she expected, a belt screeched in protest, and the little motor smoothed into a noisy, rough clatter.

Skylar fell into the seat beside her, patting the dash.

"Where's Mr. Chickawaddy?" Geraldine looked at him with a pleased smile.

"In his car, already." He impulsively tapped out a quick and repetitive rhythm on the metal dash, his freckled hands bright in the sun.

"Yeah. What did he do to fix it?" She couldn't imagine.

"Oh, it was nothing. He pushed the spark plug wire back on. Said it was loose."

"Mr. Chickawaddy knew that?"

"Sure. He said he has his Porsche torn down in his garage. It had a loose wire, too, and he only discovered it after pulling the engine apart. All Volkswagens are the same, he said." He grinned, his hand tightening the knot on the rope holding the door closed at his side.

"Sure, they're all the same," she muttered. She pressed the gas, and the car began to very slowly gain in speed.

Chapter 14

"SO, THE VERDICT?"

"Verdict?" Daggett didn't look Geraldine's way.

"You know what I mean. The reason you're out here."

She stood on the deck and looked up at him perched high on an old wooden ladder. When she and Skylar had finally limped the old VW home, its engine cutting out twice more before finally sputtering into the carport, she'd been hot and tired, with only Flotsam there to greet her. It wasn't until she'd wandered into Skylar's bedroom—they actually called it that, now—that she'd found Daggett, and then only his legs.

Now she stood below him, and she couldn't tell what he was doing.

"Trying to keep the old girl from falling down." He looked down at her, and he grinned.

"You really think she might fall?" She frowned, kicking off her shoes. They were rope-topped flip-flops—backless sandals, the dollar store had advertised—and the old, rough wood felt good on her feet.

"Bound to, what with this being Cal-i-for-ni-a." He sounded out the syllables, making them into a hick pronunciation of the word, all the vowels long except the first and third. His hand swept towards the ocean. "Whole country's going to break off, take a swan dive into the mighty Pacific, they tells me, and what's to bet, this is the first place to go."

"Won't," she said, caught up in the spirit of the moment, and laughing.

"Okay, woman. Tell me why." He put his free hand on his waist as if perturbed.

"Can't take off into the ocean, even if it wants." She fought a smirk that was more impish grin than anything else.

"Gotta have a reason. Scientists have theirs. What's yours?" He looked at her expectantly, his hair, quite rag-tag by this point in the summer, silhouetted against the sky, the silky blue framing a face that was more beautiful than any face had the right to be.

Playfully, she crooned, "Love will keep us to—ge—ther," keeping her voice right on key, and with her arms and legs doing a little twisty number she'd long ago done for a high school variety act. She burst into laughter, the sound quickly dissipating into giggles, as she turned to the railing, leaning on it, and looking out across the sea. In spite of her joviality, his words had gotten to her. She knew he'd meant them to be funny. That's the way he was, tossing worries off, making awful situations into the way life should be, as if everything was all right, no matter what the world threw at him.

However, she loved this house, and she did worry that someday it might be gone. Without the house, would there be a Geraldine and Daggett anymore? She didn't know.

She turned as his arms wrapped around her, wishing there weren't tears on her face. She didn't want tears on her face, for him to see her crying. He never cried, and she didn't want to appear weak. Weak wasn't Daggett, and she wanted to be what he needed her to be.

He kissed her on the neck, and he hummed the song back to her. After a short time he was quiet.

"I love the ocean. You know that, Geri. If I meet my end by leaping into the sea in the greatest earthquake of all time, then what better way is there to go?"

"Together?" she whispered.

"Yeah, together. We'll go together."

Well, it wasn't quite an *I love you*, but it was as close as he'd ever gotten. She hugged his arms, and for the moment, she was satisfied with that.

Chapter 15

"WELL—" and Geraldine paused, taking a deep breath. "What do you think, Daggett?"

She sat on the big rock by the mailbox, and she let her eyes run the length of the house. Daggett's house. His grandparent's house before that, the one thing retained from the McCarthy hearings, their grandson's legacy from a bygone era.

To the south, the coastline jutted out to form a small promontory, putting Mrs. Nettleworth's house proudly on a rock footing overlooking the ocean. She even had a small backyard. Daggett's grandparents had planted the front edge of their home against the steep hillside, throwing down long wooden supports to rest on concrete stanchions buried against bedrock far below.

North along the highway, there were no other houses for quite some distance. The shoulder of the road rimmed the rocky cavalcade where it dropped a hundred feet and more directly into the breaking surf far below.

The old house—trendy and modern in its day—was long

and took up a lot of highway. One end was original, she'd been told, the other added in the years when Daggett's grandparents had made a lot of money. She was unsure which was the new or the old. Both were pretty well worn, now.

Few people noticed the old structure, wedged down the side of the hill as it was. Driving by, people saw more roof than front yard. The front carried a double carport, an entry door on a deep porch, and a whole lot of white rock. She could see two small windows, the one from the kitchen, and the second from what she thought was a bathroom far down the facade. She didn't equate inside spaces to outside dimensions very well, so she couldn't be sure.

There were various other low rock walls, and a long planter—very empty and dry—along the front sidewalk. The front yard was like a sluice, one that was lower on the house side than the street. The planter kept runoff away from the house.

Everything looked fine until you got off the street and onto the drive, looking down the roofline. Then you could see how the far end sagged. It was obvious when walking through the yard, also, the sudden drops in the soil. You wouldn't trip and fall just wandering through, but line up the drop-offs with the roofline, and you could tell. The house was giving way, following the hillside into the ocean someday.

She refused to look at the carport.

"I don't know, Geri. I never had a car before. I didn't think I needed one when Ronnie offered us this one. Can they fix stuff like this?" Daggett was puzzled, clearly out of his depth.

The carport was completely empty except for the old VW. At a glance, the car looked as good as ever. The moon hubcaps were dented, but they were there. Most of the paint was visible, and while the rust was bad, in reality, there was more body than not.

The problem now was not something as simple as the connector to the spark plug. Oil had flooded the floor under the car, and more dripped out as they spoke.

The car was why she refused to look.

She could hear Daggett kick the bumper. It must be a surfer thing. Skylar had done the same thing. He could kick the fender for all she cared. Let it fall off. Her bolts were no good without an engine to make it run.

"I've asked Mrs. Nettleworth for a ride to work three times this week, but I can't keep that up." She scratched in the dirt with her toe. Each time she tried to look at Daggett, her eyes jumped away from the disaster the car had become. "Even with paying her for the gas, I feel guilty."

"Marla? Have you asked her? You cover for her so much, she can't mind."

"I mind, Daggett. She lives seven miles the other side of the shop. It's the time that it takes. How long will she be my friend if I expect this of her?"

She realized he'd moved to her side when his leg brushed hers. His elbows rested on his knees, and he reached with a stone and scratched at the dirt. The sound was rough and dusty, as if the land itself felt as worn as the house and the car that were so clearly tired of life.

"I can't touch the trust. Even if I could, it barely pays the taxes on the house. I guess to my grandparents, it was a lot of money when I was born. Now, it's not much at all." He said it very matter-of-factly, with no recriminations at all, just stating the obvious.

"You know I'm not asking that. I wouldn't." She placed a hand on his leg, giving it a squeeze. She would gladly throw in the rest of her mother's money, but there wasn't enough for a car, or even to repair a really broken one.

"I know. I just wanted you to understand I would if I could."

He tossed the stone, and it hit the rock wall by the walk, bouncing onto the porch.

"Well," she said, standing, "I can put back a little from my next check, and maybe I can find someone who will at least look at the problem without charging first. If we let the electric ride for two months, it might be possible . . ." She didn't finish, and she didn't turn to look at either Daggett or the car. Letting the electric bill run over meant paying double on it the next month. It was a downhill spiral she knew would be hard to reverse.

Somewhere off in the distance, an undercurrent of thunder shook the air, and just over the roof of the house, a dark line encroached on the horizon.

"No surfing today." He narrowed his eyes, his glance skipping across the blackened ribbon tracing the distant sky, as small pricks of lightning created transient glowworms. They undulated, taking a drink from the ocean's surface one at a time, then disappearing when satisfied.

"Surfing," she repeated, reaching and taking his hand. "No, not today, Daggett." She pulled his arm close, the car forgotten for a time. In Daggett's world, she knew, everything else was set aside for that one singular activity. It was all encompassing to him. She enjoyed it, too, but his focus, his fascination with it mystified her. It was the breath of life to him, and as long as he had the sea, nothing else mattered.

Normally, she could accept that as part of him. Today was different. It was the car, the opportunity for the regular job it had provided, and she'd made a friend there, Marla. She didn't want to lose either her paycheck or her friend. She would without a car.

"I do know someone." He pulled his arm loose, and he moved behind her, running both his arms around her, his scraggly chin brushing the side of her head. "I can call him."

The thunder rumbled again, and a sudden breath of coolness

washed them, bringing sea and sand and shells to the top of the hillside, all wrapped up in the smell of moist seaweed in a tidal pool, the small creatures inside trapped by the movements of the earth and the moon. She shivered as a breeze ran its fingers through her hair. It felt good against the stress of the car and all the benefits its loss might wipe away. She couldn't imagine who he might know. Skylar didn't have any money. If he did, he'd surely be surfing Maui instead of freezing in his wetsuit in the cold California surf.

She closed her eyes and breathed in deeply, glad for the distracting smell of the sea. Music swelled around her, and she smiled, releasing herself to her imagination. She instantly knew exactly where she was.

She turned to Daggett's empty seat and opened her eyes. She'd asked him for a glass of Champagne, and he'd whispered his willingness in her ear. Now he was off, and just for a moment, she could watch those around her, the formal tuxedos on the men and the flowing gowns on the women, the fabrics speaking of money, as great swaths of high society gathered under the ornamental vaults rising far over their heads.

The Opera House in Sydney was a place she'd wanted to visit for years, and with Daggett's unexpected inheritance from his father, they finally had the money. Twelve hours on the aircraft had been long, even ensconced in First Class, but here, now, it was worth every moment. Walking up the grand stair-cases, the arching windows offering glimpses of the southern blue skies gracing the Aussie continent had left her breathless with excitement. Daggett in his Ferragamo shoes and Armani tuxedo had been a treat to her eyes, and having him at her side felt even better.

She turned as an usher in black and white touched her ever so lightly on the shoulder.

"Yes?"

"Miss, you are with a Mr. Priestly?" The usher smiled.

She glanced at his nameplate, so neatly ordered on his lapel, and she chuckled. "Yes, I am, Paul."

"Mr. Priestly will be busy for a time. He asks you not to worry."

"Is there a problem?" Just Paul's request was enough to cause that very thing. Her heart caught for a beat, and she knew her smile faltered for a fraction of a second.

"I don't believe so, Miss. However, he would like you to pay particular attention to the events shortly to be seen on the stage. It would seem he has something special in store for you tonight."

She glanced forward as the music faded, and the light in the auditorium shifted and melted into a darkened cocoon of silence. Three spotlights flickered on, centered on an old-fashioned chrome microphone on a stand. The lights formed a white circle where they converged, but three extended arcs, red, blue, and yellow, swept the stage just behind, catching on a spangled backdrop of blackest night. Shards of colored light danced over the crowd, playing with jewel-encrusted ears and fingers throughout the vast room.

"It's beautiful," she whispered, thinking this was what Paul had meant. A murmur of appreciation started up around her, expressing the crowd's surprised approval.

There was more, though, for after only a moment, a man in a cream-colored suit, silk, she was sure, by the sheen of the fabric, walked up to the mike. His blond hair looked familiar to her, but Daggett had on a black Armani.

It was when he spoke that she knew.

"Ladies," and the voice was deep and smooth as it flowed like buttered honey from the room's hidden speakers. "Ladies and gentlemen," it called the second time.

What was Daggett doing up there? She frowned, wondering

where his black suit had gone. It had cost as much as a small car, and she didn't want it lost. He might have his inheritance now, but she wasn't so far from California as to be a wastrel.

The room grew silent. Gently, ever so slowly, music began to swell, the sound of violins and oboes, with a piccolo dancing in between, the backdrop of sound brushing the walls of the darkened space with the barest suggestion of a melody. She settled back in her chair as the man in the cream suit began to speak over the music, his voice mesmerizing.

"Ladies and gentlemen, this is the best night of my life. I've come halfway around the world to the most beautiful place on Earth, and for one reason only."

The music continued building, and the volume swelled to a crescendo. An orchestra had risen from the floor as he spoke, the instruments glittering in the multicolored lights layering the floor of the stage. A man with outsized cymbals, standing poised at the apex of the musical ensemble, was the centerpiece. Plainly, he was waiting on some unknown signal to slam them together.

The speaker continued, "Out there in the darkness, sitting next to one of you, is the girl of my dreams. I'd like her to know just how I feel. Geri, I—"

The cymbals, obviously early, crashed together, drowning out the words.

She jumped, and opening her eyes, the sky around her was blackened with clouds, with the smell of ozone permeating the air. Daggett's arms were still around her, and the air was decidedly cool.

"That one almost got us, Geri. How about we go in before the rain hits?" He leaned forward and let his lips brush her ear. "Or do you want to stand under the wild California sky, daring the gods above to take what's ours, telling them we won't let them send our house into the sea? We could do that, you know, let the storm wash over us, and memorize each bolt of lightning as it wars in the skies above."

"A poet, Daggett?" Her somber mood was broken, and she was relieved to hear laughter in her words. "Since when do you recite lines of verse?"

"Poetry?" He chuckled, although it was nearly soundless against the rumble of the gathering storm. It was felt, more than anything else, in his breath and moving body. "I don't know any poetry. I only know you, that I—"

As with the cymbals in the Sydney Opera House, a brilliant flash of lightning and a thunderous crash of unbelievable proportions washed his words away. Geraldine twisted around and put her face against his chest, as his arms pulled her tight.

"Shall we go in?" His hand rubbed her back, giving comfort.

"Please." She laughed unevenly. The bolt of lightning had been a big one, and she no longer wanted to be outside. The bleeding car, the wilting house, none of it mattered. Safety did, and that could only be found indoors.

The first raindrops hit as they stepped onto the porch. The fat globules broke messily, splaying over the dry yard, the concrete drive becoming a checkerboard of light against dark. They came faster and faster, the light fading as the falling rain soaked it from the sky.

"Let's get inside." She tugged his arm as the downpour pushed deeper and deeper into the shadows.

It was the sound of a barking dog that prevented them from moving. Running up the side of the highway came Skylar, led by Flotsam.

"Hey!" he yelled when he saw the two on the porch. His hair was wet, and his clothes were soaked and clinging to his skin. He held a darkening paper bag in one hand, vainly attempting to shield it from the water. "Anybody for a shower?"

"Run, Flotsam! It's dry under here," Daggett called, grinning to see the big animal tear away from Skylar, his leash flapping in the air.

"He's already soaked." Geraldine pushed him on the shoulder. "Leave the poor animal alone." Skylar, too, she thought, her empathy going out to him.

Flotsam had reached the porch by then, and before anyone knew what was happening, he barked twice and shook, beginning at his head, all the way to his tail. Water flooded every dry space, a miniature shower of grand proportions.

"Flotsam, no!" Geraldine held him at arm's length, her hand on his head. "Daggett, help."

Hearing Daggett's name, the dog turned to him and leaped, planting his big paws on his chest, barking and throwing out his long tongue. Daggett grabbed the dog's mouth, forcing his head and tongue away.

"Lucky you, Daggett." Skylar had reached the porch, and he grinned as he stepped out of the rain. He rubbed Flotsam's head as he held out the paper bag. "Dog food from the shop up the road."

Geraldine looked at the soaked bag, then at Skylar dripping water all around him. She began to laugh. Without warning, the bottom of the paper bag, darkened with water, split, and all the food inside scattered across the width of the porch. Flotsam dropped to all fours, and with gusto began to snap up the unexpected bonanza.

"Thanks, mutt." Daggett pulled at his shirt, the front now muddy and wet. He looked at Geraldine. "Remind me why I have a dog, because I don't know just now."

"Because you love him?"

"Ha!" he barked, yanking the wet shirt over his head and holding it high. "After this mess?"

By then the downpour was in earnest, and water poured

from the house's gutter downspouts in a flood, filling the long rock planter, and coursing through the front yard. The highway above was a river, and a passing car dumped a sizable portion of it directly into the front yard, sending a tidal wave onto the porch.

Geraldine hooted, dancing. Unable to keep her feet dry, she grabbed Daggett, and in a moment of wild-eyed looks, they toppled to their backsides, no longer dry in any reasonable manner.

Already soaked, and unable to resist, Skylar dashed into the yard to dance the dance of the redheaded god Kokopelli, his gift of rain bringing fertility to the parched fields, forests, and gardens of Northern California. Amusingly, all it took was an ear-splitting crash of explosive thunder to drive him from his watery dance back under the porch.

It was later with towels and hot cocoa, as they stood at the back windows and watched the sun break through the black clouds out over the ocean, that they began to warm. The sudden intensity of the storm, Flotsam's watery antics, and Skylar's god dance had eased Geraldine's worries for a time, pushing the broken car and its possible ramifications from her mind.

"This should be life, Daggett." Her words were whispered between one sip and the next. "No worries, watching the sun over the ocean, and nothing to pull us away."

He stood for a moment, his cup long emptied. He looked into it, one small remnant of marshmallow caught in the bottom.

He glanced at Skylar off to the side. Bare-shouldered, his own cup empty and on the floor, his freckled arms wrestled with Flotsam, rolling him to the side, and grabbing his legs to tease him. The dog was almost as big as the man-god who had danced the rain into their yard, a twin in his actions as he pirouetted across the canted wooden surface.

Sky-god Skylar and animal-god Flotsam, sharing the life-dance from above.

"This *is* life, Geri." He glanced at her, then back into his cup, before turning his gaze to the ocean.

"Your life." She swirled her remaining cocoa. "This is your life, not life."

"Your life, too. You're here. Now. With me."

She smiled at that. However, she had work at five, and she still didn't have a ride.

"Outside, you said you knew someone."

"Oh?" He had that grin on his face that he sometimes got, the one when he planned to go out on his board and do some stupid new stunt that would later be called brilliant and daring. "Like who?"

Before she could answer, Skylar yelled out, and they looked to see Flotsam with the leg of his shorts in his mouth. The big dog was dragging him across the floor, and Skylar barely held them on with one hand wrapped around the waistband.

"Like old times, Daggett?" She pointed and grinned.

"Give up, Skylar," he called. "Flotsam's gonna win. Let him have 'em, and go find another pair."

She chuckled, remembering the times Daggett had chased the dog in nothing but the buff, not giving up for a moment.

"Someone, Daggett?" She wrapped one hand into his. The sun had finally begun to sparkle off the water, but work was on its way, and if Daggett had good news, she wanted to hear it.

"Remember San Jose?"

"Sure." She frowned. That was where they met. "Two years ago."

"Over. You met him then. Corky. You said you knew him. He might help, if I ask."

Corky. Her heart was immobilized at the mention of the man's name, the man who knew her and yet didn't know her at all. Corky might help, if he asked. Daggett said it so casually,

111

just threw the man's name out into the room, as if he would be there at his beck and call.

After she'd found Corky, found out who he was, anyway, she'd planned ways to get to know him, to find out what he was like. He was on the West Coast, she learned, far from her home in Colorado. She was away at school when her stepfather took ill. Her mother, Judy, let the business slip, and then the house was gone. By the time Geraldine was out of school, the remaining money had evaporated, and she was headed west. She'd gone to San Fran, waitressing near Corky's place, hoping he'd come in. One day he had. Soon he'd come in more often, and then she'd gone to his shop to work weekends, moving up to two and finally three days during the week. They'd become friends, Corky finding a willing student for his love of surfing, and she'd been talented, he'd said, a natural. Like him, he'd bragged once. She was his second best protégé ever. He hadn't mentioned his best. She hadn't cared about that. It was his other words that she held in her heart. Like him. He hadn't known what that meant to her.

It was truer than he knew.

Finally, she'd moved further south, unable to take being so near him and yet not being near him at all, not in the way she wanted. She didn't want to be his protégé, his employee, his friend.

However, even with her emergency trips to Colorado that summer to tend to her ailing mother, she never thought of leaving the coast. Not permanently. Even if she couldn't have Corky, she wanted to be part of his world.

When her mother died, and she no longer had a reason to return to Colorado, she stayed in California.

Then she'd found Corky's son, although the relationship between Corky and Daggett wasn't biological. That was Corky, his magic, to be able to draw beach waifs to him and make them

112

his own, to create a family wherever he went, to make people love him, even as he did his own thing.

He had done that with Daggett. With her, too.

Now it seemed they'd be drawn together once again, father and daughter, Corky and Geraldine, and he didn't even know.

Chapter 16

"RAD BOARD, man! I could carve a gnarly wave with this dude!" The long-haired, bare-shouldered boy in his worn flip-flops stroked the blue board with obvious lust. His eyes glowed as he clearly pictured himself on the waves, this board making him the king of the surf. He pulled it out and held it under his arm, taking a few steps just to see how it felt, and then reluctantly replaced it on the rack.

Corky Maiterson smiled from his position high on a ladder. A well-known surfing expert, as a younger man, he'd done his own endless summer, traveling the globe, hitting all the world's best surfing locales, and burning through a small inheritance in a rather inventive way. Now the owner of his own surf shop, he sorted hats and shoes that were out on display high on the walls, colorful gems visible through the banks of glass facing the ocean, placed there for no other reason than to tempt the eyes of wandering beach-wannabes. The real jewels—custom made boards—he kept in back for the true surfers, the ones to whom carving the perfect wave was more than just a blue board that fit easily under one skinny arm. Some of the boards were one-offs by the most famous in the business, and others were hand-formed by Corky in his private shop, only available to a select few.

"Like it? It can be yours," he called to the boy. He was a salesman, after all. He had to be. This was his shop, named after him, and he loved it, almost as much as surfing. Besides, this was no beach urchin, no matter the faded board shorts and the worn shoes. The boy's hair carried a good cut, and his teeth were even and bright. His parents were probably lawyers living in a three-story condo overlooking Lincoln Park.

"It's a Walden, isn't it?" The boy's voice carried the reedy tenor of early adolescence. "Do you have any Degree33s? I heard Clyde Beatty shapes some of their boards."

"One or two in back." He was impressed. Clyde Beatty, Jr. was a master shaper from the 60s who still turned out excellent work. This boy knew his boards.

He began to back down the ladder, warming as he dropped into the afternoon sun streaming through the windows.

Then another boy hit the front door, one about the same size, wearing board shorts in similar condition, but with bare feet and dark hair as compared to light. He didn't come all the way in, just yelled, "Luke! Mom's here with the chicken. Come on!" He twisted and was gone across the sidewalk, crossing the small parking lot in a few strides, and already at the crosswalk to the beach before the first boy could respond.

"Degree33s, right?" The boy danced backwards, pointing at Corky. "I want to see 'em next time." Without another word, he crashed through the door and into the sun.

Corky smiled. Those boys were the lucky ones, with family, fried chicken, and someone who cared enough to make sure their hair was trimmed, even if they allowed them to pretend an impoverished urchin facade. Not all kids were so fortunate.

His eyes glanced at the wall above the door, at the string of framed photos there. He had surfed with the best and had pictures of him on various beaches with most of them. Sand Dollar just south of Big Sur. Steamer's Lane. Half Moon Bay Jetty. Even one at Doran Beach at an exceptionally high tide. He'd lucked into that one, gotten lost, and happened to have his board in back. Some guy at a station noticed it, and before long, there they'd been. He'd never been back, but he had a picture to prove Doran could make pretty good waves.

The most special pictures didn't have anyone famous in them. They were of kids he'd known, some boys and a couple of girls, castoffs from life come to the beach because it was the only home they knew. Most of them hadn't been homeless, but a kid didn't have to be homeless to be a castoff. Corky understood that being castoff was a condition of the heart, not one of absentee parents and homeless shelters.

Two were his favorites.

Down off Baja he'd surfed with a boy one summer, blond-headed, tall, one he would have taken home, if he could. However, the boy had family, grandparents on the coast up north near Mendocino. He and the boy had taken Corky's van south into Mexico, spending the entire summer searching for the best waves ever. They'd found a few, too, really good ones.

The other was in the picture four down, the backdrop just across the highway on Ocean Beach. She'd been working for him then, showing up several days a week to clerk in the shop, maybe haul things in from the back room, restock the shelves. He'd really taken to her, a natural on a board like he'd been as a teen, and he'd seen more of himself in her than he'd thought possible. If he'd married and had children, she could have been the daughter he might have had.

She was a prodigy, and he'd gloried in that, giving of his

early mornings and weekends, taking her out on the water, and being surprised when she taught him stuff he'd never realized he didn't know. Then she'd disappeared until he'd seen her again that weekend in San Jose.

He liked the thought that his two finest had found a life together, that maybe he'd had a hand in matching them up. Corky, the Matchmaker. Find Love on the Beach. He could sell his services, and he'd never have to work at a real job ever again. Except he would, at surfing, in a surf shop, or anything to do with the waves.

The boys from earlier had finished their chicken, and their antics on the beach caught his attention. With the shop empty and his stocking high up the ladder on hold, he took time to watch. The two rich-boy urchins had a Frisbee, and they tossed it at one another, their enthusiasm outmatching their skills. The light-haired one, Luke, leaped to catch it, missed, and watched in dismay as it hit the top of the seawall, skidding for several feet, sending a handful of seagulls airborne. Then it bounced onto the edge of the road. He leaped over the wall, not bothering with the steps, and in a quick motion, threw the Frisbee back at the second boy. The dark-haired boy grabbed it as he ran, falling down in the sand, hooting as he leaped to his feet, the plastic toy held high in the air.

They were about the size Daggett had been when Corky met him for the first time. Geri hadn't fallen onto his plate like Daggett had, all need and craving for attention. Daggett had been a sponge, soaking him up, riding on his every instruction. Geri had been a wild tabby, aloof, cautious, only willing to take him on her terms. She'd tested the waters first. Was she welcome? Did he try to control her? Was she still Geri when she walked away?

In the end she'd walked away for good, and he'd never been able to figure out why. He'd had to let her go. She wasn't his,

117

and no matter how much affinity he'd felt toward her, she was her own woman. It had hurt for a long time when she'd gone, more so than with Daggett, even though she kept in touch more than the boy did, the odd postcard at first, then a phone call every now and then. With Daggett, he was lucky to get a bit of attention a couple of times a year, and that was only if they wound up at a surfing event together.

Then had come that e-mail. He reached into his pocket and pulled it out. Yesterday after he'd gone for the day, his clerk-slash-bookkeeper had caught it, printing him a copy and leaving it out. She said she was afraid he'd not get to it for a week or more, and it seemed important.

Call Daggett. He won't call you, you old fool, and you never do call him.

That was all it said, sent from a beauty shop somewhere up the coast. It didn't say who it was from, although he suspected Geri.

"An old fool, am I?" He looked out to the birds on the seawall, finding the boys throwing sand at one another, dark against the sun slowly falling towards the sea. The shop silent, he could just hear the sounds of the boys' voices through the glass, with the occasional car on the highway interrupting the distant dialogue just enough that he couldn't tell what they were saying to one another. It reminded him of Baja, and windy mornings crawling out of an old van, falling into the sea and yelling over the crashing waves to a bright-haired boy at his side.

Yeah, he'd call. He'd call and see what Daggett needed, and whatever it was, he'd do it. Just like that. All the boy had to do was ask.

Corky folded the paper back up and poked it into his pocket. He blinked away tears. Yeah, whatever he needed, just ask. Corky would do anything for him. Anything at all.

He pulled his keys from his pocket, and with a smooth, practiced motion, he locked the doors. He hit a switch, and the open sign by the front door blinked off, its darkness telling the beachfront that the day was drawing to a close, and to come again tomorrow.

Chapter 17

"JUST LIKE that," Geraldine nodded, "and I wouldn't have believed it if the car hadn't started right up." Picturing Mr. Chickawaddy in his rolled-up jeans and flip-flops made her smile, and she badly needed to smile.

"No! Tell me he did not!" Marla had her hands in plastic gloves, the sort that come a hundred in a box, and she worked chemicals into a client's hair. The client was snoring softly, and to avoid waking her, she whispered her astonishment.

"I tell you he did. Skylar and I were by the road, completely broken down, and up drives Mr. Chickawaddy, as pretty as you please. Skylar was inside the engine trying to sort it out, and Mr. Chickawaddy disappeared back there with him. He jiggled something, and my little car just started up." She winked. "Now, if he could just jiggle the oil pan and fix my leak."

"Well, I can promise you this: I'll never see Mr. Chicka-waddy on the Public Broadcast Network and think of him the same way again." Marla giggled, and when her client snorted in her sleep and shifted her head, she glanced at Geraldine with her eyes wide. The snoring resumed, and she burst out laughing, placing a red-stained glove close to her mouth to cut off the sound. "What did Mr. Chickawaddy jiggle, if I may be so presumptuous? With your houseguest back there, and the two of them all alone—" She let the unspoken implication fall away with an impish smirk.

Geraldine turned away, fighting an urge to smile. "Marla, you are so bad! It was a wire, I think, maybe on a spark plug. Yes, I'm sure of it. Then he drove right off without another word. My houseguest, whose name happens to be Skylar, plopped down in my car, and with no more ado, we were on the road again." She began humming the old Willie Nelson song, the one with a similar line, her fingers walking along the countertop. She could afford to play for a few minutes. Her next appointment didn't arrive for another fifteen.

"Well, at least you still have your houseguest. He didn't ride off into the sunset with a dancer from the PBN. Now, when are you planning on that blind date you promised me?" Marla frowned, twisting a strand of her sleeping client's hair around one finger, and smearing a second coat of chemicals toward the roots. "You're certain he's not gay, right?"

"Mr. Chickawaddy?" Geraldine giggled, the humor of the situation not played out yet. "I know no such thing, one way or the other."

Marla simply growled. Rather than speak, she held up her hands and formed a complete circle, clearly a chokehold, and shook them, her eyes narrowed in mock anger.

"If you really want to meet him, you can drive us down to Monterey this weekend. Daggett's got a competition he'd like to attend, and Skylar's going." Geraldine had wanted to ask, but she'd been afraid Marla wouldn't want to drive them so far. She crossed her fingers.

121

"Monterey? You know, I've never been to the aquarium there. It's supposed to be pretty fantastic." She was back in her client's hair again, and she pursed her lips. Another strand of hair came up, wrapped around her finger, and she worked her chemical magic all the way to its roots before looking up. "I caught a glimpse of him—" Skylar, her words intimated, "—when I picked you up today. I like freckles, you know. And something else, before I forget. Who's Corky?"

The door chimes rang before Geraldine could gather her thoughts to answer that, and she was grateful.

"Later, Marla. I've got to take this. It's my appointment, although a bit early." The door chimes didn't stop, and then a light dusting of ceiling tile drifted through the air.

Marla's client jerked awake, her plastic shawl and halo of red, tufted hair giving the effect of a comic strip character come to life. "Yes, dear? Are we finished?"

"Almost." She touched her shoulder, keeping her hand on the plastic protector. "Lay back down, Mrs. Berneke."

"Of course, dear. I think your chair has a vibration in the mechanism."

"I'm sure it does, Mrs. Berneke." As Marla looked around, her eyes told the truth. This was a quake.

Through the front windows, they could see a couple with a baby in a stroller, and the small family group was motionless in the middle of the street. A dog ran past, barking, and as quickly, a teenager on a skateboard wearing a hat and elbow pads zipped by, a leash flapping wildly in his hand.

"The dog got away, I guess," Geraldine said, her thoughts not really on the boy or his dog. She forced away the picture of a house sliding into the ocean.

"Dog?" That was Mrs. Berneke. She didn't have a clue what was happening.

"Yes, Mrs. Berneke," Geraldine called, and then she

122

motioned to Marla to continue with the older woman's hair. When the door chimes rang again, she realized they'd stopped for a time, and she hadn't noticed. Why did she always notice the quakes when they started, but not when they ended? Was that significant?

"Geri! There you are!" Her appointment rushed through the door, dropping all her things into an empty chair. "When the quake started, I knew you'd lock up if it was bad, so I ran as fast as I could. You know I have a screen test in L.A. tomorrow afternoon. I'm flying down in the morning. I figured if you'd at least started on my hair, you wouldn't leave me half done, would you?" The pretty blonde had bright red nails, and all she'd asked for when scheduling the appointment was a wash and a wax. She smiled brightly, coming up to lean on the counter. "And now the quake's over, and I'm early. Is that okay? Oh, hi, Marla!" She waved, her nails flashing.

Another hour, and the shop was empty. Geraldine's basket was filled with damp towels. Marla had her hands free from the plastic gloves, and she pulled a fresh towel from the cabinet to pat at her face. Outside the windows, the couple with the baby were long gone, and neither woman had noticed the boy skating back by, the dog leashed and pulling him this time. The clock was nearing closing, and they climbed into their respective chairs for a break.

"Now, about Corky." Marla snapped her fingers together. Then she pulled a piece of gum from one pocket, unwrapping it and popping it into her mouth.

"Not a good subject." Geraldine waved her off.

"You and I both know Judith doesn't mind if we e-mail out, or even take them here. I sure don't mind if you do. Old fool, though?" Marla looked at a freshly washed fingernail, and she began to chew absently on a rough corner. Her gum popped twice. Her look was one of thinly veiled mock distraction.

The computer was for appointments scheduled online. Only Judith had a personal e-mail account. Anyone else could use it, but it wasn't exactly private. Now, Geraldine wished it was.

"I have clippers for that." She pointed to the nail Marla chewed.

"No, you don't. No subject changing allowed. Who is Corky?"

"Will you change the subject if I talk about Skylar?" She should have found somewhere else to send that e-mail from. Corky was an emotional blister on her heart, loved but unbearable in her need for him, and she didn't want to discuss him.

"Okay, then, if you won't give, I'll have to make it all up. I think Corky really is Daggett's long-lost father, and now that Daggett has to have his kidney removed—a gene defect from his mother's side, I've been told—he needs to borrow one of his father's. Otherwise, he only has a year to live. Does that about sum it up?" Marla went back to her finger, refusing to look at Geraldine after one quick glance.

"Go to Monterey with us?" Geraldine really didn't want to talk about Corky.

"Before or after the kidney donation?" She was still focused on her finger.

"Before. Don't forget Skylar, you silly. He's why you're willing to drive us down there."

"So, there really is a bad kidney? Corky really is Daggett's long-lost father? I can't make up stuff this good." Her focus was now on Geraldine, and her eyes were bright with interest.

Geraldine gave up and laughed. "I will let you have the father part, although not long-lost. However, all Daggett's kidneys are fine. It's my car that's terminal, and Daggett said Corky might help. Is that good enough for you?"

"Oh, but that's so boring. I like the kidney version better—"

"Sorry," Geraldine interrupted. "Scratch the kidney. No

operation. No gene defects. Nothing."

"Oh." Marla pressed her lips together. "Then, how about this? Daggett—"

"No, Marla. Are you coming to Monterey or not?" Geraldine glanced at the clock, then stood and walked to the front of the shop, clicking the lock, and flipping the open sign over to show the closed side to the outside world. She looked back to see Marla standing with her purse in her hand.

"Ready?" She dangled her keys.

"Can I throw the towels in the washer?" It was just in the back, there to keep the towels from drying overnight in the bins in case the cleaning crew didn't show.

"Did it while you were locking up. Honey, I think ahead." Sure enough, there was a click in the background, and the swishing sound of a washer running. "Can we stop for a shake on the way to your house? I'll buy."

"Sure, Marla. Nothing for me, though."

"That quake got you rattled again? Living perched over the ocean will do that for you. If you like, I've got a couple popsicles in the little fridge in back. Would that do you better than a shake?" She put her hand on the break room door, stepping in without waiting for a reply, and returning with one banana and one cherry. "Your choice."

Geraldine gave her a quick hug. "Thank you. You are the best kind of friend, one who shows she cares. Banana, please."

"Good. I like cherry best." She flipped the wrapper off and dropped it into a trash can.

When they stepped outside, the sun was hot against their skin, and a breeze washed the smells of the town across them. It was hardly refreshing. The car was parked two blocks away, and they were perspiring by the time they got there. The air conditioner was a welcome relief against the California summer.

125

As the blocks drifted by, Geraldine felt her troubles in her throat. Marla didn't work tomorrow, and that meant seeing Mrs. Nettleworth when she got home in order to arrange yet another ride. If Daggett hadn't heard from Corky tonight, she would have Mrs. Nettleworth bring her in a bit early to e-mail him again, letting him know they'd be at the Monterey competition over the weekend. Maybe they'd meet up on the beach.

She could call, she knew, get on the phone and ring him up. He'd be glad to hear from her, and she would enjoy the sound of the man's voice. However, she pictured the last time she'd spoken with him. They'd talked for an hour or more, and she'd been a basket case for the rest of the evening. He was her father, for heaven's sake, and she couldn't tell him. What if telling him changed everything, and . . . and . . . how could she handle that?

Marla pulled up in front of Daggett's house and patted Geraldine's leg, laughing softly. When she reached to the dash to turn the radio down, the drumming of the unseen surf drifted into the car. "Home, honey. It's still here."

Geraldine's eyes turned that direction. Home. There was the roof of the house, and beyond, just visible, the distant ocean stretched to the horizon. The same, always the same, ignoring earthquakes and disrepair and fathers who abandoned their sons and even fathers who didn't know they were fathers.

Even if Corky didn't respond to her pleas to contact Daggett, perhaps he would show up this weekend, anyway.

Stranger things had happened.

Chapter 18

FLOTSAM echoed through the house, his deep-throated barks coming sharp and often. A game, Geraldine thought, the boys playing inside instead of out. The quake at the shop probably hadn't been felt here at all. Everything was normal, although if they were playing outside, it would be better. She was tired, and she still had a meal to prepare, probably boxed mac and cheese, something easy. She hoped she had milk and butter.

It was when she stepped inside that she knew something unusual was up. Daggett tore by, his hair soaked, with only a wet towel around his waist. Skylar flew after him, a wrench in his hand. She had no idea where the wrench had come from. They didn't have one. Then Flotsam bounded into the room, also soaked, traveling the opposite direction. He saw her, and he barked sharply three times before shaking, sending huge water drops everywhere.

"Did you get a bath, boy?" She knelt to rub his nose. "Daggett?" When there was no answer, she called louder,

"Daggett, thank you."

His head popped through the hall doorway, his skin flushed. He was wetter than before, and water dripped from his hair. He carried a second towel, wiping his hands, although how it could help was unclear. It was soaked.

"Thanks for what?" He glanced into the hallway as if anxious to disappear into its depths once again.

"For giving Flotsam a bath, that's what. He does need to be dried off, though." She laughed.

"Flotsam?" He looked puzzled for a moment, but then he nodded. "The dog hasn't had a bath." Skylar's voice yelled from down the hall, and he shrugged helplessly to her, tearing off that direction.

When she stepped to the hallway door was when she first paid attention to the floor. It sloped more than it had when she left that morning. She glanced at Flotsam, still sitting on the floor, his tongue out, and his eyes on her. Uneasy suspicions twisted at her gut, ones built on recent memories of popping glass, settling foundations, and a washing machine that was now far down the hill.

"Daggett?"

"Yes, Geri?"

"Do I even want to look?"

"Maybe not. Excuse me—" He broke his words off, and a sudden clanking filled the house, one of a metal wrench slamming against metal pipes.

"There. Twist that one." That was Skylar's voice. It echoed with frantic overtones.

Geraldine remembered the VW. He hadn't been able to close the engine cover. He was working on the house?

"No, this one." Daggett's voice rang with insistence.

"I know what I'm doing." The banging sound was back, then frightened words. "Oh, no, it's moving again."

"Grab my hand!" Daggett again, this time yelling. There was a frantic urgency to his words, then, "Got you!"

It was the sound of triumph.

More pipe sounds echoed, followed by protracted groaning, and she heard something let loose, hitting under the house before banging onto the deck below. The raucous sound of spurting water grew loud. She was no longer sure she wanted to know just what was going on. She imagined the worst. A pipe had broken, and the repair had gone badly. The wrench had been dropped. The new pipe hadn't seated well, and it was through the floor. Perhaps the ladder from underneath the house had come loose, taking flight briefly and crashing down the hill. She hoped it was something so easy.

She suspected worse.

Her premonitions of doom were pushed aside by a plea for help.

"Um, Geri, could you come in here?" Daggett's voice, filled with desperation. "Now?"

When she moved, so did Flotsam. He jerked to his feet, barking, cutting her off, and dashing down the hall toward Daggett's voice. She stepped to a chair to place her things in a dry location off the floor.

"Back, dog! Geri, hurry!"

Flotsam barked again with a distinctly hollow sound. Geraldine frowned, now running down the hall. The dog's rump and tail stuck out of the bathroom door. When she arrived, she threw her hand to her mouth and gasped.

"Daggett! The tub! Where is it?"

Water sprayed everywhere at full force. The pipes in the wall were ripped free, and Daggett stood in the middle of it, his legs stretched over an opening just where the tub used to be. Greenery could be seen far below, the late-day sun brilliantly lighting the hillside under the house. He held onto something extending through the floor, and it took a moment for her to realize it was an arm.

"Skylar?"

"Hanging out here under the house." His reedy voice called thorough sounds of spraying water and suddenly howling dog.

"Quiet, Flotsam." Daggett barked his command at the big animal. "Geri, I need your help to pull Skylar up."

"Of course. What can I do?" She pushed Flotsam aside and stepped through the water covering the floor. The center of the bathroom was very springy, and she saw why as she drew closer. The joists underneath the tub, and in fact all under the bathroom, had torn loose. They could be seen hanging at an angle several feet underneath the opening, swinging freely, attached at only one end somewhere back under the house.

To make matters worse, the water spraying from the pipes was very cold. By the time they had Skylar back inside, soaked and huddled on the floor in the living room, she was shivering as much as the men.

"What happened?" she chattered, opening a hall linen closet to pull out several dry towels.

"Daggett was in the shower when the quake hit—"

"Honest, Geri, the quake was long over," Daggett interrupted, and he shook his head. He reached for one of her dry towels when she held it out.

"—and he yelled—"

"Did not." He frowned, cutting Skylar off a second time.

"—the tub is loose! The tub is loose!" Skylar was laughing by then. "Chicken Little could hardly do it better. The tub is falling! That's what he should have said." He held his stomach, pointing at Daggett, only ducking when the bigger man grabbed the third dry towel from her and chucked it at him, hitting him squarely in the head.

"Geri, I've got to try to get the water turned off. Skylar,

130

loser, couldn't manage that, and now the wrench is somewhere down the hill. I guess I need to see if I can borrow another." He pulled his towel tighter and marched out the door.

"I couldn't find the cutoff," Skylar called after him.

"It's by the mailbox." Geraldine shook her head. Of course he didn't know. Daggett wouldn't have thought to tell him. As she toweled her hair, she stepped down the hall and glanced in the bathroom, glad to see that most of the water was at least draining through the opening in the floor. "Skylar, how long has it been running like this?" she called back into the living room. They had to pay for all the water running through the hole in the floor, and her car still sat outside broken.

"Not long," he called back. "I tried to twist the pipes to fix the leak. When it fell through, Niagara Falls erupted, and I thought I was gonna die."

"Twist the pipes?" She sighed as she stepped back into the living room. "You don't twist on pipes. You can tighten the connections, maybe, but you don't twist on the pipes." Anyone who knew anything should know that. However, this was Skylar, right?

"I tried to remember righty-tighty and lefty-loosey. When the pipes came loose, I yelled for Daggett, and he caught me just before the tub dropped through the floor."

She knelt at his side, aware of red on the floor under his legs. "Skylar, let me see." She twisted one ankle, cringing at what she saw. There were jagged tears in his skin on both calves.

"Oh," he said, glancing at the damage. "They do sting a little bit. I didn't really notice."

She set her towel under them, pressing his legs down. They heard the water in the bathroom slowing, and in a bit, Daggett came through the front door.

"Fixed," he shouted, thrusting a much smaller wrench high in the air triumphantly. "Whew!"

"Not fixed," she called back. "Now we have no water."

"We will have water." He tossed the wrench on the floor, squatting at her side. "Hey, how'd he do that?"

She looked at him and slapped his leg, pointing to the water outside the windows. "Don't you pay attention to anything except the ocean out there? Your tub just fell through the floor. Where were you all that time?"

"Yeah, Daggett. Where were you?" Skylar's eyes sparkled.

"Playing god." He winked. "Saving me a puny human. That one." He pointed at Skylar.

"Seriously, Daggett, how will we have water?" She felt her head tighten at her temples. The pipes in the bathroom had been running full blast. "You can't turn it back on without that geyser starting up again." She patted Skylar's knee, motioning for him to stay as she stood. Her signal was mistaken by Flotsam, and the big animal obediently crawled up by Skylar, placing his head on his lap, his eyes trained on her.

She walked to the bathroom door, watching the water dripping over the floor's ragged edge, and she felt her eyes begin to burn. No car. No water. No money. How bad could it get?

She felt Daggett's arms go around her, and his chin nestled comfortably at the side of her head.

"This end of the house was an addition from long before I was born. Just before the floor fell out of the movie business—" He pointed to where the tub had been, chuckling at his joke. "—my grandfather sold one of his movie scripts. The money doubled the size of the house, adding all the glass across the back, even the decks down below. They ran the water to this end from the existing line in the kitchen. There's a cutoff under the sink. In all the confusion, I forgot."

"Even so, it seems we'll be down to one bath." That was better than no water at all, but she thought of Skylar coming through their bedroom to use theirs. There was some privacy to be lost. She might mind that a bit.

"Nah." He leaned in and brushed his lips against her neck. "See, I'm thinking about that, already. I can cap the pipes that Skylar ripped out. The toilet's still good, I bet, and up inside the wall, the shower pipes might still work. Probably, would be my guess."

She laughed at his unexpected twist on this very dismal situation. "The floor. Did you notice that?"

"We'll patch it, drill holes in the new boards for a drain. Hey, a shower! That's it. Instead of a tub, we'll have a shower. Skylar would probably like that better, anyway."

"There you go again," she whispered, turning and looking into his face.

"What?" He kissed her gently on the forehead.

"A disaster happens, and you turn it into an adventure, an improvement in our lives." She placed her open palm on his damp chest, the warmth of his skin insisting she leave it there for a long time. When Flotsam barked, calling for someone's attention, she made to step away, letting her hand run down his arm.

When it got to his elbow, he stopped her, kissing her on the cheek.

"Life is an adventure, Geri. Worrying about every disaster doesn't make things any better. It just makes us miserable." He kissed her again. "Am I right?"

The dog barked again, and she pulled away, fully this time. When she stepped into the living room, Flotsam and Skylar were just where she'd left them.

"With your legs, can you stand?"

"Sure." He kicked them into the air. "Sorry for all the water in here."

"Blame the dog." Flotsam whined, and she'd be doggoned

133

if she didn't think she saw a smile on the animal's face. She grinned as she reached a hand to help Skylar up.

Daggett was right. She knew that. Worry made life more miserable than it had to be. Still, she hoped Corky came through, especially with this new disaster to their teetering house. It would cost money to patch up, even with Daggett's makeshift suggestion, and that meant no car repairs out of her paycheck. There was barely enough for food and utilities. There was also the expense of the water with all that leakage.

That reminded her that Marla wasn't working the next day, and she still had to make time to see Mrs. Nettleworth to ask about a ride. Maybe she could return the wrench and talk to her then.

Yes, that's just what she would do.

Chapter 19

"BUT YOU'VE helped us so much already." Geraldine had her hands full, and still Mrs. Nettleworth wanted to foist more supplies on her. She was grateful, but the moment was also tinged with guilt. After all the rides to work, how could she ever repay her?

"Dear, I was twenty once. You and that man of yours can sleep on the beach all weekend, but you still have to have food to eat." Mrs. Nettleworth handed her a foil-wrapped pie. "Strawberry. I haven't emptied my freezer yet, so I have plenty, and I made you another one. And I've got you a cooler of sandwiches to last you as long as you can stand to eat them." An insulated bag at her feet bulged with hidden treats.

"You are so good to us." Geraldine pressed one hand to the side of the old woman's face and brushed her cheek-to-cheek on the other side. "What would we do without you, giving me a ride to work so often, making Daggett his favorite pie, and just everything?"

"Don't you start that up. I like my neighbors, and I like doing for them. You remember I said my son could come up from the city and put your floor back. I told him this weekend will be fine. That boy living with you can lend him a hand."

"But this weekend won't be fine, Mrs. Nettleworth. I'm so sorry. No one at all will be home. We're all going to Monterey, Flotsam, too."

"Oh, my!" The old woman laughed, one hand to her mouth. "You told me that, I remember now. You know, I watched that boy grow up, running around in his diapers, then riding his first bike, wearing nothing but his brightly colored underwear. Batman, I think. I never loved a boy so much as that."

"Carl must be one special son."

She frowned. "My son? Heavens, no! Carl thinks I'm crazy. I'm talking about Daggett. That's why I told that boy of mine to get his keister out here and help me with my floor. Floor joists hanging loose, I told him. Need rehanging." Her eyes wrinkled in mirth. "Can't help it they're underneath your house, now can I?"

"We'll try to come back early so your son will have help." Geraldine had met Carl several times. He wasn't the type to work on floor joists.

"No, you won't. Working on your house will keep that son of mine out of my hair, and I'm glad for it. He's got all of my money invested, and if he needs to call someone to come help him, he can afford it. Don't worry about me getting in, either. I've still got my key from Daggett's grandparents. Now, I see you have things still to pack, and I'm keeping you. Bye, dear, and I'll wave from my window when you leave. Look for me!" She took a deep breath, and with a smile, she began the slow walk uphill to her house.

Geraldine appreciated the sandwiches, but she hoped Marla had left room in her trunk. Four people and a dog would take up a lot of space.

"Geri!"

It was Marla, and about time, too. Geraldine waved as her friend turned off the highway to pull in the drive.

"Is that bag full of food for the trip?"

"From Mrs. Nettleworth." She motioned to the house next door with her head, where the old woman could be seen opening her front door.

"Is she the one who makes the strawberry pies?" Marla drew in a deep breath and closed her eyes. Some of the famous pie had found its way to the shop one day, and after one bite, she'd raved how it was the best thing she'd ever eaten. "Where is everyone? I hope your little visitor is still going." She giggled.

"Of course. If he didn't, would you still drive us down?"

"Naturally. I just wouldn't look forward to it as much." She was now digging in Mrs. Nettleworth's sandwich bag. "Oh, my stars, is this scrambled egg and sausage, and with cheese? For this, Skylar can stay here, and I'll go anyway. Bless your Mrs. Nettleworth. I need a neighbor like her."

Geraldine called toward the house, "Skylar! You can stay home for the weekend. Mrs. Nettleworth's son needs help with the bathroom floor."

"But you promised!" His red hair thrust through the screen door, his body quickly following. He wore clean trunks and a vibrant tank, and his hair reflected a recent wash. A look of dismay danced across his face.

Before she could respond, Flotsam knocked the screen wide, forcing himself between Skylar's legs. He carried a pair of red and blue plaid boxers in his mouth. Skylar grabbed the dog, and he pulled the boxers from his mouth, shaking his finger at the animal, a mock reprimand worthy of any good disciplinarian.

Then he noticed Marla. A grin broke on his face. Heading

her direction, he stuffed the plaid shorts partially in one pocket. "Hey, I'm Skylar. You must be Marla. Geri and Daggett told me all about you."

Marla smiled brightly. "Well, I've not heard so much about you, and you can just ignore Geri's teasing. Of course, you're going. Isn't he, Geri?"

"Everyone who wants to is going."

Geraldine knelt to re-zip the bag now that her friend had lost interest. Pushing her hair back from her face, trying to figure out how to fit the bag in, she turned to let the sun warm her skin.

Then airbrakes hissed.

She turned and saw an enormous motorhome pulled up next to the curb. It was all black glass and stainless steel. It hissed again, and the entire unit settled to rest inches off the ground. The double doors swung open with a soft whoosh, and marble-topped steps extended to rest against the curb.

"Welcome aboard." A liveried young man wearing a cap trimmed in gold-braid stepped forth, extending one hand. "You are our only guest for the first part of our trip."

She glanced around to find there was no one else in the drive. She was surrounded by grounds that were surprisingly manicured, lined with flowering rosebushes and fountains as far as she could see. Birds twittered, and a cool breeze ruffled her hair. What she saw reflected life as many people thought it should be lived, glamorous and perfect.

"Will Daggett be joining us at some point?" The ride would be sumptuous but very lonely without him. She turned her hands, noticing the vibrant red polish flowing across each extravagantly shimmering nail.

"Certainly. Mr. Priestly will join us along the way. To help me serve you better, my name is Paul, and I'll be your host today."

His gloved hand helped her into the coach, and the interior

138

took her breath away. There was more marble layered across the floors, ornate glass fixtures lighting every nook and cranny, and televisions as large as the walls allowed. A custom kitchen stretched along one wall, and the refrigerator touted stainless steel doors.

"Paul, this is wonderful. What a great trip this will be! I had no idea our coach would be so luxurious."

"Paul? Who's Paul? And I like my car, but you can hardly call it luxurious." Marla's laughter danced through her words.

Geraldine opened her eyes to find her friend standing beside her. Realizing she must have spoken the final words in her daydream aloud, she laughed. "No one. Paul is no one at all, and I like your car just fine."

"Well, you can plan a great trip with no one if you want, and I hope you enjoy it. I'm having mine with Skylar. You know, since I got here, I've been thinking. I might let you drive. I'll sit in back with that redheaded man. Before you ask, the keys are in the car, so start it anytime you like. Now, I need to borrow the loo before we're off. Just in case, you understand."

She pranced off, excitement in her steps, letting the screen door slam behind her as she disappeared into the house. Flotsam scratched at it, barking once, and a hand pushed it open just enough for him to enter.

Geraldine lugged her satchel to the back of the car. No more had she gotten the key out and popped the trunk, than she looked up to see her friend at the front door, barging through the screen and yelling, "Hey, you could have warned me. You have a hole the size of a bathtub in your floor. I nearly fell in." She breezed to the back of her car, pushing her one small bag to the side. With a quick motion, she hefted Geraldine's bag inside, shoving it to the back. "Actually, it was sort of funny. The floor sure wobbled, though."

"At least the water works. If Mrs. Nettleworth's son doesn't get the floor repaired while we're gone, that's Daggett's job when we return."

"You know my brother Bobby does construction for a living. I bet I could get him up here. Daggett might have to give him a surfing lesson, though." Marla leaned against the car, and she looked studiously at the nails on one hand. "I could paint my nails on the way, couldn't I? I brought a fresh bottle in a darker shade."

"You could not. I'll be in that car with you, and I don't want to smell your nail polish all the way." Geraldine slapped at her friend's arm when she rolled her eyes.

Daggett and Skylar stepped out of the house, and she laughed. Flotsam was behind Skylar, and he nipped at the plaid boxers hanging from his pocket. Skylar was clueless. Then Flotsam was off with them, tearing across the yard. Skylar yelled at him, but his hands were full. A red face was all the response he could manage.

Each of the men lugged a small bag, but what caught her attention were the surfboards. After all, this was a trip to a surf competition. She hadn't thought that through.

"Hey, Geri." Daggett dropped his things, his surfboard carelessly tumbling onto the remains of last spring's grass. It got rougher treatment when battling the surf.

Skylar dropped his bag and board beside Daggett's.

Flotsam ran to them, depositing his own luggage, the plaid boxers, right between them.

"Daggett!" Geraldine pointed, with a smile.

"Hey, dog!" Skylar growled his words. "I had those."

"Bad boy," Daggett said firmly. "Take those back inside." When Flotsam lay down between the boards and began chewing on the underwear, he shrugged at Skylar. "What the dog wants, the dog gets, I guess."

"Geri?" Marla had her hand on the open trunk, and she

studied the inside intently. "I'm not sure how we're going to get those boards inside. Do we really need them? You know, I wonder if we can fold them." She glanced at them seriously, pursing her lips in thought.

"Fold?" It was Skylar's turn to be dismayed, and he turned to Daggett. "You're letting me borrow one of your boards, and now she wants to fold it? What's she thinking?"

"She's not serious." Daggett stepped forward and ran his hand over the roof of the car. "I need my foam mounts. I should have thought of that already."

"We don't have to fold the boards?" Marla sounded relieved. She'd been rearranging things inside, as if she could create the extra room.

"No." Daggett walked by, slapping Skylar on the side of the head. "Forgive my friend, here. They ride on top of the car. Come help me find the board mounts and straps."

"But on Geri's car—" Skylar followed Daggett inside, talking all the time, "—we just tied them on. The ropes are still in the back seat—"

Daggett just slapped the side of his head again as the screen door closed.

"He's so cute." Marla tapped Geraldine's shoulder to get her attention. "If they can't fold the surfboards, how will we load them?"

"The boards don't go inside at all. Like Daggett said, they go on the roof. I should have mentioned it, but we never carried them very far in the Beetle. We simply tied them on with ropes. It never occurred to me how we'd transport them this weekend."

"But Daggett has a way to do this?"

"It sounds like it. Where do you want the rest of the bags?"

By the time the two men returned, the trunk was loaded. There was a hard plastic cooler for drinks, the zippered bag of sandwiches, and the strawberry pie. Contrary to Geraldine's expectations, they all fit with ease, and even Flotsam's bag of treats found a perfect nesting place. The foam mounts snapped onto the sides of the boards, four rubber-coated brackets held two straps in place, and the car was ready, except for the people.

That proved to be the real challenge.

When Geraldine climbed in the driver's seat, Daggett looked puzzled. "Are you and Marla riding in the front?" He leaned into the car, reaching to push a strand of hair behind Geraldine's ear. "I'd hoped to have you next to me. It's a long way to Monterey."

She grabbed his hand, pressing it to her face. "We're both riding in the front. Marla wants in the back with Skylar." She chuckled, imagining romance already in progress.

"And Flotsam?" He pointed to the opposite side of the car. "I don't think he'll fit in the front seat with me."

"Oops." Her chuckle this time was more of a silly school-girl giggle. They'd discussed this, and the plan had been to have Daggett share space with the dog. "She asked me to drive, and I didn't think to tell her Flotsam has to be in the back." Her fingers tinkled the keys in the ignition, the sound soft and pleasant. "You can hold my hand all the way, if you want." She brushed his hand with her lips, looking up at him and winking.

It seemed that Flotsam climbing in the back seat with Skylar and Marla didn't bother Geraldine's coworker at all. The seat was very small for three, but that meant Marla had to ride curled up next to Skylar, very nearly in his lap.

"Ooh, la, la," she whispered, smiling at Skylar, as Geraldine started the car and backed out of the drive. "Ooh, la, la, indeed."

Geraldine slowed and honked the horn as they passed Mrs. Nettleworth's drive. Hands reached out the windows of the crowded car to wave, and behind a metal screen, a gnarled set of fingers could be seen waving back.

They were on the road to Monterey, only six hours away.

Chapter 20

"THANK YOU, Paul. You are so kind." The words were murmured sleepily. It was wonderfully cool in the marble-floored motorhome as it cruised effortlessly down the highway, carrying Geraldine along. Paul had assured her a preheated blanket would warm her up. He'd draped it over her shoulders, and he'd been so right.

After enjoying her rum daiquiri, she'd watched the Redwood Highway whisk past the windows. Only when she'd seen the signs for San Francisco had she turned away. San Francisco made her think of Corky, and she hadn't wanted him to be on her mind.

She had fallen asleep somewhere between Richmond and Oakland, only waking up to murmur she was chilled, and would Paul please bring her a blanket.

"Would Miss like another daiquiri?"

"With that special rum? A double dose, maybe? What do they say, two fingers?" She didn't remember the rum's name, but it had been in a squat brown bottle with a little chain around the neck. It was so cute.

"I'll be most glad to add an extra finger to your drink. Will there be anything else, Miss?"

She waved him away, turning her face into the down pillow he'd brought her, only to have Corky come to her mind once again. She'd sent him a second e-mail telling him to look for Daggett at Surfjam. It was taking place at Carmel Beach over the weekend. Would he make it? She knew Corky well enough to know that she couldn't guess.

The pillow smelled heavenly, of oranges and mint, distracting her. She moved her hand into the emptiness beside her and thought of Daggett.

"Paul?" She called louder, "Paul, when will Daggett be joining us?"

"In San Jose, Miss. We should be there within the hour."

A tinkling sound told of the glass he placed on the marble tabletop at her side. She reached out and stroked it with two fingers, the outside already moist with water. Dipping one finger inside, she stirred the ice, bringing her finger to her lips to lick it clean.

"Daggett, you would love this," she whispered ever so softly.

"I would love what?"

She opened her eyes to see his face nestled next to hers. She was curled against him, with his arm wrapped around her shoulder. Her feet were tucked in the seat, and Flotsam stretched across the floor beneath them, covering the bottom portion of Daggett's legs.

"You're not driving?" She made to sit up, and then decided it was too difficult with her feet in the seat. His arm squeezed her shoulder, and she relaxed against him once more.

"Not since Santa Rosa. We stopped for gas. You were out."

He chuckled. "You barely came to enough to stumble to the back seat. Marla wanted to drive for a while. Too much dog, I think."

"And too little Skylar." Marla's voice interjected her opinion, as her head jerked toward the person sitting in the front passenger's seat next to her. His head was against the glass, and he was snoring gently. "Visit on, you two lovebirds. I'll mind my own business." Her fingers waggled over the seat, then reached to the glove box to pull out a piece of gum before returning to the wheel. She tapped the steering wheel mounted radio controls a couple of times, and an oldie goldie about traveling to San Jose warbled out over the speakers. Marla snapped her fingers softly to the beat, falling easily into an insular musical world of her own.

Daggett whispered, "I don't know where you were, but it must have been a good dream. You were smiling all the while."

"I was meeting you in San Jose." She shifted her shoulder. Daggett was lean and muscular, and against him, she fit like a hand in a glove. She touched his shirt, running her finger down a long fold of fabric. Resting her hand against his stomach, through the cloth she felt a tight roll of skin at his waist, just where his body folded into the seat. It wasn't special. She knew that. Everyone had one of those when sitting down, but this skin was Daggett's, and she enjoyed knowing it was his and no one else's.

"Were you bringing me anything special? Mrs. Nettleworth's pie, maybe?" He wrapped his hand around hers.

"Paul brought me something."

"Paul?"

She smiled, although she knew Daggett couldn't see it. "Paul was my host, and I asked him for a rum daiquiri. I had just stirred it with my finger then licked it dry. The taste was wonderful."

He was quiet for a time. Then he drew a deep breath and let it out fully. After a short time, he released her hand to rest his fingertips against the window, drumming his nails softly against the glass.

"Daggett, what?" She reached for his hand, but he tugged it away, keeping it at the glass. His fingers drummed once more, then were still. "You're not irritated about Paul, are you?" Now she wished she hadn't mentioned him.

"Look out there. No ocean. There hasn't been for hours. All these people, how do they live never seeing the ocean?" He whispered softly, as if speaking to himself and not to her. "I couldn't stand it."

She followed his gaze. The sun outside the car was bright, with grass and trees strewn across the landscape. There were lone buildings here and there, intermingled with occasional clusters of houses before the grass took over once again. Occasionally a car heading the same direction passed them, its need for haste more pressing than Marla's. In the opposite direction, cars flung themselves north at breakneck speeds, their goals Sebastopol or Bodega Bay or, God help them, Cloverdale.

"Daggett, I'm listening. What is it?" She felt an odd sense of foreboding hovering between them. She had no idea what had shifted in his thoughts. He'd been warm and attentive, and now he wasn't. Sometimes she thought it was the ocean that held them together, the house they shared, maybe even the income she earned. It was too hard to peel back the layers, to be open with whatever the past had done to them. She was afraid to try, afraid to lose him if anything changed. At this moment, though, she was willing to take that step, if she must.

"I'm sorry about the daiquiri." He pursed his lips, and then pressed them hard together. After a bit he allowed his mouth to go slack. "About everything." His eyes glistened, but that was all. He was not a crier, and he never went there. He'd told her that long ago.

She reached for his hand again, this time forcing him to let her hold it. She kissed it, one touch of her lips for each knuckle, finally wrapping it between her hands.

"The ocean is my life." He still refused to look at her.

She traced his face with her eyes. There was moistness on his lower lids, and she felt herself tear up. Whatever he was telling her was important to him for this much emotion to bleed through.

"If I get a job, I'll lose the ocean, and if I lose that, then I've lost myself." His voice slipped at the end.

"You have money every month from your trust, Daggett. What's this about a job?"

"I want to buy you daiquiris." This time he lifted his hand with hers inside. He raised it to his lips and kissed her fingers. "And everything else, too."

"I don't want everything else, or daiquiris. I just want you."

Had she said that, or just thought it? He didn't reply, nor did he release her hand, and before she thought to repeat it more loudly, the moment had passed, and to say it then would have fallen flat.

Anyway, at that moment, Marla turned the radio down and pointed to a sign just ahead. "San Jose coming up. Then Morgan Hill, Gilroy, and—" with a snap of her fingers "—Monterey! We're almost there. Hey, have you been looking out at the Bay over there? Doofus up here is sleeping through it all, but it sure is a beaut." Water glistened in the distance.

Without waiting for a response, the radio resumed, and Marla's head began to bop back and forth. Someone was having a good time, and it didn't matter if anyone joined in or not.

However, Geraldine knew Monterey was still another two hours away. She rested her head against the man at her side, wondering the real reason for his reaction. It couldn't be something so minor as the mention of a daiquiri. She sighed. At least he couldn't run from her for the next two hours.

At her feet, she felt Flotsam shift position, and she wondered if he needed a break. She tapped Marla on the shoulder to ask her to stop, then belatedly remembered Daggett's remarks about Santa Rosa. Surely the dog had been outside then, and she waved Marla back to her music, letting her thoughts of the animal go.

"Please be there, Corky," she whispered, barely breathing the words. "For Daggett, if not for me." She closed her eyes, hoping beyond hope. She wanted to trust in him. It was a daughter thing, the need to find trust in her father, even if he didn't know.

Then, with a determined set of her jaw, she knew he'd better be there. She wouldn't have Daggett let down. With that thought, she felt better, and as the car traveled along 101, the rubber tire treads whipping against the imperfections in the highway, she let herself be lulled into an easy, if somewhat fitful sleep. There she asked Paul not to bring her another rum daiquiri. All she wanted was Daggett, and he could only be had in San Jose.

Chapter 21

GERALDINE barely had time to fall asleep, it seemed, before the car came to an abrupt halt.

"Hey, guys, we're here." Marla slipped her car into park, and with a jerk of one hand, she ratcheted the emergency brake into place. They were in a parking lot, but the ocean was nowhere to be seen. Billows of ghostly fog blanketed them on one side. The other side was clear, the wispy fingers dissipating before they could stretch across the paved spaces.

"Where?" Skylar lifted his head, looking around. The side of his face boasted a red circle where it had pressed up against the glass. With his bleary eyes, he looked more surf bum than surf god. Squinting, he asked, "Is this San Jose?"

"San Jose? Wake up and smell the beach, sleepyhead." Marla rolled her window down a bit, breathing deeply of the cool, sea breeze. It had been hot on the drive down, but now a chill enveloped the car.

As the smell of the ocean drifted in, Flotsam also caught a

whiff, and with a surprisingly loud bark, he leaped to his feet. Baying repeatedly, he clambered towards the open window, his tail wagging, his snout pointed outside.

"Flotsam!" Geraldine laughed, pulling her feet into the seat, and piling onto Daggett to get out of the way. "Daggett, he's gone crazy."

He had, too, and he bounded into the front seat, one leg hitting a paper drink cup resting in the front console, crushing it and spilling the contents all over Skylar.

"Flotsam!" Unbuckling his seatbelt and pulling at his wet clothes, Skylar yelled the dog's name. His arm inadvertently hit the latch, and the door sprang wide. Flotsam jumped on him, and in a massive flailing of freckled arms and legs, he was soon spread-eagled in the parking lot, one flip-flop on, and the other flung off to the side. Flotsam was right on top of him, and after dancing for a moment, he hiked his back leg right on Skylar's bare knee.

Hooting laughter flooded from the car.

"Go, Flotsam! Rah, rah!" Marla pumped her fist.

"So, that's why he wanted out so badly. Thanks, Skylar. You make a great fire hydrant." Daggett leaned forward and waved through the seats, a grin on his face. "I was worried I wouldn't find one close by."

To be fair, the block they were on was hardly long enough to contain a fire hydrant. To the left was a massive, tiered beach-front hotel, and off to the right was a series of small shops. Geraldine couldn't see the water, but a sign showed that the road down which they'd come ended over the rise, and they could go no farther without driving into the ocean. The sound of crashing breakers was unmistakable. The smell of the sea, too. It was the scent of five thousand miles of pristine salt water.

"Ah, real people could live here." Daggett drew in a deep breath. Within spitting distance of the ocean, he meant. "Unlike

Bakersfield. See? There's life around us coming out of the woodwork."

He pointed. Walking through the parking lot was a couple holding the hands of two small children, all dressed in brightly-colored swimwear. Two teen boys appeared over the rise, pushing on each other, small boogie boards in their hands. One wore a shorty wetsuit, black with one gray leg. The other had on bright yellow board shorts. They laughed at a joke passed between them before disappearing once again.

Daggett climbed from the car, reaching to check the stability of the boards on top. He adjusted his shorts and wriggled his toes in his sandals, yawning and stretching his legs. When Geraldine made to climb out, he reached for her hand.

"Walk with me to the beach?"

"I'll go," Skylar called, still on the tarmac. Flotsam had the leg of his shorts in his mouth, and he fought to get to his feet.

Marla was out by then, and she stepped to stand over him, answering him rather curtly. "No, you won't. You've slept all the way down, and now that you've decided to join the land of the living, you're mine. I need a sweatshirt. Come shop-ping with me." The brisk breeze ruffled her shirt as she pointed to a surf shop at the edge of the lot.

"All the way down?" Skylar frowned at her remark. "What do you mean? Someone told me we were taking a break in San Jose, or maybe it was San Francisco. Isn't that like halfway?"

"You slept through it. See the fog?" Daggett moved his hand to grab a wisp, only to have it evaporate in his fingers.

"So? What's a little fog?" Skylar pushed at the golden retriever and growled, "Boogers! Get off, Flotsam."

The animal was having none of it, and he turned and licked at his face.

"You're looking at the ocean, man. The Pacific Ocean, come to greet us in the air. San Jose was a long time ago."

Daggett waved to the dunes just visible in the swirling fog.

"Well, they have oceans in San Francisco, too, and maybe even in San Jose."

Marla grabbed his hand. "Not in San Jose. Even I know that."

When Skylar started to stand, Flotsam nipped at the leg of his shorts once more. Daggett whistled, and the big animal let go. When Skylar turned to step into his missing flip-flop, Flotsam darted back and grabbed the one the redheaded man hadn't managed to get on.

"No," he yelled.

"Here, boy," Daggett called. He worked the shoe from the dog's teeth, and he tossed it back. Ruffling his fur, he spoke as to an old friend. "Come with us, boy. We'll show you what a real beach looks like."

"Can I come, too?" Geraldine knelt at the dog's side, and she wrapped her arms around his neck, rubbing her face against his. He felt warm, and she was certain she would want one of Marla's sweatshirts before evening. However, there would be plenty of time to shop later.

A big, surfer's hand wrapped around her neck, and she felt the warmth of Daggett's breath on her ear as he whispered, "I insist." Then his lips kissed her cheekbone just where it rose to meet her ear.

"The surfboards will be okay?" She stood and tucked her hands in her pockets, glancing at the car as they moved toward the beach. The boards were well-used, but any surfer of any experience would recognize them as quality.

"These are surfers, Geri." He motioned with his hand to the people they could see. "What's not theirs, they leave alone." He whistled to Flotsam, taking off and running with the dog to the top of the rise, hooting when he could finally see the water. Once there, he paused and looked back to her, motioning with his hand for her to hurry up. The cascading sea fog swallowed him for a brief moment before rolling off again. It was as if he stood on his private Mount Olympus, master of the world and sea, his right hand stretched over the waters, and his left over the land. Both had to obey his command as he peered down from the lofty heavens.

"I'm coming," she called, pulling one hand from a pocket and motioning him to go on without her. "Go on. Go play. Wear Flotsam out. He needs to stretch his legs." She waved him on again before pushing her hair from her face and tucking it behind one ear. As quickly, she stuffed her hands into her pockets, feeling the damp fog pulling the warmth from her body.

On the rise ahead, just where the road turned into the beach, she watched Daggett's feet tear into the sand, and with a yell, he disappeared from her sight. Flotsam's fur flying, he was gone after the man he loved. Walking forward more slowly, she reached the sand and paused to pull her sandals from her feet. She would walk barefoot, she decided. Not only would it keep her shoes clean, she enjoyed the grittiness of the sand against her skin.

Topping the rise, she glanced down the beach to find the skies in the distance clear. She was surprised at the sudden warmth of the air. The water was crystalline, and in the direction of her hotel, little beach cabanas were set up, their striped canvas roofs blowing gently in the wind. A man she recognized immediately, his dark hair slicked back, and his tailored jacket buttoned at the waist, came striding her direction, his bare feet stepping though the hot sand smoothly and confidently, a tray in his hand holding some sort of chilled liquor. His skin carried a Mediterranean cast.

"Pablo?" She laughed as she reached to lift the footed glass from the tray. He always went by Pablo when he was of Spanish descent. She sipped it. "Rum. My favorite. How did you ever find me here, Pablo?"

"Si, Senorita." He bowed, a smile on his face. Rising, he offered her a chilled towel.

"I'm sorry, Pablo. I forgot. I can only ask you yes and no questions." She took the towel and pressed it against her face. It had grown warm, and the sun was certainly bright. "Thank you for the towel."

"Si, Senorita." He bowed once more, then politely backed away, his feet leaving perfect little imprints in the sandy beach.

"Pablo," she called. He turned to her and smiled. "Have you seen Daggett? He was supposed to be right here, and somehow he's gotten away."

"Si, Senorita." He bowed again, although not quite as deeply.

"Have him meet me at the cabana. I need him to rub some oil on my back. I don't want to burn too badly."

"Si, Senorita." His head ducked obsequiously, although he didn't bow this time.

She smiled and waved him away, taking another sip from her glass. She mustn't drink too fast, or her head would spin. Then how would she ever make her way to the cabana? If she wasn't there when Daggett came checking, he'd be lost, and she couldn't have that.

It was too late, though. She had taken several sips, and anyone who knew her understood her inability to tolerate alcohol. Just a sip for her was a night on the town for most people. Her eyes blurring, she knelt to set the glass on the sand, but she missed. The glass floated right out of her grip and went flying, the precious rum concoction Pablo had so thoughtfully provided dashed to the sand. As she fell, she was appalled that she was so careless. Pablo would have to clean it up, and what a waste of good rum. Then her face hit the sand, and the sun went out.

Chapter 22

"GERI?"

A warm hand patted her face. When she opened her eyes, she realized she was looking at the sky. She felt herself wrapped in a blanket, and mist swirled around her. A number of faces peered down, watching her, worried, and she was surprised to recognize several she knew. There was Zac Dirkson, a dark-haired Aussie Daggett had once surfed with in Big Sur. The waves had been huge, and she remembered the gash he'd taken on his forehead when one especially violent collapse had smashed his board into a rock, destroying it and nearly him. The scar was still there, she noticed.

Another man over her was blond Kolbe Tatge. He'd stayed with them a while the first summer she and Daggett had been together. Rather, he had stayed on Daggett's little beach, sleeping in a pop-up, cooking wieners over a small camp stove. He'd surfed at the crack of dawn each morning, then hiked into town to find odds and ends to work at, making just enough money to keep himself in food. Then, one morning, he'd been gone. Later they'd learned his wetsuit had blown away during one extraordinarily windy night, and he'd seen no further reason to remain.

She thought one or two of the other faces might be familiar, maybe Jon Manning and Sparky something-or-the-other from Half Moon Bay up near Moss Beach, but her eyes became heavy. She heard Daggett's voice once more, a sense of panic edging the words, as she drifted away.

Pablo stood in front of her once again.

She closed her eyes and wiped her face with a chilled towel. Without looking, she held it out for him to take. She kept her eyes closed against the brilliance of the tropical sun.

"Pablo, I'm hungry. I'd like lunch."

"Si, Senorita."

"And leave a fresh drink on the table. Rum, if you don't mind, Pablo."

"Si, Senorita."

The chink of glass accompanied his words, the touch of a stem against the marble tabletop at her side. She felt beside her for her drink, found its stem, and ran one finger up to stroke the coolness of the bowl. She refused to drink it, though. She'd have to open her eyes, and the sun was entirely too bright. She did dip her finger and lick the tangy liquid from her skin.

"Geri?"

"Daggett, you've finally come." By touch, she reached her hand to find his familiar head, and she worked her fingertips into his hair.

"Geri, wake up."

"Not now, Daggett. First give me a kiss."

A round of laughter greeted her request, and she forced her eyes open. The fog-shrouded faces were still there, but the worry was gone. If she wanted a kiss, it was clear she'd be fine.

"Thanks, guys," Daggett called out, and a chorus of male

voices replied with congenial salutations, the sounds fading into the background of the surf as they scattered. "Geri, you will be okay?"

"Of course, Daggett. What happened?" She grasped at the unfamiliar blanket, unsure where it was from.

"I saw Kolbe, figured he'd come for the competition. As I got there, he pointed to you, said you'd fallen down. When we got here, you were out, and I couldn't get you awake."

She watched his face, the scraggly chin that would need a shave soon, and his raucous halo of golden hair. His eyes glistened. He was worried about her, and that was sweet.

"I feel fine. Just let me up." She made to stand, only getting so far as to raise herself up on her elbows, and was surprised to find that she had no energy to do so. She fell back to the sand, gasping for breath.

"Geri?" His voice broke this time, a clear admission of his concern.

"Where's Flotsam?" All of a sudden, she missed the big dog. He'd been on the beach with Daggett when she last saw him. He wasn't lost, surely. Daggett wouldn't be so careless. Yet, there was no dog that she could see.

"Geri, are you sure you're okay?"

"I'm not quite sure I am, Daggett. Not if you've let Flotsam run away. Where is he?" He'd ignored her question, and that irritated her.

He glanced up, his eyes searching. After a moment he found the big animal. "With Kolbe. They're tossing a Frisbee. It's you I'm worried about. Do I need to find a doctor, do you think?"

"A doctor? I don't think so." He had no idea how much that would cost.

"I can send Kolbe. He won't mind."

"I would mind." She laughed brightly, forcing it onto her face. She heard Flotsam bark in the distance and turned her eyes

157

to see him leap and catch a bright yellow disk in his mouth. Kolbe reached to the sand and picked up the remains of a hamburger, tossing a chunk of it into the air for the dog to catch, laughing when the big retriever dropped the Frisbee and snatched the food out of midair. She closed her eyes. "Flotsam has food in the car. Did you give him any after we stopped?"

"Food?" Daggett grimaced, hitting his forehead with the heel of his hand. "I'm so stupid. No wonder he was sniffing at that little girl's hot dog."

Finally, she realized what her problem was. "I haven't eaten since breakfast. That must be what's wrong with me. I had a granola bar before we left, but nothing since. I do remember being chilled when I got out of the car." She shivered again, even under the blanket.

Daggett's face eased, relieved at the easy explanation for the fainting. "Then I'm doubly stupid. Food. I can do that. Do you have any money?"

"I have some in my pocket, although most of what I brought is in the trunk of the car." His response made her smile. That was so Daggett. He never thought to carry money. How would he survive this trip without her? With one hand, she worked several bills out, sticking them outside of the blanket for him to take.

She was equally amused when he didn't run to one of the small stores near the car. Instead, he motioned, and Kolbe and Flotsam came running. The dog crashed into the sand next to her, one paw over her chest, nuzzling her neck and finally licking her chin. As soon as she put her hand on his head, he settled down, his eyes finding Daggett and watching his every motion, as his master held the money out to Kolbe, sending him to a food shack across the road.

Daggett knelt at her side, reaching his hand to rest it against her temple. "One minute, Baby. Kolbe will be right back."

"You're so sweet. Thank you."

She looked at him and smiled. She really was feeling better. Flotsam was found and giving her more attention than she wanted, and the thought of food on its way had her salivating. However, Daggett's eyes were red. She pulled one arm from the blanket and wrapped her fingers around his wrist. "What is it, Daggett?"

"When I first saw you had fallen, I thought—" His voice broke, and he looked away.

"You thought what?" She could see his eyes, the moisture pooling at the corners, and she felt her own grow damp. "Everything's okay. You do know that."

"I know." He blinked several times and then sniffled. After a moment, his face broke into a forced smile, and he turned to ruffle Flotsam's fur. "Rotten dog. Geri's mine, you know."

Kolbe came tearing up at that moment, and Geraldine didn't get her answer. She got food, instead. Daggett helped her sit, and several sips of a sugary orange soda and two hot fries later, she pushed the rest away.

"Geri, you can eat as much as you want." That was Kolbe. He held out the food, offering her more. There was a paper tray of chili chips, also.

"Thank you. I did eat as much as I want. You've brought more than I could consume in a week. It is good, though. Very good." She pulled one fry from those remaining and offered it to Flotsam. When he snapped it from her fingers, she laughed. She definitely felt better, and she sat up fully, crossing her legs on the sand and pushing the blanket back. Looking around, she questioned, "My shoes?"

"Here." Daggett leaned and pulled them from behind her, setting them at her side. "Are you warmer, now?"

"I'm not shivering. Kolbe, you are so sweet to do all this for Daggett—"

"For you," Daggett interrupted.

"For me." She rolled her eyes, laughing, and she reached to take one of the chili chips from the paper bowl. She was hungrier than she thought. She turned to Kolbe. "Are you here for the contest?"

"Surfjam Monterey?"

"Is that what it's really called? Surfjam Monterey?" She giggled, not sure why she found it so funny. Surely Daggett had known that and might have told her at some point. If so, she'd forgotten. Still, it was so silly, and in the moment, she couldn't let it go. "Why not Surfjam Carmel? Isn't it on Carmel Beach? Won't Carmel-by-the-Sea get jealous that Monterey is dropping in?" She realized she must still be lightheaded.

Kolbe grinned at her question. "I expect they might. All the dudes are here. Zac and Jon were around a bit ago, and I think you know Janjak and Sparky."

"Janjak?" She looked at Daggett. "Do I know Janjak?"

He paled. He threw his arm around Kolbe, whispering urgently. She caught part of it, something about Cristal being his previous girlfriend, and she was the one who knew Janjak. It was Kolbe's turn to pale. He coughed into his hand, cutting his eyes her direction.

"You don't know Janjak. Sorry, Geri."

"I heard." She winked, glancing at Daggett and back to Kolbe. "I guess I'll get to know him later." To change the subject, she asked, "Where are you guys staying?"

"At Veteran's. There's a whole group of us there, all camping together. Where are you dudes at?" He had begun to consume the chili chips, and he popped one whole in his mouth, licking his fingers one at a time.

She looked at Daggett with a grin. "Veteran's? Isn't that what we agreed on, Daggett?"

"Cool. This is so rad. We'll be together all weekend. Have

160

you dudes claimed your spots, yet?" Kolbe grinned in excitement, reaching for Geraldine's cup and taking a long draw from the straw. For surfers, it seemed it was share and share alike. You can't get diseases when you're at the ocean. Besides, orange. Geraldine figured it was Kolbe's favorite. Who could resist?

"Um, not yet." Daggett frowned, and he leaned forward to wrestle with Flotsam, whispering to Geraldine, "Veteran's?"

She shrugged. "Go with it." She stood, brushing off her legs and picking up her sandals. "Let's find Marla and Skylar. Off to Veteran's we go." She made as if to walk away in a military step, only to have Flotsam tear by. He'd seen the other two members of their party, and they carried burgers and more fries. He wasn't full yet, it seemed.

"Your chips and fries?" Kolbe held them up. When she turned and waved them his direction, he grinned. "Sites three through nine. The park'll fill up early, so if you can't get a spot, all you dudes are welcome to crowd in with us. See you there."

"Sure thing." Daggett looked to her. "Do you know how to find Veteran's?" When she shrugged, he turned to call to Kolbe. He was already headed down the beach, and another blond surfer type was sharing the unexpected bonanza of chips and fries.

Skylar called, "Hey, did I overhear we're staying at Veteran's? It's at Skyline and Jefferson."

"You know how to get there?" Daggett frowned, turning to Geraldine. "How could he know that?"

"I saw a flyer in the shop." He held up a burger in one hand and a sack in another. "Food, anyone?"

"Check out my hoodie." Marla held her arms out, her own burger in one hand, a plastic bag in the other. Across the front of her green sweatshirt was the famous Monterey coastline at Pebble Beach. "Woo-woo, but I'm toasty warm, now. Jealous?"

161

"Pretty," Geraldine said, a wistful look on her face. "You didn't by any chance buy two?"

"What, like this?" She handed Geraldine her burger, then she fished in her sack and pulled out a gray one decorated with a sleek old car in all its gleaming glory. She giggled. "It's summer. They didn't have much choice. This is from the auto show at Pebble Beach. Sorry, honey, but I got it cheap. Do you still want it?"

"You're my salvation!" Geraldine grabbed the sweatshirt and pressed it to her face. She drew in the smell of new fabric and fresh ink. She didn't care what was on the front. If it was warm, she would wear it.

"I'm so relieved." Marla let out a big sigh of relief, and she dug in her bag again. "They had more, and I couldn't resist." She pulled out one with a bikini-clad babe draped over a red sports car and thrust it Daggett's direction.

He frowned, holding it up. "Geri, am I allowed to wear this?"

"Not now. Later, perhaps." She took it from him, smiling. "Skylar, did you get left out?"

"Mine's in the car." He grinned, ducking his head, his face turning the color of his freckles.

When they got back to the car, they saw why. His said *I'm with her* and had a giant hand pointing to the side. Marla informed them he had promised to wear it all weekend, and she intended to be at his side the entire time.

Chapter 23

"HEY, THERE'S Zac." Daggett grinned. A bronzed man, topped with charcoal hair and carrying a surfboard under his arm, crossed the street just in front of them, barely getting past on the pedestrian light. "He's got a bonzer. I haven't seen one of those since I spent that summer with Corky in Baja. Pull over, Marla."

"A bonzer?" She made a face, catching Geraldine's eye in the mirror. She winked and giggled.

"It's a surfboard, Marla." Skylar caught on immediately to the wink.

"How can you tell if it's a bonzer?" She giggled each time she said it.

"It has five fins on the back." Sure enough, when Zac turned, there were five fins on the bottom.

He was about to get away, and Daggett squirmed through his car window to sit on the sill, calling out over the roof and past the surfboards mounted there. "Hey, Zac, wait up!"

The ebony-haired man turned, looking for the voice. Then finding Daggett, his face brightened, and he waved, yelling back in a distinctive Australian accent, "Of course, mate." He held the board up over his head.

Daggett threw him a thumbs-up, yelling over the traffic, "How far to Veteran's? If you're headed that way, we'd like to follow."

"Absolutely, mate. Come along." Standing his board at his side, he motioned up the street.

Daggett slipped the rest of the way from the car, stopping to rap sharply on the hood. Running up and throwing a quick arm around Zac, he slapped him playfully on the side of his face. When Flotsam let out a howl, sticking his head out one window then the other, the men separated.

"Your dog? The yellow one hanging out at the beach?" Zac nodded the direction of the car. His distinct accent threw away the beginning consonants of many of his words, making them into "em," "e," and "ang."

"Flotsam?" Daggett laughed. "He thinks I'm his."

"Gotcha there, mate." Zac waved his board's leash in the air, calling out to the car, "Turn him loose. He can hang with us. I can noose him with this."

"Turn Flotsam loose in the city?" Geraldine shook her head no, and as Marla pulled to the curb, she opened her door and climbed out, Flotsam already on his real leash.

"Let him come, Baby." Daggett snapped his fingers at the golden retriever, then slapped Zac on the back, leaning in to whisper a joke to him. He laughed before turning back to the others. He dropped to a crouch, slapping his hands together.

"I don't think so, Daggett." She had the leash firmly in both hands.

"Let him go, Geri." That was Zac, dropping his "h" and grinning broadly. "He'll be safe." He slapped his leg, whistling.

She didn't really turn loose, but Flotsam tore away anyway, jumping on Daggett, his paws on the tall man's shoulders, his tongue all over his neck. Blond hair and yellow fur became one for a minute.

"Go, dog, go!" Skylar yelled, pumping his arm out the window.

"Don't know you, mate," Zac called, walking over to the car and sticking a deeply browned hand through the window. "Name's Zac."

It was Marla who reached across the car to grab his hand. "Marla, Zac. I'm Geri's friend. Can I come visit you when you go back home? I've never been Down Under."

"I am home." He had a grin on his face. "I haven't been Down Under for years."

"But, don't you live in Australia? From your accent . . . I mean, it's obvious . . . isn't it?" She glanced at Skylar, now ducked in the seat, only to see him roll his eyes.

He sat up, poking his hand out the window. "Skylar. I live with Daggett."

"Ah. A protégé." Zac nodded. "Daggett's the best. I know."

"How can you be home with that accent? I watch TV. I know what Australians sound like." Marla sank back into her seat, counting with the fingers of one hand, "Accent, tan, fancy surfboard."

"He's an American, born down the road. Right here in L.A." Daggett leaned in beside him, slapping him playfully on the chest.

Zac grinned wider. "My mother was on vacation twenty-two years ago, and I popped myself out two months early, right in the middle of a vacation to Disneyland. There's nothing more American than that."

Geraldine called out to tell Marla she was walking with the guys. "We can see Veteran's from here. We'll keep the dog with us."

Daggett tossed a soft-brimmed hat like a Frisbee, and Flotsam dashed after it, his leash flopping and untended. Zac took off to join the game.

Without warning, even with the sun still streaming boldly through the air, enormous drops of rain began splattering the sidewalk.

"An earthquake?" That was Zac.

"An earthquake," Daggett repeated. "Why in the world does rain mean an earthquake?"

"You know. A water main rupture."

Then the drops came faster and harder, a blanket of water dancing on the pavement, a raging torrent. Laughing, three people and a yellow dog scrambled to huddle underneath a long surfboard.

It quit as quickly as it had started, the sun still shining, leaving steam rising from the sidewalks and street.

"What was that all about?" Geraldine laughed, leaning her head out and looking into the sky. Far overhead was a thin strand of black clouds, the only ones anyone could see, except for a dark bank far out over the ocean.

GERALDINE stepped out from under the surfboard, shivering and running her hands through her hair. While the three humans had attempted—not quite successfully—to stay dry under Zac's surfboard, the dog had gotten drenched. She laughed to see Skylar hanging out of the car looking into the sky. Even with the rain, all the windows were still down.

Next to her, Daggett was drenched on one side, and he shook his head, slinging water all over her. Zac had caught the worst of it, although he seemed to pay it no mind. He simply hiked the board under his arm and waved to the car that had yet to catch up with him.

166

Flotsam took care of what dry clothing Geraldine still boasted. Barking excitedly, he leaped into a shimmering puddle, then beginning with his head, he shook, his ears flung wide from his body. The motion moved down his neck, into his shoulders, and finally it wrapped his backend, wrenching his legs until he could barely stand.

"Daggett, stop your dog. He's gone wild." She laughed, covering her face with one arm.

When he grabbed Flotsam around the neck, all he did was convince the animal that he wanted to play, and Flotsam jumped on him with all four paws, knocking him onto his back, directly into a large puddle.

Marla's car had made it to them by then, and Skylar still hung out the window. "Hey, guys, we're going camping. By the way, we're still dry. Want to ride with us?" He grinned as he pointed with his thumb, as if hitching a ride.

"Go. Get us a spot if there are any left." Geraldine waved them along, brushing water from her arms. "We'll air out as we walk." She motioned with her hand once again. "Go. I want a place to sleep tonight."

As the car pulled away, she reached for Daggett's arm, enjoying the animated conversation erupting from the men walking with her. She smiled to herself, closing her eyes against the brilliance of the California sun. Their discussion easily could have been one they started the last time they were together, interrupted by mere months apart, and now resumed without a moment's hesitation. The past and the present knew no distinction in their relationship.

She'd never had that skill, not in reality, anyway. Only in her thoughts did the world become so malleable to her. There she could be anywhere and with anyone, even a father she could never possess as her own.

Pulling Daggett close, the scene shifted for her, and it was

Corky's arm she grabbed, instead. The sudden onset of rain, the flashing brake lights, and the shimmering reflections across the rain-slicked pavements drew her back, and the intervening years fell from the slate as if they had never been.

"CORKY, THAT was so much fun!" Geraldine shook water from her hair, and her eyes sparkled.

"Hey, girl, a break, please, for me." He dropped his board and sat heavily on the sand.

They were on Ocean Beach, the winds were brisk, and they had just come in from a series of breakers that should have killed them both. Spray peeled off the tops of the waves, coating the highway just off the beach with liquid sky, and cars flashed by, their brakes twinkling on and off as traffic lights demanded their attention. The flickering glow from the street invited them to laugh, as if to celebrate a harrowing experience that had left adrenalin running high. Geraldine's leash had held, but her ankle had a red mark that told how close she'd come to losing her board.

"You liked that?" Corky ran his thick fingers through his red hair, hardly making an improvement. He shivered, even in his wetsuit, and his breath came hard. A broad, red band printed across the chest broke the monotony of the suit, but there was no denying how much of Corky it covered. No one cared, though. He was adored by everyone he met, and her most of all.

"Again?" Her eyes glistened. She was invigorated, totally unaware of how dangerous those moments had been. She had survived, and that was what counted, that and the rushing beat of her heart, the flush of excitement running down her arms, and the cold that brushed every inch of skin not covered by her wetsuit.

It was only later that she learned the truth of the moment. The waves out there had surprised him. He'd been riding his board, barely stable even with his immeasurable skill, the face of the wave falling away in front of him for what seemed like fifteen feet, and he'd caught sight of her just as she bailed out of the biggest wave he'd ever seen off Ocean Beach. Then she'd not come up, and he'd known she was getting drilled by the heavy water. When she'd gone under, he'd felt all time stand still. Each breaker had frozen, rolling into perfect, unmoving barrels, the wind-driven spray no more than a pointillist painting strewn across the hazy sky, with each bird overhead flying forever motionless, wingtips hovering endlessly in the grey-blue of the sky. Deep in his chest, he'd known his heart would beat again only when his young protégé erupted whole from the depths of the churning sea.

Then, she'd been spewed forth, board first, the fist of the sea vaulting the slender fiberglass shard high into the air. The leash had been stretched tight, and he'd hoped, prayed, even cursed the weather, unable to find the girl at the other end, and finally, her arms flailing, she'd somersaulted through the air, undamaged and alive.

Only then had the frozen waves resumed their frenzied, gravity-forced dance, crashing to the sand below, the intensity of the storm exposing everything on the floor of the sea, if only for an instant. Then the water churned once more in its manic dance, a ballet of gods and goddesses so old they were now as forgotten as if they'd never existed in the first place.

On that day, he'd just laughed, dropping to the sand, and letting his board clatter down beside him.

"You know what you did out there?" He pointed with his head to the distant waves.

"Loved it!" She grabbed his wrist, pulling, hoping he'd stand and go out with her once again. "Come on!"

"No, no." He waved his free hand, once more pointing to the sea. "That, girl, was a macker. You know what that is?"

169

She laughed. "A macker? Is that good?"

"Sit." He patted the sand at his side. When she did, he took her hand and squeezed it before giving it back. "A macker is the biggest wave there is, and that out there was a hell of a macker. Yet, you took it in your hand, rode it to the end, and you want to go out again. Girl, I love you, you young whipper-snapper."

Then, with the spray in the wind growing heavier as they spoke, he pulled himself up, took his board in one hand, and offered her the other.

She looked at him with something akin to worship. He towered over her, his massive girth, with its red stripe across black, a bastion of goodwill, generosity, and love. He'd said it. He loved her. She knew it wasn't what she wanted, not what she needed from this man who didn't even know he was her father. But he'd said it nonetheless. He'd been proud of her, and he had said he loved her.

Her eyes teared up, and she was glad the spray had become like rain. Her face was soaked, and she could laugh the crazy feelings away.

Somewhere behind them a horn honked, and when she looked, a city trolley ambled past, blocking the passage of a car that was determined to express its frustration to anyone who would listen. When she turned back to Corky, it was Daggett at her side. The spell was already broken, the rubber band of the present snapping her back to reality.

The sun caught in her eyes, and shading them with one hand, she smiled as Daggett took off. He and Zac began tossing the surfboard back and forth through the air, catching it easily, as familiar with its shape on land as on water. Once a breeze caught it, and it nearly got away, both men running for it. Flotsam got excited, and he took off after it, wedging into the middle of the ensuing fiasco, as all three went to ground. Despite the fracas, the board was saved, and Daggett rose triumphantly, holding it over his head, lording his prowess over both Zac and the dog.

He called to her, flashing a bright smile, doing a little soft-shoe dance, spinning completely around once at the end.

When she caught up with him, she made him give the board back to Zac, and she grabbed Flotsam's leash. With her free hand, she claimed Daggett, wrapping her arm around his waist and fitting her body next to his, matching her stride to his easy-going walk. Zac walked off to the side, his board under one arm, one against three.

Daggett leaned his head against hers, and for the next few blocks, she had what she had always wanted, a family of her own, one that would always be hers, no matter what came her way.

She knew one little fly remained in the ointment. She had hoped to find that with Corky, and life hadn't played out that way. She could only hope it would with this man at her side.

She also hoped Corky showed up this weekend for Daggett's sake.

She hoped he showed up for hers, as well.

Chapter 24

"BURGERS and fries?"

The words were ones more normally spoken at the take-out window of a drive-thru, with acres of grills and vats of aromatic grease in the background. These were said over a campfire with a single iron grate and a deep pan of sizzling oil, the question thrown out into the soft light of an early outdoors evening filled with voices of friends old and new.

Geraldine's stomach rumbled with anticipation.

She offered her paper plate, supported by fire-warmed fingers, as a thick burger was laid out on a flame-toasted bun. A slice of cheese and a scattering of fries, and supper was ready.

The meal tasted just as good as any found in a fast food diner. Better, some would say. She gathered a drink in a silver can and popped the top with the tips of her fingers, collecting one in a brown bottle for Daggett. After she set her plate down on a beach log, she screwed the lid loose and tossed it into a box for such things before handing it to him. Conversation seasoned the meal, laughter sprinkling through the tree-covered camp-sites, turning simple, greasy bites into a gourmet's delight.

Even Flotsam found he was a canine king, gifted with manna from the gods. The surfing crowd gathered together for the weekend's Surfjam festivities contained the best from 350 miles up and down the Pacific Seaboard, and even a few from farther afield. They were the gods of the surfing world, although many of these gods wore rope-topped rubber sandals, grommet-laced swim trunks, and soft-brimmed caps over hair that had needed a wash two days before.

The sun dipped low into the sky, casting a russet radiance across the hills that made up the rustic campsites.

As a backdrop to the fire-littered scene, damp sleeping bags hung over tree branches. Not all the tents had been closed up during the day's sudden shower.

Off away from the surfing crowd were a number of RVs: several pop-ups; one fifth-wheel; half a dozen tag-a-longs. The bigger trailers had awnings out, with canvas-backed folding chairs and glowing lights in the windows. Not Daggett's and Geraldine's crew. They would be sleeping under the stars. They had managed a campsite, although it was away from the others a bit. That was fine with them, though. The festivities in this part of the campground would clearly go on for quite some time.

"Daggett, not another bite," Geraldine cried in mirthful alarm, pushing his hand away, as he tried to force a multi-layered slab of burger into her mouth. "No!"

"Just a taste," he pleaded, his face screwed up in mock dismay. He winked at one of his buddies. "Just one teeny taste."

"I've had a teeny taste three times. You'd think I'm an eating factory, the way you're acting." She was laughing so hard she coughed. "Give it to Skylar. He's only had two."

"Three!" Skylar held up three fingers, then he burped loudly, setting a brown bottle at his side. "I've had three, but I don't mind another."

"There, Daggett. Skylar wants it." She pushed his arm that direction, relieved when Marla took the burger and handed it to the freckled man at her side.

That was when Flotsam came running from inside one of the drying tents. In his mouth was a pair of boxers, dark blue, with an enormous smiley face on the front. He growled, shaking them from side to side, creating a twisting, self-contained skirmish as he fought with an imaginary foe. It took a few moments before the owner of the shorts recognized them as his.

"Hey, dog!" Sparky Richardson from Half Moon Bay leaped from his log. "Those are my last clean pair. Give, dog." He ran towards Flotsam, only to have the big retriever take off for several steps, then turn and wait to see if Sparky was indeed following. When he saw that he was, Flotsam took off once again, dodging the scattered tents, and then darting into the woods.

"He goes by Flotsam, Sparky." Daggett yelled the information with his hand at his mouth. He grinned at Geraldine, then yelled again, "I'd give up, if I were you. Flotsam always wins." He gave her a kiss on the cheek before he stepped over and knelt by dark-haired Zac. He began to talk in a low voice with animated gestures, and it was clear he would be in surfer's heaven for a time.

She stood. She needed to, anyway, with the bites of burger she'd consumed. Beef always sat heavily on her stomach, and never more so than after a day on the road.

Wandering the campsite, she saw a number of people she knew, and several more she hoped she would know before the weekend was done. Kolbe, of course, his hair blonder than Daggett's, was at the grill, master of outdoor cookery. He'd stepped up from his beach-front wieners on his camp stove, and she stopped by to tell him so. He laughed, reaching to flip yet another on the grill, jumping back and covering his eyes when splattering grease caused smoke to bury him. She patted him on the shoulder, thanking him for all his help that afternoon, but he waved it off. They were a family, he replied, and of course she had his help anytime she needed him.

Most of the guys—"dudes" to Kolbe's way of thinking, or "mates" when talking with Zac—didn't have girlfriends along. Some had jobs or family, or just didn't want to sleep in a tent for the weekend. One or two had brought girlfriends to events in the past, but it was hard living with a surfer. The surf was their life, and girlfriends took second place. Geraldine understood, and for that reason, she made an effort to include each of them in her greetings.

She even asked about Janjak, was he staying in one of the campsites, and when she learned he was, she asked where. Sparky was back with his underwear by then, although he was holding it high over his head to keep it from Flotsam's reach, and he indicated a medium-sized man with dark skin and tight hair, polishing a surfboard not quite his height.

"Janjak?" She held out her hand. "I just spoke with Sparky, and he pointed you out." She nodded her head in the other man's direction. He could hardly be missed, still involved in his animated tryst with the big dog.

A puzzled frown washed over Janjak's face, then a grin broke free. "Ah, from the beach earlier, outside of town. I be most glad to meet you."

She grinned. "Jamaica, or one of the other islands?" The lilt of his voice was unmistakable and beautiful.

His grin grew wider. "Port-au-Prince."

"Haiti. What brings you here?"

"Food. Women. Beautiful music." He dipped his cloth into a small can of paste, and he began to work on a section of his board.

"Beautiful music?" She couldn't help but be amused. "You come from Haiti, and you found beautiful music here? I would think it's the other way round."

"You been there? It be a beautiful place. It be true what you say about the music there." He nodded his head, bobbing it several times in rhythm to an unheard melody as his hand worked at his board.

"And yet you're here." She smiled. "I suppose there's a story behind that."

He stopped polishing for a moment, his dark eyes still on the board. "Beautiful music be more than just the sound that come from instruments and people's voices. Music be in the way people live, the love they show, the cast of their hearts. Here be music." He pointed with his rag to Sparky, and there was Kolbe at the grill, and beyond that Daggett still engrossed with Zac. His rag pointed to other small groups, the faces dim in the darkening twilight, the fire casting beautiful shadows.

"What music did you leave behind?" She felt she understood some of what he meant. Her eyes settled on Skylar and Marla. They were sharing Skylar's brown bottle, laughing, and she saw Marla try to take a drink, sputtering as she did so, spitting out what she couldn't swallow. It was music of a sort, and it warmed her inside. It was a beautiful scene.

"Bad music. Earthquake. Everybody know about the earthquake. Port-au-Prince fall down. Not so many people know about the rest." His head dropped, and his hand returned to his board.

"The rest?" The earthquake, true, everyone had heard about that, even her. "Surely the damage was repaired."

"No. Not that. No food. People in my country starve. My brother be in prison for stealing a cow. My family, so hungry, and they send him to prison a week before the quake. There be a massacre in the prison a week after the quake, and he be killed.

Two weeks he be there, and now he be dead."

"I'm so sorry." Horrified was more like it. "The rest of your family?"

"They lived in Port-au-Prince. The city fell." He shrugged, and then he smiled brightly. "I be glad I already in California, America. See? The music be much better here."

"I think I will like you very much, Janjak. I understand you knew Daggett before he and I, um, became a pair."

"A pair. Yes. You be a better match for him than the other. He love you, I think."

That made her laugh, and she looked away, finding Daggett with her eyes. He was standing, acting out a surfing move, the firelight gleaming on his skin. She turned to Janjak. "He loves the ocean. I come in second best, I'm afraid."

"I think not." Janjak kept his eyes on his board as his hand moved in a circular motion.

Something in the fire popped loudly, and they turned. Engrossed in their conversation, Daggett and Zac were standing now, gesticulating wildly. Then, they stopped and clapped each other on the shoulders, bursting into laughter. Zac kicked some dirt onto Daggett's leg, and Daggett kicked some back, reaching for an empty can on the ground to toss it at the cardboard box set up as a garbage receptacle. Together they walked to a cooler, rummaged inside, and came up with more drinks to share. Geraldine heard the hiss as the tabs were pulled.

She smiled.

"You love him back, I think."

She turned to see Janjak watching her. "I brought some strawberry pie. My neighbor made it for me. Would you like to share it with us?"

"You ask me if heaven have beautiful music, and I tell you the truth. All music be beautiful." The grin on his face was wide, and his teeth were white.

"I'll take that for a yes. Later tonight, join us at our campsite. It's just down the road. I won't let you forget."

"I be there. Beautiful music be the best."

Another friend had been made, and a wonderful one at that. Geraldine had no doubt about Janjak's ability to fit into any grouping of people. It was when she happened into Jon Manning that she was reminded of Corky.

"Geri?"

A hand touched her arm just for a moment, getting her attention, then as quickly letting go. She turned, pleased to see the familiar face.

"Jon. Here to show up Daggett?" She laughed. Jon and Daggett had been competing since they were teens. Jon was in the real world, though, still surfing, but holding down a job, too. Something in retail. L.A., and near the beach, if she remembered right.

"Maybe." He laughed good-naturedly. "This afternoon. You're all right, now?"

"Oh, I was just hungry. You know how it is. Travel all day, no one eats, then a little walk on the beach, and zonk, I'm down." She laughed. "I have the constitution of a horse, though. Thank you for asking. I appreciate your concern. Now, how did you ever get off work to come up here from the big city?"

"L.A., you mean." He rubbed at one arm as if embarrassed. "I'm not in L.A. any longer."

"Married? You?" She found that amusing. She couldn't imagine any of Daggett's compadres married, least of all Jon. They were all godparents to their first love, surfing.

"No. Not married." He sounded relieved. "My father sucked me in. The family business, you know."

"I thought your father was in farming or something like that."

"Ranching. See all that beef?" He pointed the direction of

178

the fire, and Kolbe still turning burgers.

"Yours?" She raised her eyebrows.

"Mine." He nodded. "Just east of here. It's not bad, though."

"Just not the ocean." She understood what he meant. He felt the same about surfing as Daggett. Daggett would be devastated to leave it, as if his life had been torn away.

"Yeah. But I still come out on weekends. The ocean's not going anywhere. And it's a good life on the ranch. Money. A car. A girlfriend someday." He didn't sound excited, though.

"Have you run into Corky?" Mention of Jon's father had twisted her thoughts, sending them to her own. If he came, it would probably be tomorrow. Still, Jon might know something. He'd been one of Corky's boys once.

"Not in months. In the spring I was up in San Fran, stopped in the shop. Saw your picture on the wall. Corky wasn't in, and I was on business. The ranch, remember. It steals my time. I think Zac saw him last. Ask him."

"Sure. Good luck tomorrow. I'll wish you a good run on the waves."

"Just not as good as Daggett?" He laughed.

She laughed in return, leaning in to give him a quick brush of a kiss on his cheek. "I'm glad you're here, Jon. Don't think I'm not." She backed away, turning to the rest of the group. To look at Jon, he was the eternal surfer, alternately brown and bleached, lean, still, and yet, she knew it was fading for him. If he didn't get trapped by consumerism, marriage would find him, and there would be kids and a mortgage. The beach would grow more and more infrequent until it happened for only two weeks each summer. The thought made her shiver.

Daggett had avoided that downward spiral, helped by his inheritance, of course. Corky, too, although he'd taken a different road, one that left no room for wives or children, for unknown daughters that came to find him but were unable to

179

reveal to him just who they were.

She pushed all that aside as she made her way through the park. She'd made that choice, or at had least felt forced into it, and it was the way things were. She couldn't change it, so she might as well not worry about it. And she couldn't ask Zac about Corky now, not when he and Daggett were joined at the hip.

Flotsam bumped her leg, and she knelt at his side. "Hey, boy. You ready for the big weekend?" She ruffled his fur, then stood. She'd walked far enough that she could see the ocean through a stand of trees. The park was high, and the view dropped off dramatically. There was a band of swirling fog along the shore, but in the final throes of the fading sun, orangey-red light flickered off a line of waves that stretched far offshore. A front was expected to blow through tomorrow, and that meant it would be a great weekend for Surfjam. In spite of the afternoon's shower—or perhaps because of it—the weather had come together perfectly for a weekend that would be glorious.

Geraldine was sure of it, even if Corky couldn't bother to attend.

Chapter 25

DAGGETT woke suddenly, drawing in a deep breath, for a moment unsure of where he was. Trees—pine? cypress?—filled the air with scented aromas, and the air was thick with moisture. Then a rock in his back reminded him. Monterey. Veteran's Park. Surfjam. He looked up at the sky, expecting to find the stars overhead, frowning in the total darkness. Everything was black. It was as if the sky had burned away, leaving only charred coal in the aftermath.

Turning his head, he looked for Geraldine. Of course, the campsite was as black as the sky, and nothing at all was visible. Through the trees, the lights of a trailer gleamed in the blackness. Daggett watched it for a minute as someone moved inside, then the light flickered off. The other direction a string of colored lights told of an awning left out in the darkness, the owner trusting the wind to stay sweet, and the awning to still be attached to its stanchions when the sun rose once again. There was a breeze—fairly stiff with occasional gusts—and from time to time the distant awning popped, and the attached lights bucked in the darkness, flickering as their gleam danced through the intervening trees.

Surf could be heard breaking along the shore off in the distance, a repetitive booming that seemed to reverberate through the ground. Isolated in the darkness, Daggett closed his eyes for a moment, drawing in the aroma of the trees, feeling alone—or perhaps unattached was a better word.

He opened his eyes and stared heavenward, peering into the blackness. In that moment, Surfjam was nonexistent, and his sleeping companions were no more than dreams in a faded mist. His mind began to drift, the night pulling him back towards sleep, and as his eyes turned gritty, the darkness softened, the sky turning gray instead of black, the dimness of morning just before the sun.

A handful of mocha-skinned, sunbaked Mexican boys ran over the dunes, their Spanish bright and chaotic to Daggett's untrained ear. Their shoulders and feet were bare, with faded shorts in rag-tag patterns in between. The children had been everywhere the day before, fascinated by the long, smooth surfboards, running to rescue them each time the waves tore them from underneath Daggett's and Corky's feet. They had called out in their chattering Spanish, slapping the boards, clearly wanting to ride.

They were the reason for being on the water's edge at the break of dawn. Now there were only a few. Later would crush the fun from the day.

"I'm outta here," Daggett called, pointing at the scattered boys, then grabbing his board and leaping into the surf. His skinny, teenage legs danced across the top of the waves until he was deep enough to throw his board down and begin paddling out. After a while he looked back to see Corky surrounded by the boys, their waving arms reaching for his surfboard. He laughed. At sixteen, Corky being surrounded by the local crowd of urchins and unable to reach the surf was pretty funny.

That was when he saw the fin break the water just in front of him, sinking almost immediately and leaving the surface clean once again. His arms froze, and he searched the depths, finally finding a darker hue within the waves. Fear gripped him.

He glanced at the shore, wondering if Corky was watching, if anyone would know when the beast took him in its teeth, pulling him underwater forever. Would anyone at home miss him? Would Corky miss him, searching for days, looking for the boy who had disappeared somehow into the sea? Or would he continue his trip down the peninsula, still hoping for the perfect wave?

Then he was with his mother. He must have been five, and she had decided to try her hand at parenting once again. She'd been successful for about a day, taking him to the park and buying him an ice cream.

Then night stole her mothering skills away. Curled in a chair with a brown bottle in her hand, she'd chewed her little "vitamins" from a plastic bag. The phone had rung, raucous laughter had turned her into someone else, and sometime later, a tall, skinny man had shown up at the door.

Afterwards, Daggett watched the tiny television set that got three channels, a new wad of bills cluttered up the coffee table, and unwelcome, heavy sounds came from the other side of the wall, sounds that told him she wouldn't want to get up in the morning, and he may or may not have anything to eat if he didn't scrounge it himself.

He didn't cry, not after the time she'd slapped him for messing up her good time.

He did cry at eighteen. Life had taken his grandparents, and then it threatened everything else, too. At the funeral home, the dollars required had been so much, the final hospital stay eating up what money there was left. He was alone, completely alone, with no one to turn to, no one to help.

Corky had shown up, stepped in to work his magic. Corky could always work magic, on the sea, in Daggett's heart, and then with the funeral home. His grandparents had been buried, the ground leveled, and new grass planted. Then everything that was his grandparents' was sold, except the chair and the ladder. No one had wanted those. Corky had been there the entire time, at Daggett's side, a father to a fatherless youth, keeping the sinking teen from slipping into oblivion. And when life didn't demand their attention, they had surfed the swells, floated on their boards when the breakers wouldn't break, and found a kind of companionship on the water.

Did Corky love him? He'd never said so. He hadn't had to. Daggett had felt he did, because he was there. He'd given a needy boy of his time, and when it hadn't been enough, he'd hung around until it was.

He was wide awake by then, the charcoal-blackened sky above growing heavier by the minute. He should have asked Corky for help with Geri's car. He should have gotten on the phone and called the surf shop. He'd mentioned it to Geri, and then he'd let it go, irresponsible as always. No, not irresponsible. Frightened. What if Corky said no? I've given enough to you. You've given nothing back. We're no longer a team. You were just a kid I knew, and now I know other kids. Don't bother me, kid. Leave me alone.

He reached for Geri, found her blanket, and brushed the backs of his fingers across her cheek. She let out a sigh and murmured his name. He moved his hand, not wishing to wake her. Two years. Two years and more she hadn't given up on him. How long until she did? Would the car be what did it, sending her from him, disappointed and disillusioned? How much longer would he have her?

Everyone left him, everyone except his buddies, his surfer dudes.

The word dudes made him think of Kolbe and the tent that had spent weeks on his beach. Kolbe was someone he could trust, and Zac and Sparky and all the other guys. Those friends had never let him down, and he didn't think they ever would.

Something heavy plopped off in the trees somewhere, then again. The air felt suddenly cooler on his face, and he sat up. He was still fully clothed, or as fully clothed as a man come to the beach for a surf contest. Trunks and a shirt. Without further warning, the plopping sounds came faster and faster, until one especially large drop of water finally hit him on the face. Rain! A muted clap of thunder echoed somewhere in the darkness.

"Geri," he called, reaching to shake her arm. "It's raining." He stood and began to gather his blanket. He knelt at her side to shake her once again.

"Rain?" Her voice was sleepy, then clearly she got a face full. Her tone turned brisker, even forceful. "It's raining, Daggett. How awful! Go wake the other two. I'll get the car opened up." She could be heard gathering her things in the dark.

There was no need to wake the others. The wind that had been merely brisk moments before hit with a gale-force intensity, whistling through the trees. Everything loose on the ground, including dirt and leaves, whipped into the black air. Somewhere off in one of the other campsites, a chair clattered over, and a trailer door could be heard opening. A voice yelled, "Mary Ann, I told you we should have taken the blasted awning down." Then the rain picked up a notch, drowning out everything.

By the time Geraldine reached the car, one door had already opened, and in the light, Marla and Skylar scrambled in through the passenger side, Marla first with her blanket in hand, and Skylar following, shirtless, in just his trunks. When Geraldine

185

opened the back door, Flotsam hit the opening like a wounded deer, leaping inside. She threw her blanket inside after him and fell into the seat. Daggett slammed her door just as the worst of the rain hit, the deluge smashing into the side of the car, rocking it on its wheels. He dripped as he jumped in the other side, his blanket lost somewhere. His run around the car had his shirt soaked.

"Here." Geraldine chuckled, reaching for his shirt. "Let me help you get that off."

"This is funny?" Skylar, still bleary, yawned, his hand over his mouth, as the overhead light began to dim. He felt the window. "Rain's cold."

"Poor baby." Geraldine fluffed Flotsam's back.

In the darkness, Daggett could smell him, wet and frightened. He'd never liked thunder.

"You can say that again. At least someone feels sorry for me." That was Marla, claiming Geraldine's words of sympathy for her own.

"I meant the dog." Geraldine reached up and flicked the back of her friend's hair.

"Thank you for thinking of me, anyway. I'll try to pretend I'm on an even level with your dog, if you don't mind." She laughed, wriggling her fingers over the seat. "Geri, behind you. I think I left my sweatshirt back there. Can you hand it to me?"

"If you left it back here, it's wet, now. Flotsam's down there."

"I put it in the window." The dome light flickered on, causing groans from Daggett and Skylar. "There. I see it. Hand it to me, if you will. I'm changing out of this shirt." She had already begun to work her shirt over her head.

"Um, men are present." Skylar held one hand to the side of his face, hiding behind his skinny fingers. "Are you sure—"

"I have a bra on." The light went out. "There. Happy?" She

giggled.

"We're happy. Aren't we, Daggett?" Geraldine shifted to sit against him, leaning in to let his body cup hers. With one hand she tugged the blanket, mostly dry, to cover all three huddled for safety in the back.

"Happy, Geri." He worked his arm around her. "You, Skylar?"

"If Marla lets me snuggle." Clearly his words were an invitation. There was noise from the front seat, and he called out, "Happy, now."

About that time Flotsam shifted, expelling a long and sloppy wind. The unexpected odor filled the car, and sounds of dismay came from all four corners. The big dog wasn't sent packing, though. The storm continued to buffet the car, and it was their only safe haven. Before long, the sounds muted and began to lull the four humans to sleep.

All except one.

Daggett lay with his eyes open, watching the black windows. The rain slackened, then petered out, coming fitfully for a time, and finally not at all. The night brightened, the sky clearing, and the stars blinked into being overhead. The wind stayed brisk, very brisk. Something on the underside of the car vibrated in the worst of the gusts. One of the windows apparently didn't seal well, and a low-pitched moan made Flotsam lift his head occasionally.

Daggett remembered one other thing from over the years. None of his other girlfriends would have found this funny. Geri had said she was happy, wet and right here in this car, weathering a freak summer storm. Right next to him.

He wondered if that meant she loved him.

Finally, before the sun managed to find its way to California, he drifted off to sleep. His eyes danced beneath his lids, and there was a quiver that ran down his cheek and tickled

187

his lips. It was little more than a ghost of a smile, one that was there, but only when seen under the cloud-twisted light of a magical, storm-darkened summer moon. From the fleeting expression on his face, he must have been on his surfboard, and first place seemed a sure thing.

Either that, or he dreamed of Geraldine as his, forever and ever.

Chapter 26

MORNING did not come easily. The alarm clock was Flotsam's whine, one of desperation.

Geraldine's eyes opened first. Outside, the blackness of the night had graduated to the crystalline air of a breaking dawn. Everything gleamed with dampness. When she opened the door to let the dog out, she shivered, pulling it to as quickly as possible.

"Geri, Baby?" Daggett's words were slurred. He was awake, but barely so.

"Shush. The two in the front are still asleep." She put her fingers to his lips, and she snuggled against him for warmth.

"You let Flotsam out?"

"Yes. He's fine."

"No, it's just that I need out, too." He chuckled, and he rubbed his eyes with a big hand. After a moment, he yawned.

"But it's so nice here with you." She didn't want him to go just yet. "Were you still awake when the rain stopped?"

"Yes."

"Did it last long?" She wanted conversation. His warmth, the vibrations of his voice as he answered her questions, the shifting of his body as he breathed. Those things were important to her.

"No. It ended not long after we got in the car."

"I fell asleep as soon as I got warm." She chuckled with the memory of their mad dash in the darkness. Now it seemed silly that they'd panicked with just a few drops of rain.

"I wish I could have. With the rain and rushing to the car, I was awake by then, and it got me to thinking. It kept my mind in gear."

"About what?"

"My mom. Corky. You. Can I go, now?"

"It's windy out. Pretty cool, too." With his words, the anticipation of cuddling dissipated, and she sat up, her thoughts rattled. He'd mentioned Corky . . . and her. That put her mind to processing, and not in a pleasant way.

"The wind will be good for the beach, bring the waves up. I'd hoped this front would hit before the contest kicked in." Daggett yawned again, shifting his position, then leaning over to kiss her on the cheek. "I need to get to the beach, too. I need some time in the water to warm up."

She knew what he was saying. The event organizers would make the call on surf conditions by six-thirty. If things were a go, the first heats would start by half past seven.

"Yeah, right. Warm up. You'll freeze out there." She laughed softly, pulling the blanket closer around her shoulders.

"So will everyone else. I can take it. They can't."

"You hope." There was laughter in her words. Even so, they would probably have wetsuits. Daggett didn't. His was at home, reserved for the cold winds of winter. She could just see the first of the campsites where the others were bedded down. A red tent blocked part of a green one, but there was no one out that she could see. They were snuggled in their sleeping bags, warm and toasty.

"I hope. Now, I need out." He reached with his hand and moved one corner of her blanket aside, kissing her on her neck, just where her skin turned to meet her shoulder.

"That's nice."

She was interrupted by a voice from the front seat.

"Enough, you two. Don't forget this is my car, and I'm asleep up here." Marla's hand appeared on the top of the seat, her nail polish still bright and smooth from the day before. She held up one finger. "Shush."

A sharp bark reminded them of Flotsam, and Daggett opened the door. He leaned to whisper to Geraldine, "If anyone's up down in the other sites, I'll catch a ride to Carmel with them. That way you can sleep in."

"And if they're not?"

"They will be. I'll make sure of it."

"It's getting cold," Marla complained. "It's barely five-thirty, if you don't mind. The door?" Her painted finger pointed.

"Sure, Marla." Daggett winked at Geraldine before climbing from the car. He shut the door quietly, rubbing his arms in the breeze.

In spite of his generous offer, Geraldine intended to be there to watch him surf. She wouldn't miss it for all the sleep in the world. Besides, Corky might show up. If so, Daggett couldn't be allowed to miss him. They needed each other.

As if she didn't.

191

Chapter 27

DAGGETT stood on Carmel Beach, with Zac and Kolbe poised at his side. All three men held surfboards in their hands, the tails planted in the sand. Daggett and Zac cradled their leashes casually in one palm, while Kolbe gripped his in his teeth. The wind whipped their hair. Daggett's suit flapped against his legs unnoticed.

The ocean stretched before them, freshly kissed by the sun, its surface untouched by land for thousands of miles, while the beach remained wrapped in cool morning shadows. The underwater gods pressed hard against the sand, and the winds brought about by the front forced the breakers to peel off like clockwork. Froth whipped from the tops, coating the beach with moisture. Swells farther out undulated blue-green perfection, trailing white water where they surged around jagged formations of rock thrusting from the sea. Fourteen hours in the future, Carmel Beach might worship the sun's final rays as the mighty orb of the skies sank into the cold Pacific waters, but for now, she struggled to awaken.

To the right towered Pebble Beach and the lopped off flatness of a sprawling golf course. Left, the hills leaped skyward, filled with greenery and spotted with buildings. Growling faintly in the distance, a tractor pulled a Surf Rake slowly across the sand, clearing accumulated debris for the weekend's festivities.

The beach just ahead was freshly groomed and filled with newly assembled construction specifically for Surfjam. A series of tented structures lined the upper part of the sand, the backs and sides emblazoned with the Surfjam insignia. Every additional flat space on the structures was filled with sponsors' logos. Inside would be found small areas for trainers and competitors to get out of the weather. One small, tented structure was just the size to hold a rack for entrants' surfboards.

Umbrellas dotted a long stretch of the freshly groomed beach, rental companies selling seats and shade for the hottest part of the day. Most of the umbrellas were closed, with the chairs partially folded against the snapping breeze.

Numerous surfers, male and female, walked the tideline, some in plain trunks like Daggett's, but most sporting the protection of full wetsuits. One especially young man had an older trainer at his side pointing out different areas, possibly indicating locations of submerged rocks, or where the best curls would peel from the least likely swells.

The water had Daggett's attention, and his eyes squinted into the haze. The other two had donned wetsuits for the day. The predicted front was one reason the turnout for the competition was expected to be heavy, but fronts brought cooler temperatures, and the waters off Carmel Beach were never really warm.

"Cooking." Kolbe whispered his evaluation. "No grommets allowed today."

"There'll be some sick maneuvers out there, mate. Gonna be gnarly for anyone new to Carmel." Zac nodded at the young boy with the older trainer. "Hope that one doesn't get drilled."

"Has word come down, yet?" Daggett drew in a deep breath, tasting the salt and the surf, a delicacy better than food. They still waited for Surfjam's organizers, as well as local officials, to decide whether the scheduled events could continue. The front had brought the swells, but too much wind could cause dangerous conditions. In the worst of weather, undertow was also a serious hazard at Carmel. The call hadn't been posted yet, and the water was off-limits until it was. Tickets could and would be issued for being in the water in life-threatening conditions.

Several men, older, one in beige slacks and accompanied by a law-enforcement officer, walked up to a temporary leader board. A girl in a heavy jacket sat in a collapsible chair, a bag at her side. She was reading but set it aside when the men approached. They spoke to her a minute, pointed to the board, then glanced out at the water, arms gesticulating toward each other as if in emphasis of some important observation. Finally, they nodded. The man in the slacks rapped the board with his knuckles, and the group walked away, their feet digging in the sand, clearly working hard to make their way along the beach.

"The decision's been made." Kolbe dug his elbow in Zac's ribs. He chuckled.

"We'll be shredding the waves today." Daggett pressed his lips together. He was certain the decision, when it was posted, would be a go.

"No way they're gonna give up these waves." Kolbe grinned. "Ten to twenty's perfect range."

By then the girl at the leaderboard had a marker out, and she began to fill out the information for the first heat. There was no longer any question of whether the beach was open. The competition was on.

"Glad you entered, Sweets?" Geraldine's voice drifted over Daggett's shoulder.

He turned, and a smile grew on his face. "I didn't think you'd make it down this early. How'd you get here?" It was blocks away from the campground. He glanced behind her, searching for her ride, then again looking into her face.

"Marla." She reached one hand and just touched the pale growth on his cheek. He would trim it when it got out of hand, but she liked it like this. It was so bohemian, so, so Daggett. It was him, and she wouldn't change him in any way.

"Shut-the-door-it's-barely-five-thirty Marla?" He laughed. "She's your friend. At least it'll be you she's mad at, not me."

She laughed, obviously not worried. "Skylar's the one in the doghouse. He wouldn't miss your heat. Where's Flotsam? He wasn't at the campsite, and I haven't seen him here yet."

"Living large." He pointed down the sand at some bright-eyed, early morning teenagers throwing sticks. Flotsam was retrieving.

"Who's here?"

Zac and Kolbe had run to the waves, high-stepping in with their boards. One yelled about the water not being bad—warmer than expected, he probably meant—and throwing his board down before jumping on and paddling off.

"You see them." He pointed at the people walking the water line, then at the tented structures. "I haven't been in there."

"No one we know then."

"We know Zac and Kolbe." He leaned to kiss the bridge of her nose. "Do you know Becca Walthrop?" He'd once surfed a Red Bull meet with her.

"Hm. Should I?"

"Maybe. Lives in Carlsbad. Originally from the East Coast. Atlantic City, I think. She can take the cold like no one. There."

195

He pointed.

She was a compact girl, early twenties, in a full wetsuit. She carried a board, and as they watched, she studied the waves, then seemingly on an impulse, leaped into the water, feet stepping high. After what seemed only moments, she threw her board down and caught a small wave, putting her right foot forward instead of her left.

"Goofy foot," he murmured softly, but there was nothing goofy about her riding. She cut back once or twice to find the wave's power, switched feet, then went off the top as the wave closed out.

"She's good. I don't remember her, but she's certainly got a chance at some prize money." Geraldine smiled, slipping one hand into a fleece-lined pocket. She wore Marla's gift this morning, the sweatshirt with the old car on the front.

"I haven't seen our other half." He studied her face. Skylar and Geri's friend, he meant.

"They dropped me off and went to breakfast. They also promised to bring me a breakfast burrito, cheese and egg only. I can send them after something for you when they get here, if you want."

"Can't afford to spew chunks out on the water." His attention had already shifted back to Zac and Kolbe. They carved the tops of the waves, occasionally floating the lip, then bailing out when it seemed the waves would close out on them. As Zac stood in ankle-deep water, having just come up from dodging a kook who had dropped in right in front of him, Daggett yelled, "Blow it out, Zac!"

"Go." She slapped him on the back. "You're in love today, and it's not with me."

When he looked at her, not understanding, she put her hand on his back and pushed.

"Get in the water, Daggett. I want to watch. Go warm up."

"Warm up. Sure." He laughed, and he jerked his board from the sand. As he took off, he turned to dance backwards for several steps, patting his hand on his chest just where his heart was, and pointing to her. Just as quickly, he spun on his heels and tore across the sand toward the water.

Before he could make it off the beach, a lightning-fast missile intercepted him, barking rapidly and grabbing his surfboard's leash. The board flew from his hands. Flotsam backed up, dragging the surfboard in his teeth.

"Flotsam!" He slapped his hands together sharply. "I'm surfing, boy. Give it back."

The dog had other plans, though. He had been playing with a new crowd, and they'd taught him a great game, fetch, and with anything on the beach. Sticks, seaweed, sandals. Surfboards, too.

When the boys started cheering and running Flotsam's way, the golden retriever began backing up faster. This was his biggest prize yet, and the attention from the kids had been a great start to his day. He wanted more.

Daggett wasn't having any of it. He took three quick steps then dived for the board, landing chest down on the sand with his hand on the leash.

"Blow it out, Daggett!"

He looked up to see Geraldine's fist high in the air, and a grin on her face.

Before he could make it into the water, the teens engulfed him, calling out excited questions. He high-fived several of them, returned a fist bump or two, then waved as he splashed his way into the water. He had an hour to play—or warm-up, practice, or whatever someone might want to call it. To him it was indeed play, the best and most glorious thing a person could spend his life doing, bar none.

Paddling out, just for fun he dropped in on Kolbe, hooting and kicking up spray in his face. They repeatedly surfed alongside each other while the waves held together, bouncing their boards on backed off sections, hoping for the waves to reform, until they closed out, leaving them with sections of flat water.

Afterward, they stood, the remnants of ocean at their feet only inches deep, rivulets of water running down their bodies. He could already tell the day was going to be brutal, but they were stoked. Their faces were flushed, and they grinned at each other.

"Hey, dude, let's drop in on Zac." Kolbe chuckled as he nodded toward the ebony-haired surfer out on the water. They watched as their friend backdoored a wave, surfing straight through the barrel, then floated on the white water for a time before going off the lip and bailing out. "He won't mind."

"And if he does, too bad." Daggett laughed a short bark of a sound, then without waiting, he dropped his board into the water and leaped aboard, paddling furiously.

With all the fun, the hour of warm-up time they spent before the first heat was no more than an exhilarating escapade among friends, even as the water grew more crowded. Coaches yelled instructions, many speaking into walkie-talkies, whistling and flashing hand signs to the competitors out on the water.

Spectators began to arrive, jacketed and equipped with sunglasses, coolers, and books to pass the time until the first events started. For some, it was no more than an outing to the beach. For others, like the teens entertaining Flotsam, it was a chance to be out from under their parents' thumbs. For a few, too young to participate, this would be their chance to soak up the glory, a day to anticipate their own surfboards riding the waves someday, the air horns blasting, the scores tabulated, and them standing on the podium to be decorated as the best in the world.

For Daggett, it was life, and without it he might as well be six feet under, and by that, he didn't mean the water, either.

Chapter 28

"THAT'S Daggett!" Marla jumped from her blanket and whistled at the blond-haired man out in the surf. He wore a tight shirt with a number emblazoned on the front and the back. Underneath, in a lazy cursive script, *Surfjam* scrawled across his muscular torso in letters nearly as big.

Geraldine laughed, slapping her on the back of the leg. "He can't hear you, you know." She rubbed Flotsam's ears. The teen boys from the morning had gone home for lunch, and she'd not seen them since. Flotsam had been relegated to the sand at her side.

"I can hear me." She waved Geraldine's reasoning away, and she whistled again. Then she dropped to the blanket, her feet just over the edge and in the sand. "Everyone around us can hear me, too, and that's as important as Daggett hearing me."

"Well, I certainly heard you. My ears are still ringing. How soon until Skylar takes a turn?"

Skylar hadn't had any events lined up before lunch. Now it

was afternoon, and the sun beat down on them. Even Janjak Duvalier, Geraldine's strawberry pie-sharing friend, had gone, although his scores had been less than stellar. He'd been philosophical about it when she'd gone to cheer him up. "The music still plays. It be good music, even be it that I do not win." He'd shrugged, shaking the water from his tight hair, his wetsuit glistening in the misty air.

All morning she'd searched for Corky's familiar bulk. While Surfjam was a local competition—the big events would come in the winter when the waves were more consistent—it was close to his home. After two e-mails, surely. Surely.

The conversation was interrupted when an air horn blasted the end of Daggett's time, and the scratchy speaker system announced the next competitor.

"Skylar Johnson wearing number six. You can't miss that red hair. Send him a cheer to wish him success." Scattered handclapping punctuated the crowd, and Marla huffed at the lackluster response.

"How sad was that? I'm going down to cheer my man on." She gave Flotsam a quick pat on the head and leaped to her feet. Her fingers to her lips, she let out a whale of a whistle, causing several people nearby to cover their ears. "Boo-ya, Number Six! Shred!" She turned to grin at Geraldine.

"You know shred?" Geraldine found that funny. Marla was not a surfer.

She shrugged. "Everyone else says it. I guess I can join the crowd. See ya'." She took off toward the water, joining small kids and competitors walking in eddies swirling at the edge of the sand.

Geraldine rubbed Flotsam's neck. She didn't anticipate Daggett joining her on her blanket, even with his current heat completed. He was expected to remain in the competitors' area. The event might be local, but for the locals it was very big, indeed. There were photographers, and video cameras with massive lenses had been set up at strategic spots. To top it off, apparently Surfjam's sponsors had commissioned a full length documentary, and when each competitor came off the water, an enthusiastic interview ensued.

Most competitors welcomed it. Surfers who competed tended to be a testosterone-laden crew, and the chance to be on camera stoked their egos. Daggett? Not so much, but he took things in stride. When told, he'd snorted his opinion of the interviews, then almost immediately laughed it off. They could interview him. He wasn't pretty, but then neither were most of the other surfers. The videographers would get raw footage of a bunch of wet, tired men, and if they could clean it up to put it on film, fine. Otherwise, too bad.

She adjusted her sunglasses, closing her eyes for a minute. The wind was still quite brisk and cool, but the rays of the sun compensated nicely. The mix was perfect, except for the occasional mouthful of sugar white sand when a youngster ran by.

Flotsam nuzzled her leg, and she opened her eyes. In that instant, the sand was deserted. The waves rolled in boisterously just yards away, and a huge tree overhung the beach, its branches dipping nearly to the water. Out on the reef, a massive wooden vessel sat wedged, the masts at a precarious angle, rocking as if they would topple at any time. The tide looked high, and as it fell, the reef would grind at the hull, making the damage worse.

Somehow, she knew that had been her ship, and she and Daggett had survived a devastating storm. Yet, she felt unafraid. He was with her. He had gone to find help, a rubber plantation, an aboriginal tribe, or even a fallen tree with which to construct a signal fire.

She listened for him, but the pounding of the waves against the beach drowned out everything else.

Then, somewhere within the raucous noise of the surf, she heard the tolling of a bell. Her first thought was of the ship, its rocking perhaps causing a bell somewhere inside to clatter its noisy sounds. That didn't seem right, though. She didn't remember the ship having a bell.

She stood and looked around. Noticing Flotsam's ears at full alert, she knelt to calm him as she scanned inland. Then, far away through the dense vegetation, barely visible, she made out a tower—white stucco—with a red-tiled roof. A white cross thrust from it, punctuating the sky. That must be where the bell was. Perhaps the donging meant Daggett had found help after all, and he signaled to her, letting her know not to be afraid.

She sat again, her arm across the dog. He sighed, his entire upper body rising then falling, and finally lying still. At a rustling in the underbrush, she called out, "Daggett? Is that you?"

When she got no answer, she turned to see a man in a white robe with a dark sash walking briskly her direction. He was quite tall, and his dark hair was slicked back from his face, giving him an elegant look. Once at her side, he held out a rolled sheaf of paper tied with a ribbon. She took it, and he motioned to her as if to unroll and read it.

Inside she found a sentence written in numerous languages. The first looked Italian. The third one down was in English. "I am a monk, and I have taken a vow of silence. However, if you have a smart phone, I am not prohibited from texts and e-mail." She looked up to see he held a black phone in his hand, one with a shiny glass face.

"I'm sorry." She smiled apologetically, pointing to the water. "My ship just wrecked, and all I have left is what you see. Everything else was lost."

He held up one finger, drawing a second phone from some-where deep within his robes. He pressed a button, and when the face lighted, he handed it to her. He tapped repeatedly at his phone, and words appeared on hers.

"Good morning. My name is Brother Paolo. Is there any way I can serve you?" He bowed graciously, holding a hand toward her phone.

"Um." She giggled. Paolo. This was Italy? His name *would* be, if so. She looked to the phone, wondering how to reply. With one unsure finger, she tapped part of the screen, hoping she could figure it out. Almost immediately, more words appeared. She glanced up to see Brother Paolo tapping at his screen. When he finished he directed her attention to the phone she held.

"I can hear fine. I am just not allowed to speak. Please state your request aloud."

"Certainly, Paul, um, Brother Paolo." She giggled again, feeling like a schoolgirl. She hadn't giggled this much since third grade. "My friend, Daggett, a tall, blond man who needs a haircut, maybe a shave, too, is out looking for help—"

Before she could speak further, the bell began to ring once again. Then, someone shook her arm, gently at first, and finally, more violently.

"Aren't you paying any attention, Geri?"

She opened her eyes. Marla knelt at her side. Beyond her, the crowds sat under their umbrellas, and surfers still plied the waves. An air horn went off, and the loudspeaker system called out words that were nearly unintelligible.

"Attention to what?" She yawned. She wanted to know what had happened to Daggett, and Marla had interrupted her dream. Now, she might never know.

"The church bells. Didn't you hear them?"

"Church bells?" That got her attention. She'd just dreamed of church bells, and she hadn't told anyone. Her dream hadn't even wrapped up. How would Marla know?

"Girl, how do you keep anything straight? I declare!" Marla

plopped down beside her. "I talked to a woman down there, and she said the bells at San Carlos Cathedral always ring during an earthquake. I can't believe you didn't hear them. Everyone else did."

"An earthquake? Here?" There had been too many earthquakes the past months. She thought of Daggett's house. At least they were a long way from there, if it was really a quake.

"Nah. Not here. Up in Napa Valley. We're safe." She rummaged in the cooler, pulling out a can of soda. "Skylar's doing his interview. He's going to be part of that documentary. My boyfriend, the movie star."

"He's your boyfriend, now? And he's hardly a movie star." She grabbed Marla's can and took a sip before returning it. She grinned impishly, but Napa Valley bothered her. Daggett's house. "How do you know the quake was in Napa?"

"That lady's phone." She pointed to a different woman, blonde and with a cell phone to her ear. She was packing up and preparing to exit the beach. "Her husband sent her a message. They have a vineyard in the Valley."

"Was there damage?" She wasn't sure she wanted to know. Damage in Napa might mean damage to the coast—as well as Daggett's house. Besides, if it shook church bells all the way down to Carmel, wow!

"Don't know. She didn't say. Still, it's cool, being at the beach when a quake hits. Church bells, how romantic! You'd think they were ringing for love."

"For you and Skylar?"

"Of course." Marla pursed her lips and lifted her chin. "Who else?"

Who else, indeed?

Geraldine looked across the beach, and she saw Daggett at the water's edge with Jon from the night before, and Becca, the girl he'd pointed out that morning. She waved, and he waved back, shooting her thumbs-up with both hands, a grin on his face. He'd done well, and he was excited—stoked, he'd say— about the rest of the competition.

Those bells preyed on her mind, though. Had an earthquake shaken the bells, or had it been love? And if it was love, was it for Skylar and Marla, or for Daggett and Geraldine?

She glanced at Flotsam, and seeing he was asleep, reached to her side and idly traced a bell in the white sugar sand. Inside she put the initials DDP and GGR.

Who else, indeed?

Chapter 29

THE SUN hovered just above the sea, a quivering red ball painting the water with fire. Fingers of clouds reached along the horizon, and they, too, were flames in the sky. The world was ablaze, the ending of a perfect day.

Someone south of 10th had gathered a mound of driftwood the height of a man, and as the evening air had started to cool, a small beach fire had been whipped up. Those with chairs sat around, wieners and marshmallows roasting on wire coat hangers; and still more had broken off lengths of the driftwood, forming makeshift seats in the sand. There was more than enough wood to last the entire night, one dry limb at a time.

Geraldine huddled in her sweatshirt with its car on the front, the fleecy fabric bringing her warmth. The fire helped. So did having a blanket over her shoulders, as well as Daggett at her side.

"Ah, man, I be on the water, and the wind, she push me aside. When Mother Nature want you off the wave, she take you off the wave." With a shrug, Janjak offered his excuses for his poor showing at the competition that day. His skin gleamed in the fading sunset, and the fire cast unusual shadows across his dark coloring, making him appear as a Haitian spirit god. His wide smile helped, with its mouthful of white teeth. "But I sing, and in the song, I be in first place."

He held up his brown bottle, the glass picking up the red of the sun, and fire leaped from its burnished surface. The crowd laughed and clapped. Those who knew Janjak were familiar with his Theology of Music, and those who didn't enjoyed his words anyway. Geraldine remembered his conversation from the evening before, and she found him charming.

Zac ran up behind Daggett, and he called to Sparky, motioning him over. His words were for the entire crowd, though. "It's all Daggett's fault. He needs taken down a notch. Let's throw him in the water. It'll help Janjak feel better."

Daggett reached over his head and waved him away, picking up a small stick and letting it catch in the fire. He glanced at Geri, grinning and mouthing, "They wouldn't dare," and he pointed the flaming stick threateningly at Sparky.

She just shook her head. She'd seen Zac's face, and while she knew Sparky might be easily cowed, Zac wouldn't be. She reached beside Daggett, picking up his hot chocolate. He would want it later.

She was just in time. It wasn't Sparky that came to Zac's aid, though. Skylar had come around the back side, pulling Kolbe by the arm, and they had snuck up behind Daggett. He grabbed him under his arms, jerking him backward, then Zac and Kolbe each took a leg. Lifting him as best they could, and dragging his backside when he fought too hard, they stumbled, crawled, and finally got him to the water. The crowd around the fire cheered and clapped, hooting for Daggett to be thrown in or to fight back, whichever way they leaned, and in the end, all four men wound up completely soaked.

Daggett walked back pulling his shirt off. He threw it at Skylar, who caught it easily.

"All in fun, right?" Skylar threw his arm over Daggett's shoulder.

"Right." Without warning, he strong-armed Skylar to the sand, sitting on his chest and rubbing a handful of the gritty powder on each side of his face. "All in fun." Then he leaned down and kissed him on the forehead, patting both sides of his face. He repeated with a grin, "All in fun," before standing and offering his hand.

"Have you seen Jon?" He questioned Geraldine as he eased back onto his log, scooting it closer to the fire to dry off better. "He was in a morning heat, then I lost track of him."

"He stopped by, and we talked afterwards." She held out his drink, letting him take it. It was still hot, and he would want it to warm more quickly. The water was especially cold at night.

"Did he say where he was staying? L.A.'s quite a ride from here."

Everyone knew Jon worked, and that probably meant a hotel. It also meant hot showers and perhaps a continental breakfast. Most people envied that. Not Daggett, she knew.

"Did he tell you he's no longer living in L.A.?"

"Surfing full time again? Did you tell him he could come stay with us if he wants?"

"Hey! Did you save me a spot by the fire?"

Daggett and Geraldine looked up to see Marla with Flotsam. She'd taken him for a walk up the beach, saying she'd wanted to tour the beach houses—from the beach, of course. Many had lights on, and she could see inside.

"Sure. Skylar's off rinsing sand from his face, but he's sitting right there." Geraldine pointed.

"What, did he build a sand castle or something?" She coiled

Flotsam's leash and pushed him to the ground. He dropped beside Daggett.

"Sort of," Daggett replied. "So, where's Jon staying?"

Before Geraldine could answer, Marla jumped in. "Jon, with the hunky red car? Ooh, la, la, I would like to have something exotic like that. How lucky for his dad to own that ranch! When he inherits, he'll make quite a catch."

"Jon's got a car?" Daggett sat up. "If he's no longer in L.A., how . . . where did Jon get the money to buy a car?"

Geraldine sighed. This wasn't going to be good.

DAGGETT knew about the ranch, and he also knew how Jon had sworn he'd never give in to his father's pleas to work there, never, no matter how much money his dad offered him.

Now, the car suggested otherwise.

Geraldine tapped him on the arm. "I didn't get a chance to tell you. Jon didn't do well in his first heat, and he headed home. I thought he should be the one to find you if he wanted you to know."

He dug his stick into the sand. In a gestalt of understanding, he knew the reasons for the car, the weeks Jon spent must have spent inland with a job that forced him to travel to the beach but didn't allow him time to surf. Otherwise, he wouldn't have been knocked out in the first heat. He had once been among the best.

"I'd hoped to see Corky today." His words jumped from his mouth out of the blue, and he wasn't sure why he said them. He sat back and was quiet for a moment. He did too know why. It was Jon's car, but not just Jon's car. It was Geri's lack of one, or lack of a running one. If Corky had shown up, he'd have been able to tell him about the broken car and ask for help. For Geri, he'd have done that. Today he'd been on the top of the world. He'd needed nothing but the ocean and his surfboard. His world had been complete. Now he saw the gaping hole in the perfection.

Someone threw a large limb into the fire. Sparks shot into the air, and those closest to the flames scooted backwards in a rush, several tumbling into the sand. The liquid refreshments had made more than one of the merrymakers a bit tipsy, and they took their sandy baths with good humor. One girl—local and very young by the looks of her—rushed toward the ocean to wash off, squealing unmercifully when she hit the cold water. Startled from sleep, Flotsam leaped from his spot on the sand, tearing after her. His leash was still attached, and it caught the end of a branch in the fire. It whipped out, still flaming, and left a trail of burning embers for at least fifteen feet before it dislodged from his leash. Off in the darkness, the dog yelped, and a man's voice cursed.

"Stray dogs, anyone?" Skylar appeared with Flotsam's leash in hand, skirting the sputtering flames.

At that moment, several large logs tumbled onto the bonfire, showering sparks and flaming embers into the crowd. People standing farther away laughed, holding bottles and cans high, cheering the fracas on. Some of those closer up were actually alight, and more than one container of bubbly was emptied on a friend's scorched clothing.

It was only minutes before the scene settled down. Burnt marshmallows were thrown aside, and a few of the less charred wieners nibbled until only the crusts were left. Flotsam wandered the crowd, snacking on the remains, gnawing the blackened wires clean.

Toward midnight, a collection was taken up, and soon, a deliveryman showed up with ten pizzas. Not everyone wanted to party the night through, though.

"Pizza? At midnight?" Marla had already dozed off more than once. "If we don't head back to Veteran's soon, I'll wind up asleep right here. And you do remember that I want to go to the aquarium tomorrow?"

"They remember." Skylar had one hand wrapped in hers, and Flotsam was using the man's feet for a pillow. The big dog was upside down, his back stretched across two comfortable legs.

Geraldine said she remembered, but only because Marla mentioned it.

Daggett hadn't a clue about the aquarium, and he headed off with the pizzas, carrying the boxes around to make sure anyone who had paid got their share, then offering the rest to those who hadn't given any money.

"MARLA, WHY don't you and Skylar head on back? Kolbe left half an hour ago. He should already be there, if you need anything. I'll catch a ride with Daggett and his friends." Geraldine had picked the pepperonis off her slice of pizza, feeding them one at a time to the dog. After only two bites, she'd felt the grease on her stomach and set the rest aside.

Flotsam would be very full tonight, the way it was going.

Somewhere off towards the water, someone had an acoustic guitar out, and a melody filtered out, clear in the louder sections, fading beneath the drumming of the surf when the song whispered. A pretty voice accompanied the notes from time to time. The clouds had let the moon slip through, and although it was only a sliver, the light gave the beach an ethereal beauty. The fire kept the cool of the deepening night at bay, useful for those who had no one to hold.

"You sure? We can wait." Skylar had eaten two pieces of the pizza already but had been short real funds to donate. He'd already suggested that if they held off, Daggett might return with extra.

Marla had found her window of opportunity, and she stood, pulling Skylar up with her, snuggling his arm into hers. Her

211

voice was filled with unexpected enthusiasm. "You heard her. They can catch a ride with Daggett's friends. Let's head back to the campground." She ran one hand up his arm, leaning her head against his shoulder.

They didn't get very far. In the near darkness, they stumbled over Flotsam, getting a yelp in return.

"Take him back with you." Geraldine forced the leash into Marla's hand. "Be sure and keep his leash on when you go to bed."

"But . . ." Even in the darkness, she could be seen looking at Skylar. "What will we do with a dog?"

"Stay honest?" Geraldine chuckled, although her stomach no longer felt well. It was the grease in the pizza, she knew. As brightly as she could manage, she insisted, "Go. We'll be back before long. One of Daggett's 'mates' will give us a ride."

Zac was rubbing off on her.

"Do you think there's still extra pizza?" Skylar's eyes searched, showing he hadn't given up, yet.

"Don't be a pig." Marla jerked the leash, her voice filled with teasing. "Come on, dog."

"His name is Flotsam. I thought you knew that." Skylar took off after her.

"I was talking to you." A bright laugh made it clear she was only teasing.

"Hey, slow down," he called.

"You hurry up. I've got the keys." The sound of clanking metal tinkled back across the sand.

Their words become faint, and Geraldine smiled. Her friend had the keys, and Skylar didn't want to walk—or catch an imaginary ride with one of Daggett's friends. They sounded like a couple, and she liked that. Maybe they had indeed heard the church bells of love.

She pulled her blanket closer, settling back against her log.

Her eyes found Daggett. His hair caught the faint rays of the moon, making him easy to follow. At one point, he tossed an empty box onto the fire, and it smoked for a minute before bursting into flames. Almost immediately, it sizzled noisily, the flames shooting higher as the oil soaked into the cardboard caught.

"Daggett?" She called softly to him. He waved, then stopped again, opening the final box. No one seemed to want more, and after a bit, he walked to her.

"You want any? I have a full box." He reached inside to pull out one slice, biting off the end and chewing slowly. "It's hamburger."

"I should have had that first. I gave Flotsam most of mine."

"Where is he?" He looked around.

"Marla and Skylar took him and headed back to the campground. I told them we'd catch a ride with someone else. I guess we can take that pizza with us and have it for breakfast." Everyone else could have it for breakfast, she meant. She wasn't eating anything else, ever. Her stomach churned.

"I'm glad you have a blanket." He closed the box and set the pizza aside. Without asking, he lifted the edge of the blanket and scooted underneath.

"Are you cold?" He felt good to her. She liked having him at her side.

"I don't think we'll be getting a ride. Kolbe's how I got here this morning. I can't find him anywhere." He kissed her cheek.

"You have pizza breath." She couldn't tell him that she'd told Kolbe to go on when he'd offered to wait on them.

"I do, huh? Do you like pizza breath?" He chuckled.

That was when her stomach twisted in a knot, and it let her know it wasn't taking no for an answer. She leaped to her feet, tearing off towards the water.

"Geri? Was it something I said?"

Another voice called out, "It be something you ate. I smell a man's breath after pizza, and that be one song no one want to sing."

"Sure, Janjak. Go sing someone else's song," Daggett snorted.

"Say what you wish. All songs be ones to sing."

Daggett was off to the beach by then. At the water, he found Geraldine leaning over, holding her hair back from her face.

"Are you okay?" He knelt and touched her cheek.

"I will be. The pizza didn't agree with me." She reached to the water and splashed some on her face. "We really don't have a ride back, do we?"

"We have a blanket." He chuckled. "What else do we need?"

She sighed, putting both hands to her face. After a moment she laughed.

"What?" He reached to touch her wrist. "What's so funny?"

She turned to him, embarrassed for the tears running down her cheeks. "You. It's you, doing what you always do."

"What do I always do? Screw up?"

"No, you never screw up." She chuckled, wiping her eyes. She'd been the one to make all the mistakes, sending two rides away, leaving them stranded.

"Then what did I do?" By this time he had his arm around her.

"You took a terrible situation and made it seem like the opportunity of a lifetime."

"What terrible situation? Being here on the beach, forced to spend the night with a beautiful girl under a crescent moon," and he chuckled, "with the gentle sound of the surf as background music?"

She hugged him back this time. "When you put it that way, this is the opportunity of a lifetime."

"I always thought so. All we need is your blanket."

"And each other."

"That helps." He chuckled again.

"Being with you is why it's perfect." She only whispered those words, too softly for him to hear. It was the truth, though. With God and the sea and the moon as her witness, it was the truest thing in her heart.

She didn't even think about Corky, not more than a little bit, just enough to be disappointed that he hadn't come. Corky was Corky, and he lived the life he wanted. She couldn't control that, even if she loved him very much.

She just hoped he loved Daggett enough to show up when he was needed.

That was now.

Chapter 30

DAGGETT had one arm wrapped around Geraldine. The night had grown cold, and the blanket alone wasn't enough to keep him warm. In the near darkness of the early California morning, the diesel engine of a distant tractor revved, noisy and clattering. The sound grew louder, drowning out the sound of the surf.

"Hey, you! What are you doing down there?"

Daggett threw back the edge of the blanket, peering blearily at an enormous red and green tractor. Inside the cab, gloved and wearing a striped hat, a Carmel-by-the-Sea city employee worked the controls, the big tractor pulling an equally large lime green Surf Rake across the sand. In the dim, pre-dawn light, the blaring spots from the tractor were blinding.

"What is it, Daggett?" Geraldine stirred.

His head dropped back to the sand. "I don't know. Some guy with bright lights."

"Does he want us to move?"

"Maybe. He didn't say."

Just then, a horn blared, quite loudly, and out of the window the operator yelled, "I'm making a pass through the remains of your fire. When I get back, I'm headed right where you are. Don't be there. It's against the law to camp on the beach, you know. You people think just because the city allows fires south of 10th Street, you can do anything you want. Well, you can't sleep on the beach." The diesel engine revved again, and the tractor lurched forward. When it hit the remains of the fire, the tires spun in the sand for a moment, then it caught, and it moved ahead, leaving only slightly sooty white sand in its wake.

"Want to get up?" Daggett brought one of Geraldine's hands to his mouth to kiss it gently.

"Not really, Sweets." She rolled into him, laying her arm across his chest. "I don't want to get carried away by that machine, either."

They listened as it grew fainter, the engine revving from time to time as it struggled with soft places in the sand. A new sound took its place. A car was driving back and forth on the city street abutting the park, accompanied by familiar barking.

"I know that dog." She grinned. "I think we're being rescued."

"If we hide, maybe they won't find us." He pulled her tight. "We can spend the rest of our lives here, alone, this beach our home. I'd like that." He leaned in and kissed her on the cheek.

"Until that tractor gets here, and that green frog behind it sucks us up." She giggled. "Then it would spit us out in the city dump, and how much fun would that be?"

"Spoilsport. I guess I'll have to be the one to go flag them down. They could have waited at least until the sun came up." When he stood, there was a screech of brakes, and someone yelled. Daggett grinned at Geraldine. "Gig's up. Shall we make a run for it, or turn ourselves in?" He tipped an imaginary hat at her, pretending to pull a gun from a holster. "If we commandeer that tractor, we might make it to the border before nightfall."

She stretched, laughing. "By nightfall a week from next Wednesday. Did you even watch it drive by? It'll do ten, tops."

"That's the spirit. Give up before you even get out of bed. What kind of law-breaking citizen are you?" He put his imaginary gun away and reached to offer her a hand.

"A very inept one." She took his hand and stood. "Do you think they have showers at the campground?"

Marla's car honked, and they turned to see Skylar with the door open, standing and waving. They raised their hands in response.

"Kiss me before you go." Daggett took Geraldine in his arms.

"That's an old song, you know. Jefferson Airplane." She wrapped her arms around his back.

He kissed her gently on the lips and whispered, "John Denver, don't you mean? And it's kiss me and smile for me, anyway."

"I never could keep my artists straight." She chuckled, and she kissed him back.

GERALDINE remembered the song she was thinking of. It was England Dan and John Ford Coley singing, *Just tell me that you love me,* and she almost took the risk of speaking the words aloud. She did love Daggett immensely. However, she hesitated, and the moment was stolen from her. Flotsam came tearing across the sand, barking and letting Daggett know that he'd been sorely missed.

"I guess we can't hide now." He turned to the dog. "Flotsam, boy, come here, you old hound. Did you miss us?"

"And what about us?" Skylar came marching across the barrier between the road and the beach. "Marla and I have been driving that road—" He called back to her, "What's it called, anyway?"

"Scenic Road, I think." Marla didn't look exactly pleased.

"Yeah, Scenic Road, for thirty minutes. Where were you?" He dropped on his knees by Flotsam's side, grabbing his face in his hands. "We found them, boy. You can relax, now."

The tractor had grown louder, and its horn blared at them, driving Flotsam into a barking frenzy, right in Skylar's face. Startled, he fell back into the sand.

"You want that blanket?" Skylar pointed. The big diesel motor eased to a tolerable clatter, and the black smoke cleared to a shimmering haze above the smokestack. It was stopped only feet from where Daggett and Geraldine had spent the night.

With a wave of one hand and a smile, Geraldine snatched it from the sand, shaking it as she did so. She waved at the man in the striped hat once again, stepping out of the way, the dry sand piling around her feet as she sank ankle deep with each step. Then the tractor revved noisily, pulling by with mere feet to spare.

"Not very patient, is he?" Skylar had a finger in one ear, working it. "I didn't know tractors have horns."

"If they're ordered that way." Daggett slapped him upside the shoulder.

More gently, Geraldine pulled him aside and said, "Remember Jon? He and Daggett surfed together for years. Ask Jon about growing up on his father's ranch next time you see him. I bet his family's tractors have honked a time or two."

"Well, have you told them, yet?" Marla pushed on Skylar's shoulder.

"Told them?" He looked up grinning. "Eh? I can't hear you. My ears are still ringing." He pointed to the tractor lumbering down the beach, leaving perfect lines in the sand.

"We have company back at the campsite." She pointed with her equally perfect nails toward Daggett and Geraldine. The smell of new polish permeated the early morning air. A smile had yet to break her face. "Liked to have scared the pee out of the two of us when he arrived."

"Flotsam took to him, though. That was how we knew he was okay. Corky's his name, he said. Claimed the two of you." Skylar grinned.

He went on to tell the story. During the night, an old van had lumbered into the campsite, backfiring once, frightening both Skylar and Marla. It had set Flotsam off, the barking soon waking other campers and igniting lights in a number of the RVs in the park. Only when Flotsam ran to the barrel-chested man, nuzzling his feet, and finally climbing up into his van, did the two of them relax.

Marla pursed her lips petulantly. "It wasn't so funny during the night. That backfiring van was a gunshot, a rampaging maniac out to kill those of us not smart enough to have a trailer for protection. Only Doofus here could find it hilarious in retrospect."

Skylar snickered and told the rest of what they'd learned. It seemed Corky had made it down for the competition. It hadn't been a smooth journey, though. In the hundred twenty miles he'd had to travel, he'd broken down twice, once waiting over three hours for a tow. The repair hadn't taken as long as the tow—a clogged fuel filter—and he'd been back on the road.

He'd missed most of the previous day's activities, arriving and not finding parking, then walking several miles to get to the beach. He'd seen the campfire from the night before, not realizing everyone was there.

Asking around, he'd finally found some Haitian dude who'd known where they'd spent the previous night. Then, a couple of old friends later and a few stops for refreshment, he'd managed to find the campground and the car he'd had described to him.

"Now we have a big fat man snoring in our campsite. He

claims you two won't mind." Marla was clearly unhappy about it. "But I don't care, anymore. Skylar's taking me to the aquarium today, and you get the fat man."

Daggett was laughing by that point. "With red hair, and a waist about this big?" His hands made a circle in front of him.

"So, he told us the truth." She didn't seem any happier. "And why did you two not come back last night? When that van showed up, and you weren't there, I panicked."

Her eyes had grown red, and it seemed she might cry.

Geraldine smiled. "My fault. I sent everyone who could give us a ride away. We were stranded."

"We had a blanket, though." Daggett grabbed it from her and waved it in the air.

The red tractor towing the green frog was on its way back by then, and Geraldine grabbed the blanket and ran toward the car, shaking it in the air as she did so. Corky had come after all, and that made her morning all right, even if a giant green frog had tried to swallow her in her sleep.

Chapter 31

GERALDINE saw Corky's arms out wide, and she broke into a run.

"Geri, my girl!" He wrapped her in a hug. "All my mornings should start with such a beautiful sight." More quietly he whispered, "Thank you for the invitation. I hear Daggett's done quite well."

"Did you arrive in time to catch him on the water?" Somewhere in the distance, an air horn blew, reminding them a surf competition was in progress.

When he stepped back, he winked. "I looked for *you* on the water. I never knew such a fearless girl in all my days. Remember that time on Ocean Beach? We only realized it was the remnants of a hurricane after we got back to the shop."

She laughed. "Do you remember the leak in the storeroom? I think it was the drainpipe that came loose, and we moved buckets for two days until the storm broke. Even your loft above the shop wasn't safe. One clerestory window had come loose, your couch was soaked, and I had to crash on the floor.

"However, you changed the subject. I know you, Corky. You deal with what you want, and you simply brush all the rest away." *Like your children.* She couldn't say that. Besides, she didn't hold it against him. It was just the way he was, and if he tried to be different, he wouldn't be the man she loved.

"I tried to get here in time yesterday. I really did." He dropped his eyes, shaking his head. "However, problems, problems. Drive an old van and drive old problems."

"Get a new one."

"I've got a better idea. I'll keep this one. It carries my boards." He grinned, slapping the side of the rusty heap. "Besides, it has memories. Baja. So, how's my best protégé these days?"

"Daggett blew everyone else out of the water. He could go pro, if he wanted. You'll see today. The finals are this afternoon. He's already qualified."

"I was talking about you. You can dodge a question as well as I can. Daggett doesn't want to go pro, does he?" His eyes were on the blond-headed surf god by then. Daggett wrestled with Flotsam, occasionally grabbing at Skylar's ankle, causing the big animal to nip at the smaller man's feet. "You could have, if you'd chased it hard enough."

Corky had been teaching her, and she'd progressed beyond all his expectations. In spite of that, she knew why she hadn't. She'd wanted a father, not a mentor, and she'd run for emotional survival. She'd found Daggett, and while the ocean was his first love, she hoped she came in a close second. At least, she tried to convince herself of that. Sometimes she was even successful. Now, Corky had her emotions scrambled, and she changed the topic of conversation.

"I think they have showers here. You know, Corky, I might try to find them." She laughed, running her hand over her ear

223

and through her hair on one side. She could feel the grit. "I slept on the beach last night, and hot water sounds good to me." She felt her voice break at the end. She had wanted to say, My car's broken, and Daggett needs you, and so do I. Instead, she touched him on the arm and asked, "You are staying for the afternoon? Daggett's in the finals. He'd enjoy knowing you were watching."

"That's why I came." He turned to see Flotsam leaping from inside his van with the biggest bag of bagels Veteran's Park had known in decades. "Hey! Those are my lunch."

Flotsam had a good memory, and he knew where the campsites down the road were. When Corky tore after him, sprightlier than a man his size might be expected to run, the dog took off, stopping to shake the bagels with enthusiasm, only running again when Corky got close. The real hilarity kicked into gear when several small dogs saw the fun and leaped from their owners' hands to join the fray. Soon it was a pack of half-a-dozen animals ripping and tearing at the plastic packaging. The bagels tumbled over the ground, and the animals snapped the bread up. Before long, the parade of canines had knocked the red tent down, sent one pan of frying bacon flying into the fire, and trampled several drying towels in the dirt.

Corky walked back into camp with the bag held high in one hand, the side tattered, and most of the bagels broken or gone altogether. Several of the smaller dogs, trailed by embarrassed-looking owners, leaped for the bag, hoping for more.

"Share, Corky." Daggett grinned, pointing to the pack of dogs. "We have more food."

"Do you have bagels?" he asked, disgust on his face.

Geraldine thought he looked a hoot, his shirt stretched over his ample girth, his balding head of hair cut insanely short, and a bright red sunburn slashed across his forehead. Baggy flowered shorts hung to his knees. He might not look the masterful surfer he was, but the people who had learned the sport under him would vouch that there was none better.

"Marla, Skylar. Do we have bagels in the car?" Daggett grabbed at Flotsam, catching him and snapping his leash on. Corky had begun tossing the remains of his lunch to the yapping dogs, laughing as the golden retriever tried to hog the scraps.

"We have most of Mrs. Nettleworth's strawberry pie," called Marla, "unless Janjak snuck down for more while we were out."

"I be not a thief," a voice rang from another campsite. "Honest music be all I play."

Geraldine laughed. This was a perfect weekend, and she wouldn't trade it for any other.

"HEY, JANJAK, any bagels down there?" Daggett repeated as he yelled the request, turning to Corky and throwing one arm around him. He had missed this man. He motioned to Skylar. "Go check. Zac might be good for some, or try Kolbe. He has enough food for a dozen people. He's bound to have bagels. We'll take care of you. Don't you worry, Corky."

"Daggett," Geraldine called softly. When he glanced at her, she pointed to Corky's face.

He turned to see the big man's eyes glistening.

"Going soft, old man?" Daggett grinned. "And over a few bagels?"

Corky put one hand to his face and wiped roughly under his eyes, then forced a grin on his face. "I told you once you were polished. Remember?"

"Yeah. That summer down Baja way." Did he remember? It had been the best moment of his life.

"I missed seeing you in the competition yesterday." Corky's eyes were damp again and he coughed once, then sniffled. "I'm sorry. I should have made it down. Geri said you blew the competition out of the water. I would have liked to see that."

"You're here today." He patted the older man's shoulder. Then he pressed a finger to Corky's chest to emphasize his next words. "Anyway, you should have been the one out there. You're the real gem on a surfboard. There wouldn't have been any competition. Me? I was lucky just to be polished."

"Oh, is that so?" Corky chuckled. "Those trained by the best become the best. Is that how it is?"

"Oh, you old fart. I don't see you enough, and I'm glad you're here." He gave him a quick hug and pushed him away. He pointed. In the distance Skylar headed back with a package of bagels in his hand.

"For you, Corky." Skylar held them high. "Onion."

He was trailed by both Zac and Kolbe. On the way, Kolbe ran past another small tent and stopped to slap the top. "Out of bed, Sparky. The big guns are here." He continued to pop the taut fabric, laughing, even as Sparky yelled back to be left alone.

Kolbe's slapping wasn't perhaps in the best of timing, because Flotsam had just finished his final bagel, and he thought it meant it was time to play. He leaped for the tent, nipping at Kolbe's dancing feet, and then at the tent fabric, barking, as Sparky tried unsuccessfully to hit back at Kolbe.

It was when Sparky partially unzipped the flap that things really became interesting. He gave Flotsam a target, and inside the big dog went, toppling him over backwards. The tent walls shook violently. A few unintelligible curses filtered out, then Flotsam flew through the half-opened flap, a pair of very familiar dark blue boxers in his teeth.

Sparky came half out of the tent, his hair all askew, and his face sputtering. "Wha—!" He raised one fist, shaking it at Flotsam. "That's my only pair, you dog, you!"

"He's not coming back, Sparky." Kolbe laughed.

"Go get him," he demanded, pointing. "This is your fault."

"But they're your underwear." Kolbe walked off, laughing.

"Not fair!" Sparky nearly came out of the tent before he realized there were women present. Then, growling, he dug around in the tent for a moment, coming up triumphantly. He now held a shirt around his waist, and he took off after the dog.

Sparky's chase gave Veteran's the best entertainment of the weekend, with a big golden dog flying full speed, carrying a pair of blue boxers in his mouth, and a bare-skinned, wild-haired surfer chasing him, wearing only a white tee wrapped around his waist. During the exhibition that morning, people laughed, Marla tossed a towel at Sparky, and then someone else tossed a pair of trunks his way. Soon, he was dodging boxer shorts, shirts, and anything else anyone could grab. Even Corky forgot about his destroyed bagels, as he laughed and laughed, this time wiping his eyes because the scene was so funny.

And that was why only a few people in the park noticed the latest quake that rocked the California coast, sending the bells of San Carlos Cathedral into peals of joy to announce the Sunday morning call to prayer. Those from Monterey and Carmel-by-the-Sea would have known that something was wrong, for the resounding echoes weren't those of the cathedral's regular Sunday melody. Instead, they were a jumbled cacophony of sounds, rather pretty in a discordant way, and they spoke of stirrings in the earth that wouldn't be denied.

"Listen, the bells are ringing again," Geraldine whispered into Daggett's ear. "I'm glad Corky came. It wouldn't be the same without him."

"Hm," he whispered back, a grin building on his face. "You might be right about that." It was more than that, though. His life wouldn't be the same without Corky. He was more than glad his mentor, his *father*, had come down, and he hadn't had to ask.

That was the best part of it all.

By the time it was over, Sparky had enough clothes to do

him another week, although the blue boxers with the yellow face had disappeared. Flotsam probably knew where they were, but then, he wasn't telling a soul.

Chapter 32

DAGGETT dripped water as he ran onto the sand, the heat complete, the remaining dregs of the rampaging waves dying around his feet. His heart beat a drum in his chest, and his breath came in huge gasps.

Patting his surfboard and giving it a kiss, he passed it off to Janjak, who had been at his side all afternoon. He jogged to the tented structure reserved for the competitors, dropping into a seat.

He had waved off the interviews this day, finally feeling the pressure to perform at a level that he rarely pulled from himself. The reason was obvious to those who knew him well.

Corky was watching.

The warm afternoon sun was the mistress of the day, stoking the final heats into a frenzied struggle for first place, as well as a hefty purse. The blare of the air horn, the scratchy loudspeaker system, and waves that struggled to match those from yesterday had forced Daggett to earn every move. His eyes studied the leaderboard, every point counting, certain each time that this run would be the one that knocked him from the competition.

Anyone paying attention could tell Corky saw with different eyes. So did Geraldine. Everyone in the crowd, in fact. Daggett's moves were smooth, his feet planted on his board, and he turned even his mistakes into magnificent feats of prowess. No wave dared close out on him, and not once did he get drilled. The one time he was shacked, the crowd just knew the barrel was closing up on him. Then he came through the whitewater, kneeboarding, pumping his board until he was back on the face. There was perfection in every nuance, and when his high scores went on the board, it came as no surprise.

Daggett barely noticed. He had Corky on his mind.

DAGGETT'S companions, Corky and Geraldine and Skylar and Marla, sat in chairs today, ones pulled from the back of Corky's van. The event-watching was livelier than the day before, with Corky playing pranks, squirting water down shirts, and finding ways to drop sand where no sand should ever go.

Geraldine squealed as ice slipped down her back. She jumped to her feet, yanking at the neck of her shirt until it fell through. She admonished him, "Corky, we're here to watch Daggett."

"Ah, Geri, he's just having a little fun—" Marla began, as the big man reached to chase Geraldine with more ice.

"Stop him, Marla!" Geraldine's voice held steel.

Marla grabbed Corky's arm.

"Geri, you should have seen yourself jump!" Skylar held his stomach in laughter, his face now redder than his hair.

However, he couldn't laugh and watch at the same time, and he leaped up as Marla forced Corky's hand down the back of his shirt, dropping several cubes of ice into his clothing. His shirt was tighter than Geraldine's, and the ice didn't come out until

230

the shirt came off. He fell into the sand, sending mountains of sugar-fine powder spraying over Flotsam, who simply wagged his tail and ignored him.

"Ooh, do it again, Corky!" Marla bounced in her chair and clapped. "Down his shorts this time!"

"Marla!" Geraldine's reprimand was stern, but her laughter told otherwise. "This is a public beach."

"Janjak!" Corky waved at the tightly-wound head of hair. "Are you free a minute?" He motioned him over.

"Yes, Mr. Corky, although I must watch for my friend." He pointed to the tent where Daggett awaited his final heat. With his own surfing, he'd been cavalier. With Daggett, he was all business.

"Our friend seems to be doing very well." Corky motioned towards Daggett's tent. "What do you think?" He grinned.

"I think beautiful music be playing." His face burst into a smile. "The gods in the oceans sing for us, and those that know how to dance, dance especially well this day."

"Our Daggett dances well, then?" Corky laughed, slapping Janjak's shoulder.

"Oh, very well."

Conversation stopped as an air horn blasted the afternoon, and the loudspeaker crackled into life. "Here at Surfjam Monterey—" Someone interrupted, and the speakers went quiet for a minute. When the announcer returned, he expressed his regrets. "My apologies to the local crowd. Here at Surfjam Carmel, we've reached the finals in our two-day competition. First up is our perennial crowd pleaser for the weekend. Please give a cheer for Daggett Priestly, number seventeen." The crowd was quiet for a second as the speakers crackled oddly, and mixed voices, somewhat muted, continued, "I know this has been billed as Surfjam Monterey . . . I understand, but for the local crowd, you know . . . Well, this is Carmel . . . Oh, we're

231

still live?" and with an electric pop, the speakers went silent.

Scattered laughter sprinkled the air, and then, louder, hand-clapping started up slowly, increasing in volume when Daggett appeared. Several sharp whistles went up, and Geraldine jumped up and yelled out his name.

She wanted Daggett to win, for Corky's sake as well as hers. After all, he'd shown up, and this was Daggett's moment to shine.

AT THE FIRST mention of Daggett's name, Janjak had taken off across the sand to pull the proper board from the others in their special tented enclosure. Daggett walked down the beach, his shirt tight over his torso, his number on the back, and the Surfjam logo bold at the bottom. The water was cold, but it felt good to his surf-warmed muscles. He ignored those behind him as Janjak handed him his board.

In front, the ocean stretched to the horizon, with Carmel Bay pinched on two sides by great fingers of land, Pebble Beach and Monterey on the right, and Point Lobos on the left. The surf rolled in. The wildness of yesterday was gone, and the easy sets of waves came one after the other.

The water was clean, but the choice of waves was an important one. Some of the most likely ones seemed to close out early, rolling onto the beach, others backing off as deeper water stole their force. The wave Daggett choose today could be the determining factor in winning or, while not exactly losing, coming in second place. With Corky watching, to Daggett, second place seemed an awful lot like defeat.

He ran, dropped his board, and fell onto it, his arms paddling for all he was worth. The sounds of the crowds disappeared, and all he could hear was the water. The wave was a perfect floater, although that flashy maneuver had gone out in the 90s. With a few cutbacks, he built power, commanding the wave, doing 360s, and giving up a few tailslides, until he was on the inside, riding it to a shorebreak, and finally walking away from the wave as if there had been nothing to it.

The judges knew better. He had worked a wave that some would have seen as unworkable, and he'd mastered it. The crowd supported the judges' analysis, even though the scores had yet to be posted. Cheers and handclapping accompanied his exit from the water, with those from Skylar and Marla the loudest of all as they tore across the beach to shout their approval.

Daggett smiled as he heard the crowds begin to yell, and he handed his board off to Janjak as he wiped the water from his face and shook it into the sand.

GERALDINE watched her friends take off. She knew Daggett would be exhausted. Congratulations given now, when other surfers had yet to show their mettle, would bounce off deaf ears.

"He's done, Corky." She smiled, reaching to take his hand. It was her father's hand, even if he didn't know it. "What did you think?"

"I think you could have beaten him, hands down." He leaned in and kissed her on the forehead. "Daggett wasn't my best, although I'll deny that if you tell him so."

She laughed. "You old charmer, you. You show up a day late after not telling us you're coming, and still, everyone melts in your hands. What god did you sell your soul to for such magic?"

He didn't answer. Instead, he pointed with one beefy arm. There in their sights plied the weekend crowd from Carmel, Monterey, and beyond. Some rested on folding chairs, and others sported bare feet, walking in the surf. Small, bare-shouldered children ran around like little wind-up toys, urchins, grommets ripe for hazing on other days when the city's elected officials and paid law-enforcement officers weren't watching.

Beyond it all was the water, the blue sea, the waves curling as they reached for the shore, the latest contestant giving his best to win against all comers.

That wasn't where Corky pointed, though. His arm swept past what they could easily see, out to the deep ocean on the far side of Carmel Bay, the one that stretched uninterrupted to the other side of the world.

Finally, he spoke.

"That's my god out there. Nothing is more important than the sea, and if there's a god somewhere in this world, that's where mine's found. Blue, cold, and willing to take your life if you're not good enough to face its challenges."

Then, he cleared his throat, and his introspective mood vanished. "Come, Geri. Let's go find that boy of mine. Let's tell him how well he's done." He stood, his folding fabric beach chair shifting and groaning as he pushed against it.

"Go." She waved him on. Now wasn't Daggett's time for praise, even if others wished to offer it.

"Are you sure? He needs to hear it from you, also." He held out his hand and tilted his head the direction of the beach. Daggett couldn't be seen, but Skylar and Marla could. They ignored the latest competitor on the water, instead waving and calling into the tented enclosure, attempting to attract Daggett's attention.

"He will. Go, Corky. Daggett needs you all to himself for a while. This is the world he loves, and you're part of it. I'd just be intruding. Go, now." She sat back and closed her eyes. An air horn went off, telling of another surfer finished with his final run in the weekend's competition, and cheers rose from the crowd. The clapping and shouts weren't as loud as Daggett's had been, and she smiled at that. In the warmth of the afternoon sun, the cheers became sea-shells clattering around her, the melodic sound of loosely strung wind chimes; and an intense wash of fragrant flowers filled the air. She breathed in deeply. It was wonderful.

The slightest brush on her shoulder brought her eyes open, and she glanced up to see palm trees lining a sandy beach. She wasn't in California any longer.

"Avec ceci?" The clink of glass on a small table at her side broke the silence.

"Yes?" She looked to see a tall man, dark-headed, in a formal white suit, with a black velvet collar banding the top of his jacket. He wore a name tag, Paul. "Oh, Paul. Is this for me?"

"Oui." He nodded in a nondescript way, as if he possibly knew some English, but to press his abilities too far would be to risk a breach of etiquette that would be intolerable. "Avec ceci?" he repeated with a small bow.

She laughed brightly, giving in to the obvious. Oui would be the only answer she got from him today. She waved him away, standing from her linen-covered lounge and stepping forward. White flowers were strewn everywhere, hanging from trees, even lining a path out to the beach. The sun sparkled on water so clear and blue that it strained belief. White-shelled wind chimes hung from every branch, and when the breeze blew, they tinkled in the wind.

Walking forward, she noticed a group of cloth-draped chairs off to one side, and a tall backdrop of white lilies backing a low podium.

"A wedding! How entrancing! I love it." She twirled in the sand, soaking up the beauty of the location, so perfect for a wedding. She realized she wore a white dress and held a bouquet of white flowers in her hand. "I must be part of the wedding party," she called to no one in particular.

Walking to the beach, she ran one hand along the backs of the chairs, just touching the white satin ribbons that stretched from row to row, cordoning off each set of seats until the wedding party arrived. At the front, near the flower bedecked podium, the seats had little name tags placed in each one. She laughed when she saw Marla's name next to Skylar's. Even in her dreams they were a couple. She let her eyes rove over a nametag specifically for Mrs. Nettleworth, then one for Mr. Chickawaddy. What a pair they would make! Then there was Ronnie, although Daggett's cousin had no chair at her side. Across the aisle were Zac, Kolbe, Sparky, even Janjak and Jon, all Daggett's friends. That made her smile. Her friends were on one side, and Daggett's were on the other.

She looked for Corky's name, for a moment puzzled not to find him. Then she moved to the front row, wondering if she would recognize the parents of the bride. She frowned momentarily when she realized there was only one chair reserved for the bride's parents. The wind had flipped the tag upside down, and with a careful finger, she turned it over. Corky Maiterson. How could Corky be the father of the bride?

The clues hit home. A wedding. The bouquet. Her friends on one side, Daggett's on the other. Corky as the father of the bride.

In the distance, she saw Paul. He carried a drink on a silver tray, coming from nowhere and headed to nowhere. She called, "Paul?"

"Puis-je vous aider?"

"Paul, is all this for me?" She motioned to the wedding accoutrements.

"Oui." He smiled generously, giving a slight bow. When she turned away to look at the beach, and then back to him, he waited a moment before nodding his head receptively and moving on about his business.

Oui. Of course it was all for her. Whatever she asked, oui would be the answer. Yes, Geraldine, yes, yes, yes.

She smiled, walking down the aisle as if the wedding were really in progress. With the bouquet clutched at her waist, she nodded to nonexistent guests, spoke for a moment to Mrs. Nettleworth, even gave a little wave to Janjak. Her heart pounding, she knelt and spoke heartfelt words to Corky, thanking him for coming to her little extravaganza. With anticipation, she turned to where Daggett must be, at the podium waiting on her, this most anticipated moment making her giddy—

"You cannot sleep through this, Geri." Marla shook her arm violently. "Didn't you hear the loudspeaker? It's all over, and our Daggett took first place. They're headed to the awards podium now."

"Awards podium?" She shook her head to clear her thoughts. She had been getting married, and now she was to attend an awards program?

"Here. These are for the winner. I can't believe you couldn't smell them." Marla thrust a large spray of white lilies into her hand. "Hurry. You have to be the one to hand them to him. If you don't, that bimbo from the leaderboard will get the honor."

Marla grabbed her arm, nearly dragging her from her chair. All across the beach, people were packing up coolers and knocking sand off shoes. The smallest of the grommets had grabbed old surfboards, jumping into the water to imitate the most insane moves of the weekend. Most failed miserably, but a few mastered some elements of the highest-scoring routines.

"Hurry," Skylar called, waving his hand. Corky was at his side, beaming, his eyes on Daggett. The speaker system was already scratching the air with its proffered awards.

"In our Iron Tube event, give a hand to Ian Sommerveldt from Honolulu, Hawaii, for the best barrel of the weekend. From Fort Ord, Lieutenant Matt Orson won his division for the second straight year. And from the Northern California Coast, winner of the Overall Men's Division, and also winning a spot in the upcoming Chotsky Blue Ribbon Malt Surf Series at The Point in Ventura in September is Daggett Priestly, walking away with a purse of—"

The winning prize amounted to nearly fifty grand, but the amount was drowned out by ecstatic cheers from the crowd, not the least of which came from those gathered around Corky and Geraldine. When the speaker continued, Marla gave Geraldine a push toward the podium.

"And we have a special treat for our Overall winner." The announcer laughed. "Now, where are those flowers? Ah, there they are, with the pretty lady in the golden hair. Come on up, Miss. The white lilies have been donated by Tiger Lilly Florist, located on Seventh Avenue and San Carlos in downtown Carmel-by-the-Sea. That's Lilly with two ells. Tiger Lilly Florist, voted best in Carmel by the Carmel Pine Cone. Get them while they're hot, folks."

Trapped by the proceedings, Geraldine vamped up to Daggett, doing a few steps from her "love will keep us together" variety act, and giving him a big kiss on the cheek. Immediately after, one of the sponsors walked up with a Styrofoam check as tall as he was and handed it to Daggett, as flashbulbs immortalized the event for the local news. Needless to say, the video cameras were running the entire time. They had yet to cease recording each and every event for Surfjam's upcoming documentary.

The podium began to empty immediately afterward, with small boys running up to Daggett to get a fist bump or a high five. One of the sponsors hovered at Daggett's elbow, telling him the process involved to claim his prize money.

Daggett was all smiles, stoked, and he wrapped his arms around Geraldine, before being pulled away by the adoring crowd of pint-sized urchins. Laughing, stumbling under the pull of their arms, he mouthed at her, five fingers flashing in the air, "Fifty big ones!" It was enough to repair her car, he intimated, his hands turning an imaginary steering wheel.

"Sweetie, you picked the best man in the world." Marla stood next to her with her arms crossed, having appeared out of nowhere, admiring the blond man with kids climbing over him like crabs over a new meal.

"For?" She looked sideways at her friend, wondering what that statement was all about. Marla already had Skylar, or so it seemed to her. What was the sudden admiration for Daggett?

Skylar interrupted her answer as he came up dragging Flotsam by the collar. "This dog is going to be the death of me, yet." He gasped, out of breath from wrestling the big beast. "He tried to steal someone's nachos, and I barely pulled him away."

Geraldine whistled and snapped her fingers. Flotsam ran to her and cowered, his tail between his legs. She knelt at his side and picked up his muzzle to study his face. He licked his lips in a tentative fashion.

"Look, Skylar, he's hungry." She stood, glancing around for any leftover food she could give the dog. Seeing an unfinished hamburger on one of the rented beach tables, she stepped over and spoke to the family there. With a smile of thanks, she reached and took the burger, bringing it back to Flotsam. He immediately sat, his tail wagging, and his tongue out. He snapped up the remains of the burger, and with barely a chomp to break it apart, swallowed it.

"But—" Skylar choked.

"See? He'll be okay, now. Go, Flotsam. Skylar will get you some more leftovers." She looked at the dog and pointed to Skylar. Flotsam paused, then dug his feet in and took off towards the redheaded man, barking and dancing around him with excitement.

"Well, you get to sit with him on the way back." Skylar

made a face. "I remember how he smelled the other night. I figured if he didn't eat, then he wouldn't smell, and we'll be in the car a long time if we head back tonight."

Marla snorted, whispering in an exaggerated voice, "Like I said, your man is the best." Skylar was already gone, Flotsam pulling him through the sand. She chuckled. "But mine sure is cute. He just has a few wrinkles to iron out."

"Explain your sudden admiration for Daggett."

"Oh, that." She laughed, giving a toss of her hand. "He just offered to drive home, letting the rest of us sleep if we want, and after he spent all afternoon out there winning this contest. I'd be just about dead. Although if he only does fifty, it might be six in the morning before we get there."

"He offered to drive home? I didn't hear any offer to drive home." She knelt to reach for the blanket, clearing things away so she could shake it out.

"Oh, don't be so modest for him. He called out fifty and showed you he had the wheel. How much clearer could he be? I thought everyone knew that's sign language for driving fifty on the highway. Here, I'll put that in the trunk."

Marla grabbed the blanket from Geraldine. It was a mess, bunched up, with small piles of shells and other things that had entertained them during the afternoon. As she shook it out, shells and bits of seaweed sloughed off, making a tinkling sound as they scattered. She began to fold it, humming a catchy tune.

Geraldine offered, "Maybe I'll drive. I slept most of the way down. It's my turn, I think." Anything to save Daggett the chore, although the idea of six hours behind the wheel was dreadful.

"Or, if you like," Marla chirped in with a smile, "we can always stay another night in the park. A little snuggle under a blanket would do me fine. It's your choice. If we head back, you must know it's got to be six by now, and that means midnight before we get home, even in the best conditions."

"We have to think about food if we're on the road all night. Eating out is expensive. And don't forget I have to work tomorrow night."

"Food's no problem. I saved back enough from the aquarium this morning to stop and eat on the way, my treat. Still, that means home will be closer to two. Either way, I'm game, since I get to ride in back with Skylar." She giggled, feeling in her pocket for a piece of gum. Pulling one out, she unwrapped it as she spoke. "I'm no dummy. Oh, and did I give you my keys?"

"I don't keep up with your keys. I hope you haven't lost them." No dummy? Losing her keys might say otherwise.

"Well, earlier I thought Skylar might have had them, but he said he hasn't seen them. I thought for sure I put them in my pocket after parking the car. Did you see them on the blanket before we folded it?"

"You folded it. Not me," Geraldine reminded her.

Marla grimaced. "Uh, oh. I wonder if my auto club covers lost keys."

"Did anyone say keys?" Corky had taken his chairs to his van. They turned to see his burned head back again, and he had a mischievous grin on his face.

"What do you know that we don't?" Geraldine shook her finger at him. "I know you for the prankster you are. Do you have them?"

He grinned wider, rubbing his big hand over the top of his head. "I know someone lost their keys. Yours, little lady?" He nodded at Marla, pulling a set from a pocket, and jangling them loudly.

"You were eavesdropping, you old sponger. Aren't girl things ever private?" Geraldine teased, putting her finger in the center of his chest. She reached for the keys, and he pulled them away, causing them to clink merrily.

"Eavesdropper?' He laughed, grabbing her hand and bringing it to his lips, kissing her fingertips. "I don't have to eaves-drop to know when someone loses their keys."

"So, how do you know I lost them?" Marla stepped forward. "Are these them?" She grabbed the ones from Corky's hand. Then, frowning at them, she tossed them back.

"I'm standing on them." He laughed, the sound coming from his chest and turning into a cough. His next words were rough with broken laughter. "I saw them fly out when you shook the blanket."

"Then move your foot." Marla bent over, slapping towards his leg. He leaped back, and sure enough, there they were, shiny against the white sand.

"Corky, thank you. Right, Marla?" Geraldine shook her head when her friend glared, murmuring a quick thanks and stomping off, dragging the blanket in the sand.

"And she's your friend?" He chuckled good-naturedly. He took her arm and wrapped his over it, patting her hand, and he began to move Daggett's direction. The younger man was in the surf, helping a boy about ten stand on his board. The boy was trying, but he was falling more than he was successful. Daggett was patient, giving him a chance, even with others waiting in line.

"Marla and I work together." Corky's actions left her plea-santly warm inside, as well as emotionally emboldened. Her broken car came to mind, as did the reason she'd contacted him in the first place. "Also, she has a car. Right now, I don't. Marla's how we got here."

"I figured out that you were all in her car. I didn't know why." They stopped and watched for a minute as the boy on Daggett's surfboard finally mastered standing, and Daggett cheered, picking him up and tossing him into the surf. Another boy immediately grabbed the board, hoping to be next in line. "Daggett would make a good instructor."

242

"That's high praise, coming from you." The warmth of Corky's arm against hers was pleasurable, a father's arm, even though he didn't know. Still, she enjoyed the touch. "You're the best, after all."

"Thank you. Not good enough to keep you interested, though." He chuckled. "You say right now you don't have a car. Does that mean you did?"

"Do you know Ronnie Bertram?"

"Um, I'm not sure." He cleared his throat. "Perhaps. Clue me in."

"Daggett's cousin. Ronnie's his girlfriend."

"Oh, oh. With the rusty Beetle?" He chuckled. "I never understood how she kept it on the road."

She laughed and shook her head, now embarrassed. "That's my rusty Beetle now. My broken rusty Beetle. You do know how to burst a girl's ego, Corky. I loved that Beetle."

"You bought it from her?" He looked at her with amazement. "What did you pay, if I may be nosy?"

"It was cheap. Very cheap."

"How cheap?" He had that impish grin again.

"They begged me to take it off their hands." She felt her face warm with the admission.

"Free? I remember that car, and she should have paid you money to take it away. It wasn't worth the effort to change the title over."

"She bought a new car and traded it in. The dealer wouldn't take the Beetle, and Ronnie said I could have it if I'd come get it. She did convince the dealer to change the title, so I wasn't out that. Cheap enough?"

"And now it's broken." He nodded as if he'd known it would be, and she should have asked his advice first.

"It bled to death." She remembered the poor thing in the carport, all its fluids gushing out underneath. She'd hated seeing it dying so clearly and publicly.

"I'm guessing you couldn't afford to have it fixed."

"And I've been hitching rides to work with my neighbor, and with Marla."

"You should have called me."

He patted her hand again, and to her, it felt like a father's touch. Then abruptly, she moved her arm, stepping away. She wanted it too much, and it would hurt later if she didn't keep things in perspective. She was one of his rescue children, and he treated her warmly because she was here right now, and for no other reason. His touch was not that of a father, and she'd better remember that.

To keep from hurting his feelings, she turned and smiled. "Let's go rescue Daggett. We need to talk about whether to drive home tonight, getting there at two in the morning, or to stay in the campground another night."

Corky only lived two hours away, and he was very persuasive, inviting Geraldine's entire carload to join him in San Fran for the night. His loft above the surf shop was rough, and he couldn't promise them all beds, but there was a bathroom, and he cooked a mean Mexican omelet for breakfast. There might even be new surfboards in it for the men, custom shaped by Corky in his shop. He'd just finished several new designs the previous week.

The keystone for Skylar was when Corky offered to let Flotsam ride in his van. Somewhere the dog had found a hot dog with onions on it, and already, even before they left the beach, Flotsam was passing smells that were painful to the human nose.

Geraldine was more than pleased. She got to spend time with her father, and Daggett could ride along in the van, alongside the man he considered to be his.

It was the perfect solution, one that solved all their problems. It even gave them a place to haul that oversized Styrofoam

244

check, right in the back of Corky's van.

Chapter 33

DAGGETT and Corky sat at a small table next to an equally small kitchen, silver beverage cans at their fingertips. Across the small room, Marla swirled amber fuel in her glass, a look of mock petulance on her face. Then, unable to hold the expression, she burst into sputtering laughter, rocking in her chair and covering her mouth with one hand. She was recounting events from the Monterey Bay Aquarium that morning, and this had been the best.

Skylar, sitting cross-legged on the floor at her side, burned with embarrassment.

Daggett stifled a grin, his eyes crinkling with laughter in spite of his efforts. Corky reached across the table, clasping him on the shoulder, hushing him.

"No," Geraldine interrupted, grabbing Marla's arm to get her attention. "I cannot believe it, with everyone watching? They just—"

"Yes! Yes!" Marla gasped out the words, wiping her eyes

with the back of one hand, her face red with laughter. "Right there in public."

"And you, Skylar, you yelled it out to everyone?"

"I couldn't help it. I didn't know fish actually *mate* in the water, not in the daytime, anyway, with everyone watching." His refreshment was in a brown bottle, and he reached to push it away, sliding it across the floor as a distraction. "They should swim into the ocean. They'd have all the privacy they need there."

"And just so you know next time, orcas are not fish. They're mammals. Even I know that." Marla giggled, a wave of her laughter slowly dying off, then her eyes tearing up again for another round.

"Did you expect that new babies just appeared?" Daggett called to him from across the room. "Of course they have to mate. Try it sometime. You'll like it."

"I know that. It was just that, that—" Skylar blurted, "Did they have to do it on the one morning I was there?"

Corky snorted, his own laughter threatening to erupt. He rapped the table and spoke softly to Daggett, "Leave him be. You were the same as a kid."

"I was the same at fifteen. The man's not fifteen." With a snort of derision, he took a sip of his drink and returned to a conversation already in progress. "You've never heard of him, you say? Honestly? Marla tells me he's famous."

"Chickawaddy? A dancer? With a name like that, you'd think I'd remember."

"Yeah. I see your point. Anyway, he comes into Geri's shop to have his hair done—"

"A man, at a beauty shop." Corky ran a hand over the remains of what used to be a full head of hair. "What is the world coming to?"

"Come on, Corky. You live in San Francisco." Daggett

247

chuckled. He also knew Corky interacted mostly with surfers, a testosterone-laden crowd, one for whom time on the water was more important than time in a beauty shop. Even if an oddball were to show up at his door carrying a surfboard, he'd only see the surfer and nothing else.

"Back to Chickawaddy." Corky stood, pulling the door to an old fridge open; and taking two cans out, he offered one to Daggett. Daggett waved his dissent, swirling his can to show he had plenty. Sitting, the chair creaking, Corky popped the top of his, and he took a sip. "How does a dancer come into all this?"

"You know Ronnie's Bug—"

"Geri's," Corky interrupted, taking another sip, pointing to her as he did so. "She told me."

"So, you know?"

"That it died. Not about Chickawaddy."

"Stop me if you recognize any of this." Daggett brushed tangled hair from his face. He hadn't showered, and he still had Carmel all over him. "Geri was stranded on the side of the road, and a fat cat car pulled up. This Chickawaddy dancer dude climbed out, all fancy. You know that Bug, more rust than not, barely running. He walked to the back, tweaked something, and it started right up. Didn't get dirty or anything."

"Just like that?" Corky knew there must be more. He waited expectantly.

Daggett looked impishly at him—an expression he'd picked up from the big man—before giving out his punch line. "It seems the man has a Porsche he's been rebuilding in his garage. He knew what to do, he said, because all Volkswagens are exactly the same." He grinned. "Anyone who's seen that little Beetle knows there's no similarity between any Porsche ever built and Ronnie's cast-off car. That's the funny part."

"Chickawaddy, huh? Thinks old Volkswagens are Porsches in disguise. I'll keep my eye out for him on TV." Corky let out a laugh.

"Hey, Geri, Baby." Daggett waved to catch her attention. The others had begun singing a tune—very off key—and Flotsam was yowling along. "Didn't you say your Chickawaddy dude is on public broadcast sometimes?"

"Weekends, Saturday afternoons, mostly, but some Sunday nights. Culture Theater. Turn the TV on and see." She blew him a kiss before turning back to the song.

When Flotsam let out an especially loud howl, she leaned and grabbed his muzzle to quiet him, only to have him pull away, toppling her to her side. She laughed, letting Marla help her up, waving to Daggett and Corky with a wink.

"Oops," she called to everyone.

"Never heard of Culture Theater, but I do get Channel 9. That's the public broadcast channel." Corky reached above the fridge to flip on a small set before sitting down again. He shrugged apologetically. "It has to warm up before it comes on. Now, your prize money, will you be able to use some of that to fix the car?"

"The Beetle?" Daggett pondered, turning his can in a circle on the table, before looking at the enormous check that leaned against Corky's wall. The numbers seemed huge to him. "It's fifty grand. I should hope so."

"Forty-nine and change, but I'm not counting. You'll have taxes, remember. Your expenses coming down—"

Daggett waved his hand dismissively. The trip had been done on the cheap.

"—and also what it will cost you to attend that other contest, the Chotsky Blue Ribbon Malt Surf Series. That's the big time. I do hope you plan to go."

"I don't know." He hadn't had time to process that bit of the winning news. All he wanted to do was surf, not worry about contests that weren't coming up for months. "I'm hoping I can buy Geri a whole new car."

"Your trust. It still pays you enough to survive?" Corky paused for a moment, watching the merriment on the other side of the room. "I know how fast the contest money will go."

"With Geri's pay, we're okay."

"Just not okay enough to fix her car." He pursed his lips, looking at the boy he'd taken under his wing a long time ago, now all grown up. "Even fifty grand, after it gets whittled down, might not be enough for a whole car."

The TV had come up, giving Daggett an excuse to shift the attention from his and Geraldine's finances. They could see a news announcer standing in front of a decorative stone and plaster building. The plaster had a crack snaking through it. Across the bottom of the screen, a red band emblazoned with white letters revealed that the segment had been prerecorded earlier in the day.

Daggett pointed. "You can turn to 9, now."

"Hold just a minute." Corky stood and pushed on a button, the sound rising to an audible level. The announcer's voice was somber.

"As you can see, this morning's quake, centered here in Napa, one of several that have hit Northern California in the past months, sent shockwaves across the countryside, damaging even recently constructed buildings. Some older structures fared worse—" Pictures flashed by, one showing a collapsed out-building, and still another a teetering windmill. "—although no injuries have been reported. Connie Grutenberger, whose family owns Windward Grape Winery, is here to tell her story."

A blonde woman, very pretty, stepped into the picture and began to speak into the microphone.

"I know her." Marla had stopped to watch the news report. She stood, moving closer to the TV. "I mean, I don't know her, but she was at the beach yesterday."

"You sure?" From Skylar, with a frown.

"Her husband called her to tell her about the quake. It's definitely the same woman."

For a time, the woman's voice was the only one in the room, describing the damage to her family's winery. It seemed to be mostly superficial.

"Daggett," Geraldine called, her concern building. "I want to call Mrs. Nettleworth. I need to let her know we'll be home tomorrow afternoon."

"It's after nine. Are you sure?" He glanced at a clock on the wall. "Actually, it's nearly nine-thirty. She knows where we are."

"Corky? May I borrow your phone?"

He glanced at Daggett, who shrugged. "Sure. It's ancient, though. You'll have to dial it old-style."

"I remember." She took the cracked, corded rotary from him, motioning questioningly to the sliding glass doors and the deck beyond. He nodded, and she stepped to the door, pulling the cord after her.

Daggett frowned for a moment. His eyes rested on the sliding door. Through the glass, he could see the tops of the streetlights lining the boulevard. The sound of the surf crept through the crack where it wasn't quite closed. Across the room, Marla and Skylar still whooped it up.

"What?" Corky leaned forward, arms on the table. "I can afford the call."

"All of a sudden, just like that, she wants to phone Mrs. Nettleworth. Why the sudden concern?"

"Who's Mrs. Nettleworth?"

"My neighbor."

"Ah, the house on the point and the strawberry pie. I remember. She's calling *your* neighbor?"

"Don't start, Corky. You know what I mean."

Corky reminded him, "Geri lives there. She's her neighbor, too. Is that so odd to call a neighbor?"

Daggett stood, and he walked to the sink, dumping the rest of his drink, and crushing the can between his two hands. "Do you recycle?" When Corky pointed, he dropped the can in the proper bin. He leaned against the counter watching the partially opened door. Taking a deep breath, he said, "Not odd, not really. It's just that Mrs. Nettleworth checks on us, not us on her."

"Let her be concerned. It's a female thing." Corky reached to turn the TV to Channel 9, to find a number of dancers in garish makeup and costume moving across the screen in an outlandish and very modern dance. He shrugged, turning to Daggett. "If your Mr. Chickawaddy's part of that, who would be able to tell?"

Daggett glanced at the TV, then to the phone cord trailing across the room. "The news reporter came on, then Geri . . . She's not calling because of the quake, do you think? I mean, it was nothing. A cracked wall. We've had worse lots of times."

"Ask her." Corky nodded the direction of the door.

She walked in before anyone could do any asking. A worried look creased her forehead.

"Everything is okay?" Corky rose and took the phone. When he turned to set the instrument down, there was Flotsam. The animal plainly sensed something wrong.

"If no news is okay." She snapped her fingers for the dog to come to her, reaching to rub him behind the ears when he leaned against her leg. "She didn't answer, Daggett."

"So, she's asleep." Marla. That was obvious, her words suggested.

"Maybe. Before we left, she said her son would be visiting over the weekend, so he should catch it, even if his mother doesn't." She turned to look out the glass doors, absently pulling her hair back over one ear. The crease in her forehead was still there.

Daggett stepped to her and put his arms around her, brushing the hair from her neck with his lips. "Tomorrow we'll get back, Mrs. Nettleworth will be okay, and her son will have magically repaired the hole in the bathroom floor. Just wait. You'll see."

"Do they always dance this way? I hope your Chickawaddy's not part of this." Corky's attention was snared by the TV, and he looked puzzled, snorting his disgust. Then, flipping the set off, he turned to Daggett. "What hole in the bathroom floor?"

"You haven't heard?" Skylar pulled himself up from where he sat, excitement at the memory written all over him. "You think Marla's story was good? You'll love this. I nearly fell through the floor when the bathtub went all the way through."

"Your tub fell through the floor?" Corky sat heavily. "How bad a condition is the house in?" He rubbed his hand over his head, frowning at Daggett.

Daggett put a finger to his lips, returning Corky's frown. "The house is fine, Corky."

"The bathroom's not, though." Skylar grinned, barreling ahead with his story. "I was trying to fix the leaky faucet, then, bam, I was hanging over the ocean, about to die, when I was saved by Daggett."

"Not over the ocean," Daggett corrected. "There was ground underneath."

"Daggett saved you?" Corky's eyes were still on Daggett and Geraldine.

"Yeah. The tub dropped out from under me, and he grabbed my arm just before I fell. Water was spraying everywhere." At the look of astonishment on Corky's face, Skylar turned to Geraldine, his eyes pleading. "Geri was there. She can tell you."

"It was funny, right, Geri?" Daggett kissed her on the cheek.

253

"It must have been, you coming in seeing me running around in just a towel, everyone completely drenched. Right?"

"Well, I have to admit, Skylar's not much of a plumber." She let a small grin escape, and then she turned to him and kissed him gently on the lips. "That part was funny."

Later, with the story told and the excitement worn thin, Corky's one bathroom made for slow going for bedtime rituals. Volunteering to be last in line, sometime after midnight Daggett and Geraldine took Flotsam for a walk along the beach, giving the others time to do what needed to be done. Heading past the seawall and onto the sand, they walked to the surf's edge. It wasn't really dark, not with all the streetlights lining Great Highway, but they were alone, and it felt very private.

"Wind's died down." She took his hand, working her fingers into his. "It's nice."

"We're losing the swells, though." That only meant the normal California summer was back. The weekend in Carmel had been a welcome exception.

"I surfed this one time in a storm. Right out there." She pointed.

"You?" He laughed. This he'd never heard. "Not alone, I hope."

"With Corky. I worked for him in the shop, then, and I had no idea how dangerous it was. I was having too much fun. With Corky, I was all derring-do, immortal and fearless. Now I know better."

"But you did have fun." He wrapped one arm around her shoulder, content to watch the waves for a time, letting Flotsam run the empty beach.

"Whistle for Flotsam."

He did. He started to speak just as the light on the highway turned green, and a loud car squealing its tires drowned him out.

"I'm sorry, Daggett. One more time?"

254

"I was just thinking. That's all."

Another car drove by, more slowly this time, perhaps wondering who was on the beach at this time of night. She glanced back to see it was a patrol car, and she waved. Its siren sounded a quick burst, before it accelerated away, its lights blaring.

"The police are keeping us safe tonight, either that or keeping everyone else safe from us. They probably don't like the dog loose on the beach."

"Saved by a noisy car."

"You said something earlier. I missed it." She prodded him.

He laughed, but it wasn't a happy one. "I said I'm glad I never had a father when I was a kid. I always wished for one, but now I'm glad I never got my wish."

"Daggett! Don't be glad about that. Every kid needs a father."

"I know. But you see, Geri, if I'd had a father growing up, Corky never would have adopted me. More fittingly," and he laughed sourly, not absolutely sure Corky felt the same, "I never would have adopted Corky. I made him my dad, in my head at least."

"So, you have a father." She smiled, giving him a squeeze.

"He doesn't know, though. To him, I'm just a kid who hung out with him for a few years, and then he found other kids."

"You don't think he feels the same about you?"

"Nah. The old magic is still there anytime we get together, but that's Corky, no matter who he's with. I'm just another kid." He rocked on his heels, trying to keep his words from sounding rough. He laughed, brushing it off. "He taught me to surf, though. No father could have done better for his son."

"What would it take to convince you?"

"Of what?" He knew what she meant, that he was more than just another of Corky's kids. Suddenly determined not to wallow in self-pity, he broke away to chase Flotsam, his feet digging troughs in the sand. Soon they were in a tussle, the two of them wrestling, and then running off to be chased again.

GERALDINE watched the antics with amusement. Her question had been very real, more so than Daggett realized. It was one she had asked herself more than once. Even though she knew he couldn't hear her, she answered his question anyway.

"He does, you know."

Then, her eyes burning with emotion, in a whispered voice, she repeated her words with one slight variation.

"The way I wish he felt about me."

Chapter 34

"DO I REALLY smell bacon?" Geraldine stepped from the bedroom, a yawn on her face, and her hair in disarray. "I could love you, Corky, just for your bacon alone, and Daggett will love you even more." She stepped to him and planted a sleepy kiss on his cheek.

"Those two don't even know." He glanced up from his preparations for his Mexican omelets, and he pointed a pair of tongs across the room. Marla was in a blanketed ball on the two-person sofa, and both of Skylar's legs stuck out of an unzipped sleeping bag on the floor. His red hair was unmistakable against the dark green fabric.

"More for Daggett. I'm headed to the bathroom." She yawned again, clicking the door shut behind her. She looked in the mirror, wiping a small section clean with a towel. Around the edges and across the top were grease pencil notes, phone numbers and such. She'd forgotten how Corky did that, being all about the moment, and even more about the surfing. She also remembered how she'd worked to clean up his bookkeeping in the shop down below, encouraging him to hire good help once she'd decided to leave. She dug on the counter until she found the grease pencil she knew must be there. She tacked on her own message. *Loved ya' then and always will. G.* Then, flipping on the shower, she watched the mirror fog, the message disappearing. It would still be there, once the glass cleared.

She jumped at a sharp knock on the door.

"Yes?" She flipped the water off.

"I'm taking the dog for a walk." It was Corky. "Bacon's done and cooling. I'll be right back to start the omelets. Take your time."

"Thanks, Corky." She flipped the water back on, climbing in. It was when she was washing her hair that it hit her that she didn't know where Corky had slept. He'd given his bedroom to Daggett and her. Marla and Skylar had taken the living room. She didn't remember seeing Flotsam, either.

Coming out of the bathroom with her hair in a towel, massaging it gently with one hand, she stepped to the kitchen. Taking a slice of the bacon between the tips of two fingers, she tapped it against the plate. Hard and crunchy, the way Corky always prepared it. It was the only way he knew. She liked crunchy, though.

She heard the door, and she was pleased to see Flotsam come in, his tail wagging. He came to her, his eyes on her bacon, and his whine telling how much he wanted it. She pushed him away, looking up to see Corky putting a small plastic bag on the counter.

"So, Corky, my favorite surf instructor. Where did you sleep last night?" Now fully awake, she bit off a piece of the bacon, chewing for a moment. "This is good, you know."

"I know." He picked up a piece, breaking off half of it and putting the rest back on the plate. "My bacon always is. Can the dog have part of a slice?"

"He can have mine." She had almost finished it, and she held out the final tidbit for Flotsam, smiling when he snatched it expertly from her fingertips. "He likes it."

"Still, he'll need real food. I stepped to the store and got him some." He pulled a can of dog food out of the bag. "This will do until we get to Albion. I'll pick up some more there. I don't know that I want to drive into Little River once we get you home."

She studied him as he turned to open the can, at the same time dropping her towel to a chair. He'd said that so matter-of-factly, as if he were headed up to Daggett's with them. She walked to the counter, and she leaned against it, her arms crossed. "And so, Corky, where did you sleep last night?"

"Why is that important?" His eyes were busy with the can opener. Either that or he refused to look up. He reached for a bowl, setting it beside the opened can.

"Daggett and I had your bed, and those two over there took up everywhere else. It occurred to me in the shower that I hadn't seen the dog, either. That means you didn't sleep in this loft. Am I correct?" She watched him as he put the bowl of food on the floor, rubbing Flotsam's head as he tore into it. She pressed him, "Corky? Own up."

He turned his eyes to her, a twinkle telling much. "You caught me red-handed. You always could see through me, girl. Now if we can get those two up," he nodded Marla and Skylar's direction, "we might get on the road before noon."

She put her hand on his arm. "No, you don't, old man. You're avoiding my question. You invited us here, then let us run you out of your own home. Where did you sleep? Not in the shop?"

He frowned, horrified. "No! Absolutely not. My shop is a place of business, not for sleepovers." He grinned, working

259

Flotsam's fur with one hand. "Is it, boy?"

"Flotsam was with you wherever you slept?"

"Of course. We had our sleepover, and now we're all back together again. Aren't we, boy?" He spoke to the dog in baby talk. "We're heading home in a bit."

She let out a big sigh. "Okay, I give. You don't intend to tell me. However, I do want to know what you mean by we. You make it sound as if you're heading back with us."

He cupped her chin in his hand. "I tell everyone what a bright girl you are. See, you just proved me right. Now, watch."

He took a slice of the extra-crisp bacon, and he snapped it in half. He called to Flotsam, waving it in front of his nose.

"Corky, don't tease him." She pushed him on the shoulder. "You're a meanie, if you do."

"I'm a meanie, no matter. Watch, I said." When the dog got really excited, dropping his chest low to the floor and barking once, Corky whispered, "Fetch!" Then he tossed the bacon right onto Skylar's sleeping bag.

Flotsam leaped for it, and that was when the morning came alive. The big dog landed right in the middle of the sleeping bag, sending the bacon flying. Skylar came awake kicking. He attempted to fling the sleeping bag off, but with the dog on top, rooting for his bacon, it was a lost cause. The bacon had disappeared somewhere inside, and the animal wasn't leaving until he had it.

In the scramble, Skylar did manage to inadvertently grab onto Marla's blanket. It came flying off the couch, and in grabbing for it, she crashed to the floor. She was livid at first, but then she realized who was on the floor with her. She smiled, snuggling next to him.

It was only when the bacon was discovered that Flotsam quit rooting among the bedclothes. That was when tow-headed Daggett stepped from the bedroom to find Marla snuggled up next to Skylar.

"Skylar?" He blinked, yawning. "Marla?" He blinked several more times in disbelief, finally turning to look at Corky and Geraldine. "Surely they didn't spend the night in Skylar's sleeping bag."

"That's my fault, I'm afraid." Corky chuckled, reaching for the plate. "Bacon, anyone?"

"Corky's fault?" He pulled Geraldine aside, whispering in her ear, "Corky encouraged those two to spend the night together? I can't believe that. He's never done anything like that before."

"It's really Flotsam's fault, that and the bacon." She patted his cheek, tiptoeing to give him a kiss on the opposite side. "Corky only threw it all together."

"That's supposed to explain anything?" He rubbed his hand through his hair.

"It's as good as you're going to get." She pointed. Corky had thrown another piece of bacon onto the sleeping bag, and Flotsam was on top again, causing cries of alarm and indignation. "You'd better grab the bathroom while it's free."

"Sure." He moved that way, but just before closing the door, he looked at her and asked one more time, "Bacon?"

"Just enjoy the peace, Sweets. It's the last you'll have today." She kissed him then pushed him inside and pulled the door to. Her eyes caught Corky watching her, a studied look on his face. She walked to him, taking one of his hands. "What's the sour look for?"

"Your neighbor, the one who didn't answer the phone . . ."

"Mrs. Nettleworth? What about her?" With the antics of the morning, she had forgotten about the call.

"Nothing. Nothing." He patted her hand. "I'm just wondering what we'll find when we get there." Then his face brightened, and in a too-cheerful voice, he said, "We can expect beautiful weather for the drive up. I had the radio on this morning, and we'll see sunshine all the way to Mendocino."

"We don't go to Mendocino. We'll be home before then." She laughed. "Has it been that long since you've been to Daggett's?"

"I'll find it, if it's still on the highway." He turned to needlessly adjust the plate of bacon.

"Silly, of course it's still there, right where it was the last time you visited, even if that was before I moved in." It was only a small gibe, and she grinned.

"I hope so." He gave her a hug, and as his arms encircled her, he repeated, "I certainly hope so."

She watched as he turned to drop the bacon pan into the sink, and a chill ran down her back. She wasn't sure she really understood what he meant. He hoped he could find the house beside the highway, or he hoped the house was beside the highway? His words could be taken both ways.

The bathroom door interrupted her thoughts, as Daggett came through, his same swimsuit on, but wet and cleaner, and his entire body dripping water.

"A towel, anyone?"

"Oh, Daggett, I'm so sorry." She grabbed hers from the chair and handed it to him. "This one's mostly dry."

"Thanks, Geri." He kissed her as he grabbed it, toweling off as he turned away. "Shower's free," he called. "BYOT."

Skylar scrambled to his feet, heading that way. He slid inside, closing the door hard after him. The water could be heard immediately.

"What's BYOT?" Marla called out.

Daggett leaned out of the bedroom, his one clean shirt already on. "Bring your own towel. There aren't any in the bathroom."

"Oh," she said brightly. "So I should take Skylar one?" She

had her most innocent look on her face.

"Don't you dare," and Geraldine laughed, pointing at her friend. "He can come get one when he needs it."

The bathroom door opened, and a head of red and very wet hair peered out. "Hey, I can't find a towel." Running water could be heard through the open door.

"Finished already?" Daggett stepped from the bedroom and tossed him his. "It's mostly dry." He grinned.

"No, I'm just getting started, but thanks, Daggett. The water was getting in my eyes." The door slammed, and the sounds of splashing started up. "Hey, this towel is already wet," filtered out.

"Are there any dry towels?" Marla was sitting up on the floor, and she threw her question at anyone who might know.

Together, Daggett and Geraldine answered, "Skylar's is mostly dry." Then they burst into shared laughter.

Even Corky smiled.

Chapter 35

THE OLD van's windshield was cracked, and there was only one seat, the driver's. All the rest had been taken out long ago, broken or sacrificed for functional cargo space. A built-in surfboard rack in back could be altered to make a bench—a bed in dire straits—and that served as Daggett's seat. At the moment, Daggett was squeezed on the bench with the two surfboards Corky had offered, plus the two they'd brought with them. Transporting them in the van was easier than strapping them on the top of the small car.

Corky kept an old recliner in his shop, and it now served for the passenger seat. He had rigged a simple bolting mechanism to affix it securely to the floor. Geraldine snuggled there.

Ahead of them tooled Marla's small car, with Marla and Skylar inside. Flotsam rode in the van. The Mexican breakfast had his stomach active again, and Skylar had refused to allow him passage in the car's empty back seat.

"I always thought there must be a soft spot somewhere in

that tough exterior of yours. Daggett and I could have slept in the van last night, but I appreciate you giving up your bed." She reached and touched Corky on the shoulder. Smiling, she shifted down farther in the chair's corduroy fabric, glancing out the window at the California countryside floating past. Occasional houses sat back off the road, surrounded by trees, and she had seen several roadside stands, both empty and in use.

From the back of the van, a voice called to them.

"Soft spot? If he has a soft spot, I could use some of it back here." Daggett's bench was bare wood, except for an old sleeping bag he used for padding. "And we took this heap to Mexico?"

"And back again," Corky pointed out. "You were younger then, and you wanted adventure, not comfort."

"At least I had a real seat up front. What happened to it?"

"You didn't notice it was gone at Carmel?"

"I figured you had it stored in the shop. Besides, I didn't ride in the van at Carmel." The van lurched suddenly. With each bump in the road, the surfboards shifted, repeatedly knocking into him. "Ouch, that was a hard one. Are you trying to hit them all?"

"Up at Haystack Rock several years ago, I traded it for a classic board some guy had." Corky ignored the gibe about the bumps.

She chuckled. "You traded your seat for a surfboard?"

"Hey, he needed a place to sit, and there's only one of me." They had hit a hill, and the van was losing ground to their lead car. Corky reached to the gear lever and pulled it down into mid-range. The transmission whined, then jerked, and with a dreadful roar, the van began to gain speed.

"Hey, careful there." Daggett had slipped and scrambled for a handhold. "You've got a passenger back here."

"The old girl needs to know who's boss sometimes." Corky

reached out and patted the dash.

"You should have called my recliner, Daggett." She leaned to look in the back of the van to see what the noise was, but by then Daggett was settled once again. "It's comfy. Flotsam's not complaining about being back there, are you, boy?"

He lifted his head to look at her. When no food or further attention was forthcoming, he put it back down and closed his eyes.

"Thank you, Geri." Corky grinned. He called into the back, "Did you hear that? It's comfy."

Topping the hill, he slipped the gear lever back into drive. The old van paused for a moment, then with a loud clank, it jerked and settled into the new gear. Corky acted as if it were normal, pushing his elbow out the window to catch the breeze.

"Look at that!" He pointed through the windshield, and almost immediately he hit his brakes. "I just get up to speed, and now I'm going to lose it all."

"What?" Geraldine sat up, looking ahead to see Marla's brake lights on. She and Skylar were pulling off the road to a fruit stand under a small group of trees. A modest house sat off the road down a drive.

When the van began to slow, Flotsam barked once and came to stand with his head poking through the seats.

"Shopping, Marla?" She leaned out the window as they drove up, calling to her friend as she climbed from her car.

"Fruit, for your neighbor, Mrs. um—" She snapped her fingers.

"Nettleworth?" She already had the door open. She wanted any breeze she could entice into the van.

"Yes! The strawberry pie lady. How sweet would that be, for us to take her back all sorts of fruits? She can make you and Daggett lots of pies, then." She smiled brightly, motioning Geraldine from the van. "Come on. Help me pick out some. You can select the ones you like best."

Skylar climbed out of the car, yawning, his eyes taking in the surrounding countryside. "This isn't home. Where's the ocean?"

"A hundred miles north." Daggett unfolded from the back of the van. "Oh, does it feel good to have my feet back on solid ground!"

An older couple pulled up the driveway on an old golf cart, stopping at the stand. Heavyset, their faces were all smiles, and they waved merrily. "Sorry, dears. We were catching the news about the quake." The woman had an apron on, and she wiped her hands on the front.

"Tom. Tom Quincy." The gentleman stuck out his hand, taking Daggett's when it was offered. "My wife, Bette. Don't you worry about what she says. There's no damage at Quincy's Fruit Stand. We've been here forty years, and I guess we'll be here forty more."

"Quake? Oh, we know all about the one on Saturday." Marla laughed, picking up a pear. "Can you make these into pies?"

"Oh, no, dear," Bette said, already sorting the best of the fruit to the front of the trays. "Not on Saturday."

Marla made a face. "How about on Monday, then?" She laughed again, glancing at Geraldine. "What would we call that? Monday pie?" She winked.

"Don't tease, Marla." Geraldine turned to the proprietress. "May I call you Bette? The quake on the news, we were in Carmel on Saturday and heard it did some damage in Napa Valley."

"That was the little one, dear." She was still engrossed with her trays of fruit, and she replied in a preoccupied tone. "The latest is the one from last night. It all stayed up north, they said. That's probably why you didn't feel it."

267

Geraldine glanced at Corky still in the van. It was making sense, now, his sudden decision to drive them up, the news he'd said he listened to that morning. This woman's revelation was probably the same. She grew chilled. His earlier remark about Mrs. Nettleworth. Their neighbor hadn't answered her phone, and she always did so. Then he'd said he hoped Daggett's house was still beside the road.

Daggett picked up several pieces of the fruit, as if evaluating which he wanted. "Geri, plums." He looked at her and grinned. "I've not had purple plums in a long time."

"How far are we from home, Daggett?" She glanced up and down the road to see cars heading both ways. Nothing seemed out of the ordinary.

"An hour or two. Do you have enough money to get some of these?" He bit into one. "It's good."

"Sure." She reached into the van and pulled out a small bag. From inside, she carelessly pulled out several bills, handing them to Bette.

"My, dear. How many plums do you want? All of them?" The elderly woman held the bills loosely as if they might bite. "I don't have this much change with me, if the young man only wants the one he's eating."

"Change?" Pictures of cracked walls from Napa raced through Geraldine's mind.

"This is a little better, I think." Marla pulled the bills from Bette's hand, replacing them with one from her pocket. She walked to the van and put Geraldine's cash back in the bag. "Ger, I've got this covered. You seem a little distracted."

"A little?" Skylar was finally awake. "That looked like two hundreds. Must be good peaches. I guess with his winnings, Daggett can afford all of this."

"Winnings?" Tom Quincy's face broke into a smile. "You've been in a contest of some sort? I see you have surf-

268

boards in your van. I used to surf back East. Atlantic Beach, on the Banks."

"My good friend here—" Skylar threw an arm across Daggett's shoulders. "—won a contest in Carmel yesterday. Surfjam. Killed 'em." He flashed a hand sign with his fingers curled and only his thumb and pinkie extended. "He was sick!"

"Oh, dear! I hope you're feeling better." That was Bette, calling to Daggett. "You have my condolences, young man."

"He wasn't really sick," her husband assured her. "It's surfer talk. It means he was really good."

Daggett pushed Skylar's arm away. "I don't have the money yet, you kook. Besides, this is a plum." He slurped the last of the fruit off its seed, and laughing, he tossed it at Skylar, pegging him squarely on the chest.

Marla threw her wallet into her front seat, setting her sack of fruit in the back. "Well, I've done my shopping. Shall we head off? I'm feeling the need for a little air. From my a/c, if you don't mind."

"You got peaches?" Skylar called hopefully.

"Pears," she snorted, as she slammed the door. Once he climbed in the passenger seat, the engine started, her brake lights flashed, and her spinning wheels left gravel dust floating in the air.

Daggett opened the van door and whistled. Flotsam came running. He swung the door shut as Geraldine climbed into her recliner.

"Good to go?" Corky looked at his two passengers. On the dash, a small island girl wearing a grass skirt danced a merry jig. He cranked his engine, and at their nods, he pulled the lever into drive. He waited for a moment on a big truck, and then pulled onto the highway. "Your friend thinks I've got a hot rod back here. If she doesn't slow down, we might get there two days after them."

"That's fine." Geraldine murmured. After Bette's news of the quake, she couldn't focus on anything except what she might find at home.

"It's fine if they get there two days ahead of us?" He looked at her, puzzled.

"Corky, I might climb in the back and sit with Flotsam."

"With the dog?" He winked. "You sure? Daggett might like your attention more."

"Sure. He can sit up here." She turned to climb over the recliner.

"I can stop, Geri." He touched her on the arm. "It doesn't really matter about your friend getting farther ahead. We're already too far gone to catch up."

As if he hadn't made his offer at all, she pulled herself over, sending Daggett to the front seat, and getting his surprised thanks and a quick kiss in the process. Pulling the sleeping bag off the bench, she sat on the floor next to Flotsam. She had chosen the dog instead of Daggett because she didn't need company or conversation. Scenes of the house kept running through her mind, the uneven place in the yard, the sloping floor, and the cracked window in Skylar's room. The words from the fruit stand replayed themselves in her mind. *That was the little one, dear.* How big was the quake from last night?

She closed her eyes as Daggett struck up a lively conversation with Corky, and she listened to them compare the merits of surfing at various spots up and down the Pacific Coast, as compared to legendary surfing locales all around the world. For a time, she tried to call on Paul, or Pablo, or even Paolo to take her away, whether to the French Riviera, exotic Mexico, or to a ski resort high in the Alps. She never got farther than the back of the van, though with a warm dog at her side, her father behind the wheel, and the man she loved deeply involved in a meaningful conversation with him.

It wasn't enough. She couldn't get past the earthquake that had occurred somewhere in Northern California, and Corky hadn't wanted to tell her. Instead, he was making a four-hour drive from San Francisco—and then back again—when no one had asked him to.

She was glad he was with them. If there was bad news when they arrived home, she'd need him to be there for her. Daggett would, too. They would all three need each other.

Even Paul would have to agree, if she could ever get him to bring her some of that rum and coke she never seemed to get enough of.

Chapter 36

"DAGGETT, everything looks the same!"

Geraldine had finally dozed, and now she sat up to find the trip nearly complete. The scene out the window was a relief.

"Of course it does. We've only been gone two days." He had his right arm out the open window, and he let his hand float in the air, dancing up and down as entertainment. The curls at the nape of his neck spun in little pirouettes, ballet dancers in the wind. "I bet the beach is still there, too."

"Beach?" Corky ribbed him. "After being down in God's country, you still call your little niche in the coastline a beach? That's a good one."

In the distance was Mrs. Nettleworth's house, and Geraldine was pleased to see it silhouetted against the skyline. Closer, she could see the taillights of a car in the drive. She'd said her son was coming up. His car surely meant all was well there.

At her side, Flotsam could already smell the sea. His nose

was in the air, and after a moment, he scrambled to his feet, working his muzzle between Daggett and the open window.

"Can you smell it, boy?" He moved to give the dog room. "It smells like home, doesn't it?"

"I hope Mrs. Nettleworth didn't make her son work all weekend on that broken bathroom." Geraldine kept her eyes trained ahead. She couldn't see the house, yet.

"I hope she did." Daggett rubbed his hands together. "Then I won't have to."

"Corky, can you believe this man? He's willing to let someone else do his work. How's that for a man you helped rear?" Even as she joked, she searched. Everything would be fine. She knew that. It was just that until she could actually see the house, she wouldn't really be able to relax.

"A man after my own heart." He reached and patted the younger man on the leg with a chuckle. "Sure, a true surfer."

"You two are terrible. If he has, then we have to be really nice to Mrs. Nettleworth for a very long time." She felt giddy. The worry about the quakes was fading. All the damage—what there was—must have been in the interior of the state, bypassing the coast completely.

They slowed for the turn down Daggett's steep drive. The low roof, all that could be seen of the house from the road, became visible. Beyond, the sun glinted off ocean swells that repeated themselves until they disappeared against the far line of the horizon. When Corky swung the van into the drive, there was a sharp little jerk in the van's suspension, but there sat the VW underneath the carport, its earlier stains of spilled lifeblood beneath it, marking its untimely death throes.

"Gents and ladies, I think we beat them, unless our lead car was headed somewhere else. Skylar lives with you, doesn't he?" Corky pulled up behind the broken Beetle, shifting the old van into park.

"He's taken over my old room." Daggett turned to Flotsam. "Need to go, boy?" That brought a quick round of sharp barks, and he laughed. He snapped open the door, and before he could swing his legs out, Flotsam had already climbed over the back of the recliner, pushing past him to get outside. He ran into the yard, sniffing along the house foundation for anything that might be new.

"Geri, is that crack an old one? I haven't been here in a few years, but I don't remember it." Corky's eyes were on the house.

"Crack?" Her anxieties crawled back into her throat. "Where?"

"In the brick. See? Your planter." He released the door latch and swung it wide. Then he turned to her and laughed, brushing his concerns aside. "Probably it's not. This is an old house, and old houses settle. I've got cracks in my place back in Frisco, and not one of them from an earthquake. The builder was at fault. Get it? Fault, as in San Andreas?" He stepped from the van, stretching and yawning.

"I get it." She smiled. Still, she didn't remember the crack.

"Oh, and I see something on your front door, a piece of paper. Maybe it'll tell us where your friends are." He closed the van's door, and when it didn't catch, he opened it again, this time slamming it. It stayed shut.

She turned at the sound of the back doors opening.

"Unstrap the end of the top board for me, Geri." Daggett leaned in, his raucous head of yellow hair going from brilliant sun to shade, leaving the skin on his face suddenly darkened. He grinned, his teeth white against his brown. "I wouldn't want Corky to drive away with my new surfboard. Skylar's, I don't care so much about." He chuckled, giving a yank on his end, the strap falling loose.

"Daggett!" But she smiled as she pulled her end of the strap.

"Dude needs to be here to unload his stuff." He pulled one

274

of the new boards out, leaning it against the side of the van.

"I don't know who scribbled this note, but it's a mess." Corky appeared at the back of the van, shaking the paper in his hand. "It says, *Glue and Daze, Come plus zero pot bod. Here plus zero*—oh, that's not plus zero, it's to—*zero hop plus*—no, it's the word to, again, *choke meek's schedule.* I can at least read that word, thank goodness. Schedule." He looked up, a gleam in his eyes and a grin on his lips. "It goes on, *Boo ya, Luarla.*" He handed Geraldine the paper. "Make some sense of that."

She studied it for a minute, then she chuckled. "It does not say Glue and Daze, Corky. It says Geri and Daggett." She cut her eyes to him. Daggett grinned. She continued, "It actually says, Gone to get food—then to shop to check week's schedule. Love ya, Marla."

"You can read that?" Corky shook his head.

"I work with her, remember? She takes down my appointment information when I'm not in. I have to be able to decipher it. You, Corky, take the second board. I'm pulling the strap on this end." She pointed, and without waiting, she pulled the strap. The surfboard fell loose in her hands, and she passed it out to Corky. She climbed out when all four boards were gone.

"Daggett, I'm headed over to see about Mrs. Nettleworth. I need to return her pie plate, anyway." She reached into the van and inside a bag at the back. The plate was wedged just at the top.

"Sure." He turned to the new boards. "Corky and I will get these put away while you're gone."

"So he says, if he can quit ogling them." Corky slapped him on the shoulder. "Come on, boy. Let's get the house unlocked, then we can see about what's wrong with that car of Geri's."

She called back as she stepped up the drive, "It's dead, Corky. Not even you can bring it back to life." She laughed. Home was still here, and in one piece. Not even her dead car bothered her.

The crack she stepped over as she reached the street did. Glancing down the yard, she could see where it cut through the ground, wide enough to slip a hand inside, past the concrete drive, and across the other side of the yard. The side of the hill had dropped by at least two inches.

Barking erupted behind her, and she turned to see a large, golden dog coming her direction. "Flotsam!" She slapped the flat of her hand against her leg. "Come go with me, boy!"

He reached her side, but instead of eagerly following her to the house up the road, he nuzzled her hand, whining.

"Let's go see Mrs. Nettleworth, boy." She clucked her tongue. "She has treats for you. Treats, Flotsam? Our house won't fall down before we return. We've got solid rock right under our feet, right?" And perhaps her neighbor could tell her more of what was going on with the yard.

It was no good. After a few desperate whines, he turned and hightailed it back to the house, turning once at the end of the drive to see if she would follow him. When she didn't, he barked once, a loud, high-pitched sound, and he disappeared toward the house.

"That's odd," she said to herself. Then she saw a blind in one of Mrs. Nettleworth's windows move, and she waved. Someone inside returned the salutation. She couldn't believe she'd been so worried over one unanswered phone call. Her neighbor and friend was all right, in spite of everything.

After all, she reminded herself. Daggett is here, and so is Corky. How can anything go really wrong?

Chapter 37

THE SQUEAL of car tires and a honking horn took Geraldine by surprise. She turned to see Skylar hanging out of Marla's car, balancing three pizza boxes in his hands.

"Hey, Geri! Look what we got!" He waved, nearly dropping the boxes, before Marla dragged him back inside.

"You're very welcome, Skylar." She raised one hand in response. "I'm headed over to return the pie plate." She held it up.

"Look, we found some fireworks." He held out a small bag.

"My fault." Marla laughed, pushing Skylar out of the way. "We saw Mr. Chickawaddy climbing out of a real limo at the pizza place. He was all dolled up for a performance, and he gave us these fireworks for the beach."

"I've seen his car, Marla—"

"You haven't seen this one," Skylar interrupted. "This was a real one, with extra doors and a driver."

"On the way back, we got carried away, teasing each other

about why Mr. Chickawaddy would have fireworks in the first place."

"To fly higher—"

"Into the stratosphere—"

"The greatest dance step ever taken—"

"One small leap for a man—"

"One giant explosion for mankind!"

Marla grabbed Skylar's arm, and they burst into a round of hysterical laughter fueled by the joke.

"If you two are through making fun of Mr. Chickawaddy, I have an errand to complete." She held up the empty pie plate.

"Ger, did you see my note about work? We both have off tonight, but you have to go in early tomorrow." She giggled. "Mr. Chickawaddy told me he's glad you're back. He's your first appointment in the morning. A studio is filming, and he's a feature performer. How about that? Now, are you hungry for pizza?"

"After my nerves settle down, maybe. Right now I'm returning this pie plate." She held it up, pointing with her free hand to the house just behind her. "It belongs to Mrs. Nettleworth, remember?"

"Hey, I've got that fruit I bought. Hang on a minute and I'll go up with you. I can deliver it in person." Marla turned to Skylar, pointing her finger in his face. "You can take the car back to Geri's house. Don't you dare grind my gears."

She opened the door and set the emergency brake, waiting until he stepped around before climbing out. Then she reached in the back seat to retrieve her sack of fruit for Mrs. Nettleworth's anticipated fruit pies.

"Careful," Marla admonished him, with one finger pointed his direction.

"Cross my heart. I've always wanted to drive a standard." Skylar beamed, looking around the dash as if he'd never driven a car before.

"Always wanted to? Don't tease about that."

"Marla!" Geraldine called once more. "I'm going without you."

Marla leaned over Skylar to the glove box and pulled out a package of gum, sliding one piece out and returning the rest. "You be good to my little car, Skylar Johnson. I'm only giving you permission to drive it this once, and only for two hundred feet." She stepped away and closed the door.

The gears clashed noisily as the little car began a very jerky dance toward the driveway next door. He killed it once, a guilty expression on his face.

"Have you never driven a standard?" Marla yelled down the road to him. "I can't afford a new clutch. And release the emergency brake!"

"I've never driven at all," he yelled back, his face bright with enthusiasm.

"So, does this mean you intend to trade for a new car soon?" Geraldine took Marla by the arm, amused, and pulled her forward. "I think you should consider a blue one next time."

"I like the car I have now. Why?" She began digging in the bag of fruit.

"Oh, nothing. It's just that I think he means it. I've never seen Skylar drive." She reached to knock on the door. "But if you intend to trade it in, I guess that's not important."

"You're serious, aren't you?" She turned to see her car jerking uncertainly toward Geraldine's and Daggett's drive. It wasn't moving very fast, and by that point, he had restarted it about five times.

Before she could complain more, Mrs. Nettleworth's front door swung wide.

"Good afternoon. You are, I believe, Geraldine, from next door?" A solid man in his late forties, medium height, held out a hand. Office work and too many quick meals had taken their toll on him, shown in his paunchy waist and the beginnings of a fleshy neck. His eyes were red and blood-shot.

"Carl. Your mother said you'd be coming in this weekend. It's good to see you again. You have a good memory for faces." She nodded with a smile.

He smiled loosely, throwing off her casual greeting, as he held out a soft hand to Marla. "Carl. Carl Nettleworth. I don't believe we've met."

"Marla," she replied, shifting the sack to her left hand and reaching to shake. "Mrs. Nettleworth is your mother, then. I've brought her fresh fruit." She held up the sack with a smile, only to see Carl's mouth pinch together as he turned to look back inside the house. The mention of his mother obviously bothered him.

"I'd be pleased if you would both step inside for a moment. The heat. It's oppressive with the door open." He pulled the door wide, and the cooled air from the interior washed over the women. "Mother told me she offered to watch your house over the weekend. I'm sorry she couldn't follow through." He shifted the topic abruptly. "You know, I suggested that she should move away from the coast years ago, and she told me I was crazy. This was her home, and she wouldn't live anywhere else. Now look at what's happened."

By this time Geraldine had a hard place in her stomach. Carl had done no more than beat around the bush with suggested insinuations, but after not being able to reach his mother on the phone the previous evening, an ominous feeling gnawed inside. Having reached the kitchen, she set the pie plate on the counter and pressed him for something more specific.

"Carl, is your mother here?"

He shook his head. "I'm afraid not." He turned to look through the living room and out the bank of mullioned windows on the back side of the house. The blue of the ocean could just be seen through diaphanous sheers. "She's going to miss this, I guess, but there's no way she'll ever be able to come back."

Marla still held her bag of fruit, and she turned to Geri. "I'm not catching something. Why can't Mrs. Nettleworth come back? I've got a bag of fruit here that says pies."

"Marla," she cautioned, holding one hand up. "Carl? What happened?"

"I'm sorry. I forgot to close the door. It's the heat today." He stepped back into the entry hall to push it to. "I forget you don't know. The earthquake, the one Saturday. Were you aware of it?"

"Of course—" Marla began, only to be cut off by Geraldine's hand.

"We were in Carmel," she informed him, "but yes, we were aware of it. We heard there might have been another since then."

"Mother was already in and out of surgery by the most recent one—"

"Surgery?" It was Marla's turn to cut someone off. Geraldine raised her hand again to silence her.

"It's Mother's hip. Saturday's quake wasn't bad, really, not as far as property damage went. At least it didn't do any damage to Mother's house, anyway. The old place is as solid as they come." He pointed to a corner of the room. A crack zigzagged toward the ceiling. "That happened last night. Mother doesn't even know it's there."

"Carl," Geraldine began, ignoring the damage. "Tell us about what happened Saturday."

He sat heavily in a chair, clearly irritated about the whole mess. "Mother was out for the mail. You know how she walks, and that driveway isn't very level. Living here's not been good for her for a long time. When the quake hit, she was by the mailbox, and it was just enough to surprise her. Apparently, she took a tumble. I was late getting here. I'd planned to come up in the morning, but I had a business appointment run late—" He paused, a look of guilt in his eyes. He pressed his mouth together in a thin line, then blurted, "To be truthful, I decided to play a round of golf before coming up. I knew she'd planned a job for me to do, and I didn't feel like it. She must have lain in the driveway for hours before I showed up." Tears welled in his eyes. "I feel like a heel."

"She's okay, though?" Please, she prayed.

"As feisty as ever. You've lived next door to her. You can't have missed that." He laughed, this time brushing both palms against his face, making sure the embarrassment of the tears was gone. "As soon as she came out of recovery, she told me to get back here and start to work on those floor joists that were loose. As you can see, the house is fine, except for that." He pointed to the crack. "She doesn't know about that, so I know that's not why she sent me back. I've looked everywhere in the house, even in the basement, but I can't find any joists to fix."

"How long until she can come home?" Geraldine's heart pounded. She felt guilty. If Mrs. Nettleworth hadn't asked Carl to work on the floor, he would have been here when she fell, or maybe she wouldn't have fallen at all. Perhaps he would have collected the mail for her.

"That's the bad news, although Mother will probably tell me I'm getting what I've wanted all along. The surgeon doesn't think the hip repair will take. Bone degeneration. Osteoporosis, he called it. I'm looking for an assisted living facility close to home. She'll be pleased if you can come to Sacramento to see her once she's settled in." He smiled brightly.

"Oh, but your mother will miss this." Carl must see that. "You're sure she can't come home at some point?"

"I'm afraid not." He'd shifted gears already, his duty done, and he stood. "She's past that stage. I'm locking up the house and heading back home just as soon as possible."

"I guess I should take my fruit with me," Marla ventured.

"Probably," he said. "It'll ruin with no one here."

Geraldine offered, "If there's anything I can do to help, Daggett, too, all you need to do is call. We have a house phone."

"I'm glad you asked." A look of relief crossed his face, as if he'd wanted to ask and now felt free to do so. "Can you take a key to Mother's house? I'll need to have someone in to see about getting that crack repaired, and afterwards I'll be getting tradesmen over to get it on the market. At least real estate prices are high here on the coast. Keeping up this place has burned through most of her investments, and Mother will certainly need all the funds she can access to pay her living expenses."

"You won't be keeping it just in case? It would make a great weekend home." If not, Geraldine was sick for Mrs. Nettleworth.

"I don't think so, and I doubt I'll be back, unless there's an emergency. The coast is a long way from the city, just to come out and check on this old place." He already had the key out and held it to her. "Would you mind terribly just unlocking the door for the workmen from time to time?"

"Of course," she reassured him. "I've left your mother's pie plate on the counter. She loaned it to me this weekend."

"Take it home with you, if you don't mind." He picked it up and handed it to her. "Mother would love for you to have it. Now, if you'll excuse me, I've already shut the water off at the street, and I think I'll try to get on the road before any more of the day gets away from me." In that clear dismissal, he touched the thermostat controls, and the wash of cooled air from the floor vents ceased. Holding the door for Geraldine and Marla, he followed them out, locking it behind him.

As his car pulled from the driveway, Marla turned to Geraldine and remarked, "He has no idea if his mother wants you to have that pie dish."

"Marla!"

"Did you even watch him in there? He felt guilty, but he didn't feel sorry. Those tears he cried were crocodile tears. He gave you that dish to pay you for keeping him from having to come back out here to take care of his mother's house. He used you to wash his hands of his responsibility." She tore off a piece of the fruit bag and used it for her gum. Then she pulled a pear out, and she bit into it. "Anyway, I got to keep my pears. That's something."

Her point was well taken. Carl had acted in the way his mother had always portrayed him to be, but Geraldine had seen that on his previous visits. It revealed itself a little more clearly today than it had in the past, it wasn't fresh news.

She stroked the edge of the pie plate, remembering Mrs. Nettleworth walking all the way down her drive and along the street to hand it to her. Now the plate was hers.

As Marla had said, at least that was something.

Chapter 38

"YOUR CAR'S in one piece, I see." Geraldine nudged her friend, nodding down the drive.

"Wasn't that sweet of him to park out of the sun?" Marla pointed to where it sat mostly under the shade of the carport. It was crooked, and it should have been pulled up another several feet, but he at least had managed to keep from hitting anything. She giggled. "He might make someone a good boyfriend some-day."

"It would help if he had a job," Geraldine teased, walking by the small car. The driver's window was down, and the door hadn't been closed properly. "Two cannot live as cheaply as one, no matter what old people try to convince you of."

"Oh, he will have a job, if we ever make it that far." Marla opened the car's passenger door, pulling out a fresh slice of gum from the glove box, and holding it up for Geraldine to see. "He leaves my gum alone, too. Always a good quality in a man." She unwrapped it, popping the new piece in her mouth.

"I'm glad you have such high standards. Let's see if the guys are into the pizza, yet." For once, she actually felt hungry. She thought she could consume an entire slice this afternoon. "Did you and Skylar pick up anything to drink?"

"Oh, I knew I should have had him get some two-liters. Hey," she suggested, "I'll send Skylar back out. He can pay for them."

"Skylar?" She paused at the screen door, her hand on the latch, and she looked askance at Marla. "You want Skylar to take your car for sodas? And whose gears ground all the way from Mrs. Nettleworth's drive with him at the wheel? Go for blue when you trade." She laughed.

"Oh, those gears. They did sound pretty bad. Do you want to drive it to the store, instead?" She peeked in the car. "My boyfriend—" She glanced guiltily at Geraldine and cleared her throat. "—um, Skylar left the keys in the seat. I can trust you behind the wheel."

"No thanks." She pulled the screen wide. "If I have to drive to the store, I'm good with water. I can get that from the faucet."

Just then, the house groaned, and something loud popped. Barking followed.

Geraldine called through the door, "Daggett? Are you in there?" She turned to Marla with a puzzled look on her face.

"Ah!" Marla had it figured out immediately. Her voice bubbled with excitement. "They've started the party without us."

"Party?" Geraldine frowned at her. "What party?"

"The pizza party." She came bouncing up to the door. "Remember the fireworks?"

"Fireworks? Inside the house? Daggett wouldn't—"

"Get real, Ger. They'll be out back." Her eyes twinkling with anticipation, she motioned for her to hold still for a minute. She backed up and yelled, "Skylar? Daggett? Hey, are you guys out back? Corky, have you started the party, already? If so, can we join?"

"Hey, Marla," Skylar's voice called to her. "Look down beside the house."

The women peered around the carport. They could just see him at the end of the deck, and he waved. Behind him, Flotsam sniffed along the deck's railing, as if he was rooting out problems that only he could smell.

Skylar glanced back out of sight before calling, "Um, Daggett says to be careful when you cross the living room. The floor's taken some damage. Corky thinks we can fix it, though."

Then Daggett's voice called to him, and Skylar waved at them, cracking a lopsided grin before disappearing.

"What was that all about? Damage?" Geraldine frowned, butterflies setting her insides churning.

"I guess we'd better go through the kitchen." Marla shooed her inside. "At least it's getting fixed."

Geraldine's butterflies had turned wicked, fluttering crazily in her stomach. She felt an unwelcome wave of laughter bubbling up inside, barely hiding the feeling of hysteria washing over her. "If you recall, Skylar 'fixed' the tub, and now we don't have one any longer."

She remembered the washer, too. Was it the living room this time, or perhaps the bedroom? Was today the day for the entire house? She pictured it tumbling end over end, winding up floating out on the ocean. It was all too silly, but she suddenly felt desperate to distract herself. She imagined calling the local boating supply and ordering up an outboard engine . . . or a mast and a mainsail. She and Daggett would sail their new houseboat to all the surfing venues. All they'd need would be a place to tie up.

"Well, Daggett and Corky are down there with my boyfri— with Skylar. He can't do too much damage." Marla moved to the sink and flipped on the water, quickly filling a glass. "Come

287

on, Ger. We have pizza, already. We're not letting that go to waste. The guys must have it outside."

"Well, at least that still works." She pointed to Marla's glass of water, then moved to the wall, flipping on the overhead light. It also worked, and relief washed through her. She let her hand slide down, and the room darkened once again.

Marla laughed. "What, the water, or the lights? Did you think they wouldn't?"

With the crack she'd seen in the yard, that's exactly what she'd thought. Of course, the table was still in the dining room, the boards under the legs on one side. There was no change there. Out past the wall of windows in the living room, the view of the ocean still gripped her with heart-stopping beauty. No change there, either. She was letting her worries get the best of her, and she had to stop that.

"Here, let me do something with the fruit. I hope you don't mind sharing." She pulled a small bowl from a cabinet, and she dumped Marla's bag inside. Then, pulling one of the pears out, she polished it for a moment before taking a bite.

Marla reached for the fruit bag to fold it just as an ear-splitting noise echoed through the house. It sounded suspiciously like breaking wood. They looked at the living room floor to see a section of one of the oak floorboards come loose. Light filtered through, bright against the shadows of the room. Daggett's face could be seen below, one eye looking up through the gap in the board.

"What are you guys doing down there?" Geraldine called through the hole.

Just behind Daggett, Corky was dragging an outsized timber across the deck. Then Skylar's face appeared next to Daggett's, and he grinned, calling out, "We have food. Do you want some?" Up through the hole, the end of a toasted breadstick appeared.

"Hey, thanks!" Marla reached for it, pulling it carefully through the hole. "Oh, I am so hungry. You are a honey!"

"Daggett? Is it safe?" Geraldine heard boards rattling around under the house, and through the opening, she could see shadows moving about.

"Um, we're putting a loose board back in place." He turned and called to Corky. "We can just put this big board back, right? Geri wants to know if the house is safe." He peered through the hole. "Yeah, just be careful—"

"Hey, girl." Corky's closely cropped head appeared beneath the hole, and his face was covered with sweat. "It's safe to wander around the house, except in this one spot. If you do walk directly across the living room, you might expect to be a little seasick until we get this board under here worked back where it belongs." He smiled, then backed out of view, calling to Skylar, telling him to bring him *that*, whatever *that* was.

"Daggett—" she began.

"Don't worry," he said. "Come on down, if you want some pizza. I promise we won't make you two help."

Heading down the steps, it seemed it wasn't just Daggett's broken board that needed help. The fifteen wooden steps had separated at the old repair, leaving a gap twice the normal width. The deck railing had torn loose on one side, dangling out in space, and the living room floor joists looked even worse than those underneath the bathroom had been before the trip to Monterey. Above it all, glistening in the afternoon sun, was the cracked window in Skylar's room. Part of it was missing, although missing was not really the word at all. Displaced described the situation better. The glass hadn't gone very far; it was simply shattered all down the hillside, reflecting in myriad sparkles of miniature suns, with small bits still attached to one another by fragments of torn lamination material.

"Daggett, what happened?" Geraldine could hardly breathe.

289

Carl next door had shown them the crack in his mother's wall, insisting that it had been all the damage the house had taken from the overnight quake. Geraldine had been lulled into believing that this house would fair just as well. Now, it seemed as if her worst nightmares were coming true.

"Don't worry, Baby. We're repairing it." He put his arm around her shoulder.

"Can this be repaired by us?" By us, she meant without much money. When he didn't answer, she glanced at Corky. "Corky?"

He glanced at Daggett, then pressed his lips together and rubbed his beefy hand across his hair. "Old houses settle. Of course we can repair all this. Daggett's got Skylar and me to help. There are some extra boards underneath, see, there with the ladder, and all we need to do is brace those that are loose. We may have to buy a hammer and some nails, but yes, it can be repaired." He turned to look up at the broken window. "That may require a professional's help."

"Um, Geri, do you think the lady next door will mind loaning us a hammer?"

"Mrs. Nettleworth, Skylar." Daggett frowned at him.

"I think she has nails, too. I saw tons of everything when I borrowed her wrench to work on the tub."

Geraldine held up the keys she'd gotten from Carl. "I have the keys to her house."

Daggett frowned again. "Mrs. Nettleworth's keys? She's not home? She's always home."

"Carl took her to Sacramento." She didn't want to elaborate at the moment, not with the shock of the house hanging over her head. Even with Corky's assurances, she didn't feel exactly comforted.

"Poor Carl. Do the keys really mean we can borrow her tools?"

"I don't think she'd mind." No, Geraldine didn't think Mrs. Nettleworth would mind at all. Her house and all the things in it were lost to her already. She turned to face the ocean, wondering if she could endure knowing this view might someday be taken from her.

Then Daggett stood at her back, and he wrapped his arms around her, looking out at the majestic panorama spread before them. "The sea. That's me, too. I see it, and every time, I can't believe it's all mine." His fingers ran along her neck, pulling loose strands of hair aside, and his whispered words were for her alone. "Let's forget the house, let it fall down the hill, and go surfing instead. It's a perfect day to be on the water."

She laughed. He was doing it to her again, making the horrible into the manageable. She turned and kissed him gently on the lips, but she pushed him away. "Go, Daggett. You've got people here to help you fix all this. The next time I decide to go to the beach, I want to get there on my own two feet, not tumble down in a house that collapses on me because you didn't make time to repair it."

"Okay," and he chuckled, raising his hands and backing away. "I offered."

"Back over here, boy," Corky called. "Bring those keys with you. If your neighbor's willing to loan, we're going next door for tools."

As they headed up the steps, Marla came floating down past them. Her eyes had found the pizza boxes, and she called out with gusto, "Pizza, oh my love, there you are! Hey, Ger, I found some sodas after all. In the car. I forgot all about having some left in the cooler." She set them on the deck and pulled back the lid on one of the pizza boxes. "Oh, cheese! I love you, cheese!"

"Oh, you do?" Geraldine smirked, Daggett's words still in her ears. She reached to wipe the remains of moisture from her eyes.

"It's your favorite, too," Marla called. "Now get over here and eat." She patted the floor of the deck. As Geraldine walked over to join her, Marla looked around, finally seeing the damage to the deck and the underside of the house. "Heavens, girl, and I thought that crack in Mrs. Nettleworth's wall was bad. This place is a mess."

"Aren't we all, *girl*?" She laughed. Daggett's arms and his words had lifted her mood, and she felt hungry once more. "Oh, no," she called, teasing, when she saw Marla selecting the best slice of pizza out of the cheese box. "I get first choice."

Well, she didn't, because possession makes nine tenths of the law, but she enjoyed giving Marla a hard time about it. And together, they didn't care if they finished it all before the men returned. Corky, Daggett, and Skyler could just grow up and get a grip. After all, they'd had their chance, and late bloomers couldn't be choosers.

Chapter 39

GERALDINE'S eyes came open in darkness that was complete. Instantly awake, she knew the movement of the bed for what it was, a quake. Instinctively, she reached for Daggett, only to find his side of the bed empty. Fear gripped her.

"Daggett?" She called softly into the darkness. Outside the window, the sky along the ocean's edge was darker than the rest, and she knew it would storm before morning. Heavily, too. When the storm hit, there would be no working outside to make repairs to the house. Corky coming up had been a boon, getting the house back in order, and she had told him so.

Throwing her sheet back, she climbed from the bed and wandered toward the living room. She paused at the laundry room, listening for Flotsam. Distant popping noises echoed in the house. Some settling sounds were normal, but these weren't the same. She couldn't put her finger on it, and it sent a chill down her back.

"Flotsam, boy?" Hearing no response, she moved on. When

she reached the living room, Daggett stood at the long bank of windows, looking out to the sea. He turned her way.

"Hey, Geri. I didn't mean to wake you." As she moved to stand beside him, he motioned to the shadowy world on the other side of the glass. "Look at the water out there. See that dark band? A great black god is eating the sky, and when it finally consumes all the stars, it will rule the world with an iron fist."

"How poetic! Is the blackness a good god, or an evil one?" She still felt the chill from earlier.

A clicking noise disturbed the silence, a dog's toenails on hardwood, and Flotsam brushed her leg. He whined and forced his muzzle into her palm, twisting his head until she ran her hand down his back. Satisfied, he dropped away, sniffing at the baseboard along the windows, whining from time to time.

"What if—" Daggett's arm slipped around her shoulders, "—that blackness out there ate the entire world—"

"Daggett!" She interrupted him, placing her hand on his chest, the chill down her back growing stronger. "Be sensible. The entire world?"

"Why not?" He grinned and placed one hand on the glass, his palm open and his fingers splayed. A finger of lightning in the approaching cloudbank traced an eerie white line across the sky. Then, far to the left, another jagged bolt of lightning speared the darkness, revealing how quickly the clouds were moving in. Throbbing, rolling thunder shook the glass all along the back of the house. After several moments, the vibrating rumble from the second round of lightning echoed past.

"Your black god is angry tonight." She pressed her body against his, letting his warmth become hers. "I hope he *doesn't* eat the entire world."

Flotsam whined, and the floor beneath them shook. Additional bright fingers of lightning punctuated the clouds in the distance, filling the sky. Clearly, the storm was preparing to consume their fragile slice of the California shoreline. Thunder, louder now, rumbled. The floor shook again, harder, and vulgar splats of wind-driven rain hit the windows.

"I think it's here, Baby." He rubbed her shoulder. "Rock and roll."

The floor vibrated again more violently, then jerked hard.

"Daggett?" The rain started down in earnest, sheets of water blasting the glass, but the lightning held off for several minutes. Geraldine remembered what had gotten her out of bed. She was certain then she'd felt a quake, and except for the storm, that last jerk had seemed just the same. "That didn't feel like thunder."

"It's only the storm gods shaking their fists at us." He chuckled. The expression on his face was the one he got when riding the face of an exceptionally large, gut-wrenching wave. "Besides, you're with me. I'll keep you safe."

A crash came from the direction of Skylar's room, something falling over, followed by the sound of a door slamming back into the wall. The house shook again as if terrified of the storm, and a light appeared through the doorway.

"Geri? Daggett? You in there?" Skylar's frightened voice echoed in the hard edges of the house, setting off Flotsam. The animal's howl filled the room.

The phone rang. Geraldine jumped, the jangling noise of the old phone loud even against the onslaught of the weather outside.

"We're here, Skylar," she answered. The phone jangled to life again, and she called to him, "Can you get that?"

"Sure. Did you feel the house shake?" He was clearly frightened.

The phone rang again, and Daggett called out, "Answer it, Skylar. Please."

"Sure." His bare feet could be heard slapping across the

worn wooden floor, then the ringing stopped. "Skylar here. Marla? Um, yeah, Daggett and Geri are here with me. No, Corky's still asleep, I think. Um, we're having a big storm here. It'll probably hit soon at your place, if you don't have rain, yet. I'll ask." He held one hand over the receiver and called to Daggett and Geraldine. "You guys, did you feel what just happened? Did it feel like another quake to you?"

"Just now?" Daggett laughed. "It's a thunderstorm, Skylar, not an earthquake."

"Well, Marla said it's not raining at her apartment, and it felt like a quake to her."

The house shook again, the vibration strong even against the pounding of the storm outside, and one of the windows let out a loud cracking noise. An unexpected and out-of-place shrill whistle of wind coming through the glass pierced the room.

"Daggett—" That was all Geraldine could get out, before Flotsam began to howl once more.

"What is with that dog?" Corky appeared in the doorway, backlit by the hallway light. He had on sleeping pants and an undershirt. His big hand ran over his eyes, and he blinked away sleep as he chuckled blearily. "Is the whole house up? Skylar, are you inviting Marla over, too?"

The house shook once more, violently.

Skylar whispered into the phone, "Marla, did you feel that one?" He was silent for a time, before calling her name into the handset once more, and then hanging up the phone. He walked to wordlessly place his hand in front of the crack in the glass. The crack wasn't silent at all. Or especially dry. It whistled and spat water at him.

"Skylar? What did Marla say?" Geraldine watched him for a moment before calling his name again. "Skylar?"

"She said no, she didn't feel her place shake that last time, then the line went dead."

"You mean she hung up on you?" She growled. "That woman! I'll call her back in a minute."

Daggett laughed. "I bet she'll wish you hadn't, too."

"No." Skylar paused, then his words flooded out, "You can't. There's no dial tone, nothing." He wrapped his arms around himself, and his face was pale.

She took a deep breath, thinking. The talk of quakes and the jarring of the house were wearing on her nerves. However, while the phones might be out, the electricity was at least on. If the utilities still functioned, nothing too serious could be wrong.

No sooner did that thought flit reassuringly through her mind, than the light in the hallway blinked off, throwing the room and all the people inside into a blackness so thick it swallowed them. Corky reached back inside the hallway to flick the switch, but nothing happened.

"Hold on. Let me check the breakers. This always happens when it storms." Daggett's movements were lit by staggered flashes of lightning as he disappeared down the hall.

Geraldine felt the cruel butterflies come alive once again in her stomach, and they sickened her with dread. Moving to the kitchen, she felt in the dark for the faucet and flipped the water on. Placing her hand underneath, she prayed for water, but was not particularly surprised to feel no more than a dribble that quickly dropped off to nothing.

The house shuddered again, rattling the dishes in the cabinets, and when it stopped, she walked carefully back into the living room. "Corky? Does the floor feel more unlevel to you?"

"Possibly," he began, only to be cut off by Daggett's breathless reentry into the room.

In the darkness, his feet stumbled on the patch they had put on the broken floorboard, and he cursed softly. Excited, Flotsam barked several times, running to him with his clattering toenails.

"No, boy," he huffed. "It's not playtime." He called to the others, "Sorry. No lights. I flipped all the breakers off and back on. I guess the power is off everywhere. Can anyone see if any of the neighbors have lights?"

"The water's out, too," she called.

"That makes sense," he replied. "It takes electricity to run the township's water pumps."

"It shouldn't," Corky said. "Or, anyway, it wouldn't make a difference for a long time, anyway. Municipal water systems use gravity to provide water pressure."

"And so? What does that mean?" Skylar tapped one of the panes of glass across the back of the house. In the dark, with the storm soaking the world outside, the blackness felt oppressive.

"Have you ever known the water to go out when the power quits?" Corky's reasonable voice was hollow in the room.

"I never pay attention to stuff like that. Has the electric ever gone out since I've been here?" Skylar's voice sounded brittle, like he still watched the glass. Moaning punctuated his question, picking up then dying away with the wind.

"Um, Geri?" That was Daggett, as he deflected the question to her.

"It's been out once or twice, but mostly when everyone's asleep or gone." The sink bothered her. What Corky said was correct. They'd never been without water before. Why now?

"Hey, we've got candles, don't we? From that party back in June." Lightning flashed close by, peeling across the sky for a long minute, and the immediate clap of thunder made everyone jump. In the brilliance flooding the room, Skylar's face was clear, and he turned and grinned. "We can have another party, with just us."

"Yeah, sure," she replied absently. "A party." Her mind was still on the kitchen sink.

"Geri? The candles?" Corky called to her softly. "Do you

remember where they are?"

"Um, they're out on the carport in the storage locker. Swing the block free at the top, and you should find them on the shelf. Corky, do you mind helping Skyler?"

When they stepped out, she moved to Daggett's side. She worked one hand into his, entwining their fingers, and raising it to her lips. She kissed it gently and let it fall.

"What is it, Geri? We've got lights coming." He chuckled. "Everything's all right."

"The sink. It bothers me that the water's off."

He laughed at that. "Look outside, Geri. There's all the water you could ever need." Lightning flashed, and through the rivulets flooding down the window, they could see the rain filling the sky.

"That last quake we felt—"

"Geri," he cajoled. "This is California. If we didn't have quakes, it would be New Jersey. Do you really want to live in New Jersey?"

"But Marla said she didn't feel that one. Skylar was on the phone, and he asked." Her voice was tense with desperation. "She only lives a few miles from here. If we felt it, she should."

"Then it didn't happen."

"That's what I'm afraid of." She breathed her words, instantly hoping he hadn't heard. Something hit the window hard just in front of them, causing her to jump. It was a bird, leaving a dark smear that showed even darker as lightning danced in the night. Then the wash of rain slowly cleared it away, the remains of the bird slowly sliding down the glass.

He placed his arm around her, pulling her tight. "Corky and Skylar will bring us light, and we'll sing campfire songs. How does that sound?"

"Campfire songs?" She snorted derisively. "You build a campfire, and we'll all go up in smoke. You know the flue's cracked. I have a better idea," she suggested. "Do you think we should all go and check on Marla?"

"Marla?" Lightning danced across the ocean, and he frowned. Then his expression changed, and he laughed. "Why?"

Get out of this house, she'd meant. She'd noticed the floor. It sloped more than it had, and with the storm outside, she was frightened.

Skylar came running in, soaked, the front door slamming behind him, and he threw several boxes on the floor. "Candles, everyone! I bet you didn't know we had this many." Laughing, he headed back outside, leaving puddles of water that in the aftermath of yet another lightning strike glistened on the floor everywhere he'd stepped.

"We don't have that many." She frowned. "I only had one carton." She knelt to one of the boxes, opening it, and feeling inside for a lighter wand. She didn't find one, but there was a box of matches. She attempted unsuccessfully to strike one.

"Matches?" Daggett was at her side. "Here. Let me." In his fingers, it flared, and he held it to his face as if it were a game. "Can you see me now?" He grinned, his features grotesque and unnerving in the flickering dimness.

A blast of wind hit the house, and the structure jumped.

She noticed the air coming up through the old crack in the floor. Moisture glistened there, water somehow blowing up and inside the building. She remembered some long-ago peas that had rolled into that crack, and the odd thought came to her that wouldn't it be funny to see them shooting back out like little green missiles.

The flame in Daggett's hand flickered as she grasped his wrist to steady it, feeling in the box for a candle. Pulling out one that was stubby and had never been used, she lifted the wick straight with her thumb before pulling his arm down to touch the match to the waxy protuberance. In only a moment, it sputtered wickedly, then settled into a gentle flame.

"Place it away from the wind so we don't burn the house down. Try the hearth." She released his wrist, offering the candle to him.

"The fireplace hearth?" The dark hole hovering over it was a black pit through twin tempered glass doors. "Not in this weather." He laughed, taking the candle from her. "More likely it'd put it out. The damper's also gone." To prove his point, he opened one glass door, and the wind outside could be heard whistling down the metal flue. "See? I haven't forgotten."

"On the window ledge, then." She handed him the candle and reached in the box for another, pulling out one in the shape of a frog. Even in the dim light, she could see that it was green with yellow spots. Her voice overly bright, she called, "Look! We have a frog! How adorable!"

"Let's light his fire. Hold it still." Daggett held his candle, turning it so the wick touched the one on the back of the green frog. In the turning, the melting wax dripped off the top, splattering all over his leg. "Yikes, that's hot!" He made to brush it off.

"Baby!" She laughed, pushing his hand away. "You smear it, and it'll only burn worse. Besides, women have their skin waxed every day, and they never whine like that. Now, let's get some more of these started. I want light in this house."

Seeing the frog candle, and with Daggett's comical antics, she now felt better, deciding her nerves had been from the storm outside, and all the rest had been her imagination.

They turned when the door opened up again, and Corky came in dripping water, with several plastic bags in one hand and a box of silver and blue canned refreshment in the other. Following him, Flotsam barked incessantly at the bags.

"Hush, Flotsam," Daggett called. He pointed to the blue and silver box. "I know you didn't have time to drive to the store,

Corky. Where did that come from? Do you keep a stash for emergencies?"

"We've got company." He nodded towards the door, bringing the sacks and setting them on the floor at Geraldine's side. "This company brings food." He grinned.

"Food?" She could smell it by then. Chinese. She pushed the dog away when he tried to nuzzle the bags, relieved to have Daggett lean in and snag them out of the animal's reach.

"Just because it's on the floor doesn't mean it's yours, Flotsam. Now, Corky, own up. What company?"

"Hey, all!" In buzzed Marla. "I thought you guys must be hungry." She was in a bright green raincoat, with full galoshes and a matching hat. Water dripped everywhere, and she pulled the hat off. Underneath, her hair wasn't much drier. She held the hat out, a pool of water growing underneath, as if she didn't quite know what to do with it.

"Heavens! You crazy person!" Geraldine jumped up, taking the hat and shaking it off. Water splattered the walls. Then she laughed, giddy in the moment. "I'm just making it worse, aren't I?"

"I think so, honey." Marla giggled, her brightly made-up nails gleaming in the candlelight. "Is your fridge still working? I brought some frozen popsicles, too."

Daggett had one of the bags emptied by then, and he had a box of chow mien out with the lid open. Not much for Chinese, he frowned at the unfamiliar smell and pushed the lid closed.

"Where are the popsicles?"

"Skylar's got them. I was getting wet, so I left him to unload the trunk."

Down the entry hall, Corky's voice called out the door into the drumming rain, "Hurry, boy! I'm inside, and I'm still getting soaked. Get your skinny shorts in here!"

"You could have parked under the carport and stayed dry,"

302

Geraldine chided Marla. "Nobody else is going to park there, you know."

"No, she couldn't," Corky grunted as he appeared in the door.

Skylar was just behind him, and he shook his head, his hair sending streams of water everywhere. A huge box was in his arms. Corky grabbed him around the neck, taking the box and pushing him toward the hallway.

"Go dry off, boy." Corky was barely any less soaked.

"What do you mean by that?" Geraldine was puzzled.

"By dry off?" He chuckled. "That should be obvious, I think."

"No, the other thing, that Marla couldn't park in the carport."

"I don't guess you've seen the crack in your driveway." Marla looked pointedly at her as she slipped her galoshes off.

Geraldine had seen it, that it ran the length of the yard. She had let it slip from her in the intensity of the storm. Thinking of it now made her shiver.

Daggett held Flotsam's collar, and he tugged the animal away from the takeaway boxes. "Hey, keep the food safe until I put the mutt in the other room. He'll get into it, no matter what we try to do about it."

"Just a minute, Daggett." She turned to Marla. That crack had stopped her friend from pulling in the drive, and it shouldn't have. It had only been two inches. "What do you mean you couldn't pull in the drive?"

"Yeah. I was about to pull in the drive when those two—" She pointed at Corky and a shirtless and much drier Skylar just coming back in with a towel, "—came out and waved me off. I wound up at Mrs. Nettleworth's, instead." She grabbed Skylar's towel, pressing it to her face. She rubbed it vigorously over her head, shaking to fluff her hair when she was finished. "That's what I get for driving a small car that hugs the pavement: a long walk from next door." She held the towel out for anyone else to use.

Corky reached for the towel, and he rubbed it over his head, burnishing a pate that hardly had enough hair to care. "For now, let's get some light and eat, before the food gets cold. Skylar, get to lighting those candles."

"Oh, honey, you found the little frog. I just love that one." Marla squatted beside it and held her hands out as if warming up.

"You can pray all you want," Daggett quipped, "but I don't think you're going to get an answer."

"Watch me." She closed her eyes and began to chant in a musical lilt, "Oh, little green godlet. The rain outside is a frog strangler. Does it please you?" She giggled, opening her eyes for a moment. Skylar was still lighting candles, and he was setting them all close to the little green frog. It did look rather like a small spotted deity.

"It doesn't please me," he mumbled in an irreverent tone, as he set yet another candle on the floor.

"Shush," Marla hissed with a grin. "Little godlet, send us a sign you're listening to my words—"

A bright flash of lightning interrupted her entreaties, and before the people in the room could cover their eyes, thunder crackled against the glass, rattling the broken pane with a rough, grinding noise. A new wave of rain whipped against the house, briefly drowning out any conversation before subsiding enough that talking could commence.

"I think you got your answer," Corky's deep voice murmured.

However, more was coming. No more had Corky finished speaking, than the entire floor jerked sideways once, then, just for a moment, seemed to fall out from under them before stabilizing. A deep-throated groan started somewhere off towards the master bedroom, growing in intensity until something popped very loudly. Then all was quiet except for the storm and Flotsam's frightened whine.

"Are we safe?" Marla's words were whispered, but in the shock of the moment, no one had any trouble hearing them.

"I'll see." Daggett's voice didn't sound frightened at all. He released Flotsam, and he leaped up, slamming his feet solidly on the floor. The boards held. "Corky and I did good repairs, Marla. Trust us."

"And not me?" Skylar called out. "I thought I helped, too."

"Oh, no! Maybe we *will* all fall into the ocean, after all!" Daggett laughed, snapping his fingers and calling to the dog, "Come, Flotsam! Let's find our surfboard. It looks like Skylar's handiwork is going to dump us into the sea. I want to be ready when it does."

When Skylar leaped on Daggett to redeem his injured reputation, the bigger man quickly had him down with his face to the floor. As they wrestled in the half-darkness, Marla laughed. The antics had wiped the tension from the room. She turned to Geraldine.

"I got some sweet-and-sour pork. Have you ever tried it?"

"I will tonight. I didn't know you liked Chinese takeout." She dug in the boxes until she found one that smelled like sweet-and-sour. Like Daggett, Chinese had never appealed to her much. "Corky, would you like some?"

"Certainly." He stepped forward, gratefully taking a small container. "I'm hungry enough that anything sounds good."

Marla snuggled next to Geraldine, a box of the takeout in her hand, and their backs to the windows. The flickering candles beat back the darkness in the room. Occasionally, a bolt of lightning threw everything inside into stark relief before fading away again, leaving only thunder in its wake.

Corky had the box of liquid refreshments open, and he rolled a can to each of the women, opening his own as Daggett and Skylar continued to wrestle each other for supremacy.

"So, why are you here, may I ask?" Geraldine spooned a small bite of pork into her mouth. She hadn't forgotten her earlier urge to head to Marla's, or the reasons why she had wanted to. However, with the familiar company and the food, she thought herself silly, now.

"My bringing dinner isn't reason enough?"

"If you want." She sipped her drink. "I didn't hear Skylar ask you to come over when he was on the phone with you, though. Hm?"

"Okay, honey, I'll spill the beans." Marla had her voice low. "I was worried, okay? The phone went dead, and Skylar said there was a quake here, one that I never felt at my place. So, I decided to bring you all pizza."

"Pizza?" Daggett let go of Skylar, only to have the red-headed man rear up and try to take him down. Daggett just ignored him. "Did I hear pizza?"

"You heard it, but I didn't get you any. The only place open was this." She held up her food container. "I bought all they had left."

"Well, thank you," Geraldine said, reaching one hand to pat her friend on the knee. "Even though we're just fine, I appreciate the thought. And you know," she chuckled, "with this storm, I'm guessing I won't have to go in to work today. That'll be nice, since no one's getting any sleep, anyway."

"No, Flotsam!" Daggett's call exploded into the candlelit scene. He threw Skylar aside and crashed across the room, scattering several candles over the floor, their flames sputtering out. The big animal had snuck over and was happily digging his nose in a carton of takeout.

"See?" Geraldine pointed at the scene with a smile, seeing

Daggett dancing around while attempting to wipe hot wax off his legs and arms. "Tonight is just life as usual in the Priestly household. How can I worry about anything important with that going on?"

"I can be the one to worry, though, just a bit?" Marla spooned a bit of food into her mouth, but she chewed it very slowly.

"Sure, if you want." Geraldine chuckled. "Although about what, I can't imagine."

ACROSS the room, Corky's eyes watched the two women, easily following their muted conversation. He'd been one of the ones outside waving Marla's car away from the drive, and what he'd seen there had his stomach in a knot. Just past the front porch, he and Skylar had stepped up a break in the front walk that was closer to a foot tall, rather than the few inches Geraldine had seen earlier. It had seemed to cut right into the pad underneath the carport, although in the dark, it had been hard to tell. As soon as they'd eaten, he hoped to convince everyone that somewhere else might be a better place to spend the rest of the night.

He wasn't a panic button type of guy, though. Anything they did would wait until after they ate. Daggett had jumped on the floor hard, and the boy had been right in one thing: They had done a good job shoring up the timbers underneath the house. It hadn't shaken or made any unusual noises when he'd landed on the floor. Even if there was a problem, surely nothing could be so important that fifteen minutes or half an hour could make any difference.

So, for that reason, he sat back and enjoyed the company of the people he cared most about, and he pushed aside the concerns of the world outside.

There was always time. Always.

Chapter 40

THE HOUSE hanging over the hillside atop the Pacific Ocean looked festive. After multiple cans of refreshment and no further settling of the floor, the urgency of finding another place to stay for the night slowly faded into the background. The gathered friends—a family, some would say—food, and good times had brought warmth and conviviality to the old Priestly house. More candles than the occupants could shake a stick at lined the windowsills and countertops. Each box Skylar had brought in from Marla's car had been stuffed with wax columns and figurines, and they were all alight. It might be pushing three in the morning, but a party was in progress, and everyone was included.

How could anyone run from that?

Even the rain still pouring down outside did nothing to shake the good mood filling the warmly lighted interior. It was dry, and the lightning had long since subsided, leaving only the occasional rumble of distant thunder to accompany the beat of the water hitting the roof. Flotsam snored off to one side, his feet spread comfortably in the air, and his face twitching from time to time. He dreamed of surfboards or rabbits or someone scratching his stomach.

Once or twice a truck could be heard driving by, the distinctive growl of a diesel engine penetrating even the water-soaked walls of the house. When Corky pointed it out, Daggett brushed his concerns off. The nearby township had a wrecker-slash-snowplow, and in storms it sometimes patrolled the roads to clear downed branches and power lines. He pointed to the candles as if that made the diesel's presence obvious.

He couldn't see that all the other houses on Highway 1 had electricity. Doorbell buttons glowed cheerily, yard lights burned brightly in the driving rain, and through opened shades, the lamps of the night owls revealed television sets and computers aglow. Only Daggett's place might have seemed amiss to all those passing truckers, the electricity cut off, the windows dark even in the darkness of the passing storm, were it not for the candles. The windows of the old Priestly residence glowed as if every light in the house was on.

"Corky, you should have been in Marla's car!" Skylar sat cross legged, an empty can at his side. His eyes were red with laughter, as he regaled the older man with the adventures of their trip to Monterey. "That dog," he pointed empathically at Flotsam, "took up as much room as two of us, and you saw how small Marla's car is—"

"Hey!" Marla interrupted the tale, slapping him on the arm. "I didn't see you paying for the gas. Besides, it's big enough for me, when I'm not carrying five people with me."

"Five?" Corky's brows drew together in puzzlement. He pointed at the people in the room with him. "One, two, three, and you, Marla. How do you get five?"

"Skylar, Daggett, Geraldine, Flot, and Sam." She giggled,

reaching for her can. She shook it. It wasn't quite empty, and she took a sip.

"Hey, Sam!" Daggett called to the big golden retriever snoozing off in the corner. When the animal failed to respond, he clapped his hands together. "Flotsam!"

Flotsam's face grimaced, then he opened one eye to look at Daggett.

"Leave him alone." Geraldine grabbed Daggett's knee, squeezing it and laughing. "He has no idea what you want, and besides, you don't want anything. Poor Flotsam."

When she said his name, he drew himself to his feet. He sauntered to her, his toenails clicking on the floor, finally flopping down, his head in her lap. His eyes looked around the room, resting momentarily on each person present.

"You're a good boy," she crooned, rubbing the dog behind the ears. "Let me see if I have any pork left for you." She picked up her empty takeout container and dug in it with her spoon. She offered a small bit to him, but he refused it, yawning, and she dropped it back into the box, setting it off to the side.

"Am I a good boy?" Daggett crouched behind her, and he used his hands to pull her hair from her neck. Gently, he leaned in and kissed her just below the ear. "I could take a treat or two about now."

"Down, boy!" She reached up and slapped him on the arm, but she smiled. "You don't like pork, and you know it."

"It depends," he chuckled. "On two legs and with beautiful hair, I like pork just fine." He ran the fingers of one hand along her jaw, just stopping to touch the corner of her lips.

"I heard that," Marla called. "Ger, I'd bite those fingers, if I were you. I think he called you a pig."

"A pig?" Skylar had snatched up Geraldine's takeout box to dig out the bits of pork. Now he was on the far side of the room, holding it to a candle to see what else was inside. He looked up, his face shadowed eerily by the flickering candlelight. "Who's a pig?"

"Who's still eating?" Corky's voice rumbled. "Tell me that, boy, and we'll know who the pig is."

"Me? I'm the pig? How did this happen?" He had a look of amazement on his face. "I'm just finishing off the rest of Geri's sweet-and-sour." His question didn't stop him from poking another spoonful of sauce and meat bits into his mouth.

The others laughed. With his red hair askew and dancing in the odd shadows of the candlelit room, they had just cause. He did look funny, his freckled jaw chomping merrily on the final bits of sweet-and-sour pork. The shadows jumping wildly behind him were even better.

Corky rolled his bulk from the floor, and he stepped to put an arm around him. He pulled the cardboard container from his hands. "You've had enough, young man. Let me dispose of this, and you go sit by your girl."

"My girl?" He looked around the room, puzzled.

Corky gestured with the empty box to Marla. "You need to figure this out, boy. Right there. If you don't realize she's your girl, then trust me, she does. Act like you know what's going on."

When the young man didn't move, the bigger man gave his shoulder a shove, turning to walk into the kitchen. Several candles were on the counters, and he opened the cabinet under the sink to drop the takeout box into the can underneath. Geraldine walked up behind him with several more of the containers ready for disposal.

"Ah, thanks, girl. I appreciate your help." He smiled and took the packages from her, dropping them inside with the first one before closing the door and standing. He reached to flip on the water and rinse his hands, only remembering it was off when nothing came out of the faucet. He chuckled. "No water."

311

"You noticed." She leaned backwards against the counter, crossing her ankles, and pushing her hair behind her ear on one side. With a grin, she motioned toward the ceiling light and the candles on the countertops. "No electricity or phones, either. It seems we've been thrown back to medieval times, even to eating on the floor."

"Chinese takeout is not exactly medieval, but I get your point. Does this happen often?"

"Everything out at once? Never, not since I've lived here." She paused, her eyes on the floor, studying the pattern of the wooden boards. "I'm not sure why you decided to drive up with us yesterday, but I'm glad you did. Daggett never would have been able to fix the floor without you. He loves you, you know." There. She had said it. She looked up to find Corky watching her. His eyes gleamed in the candlelight.

"And you?"

"Me?" She turned and picked up one of the candles, peering into the flame. "What about me?" His question thrown back at her had more than one context, and both caught her off guard. Did she love Corky? Of course, even if the big man would never understand just why. Or had he questioned whether Daggett loved her? Of that, she wasn't so certain.

He chuckled. "Don't be coy with me. We're too much alike, you and me. When you answer a question with a question, I've hit close to home. You live with that man out there. Does he love you?"

She set the candle down, glancing into his face for a moment while deciding on a tactic to use. Then she drew in a deep breath and pushed her response across the flickering shadows in the room. "You helped raise him. You tell me. What does Daggett love?"

"The ocean. Surfing. This house. You, I hope. He acts like he does." He paused as Flotsam walked in, sniffing at the

312

cabinet where the takeout containers had gone, and whining before moving back into the living room. "And that dog. He sure loves that dog."

"And you."

Corky laughed.

"Hey, what's going on in there?" Marla called from the living room. "We don't have enough people here for two parties."

"Clearing things away, Marla. We'll be there in a bit."

"Okay, honey. We'll be waiting, uh, um, patiently." She could be heard giggling.

"Why did you laugh, Corky?"

"I guess we're more alike than I thought. Here you're telling me that boy loves me, and I've wanted nothing more since I took him under my wing when he was fourteen. I'm just an old surfer, though, and old surfers have to follow the waves, no matter what they cast aside."

"Even a son?" Or a daughter? She kept that quiet, though.

"Oh, girl, you don't know how good that makes me feel. I know Daggett's not mine, but I've always thought of him that way." He leaned in and gave her a kiss on the cheek. Then, he winked at her. "And of you as a daughter, even if you did run away just when you were coming into your own."

She laughed, keeping it soft so it didn't drift into the living room. This was a moment to treasure, hearing those words from him, that he thought of her as a daughter. Oh, what he didn't know!

"You find that funny?" He cupped her chin in the palm of one hand. "I saw me in you all those years ago. First at that restaurant, then when you showed up at my shop, you reminded me so much of a woman I'd met years before, one I'd romanced and would have won, except she felt the ocean owned me. She never could believe I loved her, and she disappeared one

313

morning. I never knew what happened to her."

"You loved her?" Tears threatened her eyes by this time. "You never tried to find her?" It was her mother he spoke of. It had to be.

"Oh, look what I've done. Girl, don't cry for me." Corky drew her into his arms, patting her on the back. "That was long ago, and it's over and done with."

She pushed him away, wiping at the bottoms of her eyes with her fingertips. "Over twenty years ago." She laughed, trying to keep the moment light. "What can it matter now?"

"That's my girl. Good guess, too. It was nearly twenty-three years. I've never forgotten my Judy, though." He smiled, clearly warmed by the memory.

"Not so much of a guess. Corky, I have something to tell you, something you deserve to know. I guess I should have told you long ago." She hesitated, her eyes moist again. She wasn't sure where to start, and once she told him Judy was her mother, she'd never be able to take it back again.

"Yes, Geri?" His voice was warm and encouraging, and he chuckled. "What do I deserve to know? I thought I knew everything."

"Not this." She took a deep breath before diving in. "I know Judy, your old girlfriend. She was—"

She didn't get to finish her revelation, though. A great shearing noise shook the house, with the sound of groaning wood and flexing metal. The dishes in the cabinets began to rattle, and several of the cabinet doors flew open. The candles danced, one flinging itself to the floor, the wax spattering everywhere.

"An earthquake!" Marla yelled from the living room.

Flotsam barked several times in succession, appearing in the kitchen, then running to the front door to bark again.

Geraldine and Corky locked eyes, and with no further

warning, the kitchen floor dropped from underneath their feet. Corky fell against her, catching himself on the countertop at her side. Dishes began to tumble to the floor, shattering in the process.

"Hold on, Geri," he called over the clatter of breaking crockery. Somewhere in the house, a window shattered, and the increasing volume of the pounding rain brought a new accompaniment to the music of the night.

The structure grew still. The floor that had been unlevel before now tilted at an obscene angle. A broad crack zigzagged crazily across the ceiling and disappeared into the wall on the living room side. The kitchen window was covered with brown mud, and it sounded as if a jet of water was aimed directly at it. Flotsam still barked repeatedly at the front door, the sounds sharp and frightening.

"Geri?" Daggett's voice called from the living room. "Are you and Corky okay in there?"

"We're fine. You?" All of them, she meant, Daggett and Marla and Skylar. She wanted every one of them to be fine.

"Okay, honey." Marla laughed nervously. "I think."

"I'm good. Should I check on the surfboards?" Clearly Skylar was in good form.

"Geri, maybe we should, um, try to find somewhere else to stay the night." Daggett stood in the dining room, one hand grasping the doorjamb. He had a burn on his arm, and his shirt was torn.

"Your arm!" She moved toward him, holding to the counters to steady herself. "You're burned."

"Just a candle. I rolled onto it. Two of the windows are broken, maybe more in the bedrooms."

"Here." She grabbed his arm, pulling him into the kitchen. Opening a cabinet that had yet to disgorge its contents, she pulled out a small first aid kit. "Let me put something on that."

"It's fine, Geri. Getting out might be better—"

"It's not fine!" She slapped the plastic box on the countertop hard. "Now let me do this."

As she put cream on the red spot and pulled the wrapping off a bandage, she thought of this house that Daggett loved so, and she remembered Corky's comment about her mother. He'd loved her mother after all, and her mother had never known, always believing his first love was the ocean.

She realized she felt the same about Daggett. If all this were gone, would their relationship be over, too? Corky had asked her if Daggett loved her, and she hadn't been able to answer, turning the question back on him.

Finished, she put the first aid supplies back in the box and returned it to the cabinet.

"It's okay, now, Geri. Thanks." Daggett put his arms around her and pulled her tight. He kissed her forehead three times before letting her go.

"Daggett's right, Geri." Corky put his hand on her shoulder. "We might best head for higher ground."

"Higher ground? Corky, we're at the top of the hill." Skylar appeared at the door, still bare-chested. Freckles covered him to his waist, glowing brilliant orange in the candlelight.

"That's what I'm afraid of, son. Check the front door. The dog's going wild, and that means he senses something. It might be important." He patted Geraldine's shoulder and stepped past her, catching himself on the dining room table. It was now against the far wall, one leg buckled underneath. The chairs were scattered, overturned or upside down. "Marla, are you okay?"

"Sure, if you can give me a hand." She moved a candle out of the rain.

The cracked window from earlier had held, but two others were shattered. Massive shards still hung in the frames, but much of the glass was gone. The floor in front of the windows was wet, with the water running back towards the wall, disappearing somewhere underneath. Overhead, the crack from the kitchen ceiling continued across the living room, ending just over one of the shattered windows. The house gave every suggestion it was breaking in two.

"I think we're going to try to get out of here as soon as we can." Corky dropped to the floor, moving carefully her direction. He chuckled. "I don't want to slip and fly out the window."

"You don't want to be Superman?" Marla reached for his hand. "Why in heaven's name not?"

As their hands grasped, Skylar called from the entryway, "Hey, guys, you need to come see this."

Before anyone could respond, an ear-splitting cracking sound came from underneath the house, and the entire structure lurched on its foundation, dropping and skewing sideways. With a canine howl and a high-pitched scream, Flotsam and Skylar were vomited into the living room by a geyser of mud bursting through the front door. They landed piled up against the cracked window.

"Skylar!" Marla shouted, then the window at the back of the house shattered, and Flotsam and Skylar were gone into the darkness.

The house stilled itself, but all was not quiet. The storm beat against the mangled structure, and throughout the building, boards creaked with ominous sounds. Marla sobbed in despair, and over it all, the wild wind whistled inside, bringing with it the smells of the sea.

"Oh, god!" Geraldine whispered, putting her hand over her mouth. "They're gone!"

Then the cracking sounds started up again, and once more, the floor dropped violently from under their feet.

Chapter 41

"PAOLO?" Geraldine stood from her chaise lounge and pushed her wet hair from her face. She looked up into the sky, only to have rain hit her in the eyes. Blinking the drops away, she looked up and down the beach. Surely this was Portonovo. The Adriatic Sea was unmistakable, the white breakwaters pinching the coastline, and the verdant hillside rising sharply just beyond the beach. It should be Paolo serving her needs today.

"Paul?" Perhaps she was confused, and this was the French Riviera. "Paul, are you there?" Her wrap was soaked, and the rain hadn't let up for some time. Even her rum was filling with water, and she hadn't had a chance to taste it.

Stepping to the waves, the wet sand clinging to her sandals and working underneath her toes, she let the water run up around her feet. This couldn't be Cuba, or Mexico, either. The greenery said as such, but still, neither Italian Paolo nor French Paul was answering.

"Pablo? I need to find Mr. Daggett. Pablo, are you there?"

Be Cuba, please, or Mexico!

She began to walk along the sand. The resort was only steps away. She'd come out this morning to soak up the sun, and the clouds had dropped rain on her without any warning whatsoever. Now she'd need to send her things with Pablo—or Paolo or Paul, whoever was here to assist her—to the resort's laundry to be cleaned and dried. It was inconvenient, but so much in life was. At least the service was available, and at no extra cost to her. With the package Daggett had purchased—all inclusive— there was no request that Geraldine and her party would be denied.

After a short walk, the rain coming harder, she began to wonder that she hadn't reached the resort. There should be stone steps leading directly from the sand, ones opening to a red-tile-roofed portico. Fresh towels would be available, manned by an attendant—not one of her Pauls, apparently—who would take her wet things from her and deliver them directly to her room in pristine condition.

"Stone steps, where are you?" She felt chilled, and she began to worry that she had somehow walked too far. Shivering, she turned from the beach and headed toward the greenery. For some odd reason, she now understood the problem. The rain had caused the flora to suddenly accelerate its growth. The resort must be hidden behind the towering foliage.

"How inconvenient for guests," she muttered. "What if the resort were to lose someone in every rainfall? What sort of rating would that earn them? Only three stars?"

Breaking through the wall of greenery, she fully expected to see the resort's tile-roofed exterior stretching far down the beach, the ornate balconies tiered one upon another, with her own French doors open and the pale lace curtains fluttering, the ends wetted in the unexpected downpour. The rain must be heavier than she thought, because behind the first wall of greenery was only another wall of verdant growth, blocking her view of anything more. She raised her sleeve to wipe her eyes, and then realized it would do no good. Her garment was soaked.

She shook the rain from her face. Pushing ahead, she began to tremble with desperation. There was no resort. She was lost, and the rain continued to pelt her, no matter how she tried to keep it out of her eyes. She wasn't sure, but she thought she might be crying.

"Daggett?" She stopped and called his name loudly, looking around for him. "Daggett? I'm lost. Please come find me, Daggett."

"He's right behind you." A hand grasped hers, and its grip was strong and reassuring, clearly masculine. "Geri, you need to wake up, please."

"I'm lost. Where's Daggett?" She was awake. Couldn't this man tell? She was awake, in the jungle, and very wet. She could feel the hand, but the man was nowhere to be seen. She glanced around. "Where are you?"

"I need you to open your eyes, Geri. I think you might have hit your head."

"It's only the rain in my eyes." She felt someone shaking her shoulder, and pain shot down her neck. The familiar scent of wild roses and vanilla flooded her nostrils. It was only then that she realized she did, indeed, have her eyes closed. She opened them to near darkness, barely able to make out a face just in front of her.

"Corky?"

"I'm okay, Geri. Daggett's right behind you. He hasn't come to, yet. How do you feel?" He pushed broken crockery aside and shifted closer, squeezing her hand. "Can you move at all?"

"I think." She remembered. The rain, the house. Skylar and Flotsam. Oh, god! "How bad is it?"

"We're okay, you and me. I was talking with Marla a few minutes ago. I can't get to her, yet. I want to try to wake Daggett first. I can hear him breathing, but he hasn't answered me."

"You think he's okay, then?" Please, God, she prayed.

"I hope so. That's what I've got to find out."

"Skylar?" She held her breath. Had he really vaulted through the window, lost to them forever? Please say it was a dream.

"I don't know, Geri. I'm sorry. I'm doing all I can." He made to release her hand.

"Not yet, Corky." She grasped his big hand with all her strength. "Don't let go yet. I've needed you all my life, you big buffoon, but never as much as I do right now." She chuckled, feeling desperate tears roll down her face. "And why does it have to still be raining?"

"It isn't. You've been out some time, and the sky has cleared. There are stars where I can see overhead. It'll be cold before sunrise, I'm thinking."

"It's cold, now. Where's the water from?" She could hear it on what was left of the roof, and it dripped all around them.

"The city is wasting all its water on your house, I assume. Daggett might have quite a bill, once all this is over." He squeezed her hand one last time. "Marla, are you holding up?"

"If you mean breathing, then yes. Holding up? No. Skylar! Geri, are you there?" She began to sob uncontrollably.

The house creaked loudly, and off somewhere, something let go, tumbling noisily down the hillside. Geraldine realized she could hear the surf far below as it pounded the beach.

"I'm here, Marla. I'm sorry about Skylar." Rolling over gently, she cringed at the pain in her neck, but found that with care, she could think past it. She bumped something sticking up through the floor, momentarily puzzled before realizing it was one of the supports that had once held up the house. If it had come through the floor a foot closer her direction, she would have been skewered. Listening, she realized Marla's crying had quieted to barely nothing. Shock, she figured.

Corky made movements toward Daggett, but when he bumped Geraldine, he sighed softly. "I'm sorry, my girl. The ceiling hasn't left us much room, and you and I can't occupy the same space at the same time. If you can slip downhill, I think I can get through."

She was having none of it, though.

"Daggett?" She called to him as she inched across the floor. When she reached him, she felt of his body, finding he was on his back. Touching his arm, she caressed the bandage she had applied. It brought tears to her eyes, remembering how she had raised her voice to him, and he had hugged her in return. She shook his arm, her voice pleading with him. "Daggett, please be okay. Please. Wake up, Daggett."

"Can you tell if he's restrained in any way?" Corky was right at her side, and his voice was low.

"Restrained? Oh, like has the ceiling fallen on him." She hadn't thought of that. She reached her hand as far as she could and found the space above him open in every direction she could feel. "I think he's clear. At least I can't touch anything. I think he's lying against the wall on the far side."

"That's probably why he's not crushed. Sorry. I shouldn't have said that. Stay with him. I want to go help Marla." He began to crawl away, the sounds of broken dishes and plaster marking his passage.

"Daggett," she began, pressing her palm to one side of his face, "I love you." She inched forward until she was partially on him, and she leaned in and kissed him on the lips. "Daggett, wake up! I need you here with me." She kissed him again, hard, only to feel his head twist away from her, and for him to start coughing.

322

"Whoa, Geri," he coughed again, then gasped once. "Let me catch my breath. What a way to wake up!" He shifted his position, and then froze. "The floor . . . is that the ceiling right there?"

"Corky is checking on Marla. She's okay, we think."

"Skylar?" He paused. "I don't hear Flotsam."

"I don't guess you saw . . . the mudslide. Did you see that?" She could barely get the words out.

"Mudslide? Maybe. Through the front door?"

"That one." She placed her head on his shoulder. "It took them, Daggett. They're gone."

"Down the hill?" His words were matter-of-fact.

She nodded her head, afraid to speak.

"Corky?" He called loudly. "Can we help Skylar and Flotsam?"

"Not right now, boy. We've got to get the four of us to safety first."

"How much danger are we in?"

"Let's just say that I've surfed Waimea Bay, and I was safer there than here."

Daggett laughed. "Waimea Bay, huh? I know dudes who won't touch Waimea. I guess we're in pretty deep, huh? Think we'll make it out of here?"

"If I have anything to do with it. Can you move? I'm here with Marla, and if I can get some help, I think we can free her foot. It's wedged in under a section of plaster from the ceiling."

"Move?" Daggett laughed roughly. "My house is collapsing down the hillside, so it seems my options are pretty limited. Lay here and eventually die. Move. I think I can move, Corky."

"Good. Then get down here and help out. Marla can't get free, not without our combined strength."

It took a number of minutes to squirm Marla's direction. Exposed nails and dead wiring cluttered their pathway, and the floor was steeply canted. Also, the closer they got to the back side of the house, the lower the ceiling sagged to the floor. When the structural glass in the windows had shattered, the entire outer wall had collapsed like an accordion.

By the time the plaster was knocked free, the sky had started to lighten just enough to tell that dawn was on its way.

"Ger, can we get out?" Marla's leg was whole, if severely bruised, but emotionally she was a mess. "I want out. Now. Corky?" She grabbed at him, holding his arm tightly as if afraid she might slide out the back of the house and into the sea below. "Don't let me go, Corky. Please."

"I won't. I've got you." He put his hand on hers, squeezing tightly.

Daggett crawled Corky's direction, tapping him on the shoulder and pointing uphill. "I'm climbing towards the front of the house. There's light coming through, and I might be able to get out. If so, maybe I can reach the street." When he nodded his assent, Daggett began backing up, only to find his way blocked by Geraldine.

"Not by yourself," she hissed softly. "If you're going that direction, I'm going with you." She wasn't losing him. She remembered a conversation they'd once had. *I love the ocean. You know that, Geri. If I meet my end by leaping into the sea in the greatest earthquake of all time, then what better way is there to go?* She had replied, *Together?* She'd loved his response. *Yeah, together. We'll go together.* If they died on this summer morning, they were going together. She didn't want to live without him.

He grabbed her hand and kissed it, smiling at her. "I want you to come. With you at my side, I can do anything." He grinned, and he began squirming across the living room floor, his arms and legs moving in a crab-like gait, pushing broken slivers of the house aside as he worked his way past.

324

As they forced aside the chair that no one had wanted, finding it crushed in the melee that had devastated the house, she murmured, "I liked that chair, even if it's in the way now."

Handing her a broken chair arm, the wood twisted and split, Daggett paused and chuckled. "Bet you you're glad I didn't keep much else. We'd never reach the front door if I had."

"Stop that." She wedged the chair arm into a tight place to where it wouldn't fall on those behind them.

"What?" He was up on his elbows, one knee drawn forward, ready to move on. The front door was within sight, canted sideways, but open enough to allow them to crawl through. He paused, looked at the possible exit, then turned to her. "Stop what?"

"Finding the good in everything." She felt her eyes fill with water, and she pulled her arm up to wipe them on her sleeve. "You do that, you know, every time I'm ready to throw in the towel."

He scooted back her direction, taking one hand and pulling her up to kiss her on the nose. "Would you rather we had broken furniture to worm through? I don't." He kissed her again, this time lightly on the lips. "Besides, I've got you here with me, and what can be better than that?"

"While your house is falling down the hill?" She sniffled, blinking away the last of the tears, and she forced a smile on her face. What he said was sweet, but nothing about this night seemed very good at all.

"Geri," he said, looking her in the eyes. "Today my house might wind up in the ocean whether I like it or not. That's not good or bad. It's just the way it is, and I have no control over that. But having you here, that's the best thing that's ever happened to me. I can live without my house. I can't live without you."

"You . . ." She reached and placed her hand around his neck, unable to speak. Looking into his eyes, she smiled. "You are the most insane man I know. Go. Let's get to the front door before this place does fall into the water."

They made it far enough to see where the water tap that had once serviced Daggett's house gushed with reckless abandon into the early morning air, spraying wildly into the sky. It was a good forty feet over their heads. Above it, the carport remained in place, the roof broken off roughly, but still held up by its stone and steel pillars. Over the exposed schism between the sheer face of the hillside and what had torn away, the front bumper of the Beetle hung precariously, one of the front tires visible from where Daggett and Geraldine clung. The bedrock that had supported the old house for over half a century had sheared away, dropping its burden as if it were no more than an empty purse. Even the concrete stanchions that had tied the house into the hillside were gone, buried somewhere underneath the tortured structure they had once held aloft.

"Can we make it?" The view tested her faith. The way to the road was nearly vertical, a climb up wet, glistening dirt and rock.

"We have to." He grabbed her around the shoulders, then pulled her close and kissed her. "People are depending on us."

"We can't let them down, can we?" It still seemed over-whelming to her. Sometimes things just couldn't be done. This was surely one of them.

"No, we can't. Let's go." He squeezed her neck, and then he reached for the doorframe. He pulled himself up until he was sitting on the threshold. He held out his hand for her to take.

Instead, her eyes grew wide, and her face turned white. She pointed behind him. When he turned, there was the monster that had frightened her. Above them, a huge section of the exposed hillside was turning loose, and it looked as if it was coming just for them.

Chapter 42

"DAGGETT!" That one word was all she had time to yell before the wall of mud hit the house. It impacted hard, much of its thick, batter-like substance crumpling what was left of the front of the structure. The rock facade could be heard letting go, the sharp clinking sounds of masonry giving way under intense pressure. The kitchen window, forced from its frame during the initial collapse, belched brown phlegm into the interior of the house. The front door was ringed with oozing debris, and even more coated the entry hall. The floor, once prized oak, now resembled a bog. She was spattered, and she wiped the mud from her face.

"Daggett?" She began to claw upward, the mud fighting her at every turn. "Daggett!" she screamed, hoping beyond hope that after all this, she hadn't lost the one man she had truly ever loved. As she reached the doorway, a brown mud-monster peered inside, its face and arms visible only as a dark blob against the dim sky, with two bright eyes buried in the morass of wet dirt.

"I'm okay, Geri." The mud lips broke apart, and Daggett's voice came out. A mud hand reached to the mud face and wiped at the mud eyes, revealing blond eyebrows streaked with brown.

"Daggett?" Relief flooded her, and in the crashing release of endorphins, she giggled. "You are a sight. The creature from the Black Lagoon's come to life, and he's with me now." Then tears began to flood down her face.

"What's wrong, Baby?" Daggett's mudman arms reached for her, and he hesitated when he noticed how bad they were.

She didn't hesitate, though. She flung herself from the doorway with as much rapidity as the slippery mud would allow, and she threw her arms around him. "I was scared, Daggett. The wall of dirt turned loose, and then there was mud everywhere, and you were gone. What would I have done if you'd disappeared like Skylar? I couldn't bear to lose you." She was sobbing by then.

"Baby, it's simply a little mud." He brushed her hair from her face, leaving brown streaks wherever he touched. "I'm not hurt. Are you?" He kissed her on each cheek, his muddy mouth leaving lip-shaped dirt smudges.

"No. I'm a mess, though." She drew back and looked at herself. Her front side was covered with the oozing chocolate mess. She smiled weakly and looked in his face. "I guess I overreacted."

"I like it when you overreact. Anyway, you should have seen yourself before you jumped up here. You weren't exactly pristine." He chuckled ironically and pointed up the hill. There sat Mrs. Nettleworth's house, prim and proper, its rather more solid foundation on its rock promontory still holding it nicely aloft, the craggy face of the cliff below it jumbled with massive boulders and verdant greenery as it cascaded down into the ocean. "Look there, Geri. Life as normal. That way, too." He pointed north. Just past the raw, ragged cliff face where the house had ripped free, the land rose from the ocean below in a sudden and sheer assent to meet the edge of the highway undulating lazily down the coastline, until in the distance, the craggy shore jutted long fingers once more into the watery depths. Distant houses could be seen dotting the coast, held securely in the grip of dirt, stone, and pylons driven deep into the earth. Trees waved crazily in the wind, telling of building weather on its way. Lights were on, and once, a car's headlights flickered on a curve. After a moment, it could be heard driving past overhead.

"They have no idea, do they?" She glanced up, listening to the sound. "You could barely see the house from the road before. Now, there's nothing to make someone stop."

"I guess not." He squeezed her tightly with a big smile, the mud on his face already drying and beginning to crack. "It's just you and me, Baby."

From inside the house, Corky's voice called, "What happened out there?"

"We're fine," she returned. "Are you managing all right?"

"We're stable, for now. Marla wants to know if you have any news of Skylar."

She looked at Daggett, blinking away yet another rush of tears. "We're looking," was all she was able to send back. "Be safe getting out, you two."

The water continued to spatter from the line overhead, and Daggett found a small puddle, swirling his hand in water that was hardly clear, but brushing it across his face nonetheless. He pointed above them to where the mud had torn loose, exposing bands of darker, hardened substrate, to form what potentially could be interpreted as a series of steps in the hillside. Farther overhead, a ledge jutted into the air, formed from what was left of the front yard.

"Do you think we can make it?" She pointed at the steps.

He glanced up, reaching to run his hand through his hair and finding it was covered with mud also. He pointed to the ledge. "I don't see how we can overcome that."

For a moment they were silent, the booming of the surf creating an undercurrent of sound in the morning air. Not far away, the water cascading from the city pipes drummed on the house. A large white bird took to wing, sending a high-pitched screech to announce its presence.

She chuckled and sighed, brushing both hands across her cheeks. When Daggett looked at her questioningly, she pointed to where the remains of the carport stood over their heads. "Small favors. At least you still have the check in Corky's van."

"From Monterey?"

"You did win, you remember. Nearly fifty grand."

"You didn't kiss me in Monterey. We were in Carmel." He glanced at her with a solemn expression. Finally, he laughed, shaking his head.

"What? Did I miss something?"

"I put the check in the house. And the house is down there." He pointed in front of them and across the hillside where parts of the demolished structure could be seen farther down.

"It wasn't a real check, was it? You'll have money to put something back together."

"We'll have money." He pulled her arm tight, rubbing her hand with a mostly clean one. "We need to get everyone out safely, first. Got any ideas?" He glanced back up the hillside at the towering wall of rock and dirt, and the impossible ledge blocking their assent that way. His expression didn't look promising.

"Maybe down? Perhaps we can make it along the coastline to another house and climb up." That frightened her, though. If the house had fallen this far, what would stop it from traveling the rest of the way, possibly right on top of them?

"If we have to, then down it is. We could swim . . ." He paused, the look on his face telling that he didn't really like that idea.

"I can do that." She smiled. "With two of us together—"

"There's an undercurrent to the north, and swimming means going north. So, swimming might not be especially smart. I almost drowned there when I was eight. Perhaps we could climb to Mrs. Nettleworth's. That's well over a hundred feet of very rough climbing, though." He pointed. The unkempt growth up the steep and undulating hillside looked as forbidding as he suggested. "I never was able to climb that, and I tried several times."

"That? Why?"

"I was a kid. All kids sneak out from time to time. That always drove me back home, though." He chuckled, the one small moment of levity bright against the ruin all around them. "Remember Skylar chasing his surfboard when the wind blew it up there? He almost didn't make it."

"Do you see any signs of him?" Her heart caught with the mention of his name. In all the other disasters of the night, the sudden crushing of the house and the mudslide, Skylar and Flotsam had been momentarily pushed aside. No longer. She stood, looking down the hillside as best she could. Not much was visible over the broken mass of the house. She realized it had gotten cold, as Corky had suggested it might, and she rubbed her arms. She laughed, more of a snort than a true expression of humor, as she looked at the mess all around her.

"So, now what's funny?" Daggett pulled himself up beside her.

"I was thinking how I'd like to have a jacket, and down there, Skylar's—" She choked off her words, unable to say it, pressing her fingers to her lips.

331

"Maybe alive?" He lifted his hands to his mouth and called out, "Skylar! Flotsam! Can you hear me?"

Faintly, in the distance, the sharp reports of a barking dog came back at them.

Geraldine leaped forward, nearly stumbling in an instinctive effort to make her way past the disaster of the house and down the hillside. She caught herself, looking at Daggett with hope on her face. "That's Flotsam. He's alive."

He had a wide grin on his face. "You think? How about Skylar?"

Her face fell. "Do you think it's possible? I saw them go out the window, Daggett. I can't hope—"

"We have to hope. Let me tell the others." He dropped into the house, calling out in a loud voice, "Marla, Corky! Flotsam's alive. We're heading out to look for Skylar. Are you guys making progress this direction?"

Cheers answered him. Corky called out that he could see him, and his hand waved from inside the broken structure. Hope lived again. In a disaster such as they'd just survived, hope was what they needed, and at this point, it was pretty much all they had.

Chapter 43

THE BARKING was louder, more frantic, and Daggett held up his hand for Geraldine to hold off for a minute. "Wait back there. This board has nails all over it." He tossed the board aside, letting it fly off into the brush.

They were on the old trail towards the beach. From below the house, the raw dirt had melted down the hillside, pulling timbers and unrecognizable parts of the house with it. The top part of the trail was gone, covered in lahar-like debris, the side of the hill and its verdant growth of shrubs and wild roses slumping precariously toward the sea.

"Flotsam?" She called the dog's name, waiting each time for the rapid barking that followed. "Skylar?"

"Skylar?" Daggett echoed her call. "Skylar? Can you hear me, Skylar?"

Calling the young surfer's name was disappointing. It brought no response.

Geraldine slipped in the mud, crying out, "Daggett!"

Throwing her hand out to grab a tree branch, she wound up lodged in a rose bush, surrounded by the bright pink blooms. "Daggett, I need your help. Please come back."

"That's a slick spot." He climbed back to her and reached out a hand. "Come on up. I need you with me. We can only do this together."

She pulled herself erect, brushing at new scratches on her arms and legs. "It sounds as if Flotsam's that direction." She pointed to a tumble of brush, the broken branches of the trees showing where something had fallen through.

Following her finger, Daggett scratched his head, frowning at drying dirt as it broke free in his hand. After a moment of consideration, he let out a long-held breath and snorted his assessment of the situation.

"What? You don't think so?"

"It's not that. I don't want it to be so. There's a sheer drop-off just there. It eats old washing machines and surfboards with equal equanimity. A black hole." He shook his head then called, "Flotsam!" The barking took up again, clearly from the black hole, and Daggett grimaced. "Looks like you're right. Down we go."

An ominous creaking from above grabbed their attention. The pair looked up. The sky had brightened into a clear morning, and the glare against the teetering house made them squint.

"You think it's going to come down? If so, I hope Corky and Marla are out." Geraldine wrapped Daggett's arm in hers.

"I agree. Finding Flotsam and Skylar is important, but not being crushed by a falling house is a good reason not to rush ahead with too much abandon." He kissed her cheek. "Maybe it'll hold up for a while longer."

Glass tinkled, and with a loud screech, combined with the awful sound of wood upon wood, something large tumbled from the far end of the house. It flew free, white and brown, before separating and tumbling end over end.

"Your bed." Daggett said the words, and his face carried a look of loss. "Your bed," he repeated more softly. It was the only thing she'd brought to the house. He watched it tumble down the hill, divesting itself of its bedcoverings, and finally, hitting an old tree, ripping and shedding its internal stuffing as it came to rest.

"Our bed, Sweets," she whispered. She asked again, "Is the entire house coming down?"

"Apparently. Eventually." He was transfixed by the bed, its loss more potent to him than the devastation of the house he owned. He murmured, almost too softly to be heard, "One piece at a time."

"Should we have stayed to help the others out?"

"Corky!" He snorted. "You heard me offer. Instead, I got my ears pinned back. 'Go, boy. Get that dog and that friend of yours. I can handle Marla.'" He chuckled sourly as he began to work his way to the crevasse where Flotsam seemed to be located. "One day I'm going to tell Corky he's my real father just to see what he does."

"Your real father?" She stopped. "I tried that, and you see where we are, now."

"You did that? You told him he was your father?" He laughed at her words.

"Not exactly. I just tried. Then the world fell apart. But that's another story. Would you really tell him that?"

"Yeah, I'd tell him I found an old letter from my mother or something, and she told me my real dad was Corky Maiterson." They reached a drop-off that stepped down onto a ledge. "Here, let me take your hand." He leaned over a moss-covered rock, looking down as far as he could see. He called loudly, "Flotsam?"

Barking, distinct and urgent, returned to him. Through the

335

thicket, far below, a shimmer of gold could be seen.

"I've found him! Come, boy!" He whistled, snapping his fingers. "Come, Flotsam!"

The barking renewed, but the golden ghost within the black hole didn't seem to move.

"He's not coming. Why's he not trying to find a way up?"

"Trapped, maybe? I hope something's not broken." He turned to her. "How will I get him up if he's got a broken leg? Or his back?" He turned pale.

"He sounds fine. I think it must be something else. Do you think we can get down?" She had already paled at the steepness.

"I have to try." He shifted his body and dropped his legs off the rock, catching his feet on a nearby tree branch. "Wait for me. I'll be right back."

"Wait for you? With that house hanging over my head? I'm going with you." She knelt on the rock, digging her nails into the moss. "I'm not letting you out of my sight."

"I can't convince you otherwise, can I?" He leaned against the rock, his eyes looking into her face. Then, he grinned, shaking his head. "You know, I like having you at my side. Come on, woman. We're going to rescue a dog. My dog."

"Our dog," she muttered, as she turned and dropped her legs on the branch. "That dog is mine as much as he is yours, and we're going to rescue him together."

"DAGGETT? What's that?" Geraldine's heart stopped for the umpteenth time in one day. Their trip down the ravine had been tortuously slow. Hers and Daggett's arms and legs were laced with scratches and abrasions, and they were exhausted, but they could plainly see Flotsam through the undergrowth. Two more near-vertical descents and they would be at his side. The breakers crashed not thirty feet below them, the rocky shore dropping in a deadly lurch into the depths of the water.

This was no shallowly laid out beach. This was the place of the undertows that had long ago nearly taken Daggett under.

"What, Geri?" He wiped his face on his arm, the remnants of the dried mud making matters, if not worse, then no better than they were.

"Over there." She pointed, unable to say more. Thoughts tumbled in her head: *Something white, Daggett, and freckled and red.* Too much red. She couldn't bear it, and she turned away.

When he looked the direction she'd indicated, he paled. "No! Skylar! No wonder Flotsam wouldn't come to us." He scrambled madly to a small tree, and he leaped to it, letting himself fall a branch at a time. A second tree and he was there, visible through the greenery, kneeling over the fallen form. "Geri," he called, "we've got to get help."

"How, Daggett?" She looked up the way they'd come. All she could see was trees and rocks and sky. It had taken them hours, surely, to make their way down. No one even knew they were here.

Then coughing started, and she heard Daggett speaking. "You can make it, man. Flotsam's been watching over you. Just lie flat and don't move. Just stay there. Things will be all right, I promise."

She eased her way down the steep descents, working past one handhold at a time, until she came to the opening where Skylar lay. She felt Flotsam's head push up under her hand, as if attempting to comfort her. Daggett, poor, filthy Daggett knelt over Skylar's ragged form, one hand under his neck, the other pushing hair back from a badly battered face. The hair was shiny and wet, matted with blood. His skin was whelped and splintered, cut and bleeding in more places than a cage wrestler's. One leg twisted awkwardly under the other. His chest barely moved.

She knelt to wrap her arm around Flotsam, only to have him whimper. She looked down to see blood on his coat, and he held one leg off the ground. When she touched it ever so gently, the big dog jerked the leg as if in pain.

"You poor thing," she whispered. "You're hurt, too, and all you thought of was Skylar. You kept calling us and calling us to let us know where you were."

"Geri?" Daggett called to her. When she looked up, tears streaked his face. "Geri, we have to get help somehow. He can't hold on much longer. I can't bear to lose anyone else in my life. You and Skylar and Corky are all I've got."

"And Flotsam." She forced an encouraging smile on her face. "And maybe Marla."

His face remained twisted. "You don't understand. If I lose Skylar, it all starts over again." His voice broke, and his head fell.

She disengaged from Flotsam and stepped to him, kneeling and putting her arms around him. "What starts all over?"

"Losing everyone important to me. Everyone I love. If I lose Skylar now, what's going to stop me from losing you?" His eyes rose to meet hers, and they were red-rimmed and wet. "I can't lose you. I can't live without you, not one day."

"You crazy, crazy man." She pulled him close, burying her face in his dirty hair. "You can't lose me, because I won't let you. I've loved you since the day I met you, and I was afraid of losing you, you big oaf." She separated, laughing. "I did hear you say you love me? I'm certain of it."

He pulled his hand from under Skylar's neck to gently stroke the good side of the injured man's face. "Did I?" He glanced up, but this time there was hope in his eyes.

"Oh, you! If keeping this man alive means I get to keep you, then Skylar isn't dying, not if I have my way about it." She pressed her mouth into a thin line, and she gave him a look of

338

exasperation. "I'll swim for help, if I have to."

"We can send Flotsam for help, tie a message to his collar." He gave a rough chuckle, his emotions choking him, and it turned into a cough. "Can you find a glass bottle anywhere, one with a pen and paper inside? When Flotsam gets to shore, it'll be no good if the paper's wet, and they can't read our location."

"I really could swim. I'm a strong swimmer. I can make it." She wasn't sure, but Daggett's admission of love, if inadvertent, had her adrenalin running high. She felt it was worth any risk to keep Skylar alive.

It was the siren overhead that gave them true hope. It also set Flotsam to barking once again. Even then, they couldn't miss the bullhorn that called to them. Apparently, someone had noticed the house was gone, and the local rescue team had been called.

She looked at Daggett to see a smile open up on his face. "They'll have to pull Skylar out first, you know." She reached her hand to Daggett's face, pressing it against his cheek.

"Hours and hours before we get free." His eyes never left her face.

"We'll wait until they take Flotsam up, too. Then we might try to climb up."

"Or not." He was grinning by then.

"Or not?" She raised her eyebrows.

"Surf's up, today." He pointed to the water, and sure enough, the breeze had moved offshore, and the waves were building. "We'll tell them to drop us a couple of boards."

"Is that all you ever think about?"

He winked. "Not anymore." He leaned in and gave her a kiss, a long, on-the-lips sort of kiss that said love and everlasting and I'll never leave you and I don't want you to spend one day apart from me.

Her kiss back spoke the very same words.

Chapter 44

THE FIRST ambulance was long gone, transporting both Marla and the broken Skylar to better medical attention, before Daggett and Geraldine reached the road far above. A firetruck had its lights flashing, several patrol cars blocked the lane nearest the ocean, and in Mrs. Nettleworth's drive by Marla's car was parked the longest black limousine ever seen in Northern California. Sitting in the second ambulance, a paramedic treated Geraldine's cuts and bruises. Daggett was at her side, and the bandaged Corky looked in on them.

Geraldine asked about Flotsam.

"He's fine. The man in the car up the hill transported him to a vet he knows, even promising to pay the bill. You're a lucky girl." Corky leaned in and grabbed her ankle, causing the paramedic to glare at him with a frown.

"It's all right." She waved the medical technician's concerns aside. "He's my dad, and he takes good care of me." She looked at Corky to see a smile break across his face.

"Your dad, huh? I'm okay with that." Corky chuckled. At a sound outside, he turned, then motioned someone up. "Here's your friend. He's the one who brought the emergency crews in. He saved us all."

A glittering Mr. Chickawaddy stepped to the door of the ambulance. "My dear, my dear, I am so glad to see you are in such fine shape." He reached a jeweled hand to the side of the door and moved gracefully inside.

"Sir, I must ask you to step back." The paramedic made to stand, only to be stopped by a raised hand, this one sparkling with even more jewels than the first.

"In a moment, my boy. You see, this is my dear friend, and I must speak with her. I will be gone in less than a flash."

"Mr. Chickawaddy, what are you doing here?" Geraldine glanced at Daggett, only to see him shrug.

"I was out for a drive. I do have an appointment at the salon this morning, you remember, or I guess I did." He chuckled, his barking laugh sharp and clear. "I'm certain to have missed it, do you suppose? Oh, my, my. My apologies. My jest was in poor taste."

"Oh, I liked it very much. Go on." She smiled. He could make all the jokes he wanted in exchange for rescuing them.

"You see, I was early, and I seemed to remember you speaking on occasion of living on the coast. I told my driver to take a little spin down Highway 1, and then I saw the most unusual sight. There was your little car, sitting under a carport, with no house attached." His eyes twinkled. "I remembered, you see, that adorable young man who couldn't seem to find your spark plug, and I told my driver to pull to the side. When I looked down the hill, I saw your . . . your father, I believe you called him . . . climbing out of that horrible mess down there." He visibly shivered. "I had to do something, and I immediately told my driver to call for the nearest help. Now I'm late for my noon rehearsal, and I couldn't care the least. What's a rehearsal, when the lives of my dearest friends are at stake?"

"That is so sweet, Mr. Chickawaddy." She held her hand out, and he reached to it and touched the tips of her fingers with his.

"However," and he raised his head, his nose pointing into the air, "I cannot miss the rehearsal completely. As you can see, the studio was kind enough to loan me a car for the week. We are filming in two nights, and my performance must be perfect. I cannot let them down. Now that I know you are well, I bid you adieu." He gave a barely perceptible bow and removed himself soundlessly from the ambulance.

Daggett grinned. "And now I've met Mr. Chickawaddy." He laughed. "I am so glad I've met Mr. Chickawaddy. You have the best friends, Geri. The best, ever."

Epilogue

"SO, YOU CAN hobble, I see." Corky peered across the small living room he called home to see the redheaded mooch everyone knew as Skylar making his way on crutches towards the balcony. Until Marla's new beauty shop two blocks over broke even, Skylar and Marla were sleeping on his fold-out. "I can stop bringing your meals to you, I guess."

"Yeah, I can walk, Corky." Skylar reached one hand to unlock the door, and he slid it aside. "It's surf I can't do, and out there's where I want to be."

The sounds of the ocean filled the room. So did the sounds of the cars on the highway below. A new sign graced the front of the building: Priestly Surfing School. Below it two names were listed: Daggett Priestly and Skylar Johnson, Instructors, although Skylar had yet to instruct anyone. His was an advisory capacity as yet.

The beach across the highway was crowded, a last fling at summer, and sun-browned people were queued up on the water, surfboarders one, ready to accept any wave, no matter how small. Only the best of those lined up would make any showing today, but all would have fun. They were surfing, and what better life was there?

The sharp barking of a dog brought the men's attention back into the room. The door burst open, and in bounded an energetic golden retriever puppy.

"Jetsam," Marla called. "Come back here. I'm sorry, Corky. He's wild." The leash dangling from her hand was supposed to be on the dog. She set the bag from a little Chinese eatery on the small table.

"And who taught him to be that way?" Corky jerked his head at Skylar. The redheaded man held out an old sock, and he teased the dog, finally throwing it across the room, smiling when the animal chased it down, sliding halfway across the floor while attempting to come to a stop.

A pounding noise erupted from the wall. It moved towards the front of the building.

"Someone wants you, Skylar." Corky pointed towards the balcony. "Daggett, I'm sure." He tried to sound exasperated and gruff, but a grin tweaked the corners of his mouth. "Git, boy, or that noise'll never stop."

Outside, Daggett leaned around the wall that separated the balconies of the two apartments. "Hey, no lessons are scheduled today. Geri and I are heading to the beach." He smiled and tilted a surfboard out to where Skylar could see it. "We're planning to join the grommets out there and show them just how it's done. Maybe tempt them to sign up for classes."

Setting up the new business was where part of Surfjam's prize money had gone.

"Oh, dude!" Skylar slumped. "I want to be out there." He glanced back into the room at the bag Marla had carried in. "Besides, Marla got Chinese takeout again. That's the third time

344

this month. She thinks I love it." His face revealed his desperation.

"Have you told her you don't like Chinese?" Daggett grinned.

Skylar was aghast at the thought. "I couldn't do that! I might hurt her feelings." He shifted on his crutches, finally setting one aside and propping himself on the railing. "Besides, I don't have a job. She does."

"Skylar!" Marla's voice called from inside the apartment. "I brought you a paper. Look how many ads are in the help wanted section." She stepped outside and flipped the paper open, laying it out on the small table at his side. She placed a highlighter on it, giving him a kiss on the cheek before waving to Daggett. "Hi, neighbor. Is Geri there? I brought her keys back. I like the new car." A shiny red, almost-new Beetle nestled in the parking lot below next to an old rusted one. It was the other part of the prize money.

"I'm here, Marla!" The voice drifted out of the apartment, accompanied by the sharp barking of a large dog. "So is Flotsam, as you can tell." Geraldine appeared on the balcony. She held her hands out for the keys.

"I think I'd like a blue one, though." Marla tossed them over, giggling when Geraldine nearly fumbled them over the edge.

"Come over later. I'm ordering up pizza. We can make a party of it." She held up the keys triumphantly.

"Pizza!" Skylar slowly closed his eyes in anticipation. "Sausage, pepperoni, and hamburger. Three meats in one."

"Silly," and Marla laughed, punching his arm. "I have Chinese. It's your favorite. You always say so." Before stepping inside, she called over the wall, "We'll be there, Ger!"

Daggett reached around the abbreviated wall and pushed on Skylar's shoulder. "You told her you love Chinese? Are you ever a glutton for punishment!"

About that time, Jetsam ran onto the balcony, leaping against Skylar for attention. Even for a puppy, the dog was powerful, and Skylar was caught off guard. With a high-pitched scream, he teetered backwards, both arms flailing in the air.

Daggett leaned out and slapped his hand against the other man's back, hitting him hard enough to rock him forward and back to safety.

"Hitting on Skylar?" Geraldine leaned back on the railing, amused at the antics between the two men. "He's barely better from the last fall he took. However, if it keeps him alive, I guess it's all right. We don't want him to take another dive."

Daggett laughed. "Wouldn't do to lose him, would it? After all, he's the only one in the world who thinks I'm a god." He pulled her to him and kissed her.

Flotsam had the same idea, and he jumped in for his share of the action. Daggett was equally unprepared, and for a heart-stopping moment, he teetered on the edge, with the parking lot far below.

Geraldine's hand pulled him back, pushing Flotsam away. "He's not the only one." She wrapped her arms around him, kissing him on the forehead, nose, and both cheeks. "But no matter what, you couldn't lose me, because I'm yours forever."

Then she kissed him on the lips, long and hard, promising him tomorrow, the day after, and the day after that, all the way to the ends of their lives.

www.ingramcontent.com/pod-product-compliance
Lightning Source LLC
Chambersburg PA
CBHW072121250626
47159CB00007B/2523